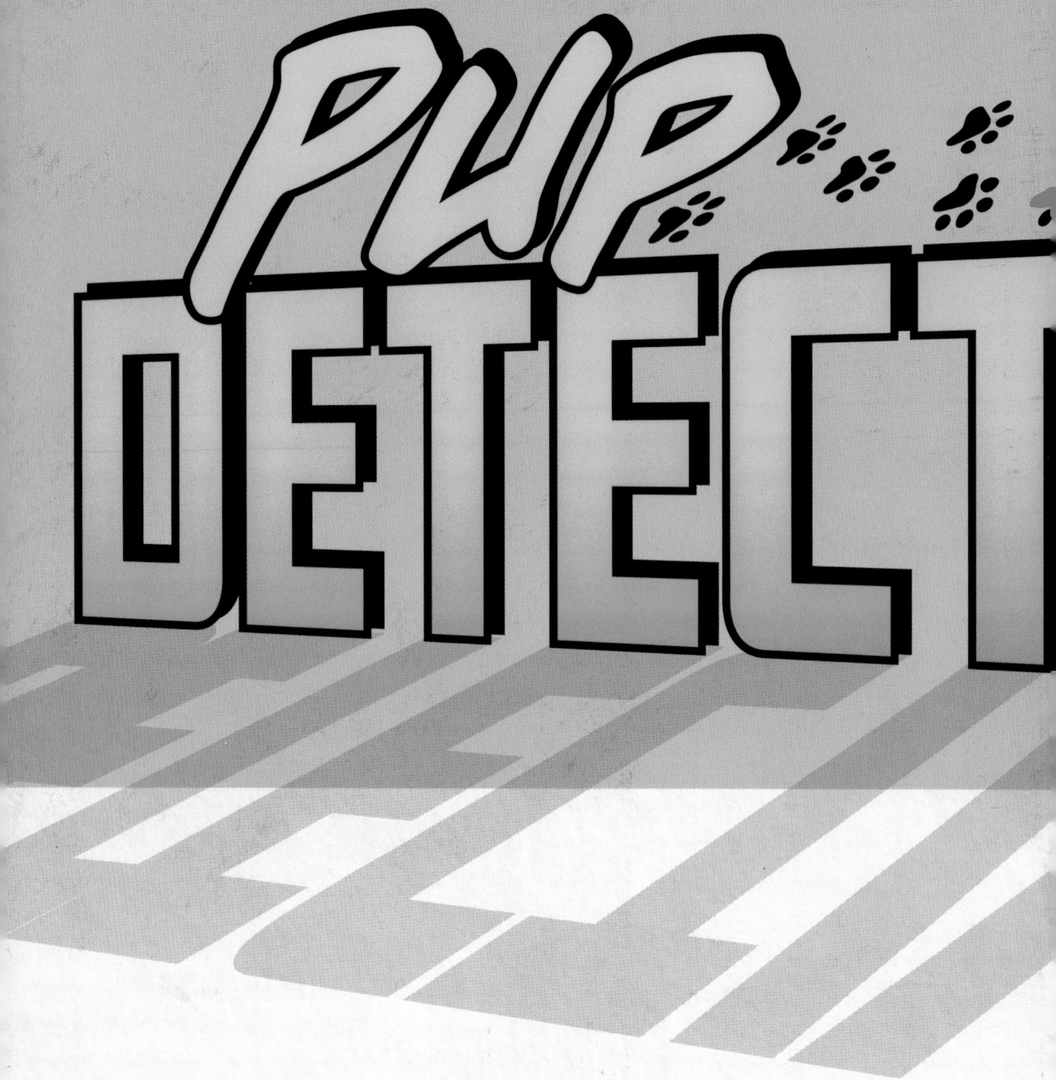
PUP
DETECT

MYSTERY MOUNTAIN GETAWAY

Written by **FELIX GUMPAW**
Illustrated by **WALMIR ARCHANJO**
at GLASS HOUSE GRAPHICS

LITTLE SIMON
NEW YORK LONDON TORONTO SYDNEY NEW DELHI

LITTLE SIMON
AN IMPRINT OF SIMON & SCHUSTER CHILDREN'S PUBLISHING DIVISION
1230 AVENUE OF THE AMERICAS, NEW YORK, NEW YORK 10020
FIRST LITTLE SIMON EDITION OCTOBER 2021
COPYRIGHT © 2021 BY SIMON & SCHUSTER, INC.
ALL RIGHTS RESERVED, INCLUDING THE RIGHT OF REPRODUCTION IN WHOLE OR IN PART IN ANY FORM. LITTLE SIMON IS A REGISTERED TRADEMARK OF SIMON & SCHUSTER, INC., AND ASSOCIATED COLOPHON IS A TRADEMARK OF SIMON & SCHUSTER, INC. FOR INFORMATION ABOUT SPECIAL DISCOUNTS FOR BULK PURCHASES, PLEASE CONTACT SIMON & SCHUSTER SPECIAL SALES AT 1-866-506-1949 OR BUSINESS@SIMONANDSCHUSTER.COM. ART BY WALMIR ARCHANJO AND JOAO MARIO TEIXEIRA DE ARAUJO • COLORING BY WALMIR ARCHANJO AND RAFAEL RAMOS • LETTERING BY MARCOS MASSAO INOUE • SUPERVISION BY MJ MACEDO/STUPLENDO • ART SERVICES BY GLASS HOUSE GRAPHICS • THE SIMON & SCHUSTER SPEAKERS BUREAU CAN BRING AUTHORS TO YOUR LIVE EVENT. FOR MORE INFORMATION OR TO BOOK AN EVENT CONTACT THE SIMON & SCHUSTER SPEAKERS BUREAU AT 1-866-248-3049 OR VISIT OUR WEBSITE AT WWW.SIMONSPEAKERS.COM.
DESIGNED BY NICHOLAS SCIACCA
MANUFACTURED IN CHINA 0821 SCP
10 9 8 7 6 5 4 3 2 1
LIBRARY OF CONGRESS CATALOGING-IN-PUBLICATION DATA
NAMES: GUMPAW, FELIX, AUTHOR. I GLASS HOUSE GRAPHICS, ILLUSTRATOR.
TITLE: MYSTERY MOUNTAIN GETAWAY / BY FELIX GUMPAW ; ILLUSTRATED BY GLASS HOUSE GRAPHICS. DESCRIPTION: FIRST LITTLE SIMON EDITION. I NEW YORK : LITTLE SIMON, 2021. I SERIES: PUP DETECTIVES ; 6 I AUDIENCE: AGES 5-9 I AUDIENCE: GRADES K-1 I SUMMARY: WHEN RIDER WOOFSON AND THE P.I. PACK ARRIVE AT THE TOP OF MYSTERY MOUNTAIN, THEY FIND THEIR CLASSMATES HAVE LEFT, SCARED AWAY BY A SNOW MONSTER, SO THE DETECTIVES DECIDE IT IS TIME TO INVESTIGATE EXACTLY WHAT IS SO MYSTERIOUS ABOUT THIS MOUNTAIN. IDENTIFIERS: LCCN 2020049152 (PRINT) I LCCN 2020049153 (EBOOK) I ISBN 9781534484870 (PAPERBACK) I ISBN 9781534484887 (HARDCOVER) I ISBN 9781534484894 (EBOOK). SUBJECTS: LCSH: GRAPHIC NOVELS. I CYAC: GRAPHIC NOVELS. I MYSTERY AND DETECTIVE STORIES. I DOGS—FICTION. CLASSIFICATION: LCC PZ7.7.G858 MY 2021 (PRINT) I LCC PZ7.7.G858 (EBOOK) IDDC 741.5/973—DC23. LC RECORD AVAILABLE AT HTTPS://LCCN.LOC.GOV/2020049152. LC EBOOK RECORD AVAILABLE AT HTTPS://LCCN.LOC.GOV/2020049153

CONTENTS

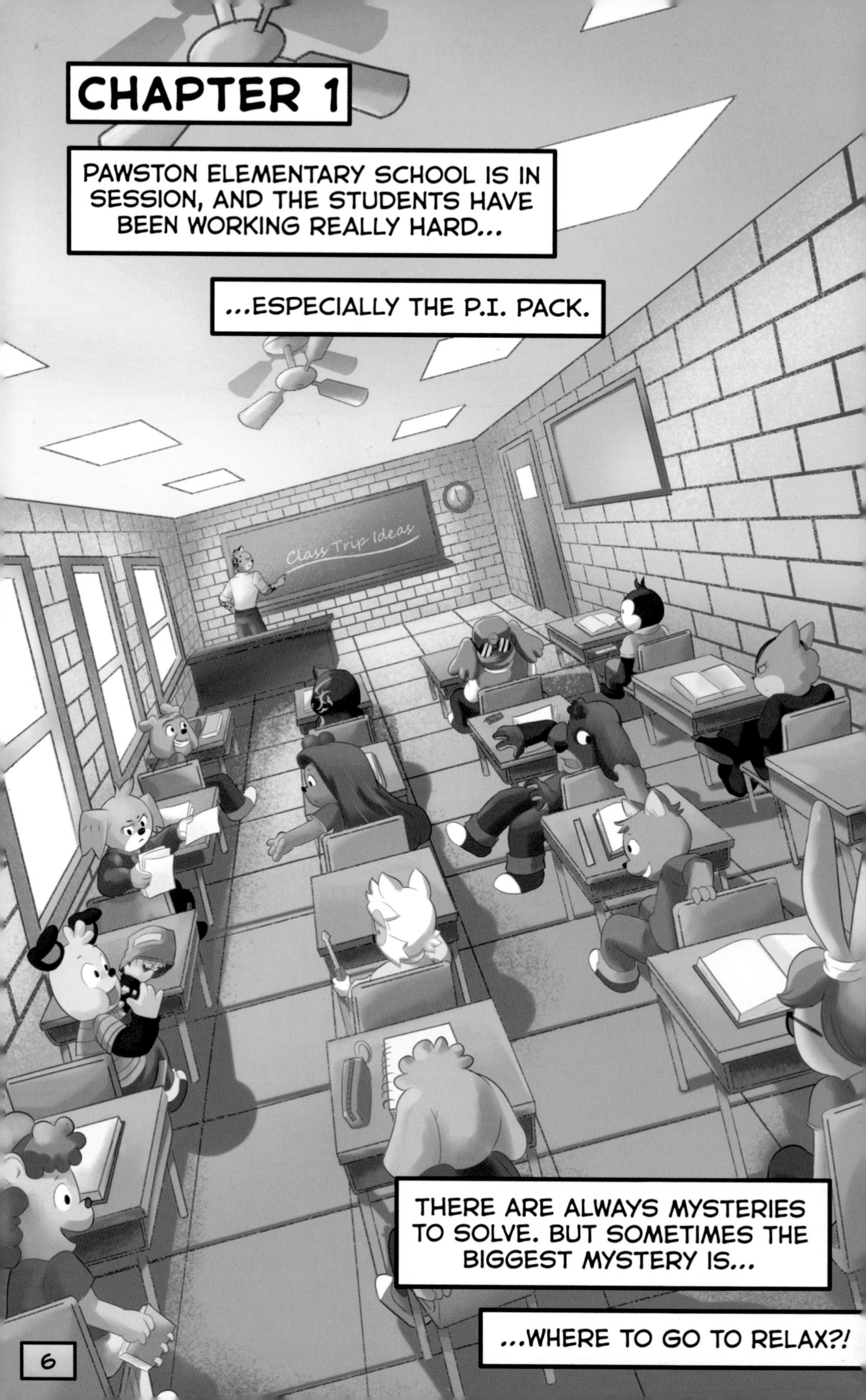
CHAPTER 1
PAWSTON ELEMENTARY SCHOOL IS IN SESSION, AND THE STUDENTS HAVE BEEN WORKING REALLY HARD...
...ESPECIALLY THE P.I. PACK.
Class Trip Ideas
THERE ARE ALWAYS MYSTERIES TO SOLVE. BUT SOMETIMES THE BIGGEST MYSTERY IS...
...WHERE TO GO TO RELAX?!

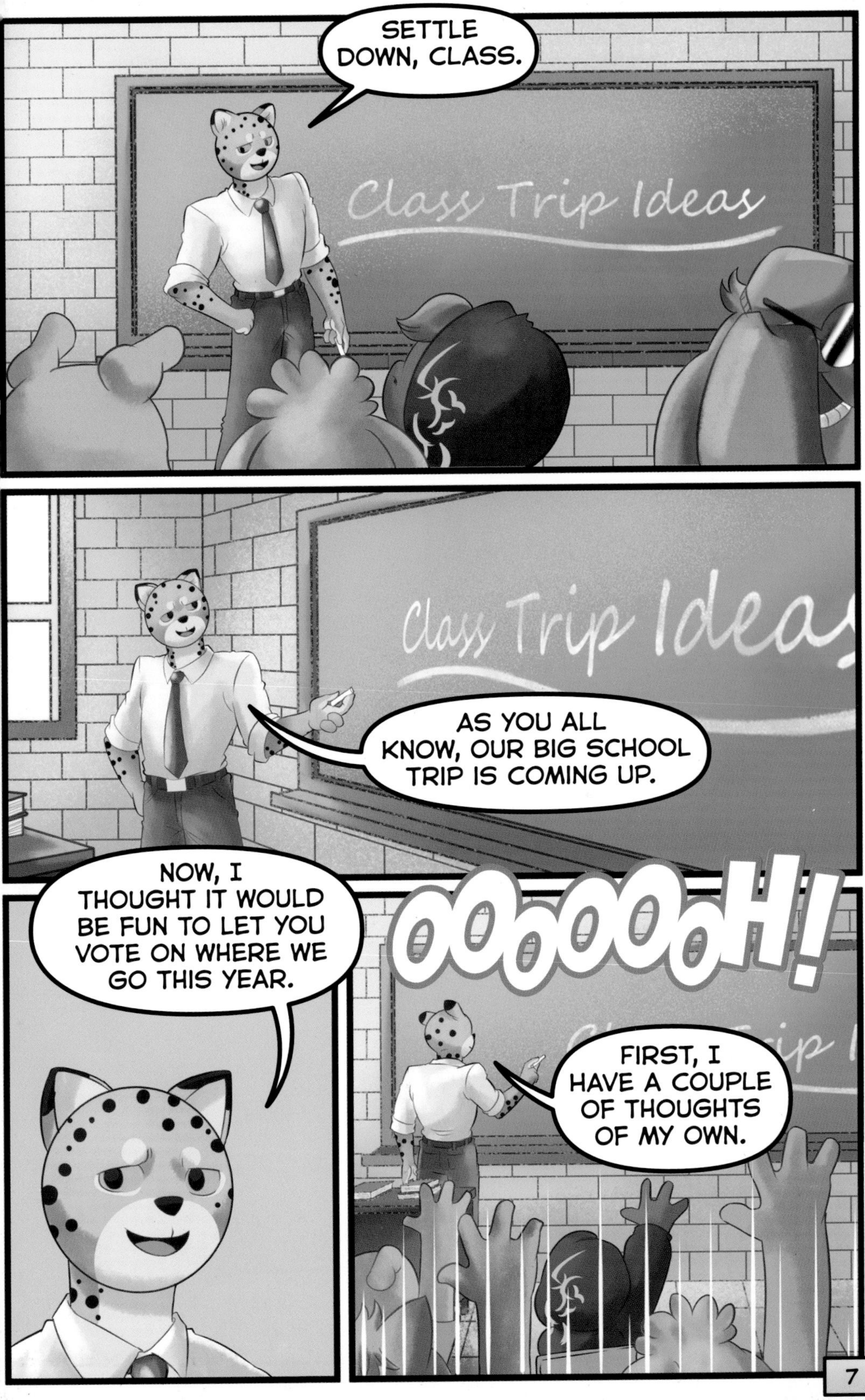
SETTLE DOWN, CLASS.
Class Trip Ideas
Class Trip Ideas
AS YOU ALL KNOW, OUR BIG SCHOOL TRIP IS COMING UP.
NOW, I THOUGHT IT WOULD BE FUN TO LET YOU VOTE ON WHERE WE GO THIS YEAR.
OOOOOOOH!
FIRST, I HAVE A COUPLE OF THOUGHTS OF MY OWN.

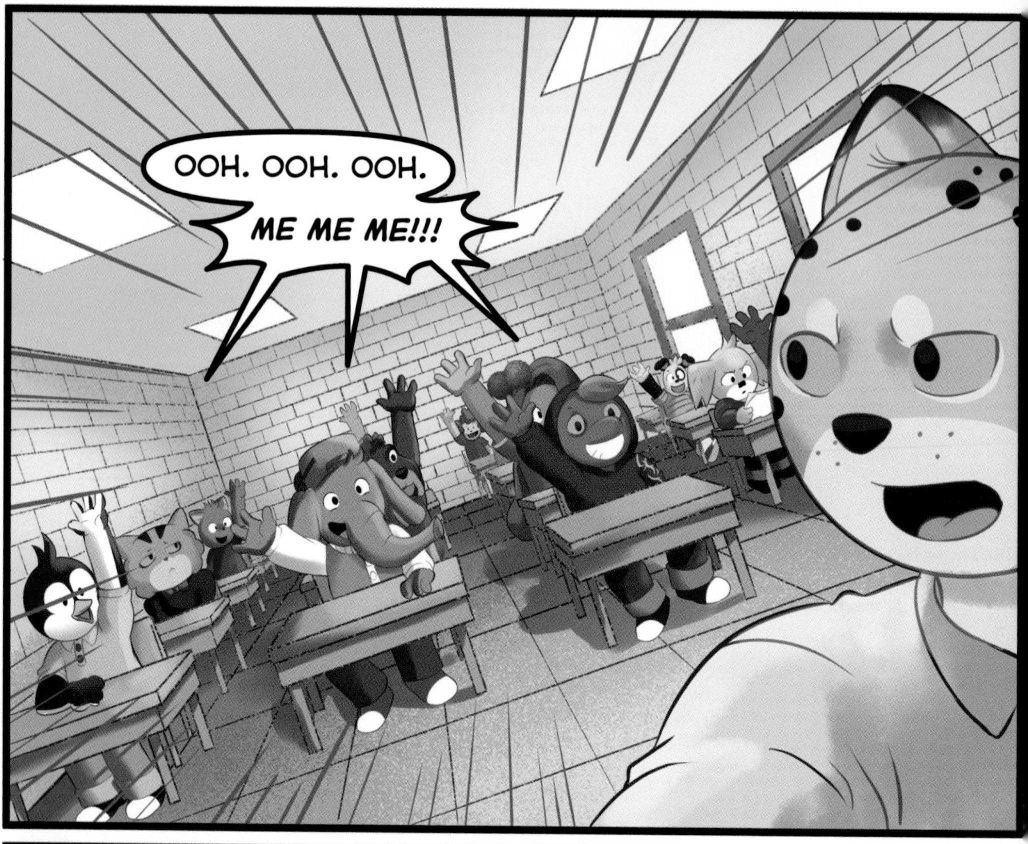
OOH. OOH. OOH.
ME ME ME!!!

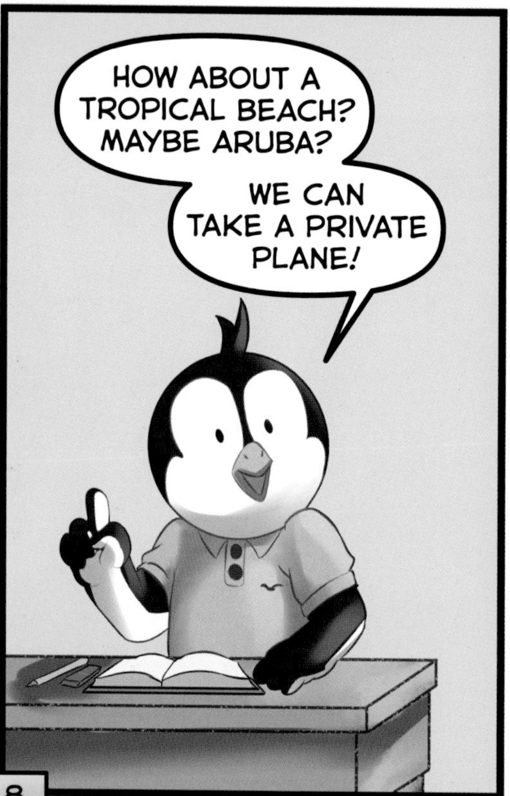
HOW ABOUT A TROPICAL BEACH? MAYBE ARUBA?
WE CAN TAKE A PRIVATE PLANE!

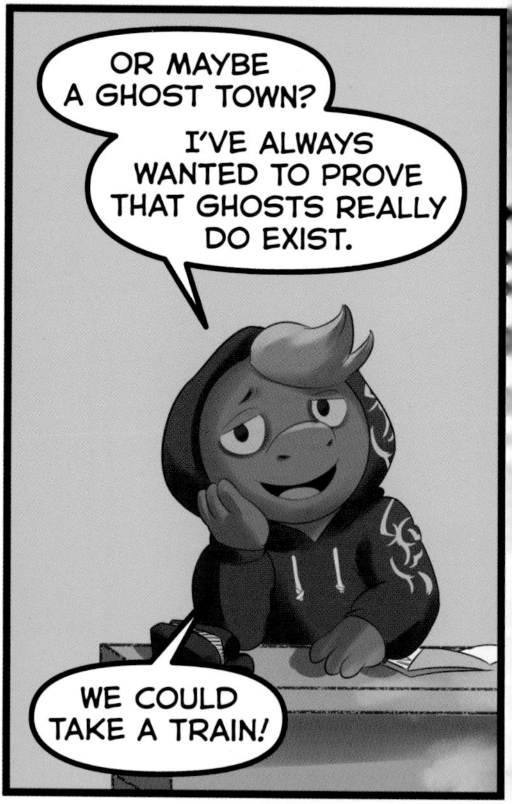
OR MAYBE A GHOST TOWN?
I'VE ALWAYS WANTED TO PROVE THAT GHOSTS REALLY DO EXIST.
WE COULD TAKE A TRAIN!

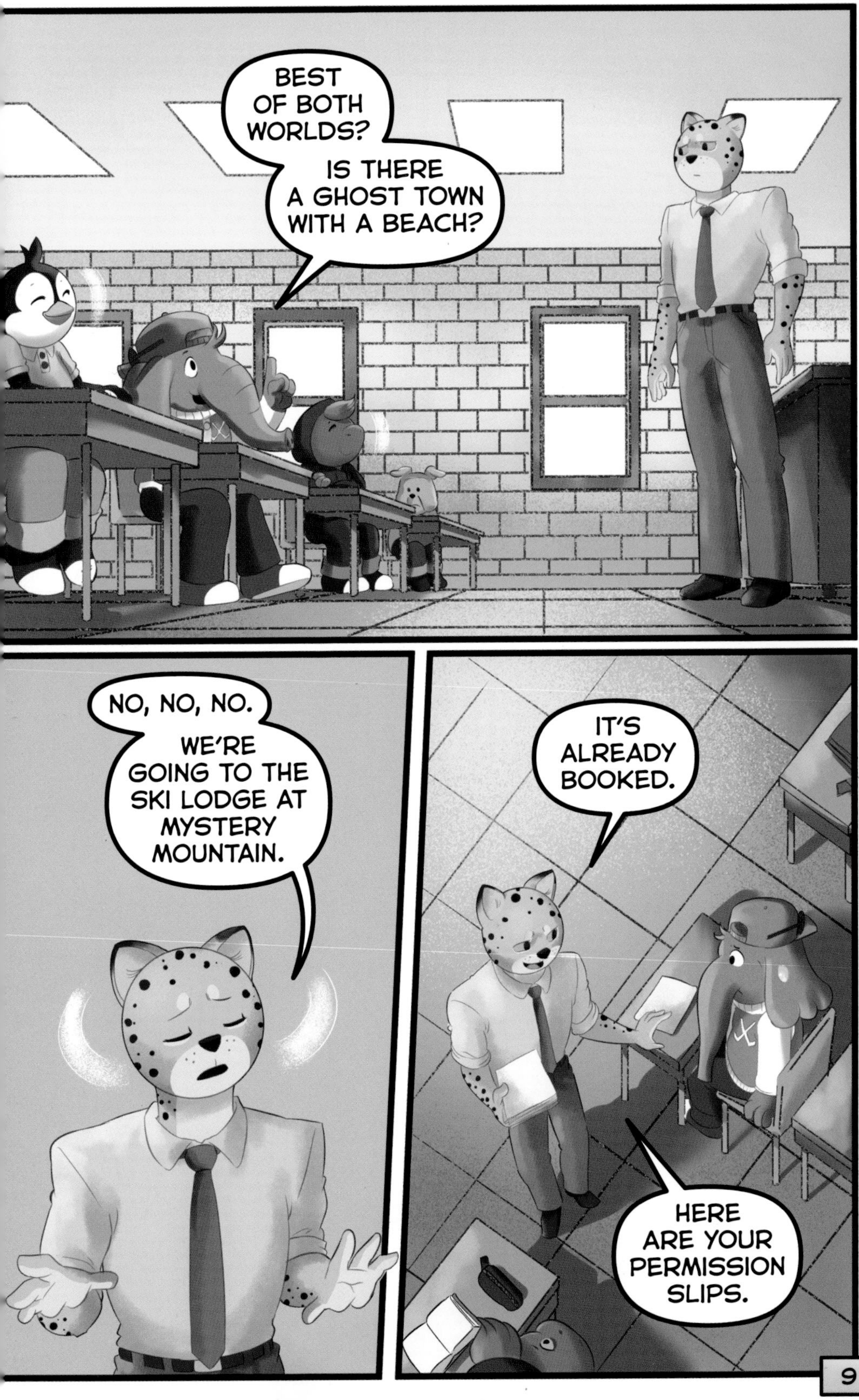
BEST OF BOTH WORLDS?
IS THERE A GHOST TOWN WITH A BEACH?
NO, NO, NO.
WE'RE GOING TO THE SKI LODGE AT MYSTERY MOUNTAIN.
IT'S ALREADY BOOKED.
HERE ARE YOUR PERMISSION SLIPS.

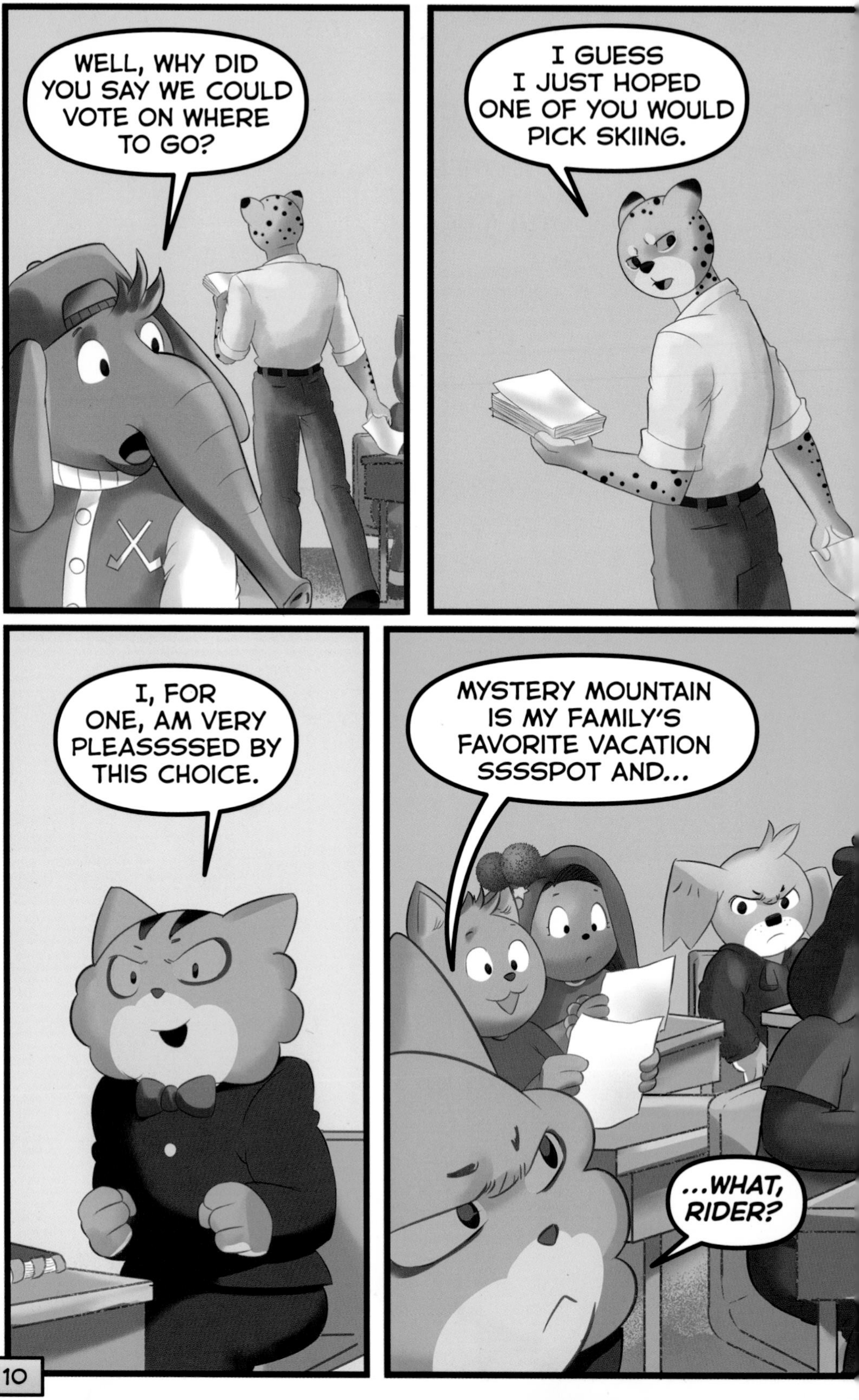
WELL, WHY DID YOU SAY WE COULD VOTE ON WHERE TO GO?
I GUESS I JUST HOPED ONE OF YOU WOULD PICK SKIING.
I, FOR ONE, AM VERY PLEASSSSED BY THIS CHOICE.
MYSTERY MOUNTAIN IS MY FAMILY'S FAVORITE VACATION SSSSPOT AND...
...WHAT, RIDER?

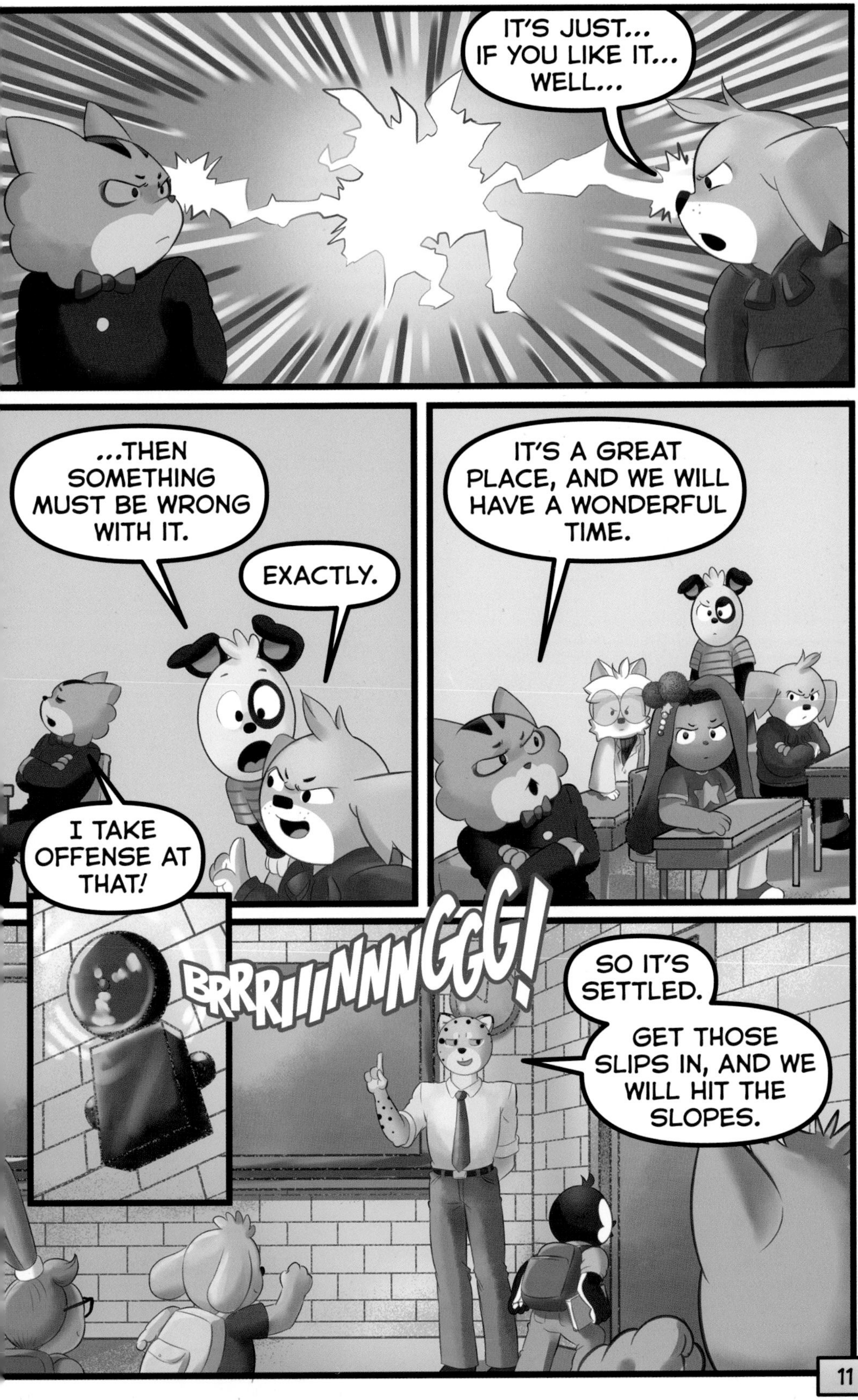
IT'S JUST... IF YOU LIKE IT... WELL...
...THEN SOMETHING MUST BE WRONG WITH IT.
EXACTLY.
I TAKE OFFENSE AT THAT!
IT'S A GREAT PLACE, AND WE WILL HAVE A WONDERFUL TIME.
BRRRIIIINNNNGGG!
SO IT'S SETTLED.
GET THOSE SLIPS IN, AND WE WILL HIT THE SLOPES.

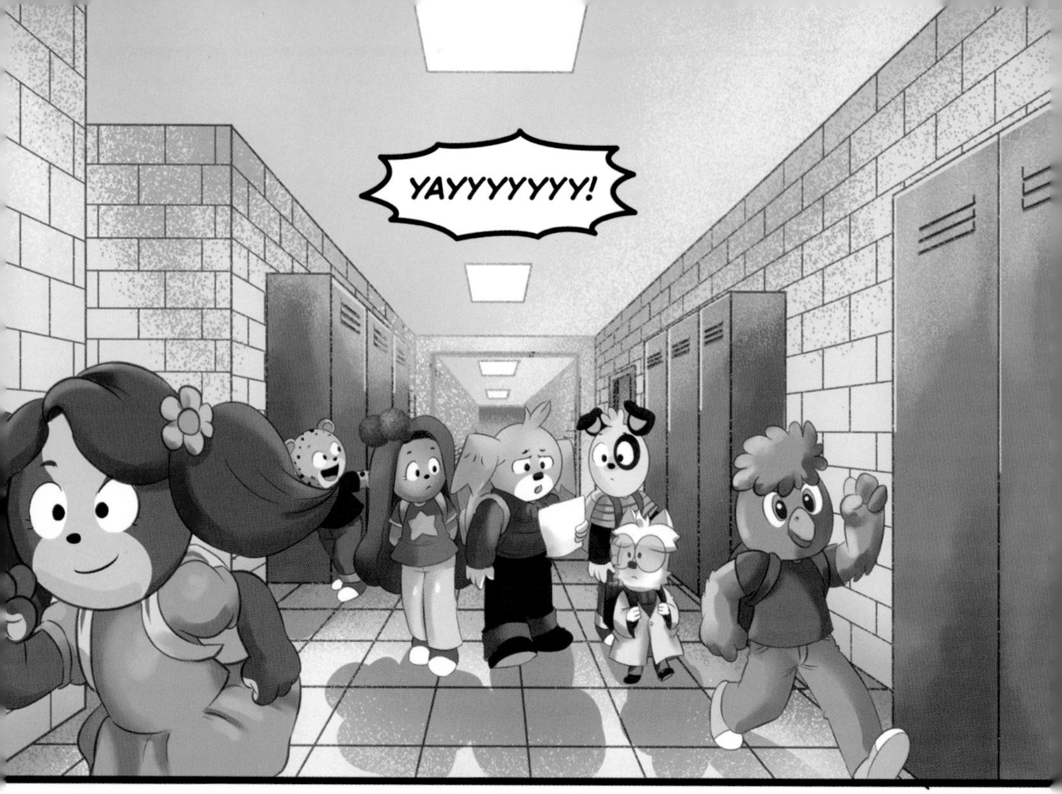
YAYYYYYYY!

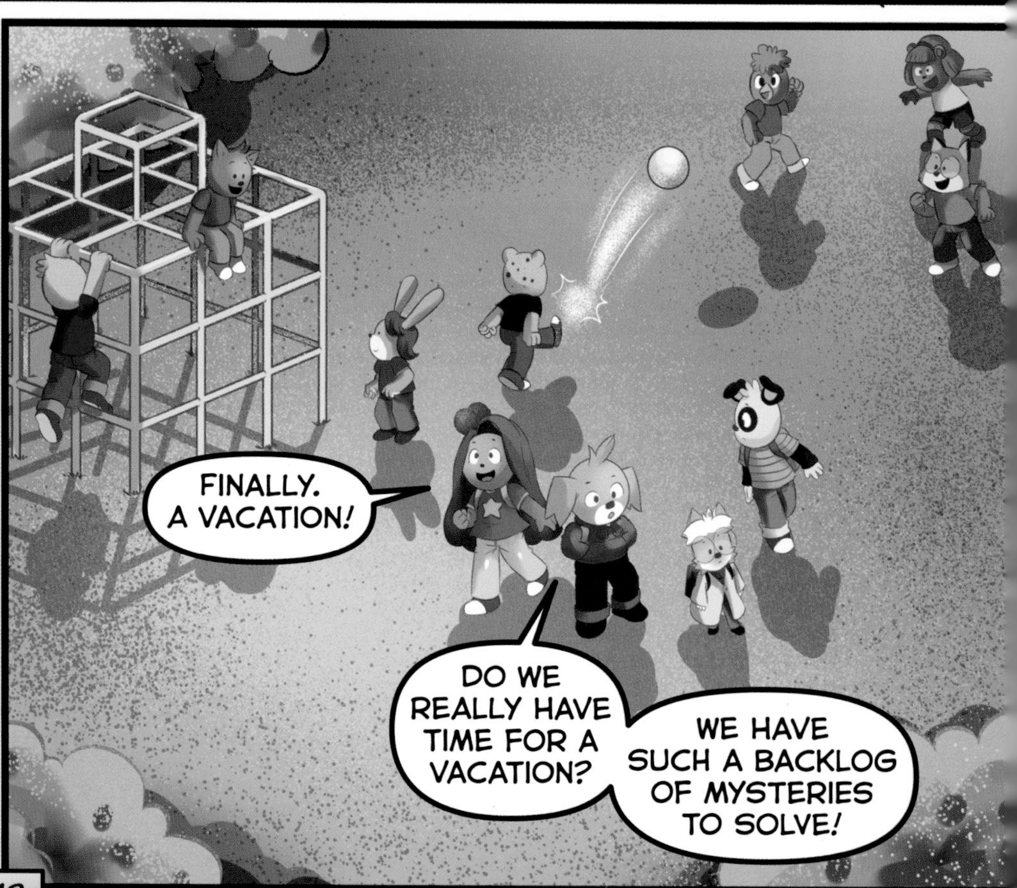
FINALLY.
A VACATION!
DO WE REALLY HAVE TIME FOR A VACATION?
WE HAVE SUCH A BACKLOG OF MYSTERIES TO SOLVE!

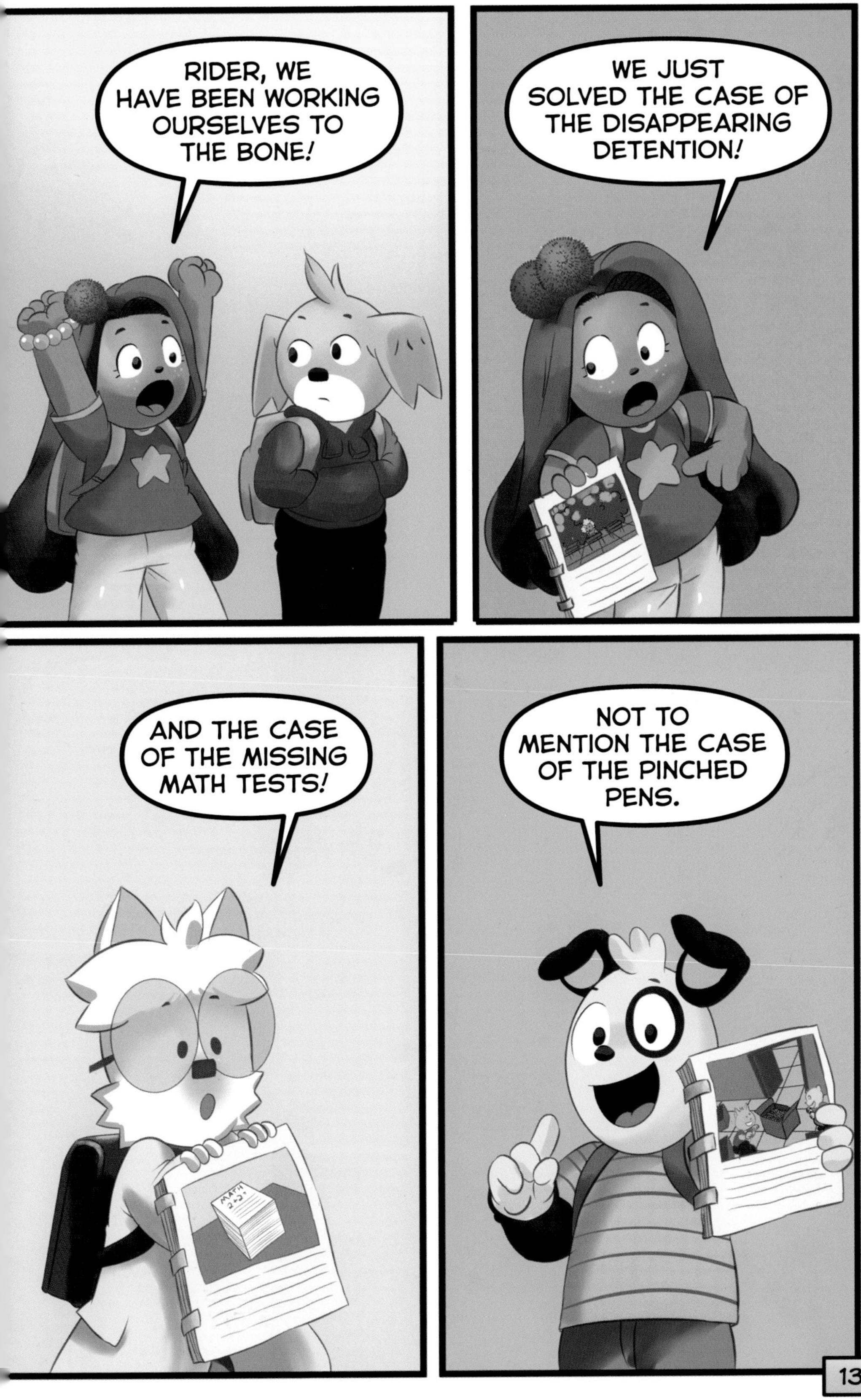
RIDER, WE HAVE BEEN WORKING OURSELVES TO THE BONE!
WE JUST SOLVED THE CASE OF THE DISAPPEARING DETENTION!
AND THE CASE OF THE MISSING MATH TESTS!
MATH 2+2=
NOT TO MENTION THE CASE OF THE PINCHED PENS.

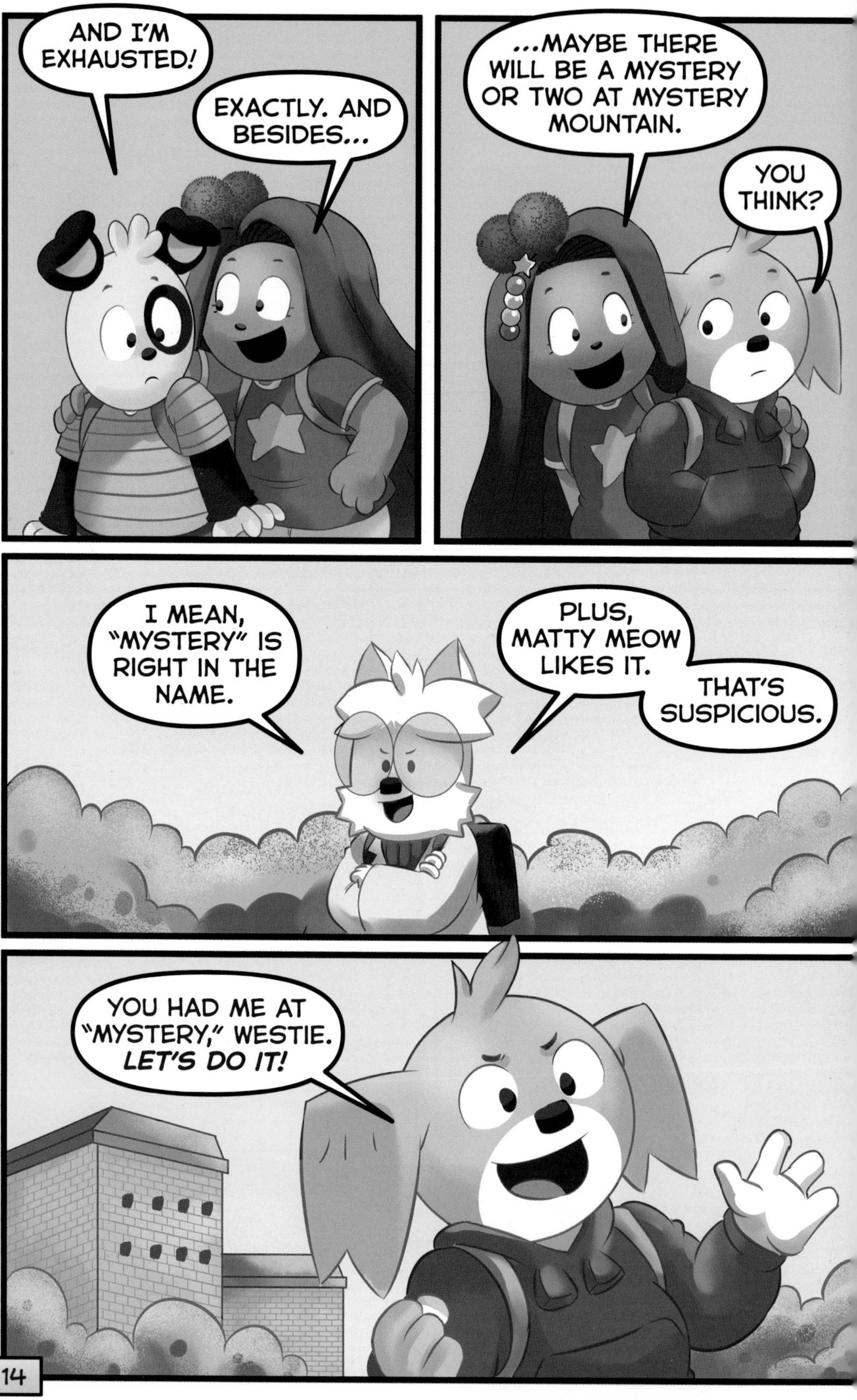
AND I'M EXHAUSTED!
EXACTLY. AND BESIDES...
...MAYBE THERE WILL BE A MYSTERY OR TWO AT MYSTERY MOUNTAIN.
YOU THINK?
I MEAN, "MYSTERY" IS RIGHT IN THE NAME.
PLUS, MATTY MEOW LIKES IT.
THAT'S SUSPICIOUS.
YOU HAD ME AT "MYSTERY," WESTIE. LET'S DO IT!

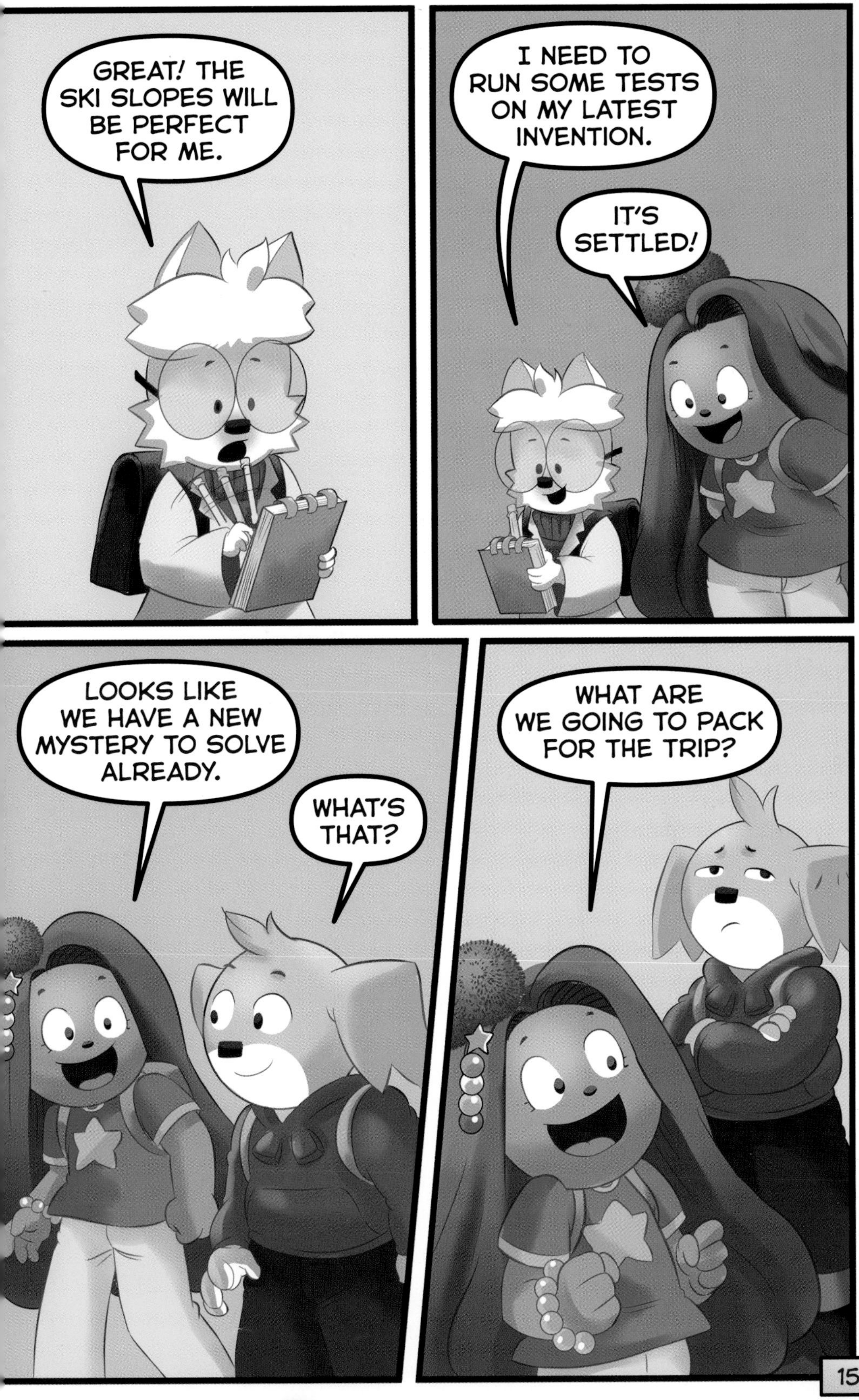

GREAT! THE SKI SLOPES WILL BE PERFECT FOR ME.
I NEED TO RUN SOME TESTS ON MY LATEST INVENTION.
IT'S SETTLED!
LOOKS LIKE WE HAVE A NEW MYSTERY TO SOLVE ALREADY.
WHAT'S THAT?
WHAT ARE WE GOING TO PACK FOR THE TRIP?

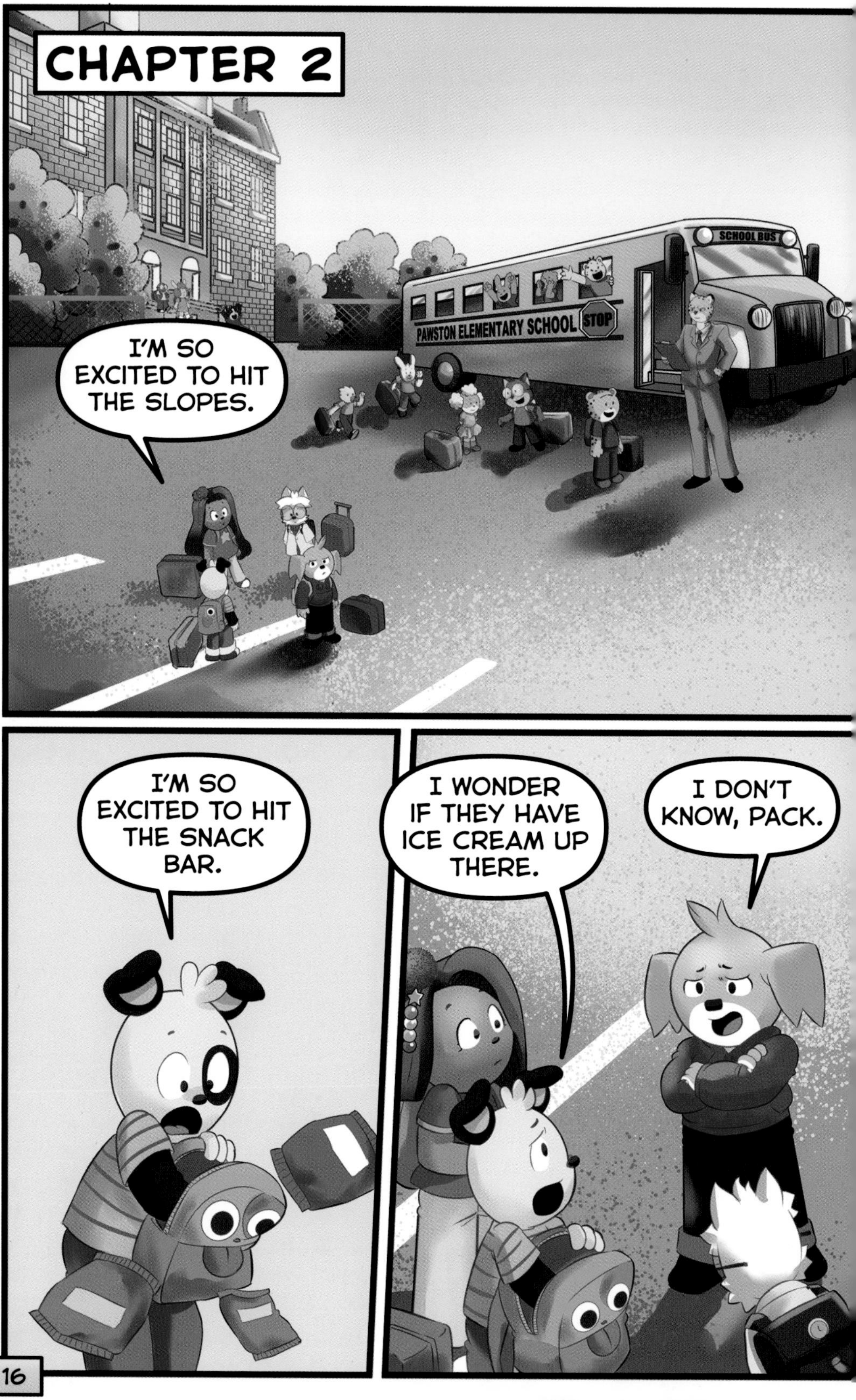
CHAPTER 2
SCHOOL BUS
PAWSTON ELEMENTARY SCHOOL
STOP
I'M SO EXCITED TO HIT THE SLOPES.
I'M SO EXCITED TO HIT THE SNACK BAR.
I WONDER IF THEY HAVE ICE CREAM UP THERE.
I DON'T KNOW, PACK.

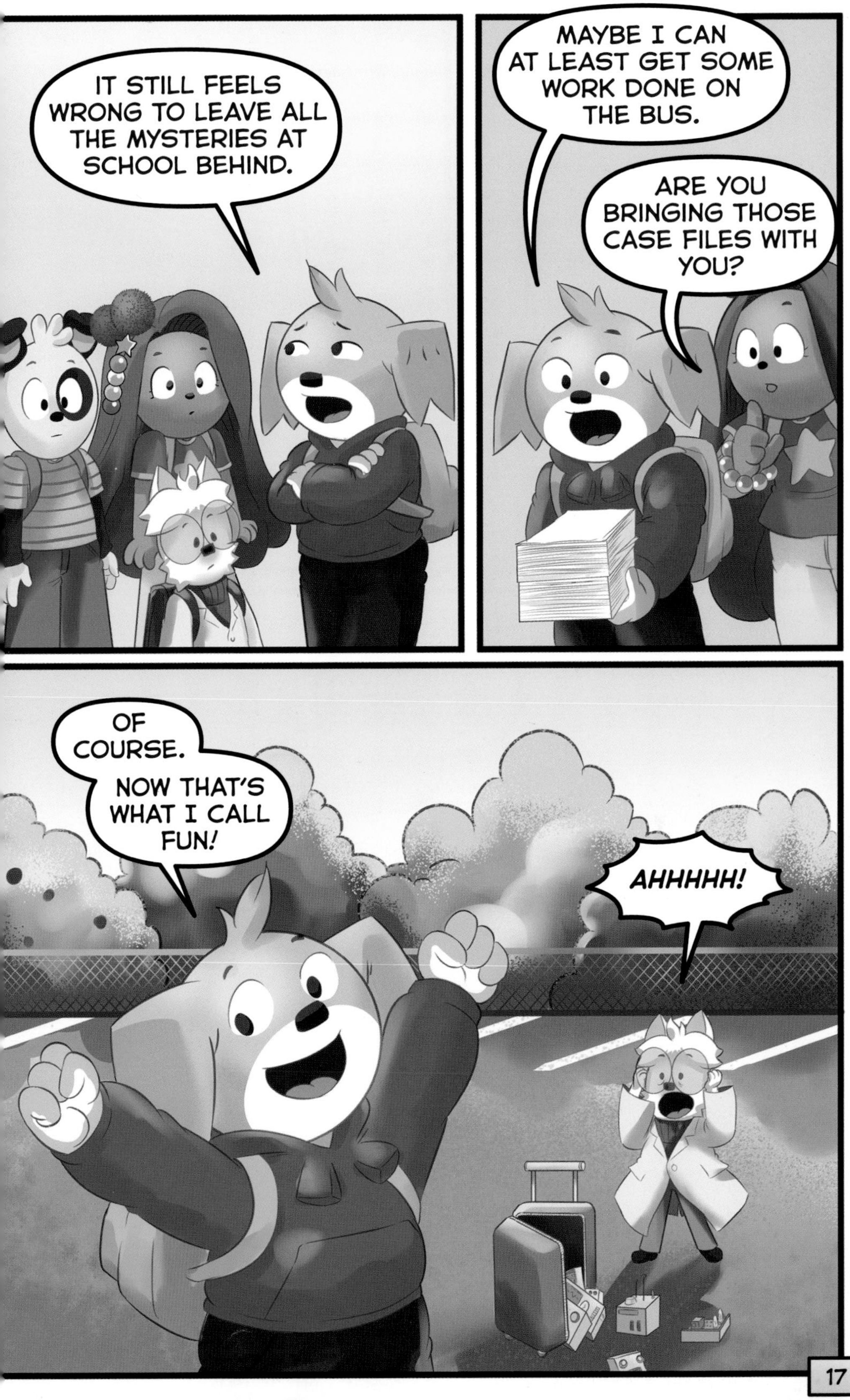
IT STILL FEELS WRONG TO LEAVE ALL THE MYSTERIES AT SCHOOL BEHIND.
MAYBE I CAN AT LEAST GET SOME WORK DONE ON THE BUS.
ARE YOU BRINGING THOSE CASE FILES WITH YOU?
OF COURSE.
NOW THAT'S WHAT I CALL FUN!
AHHHHH!

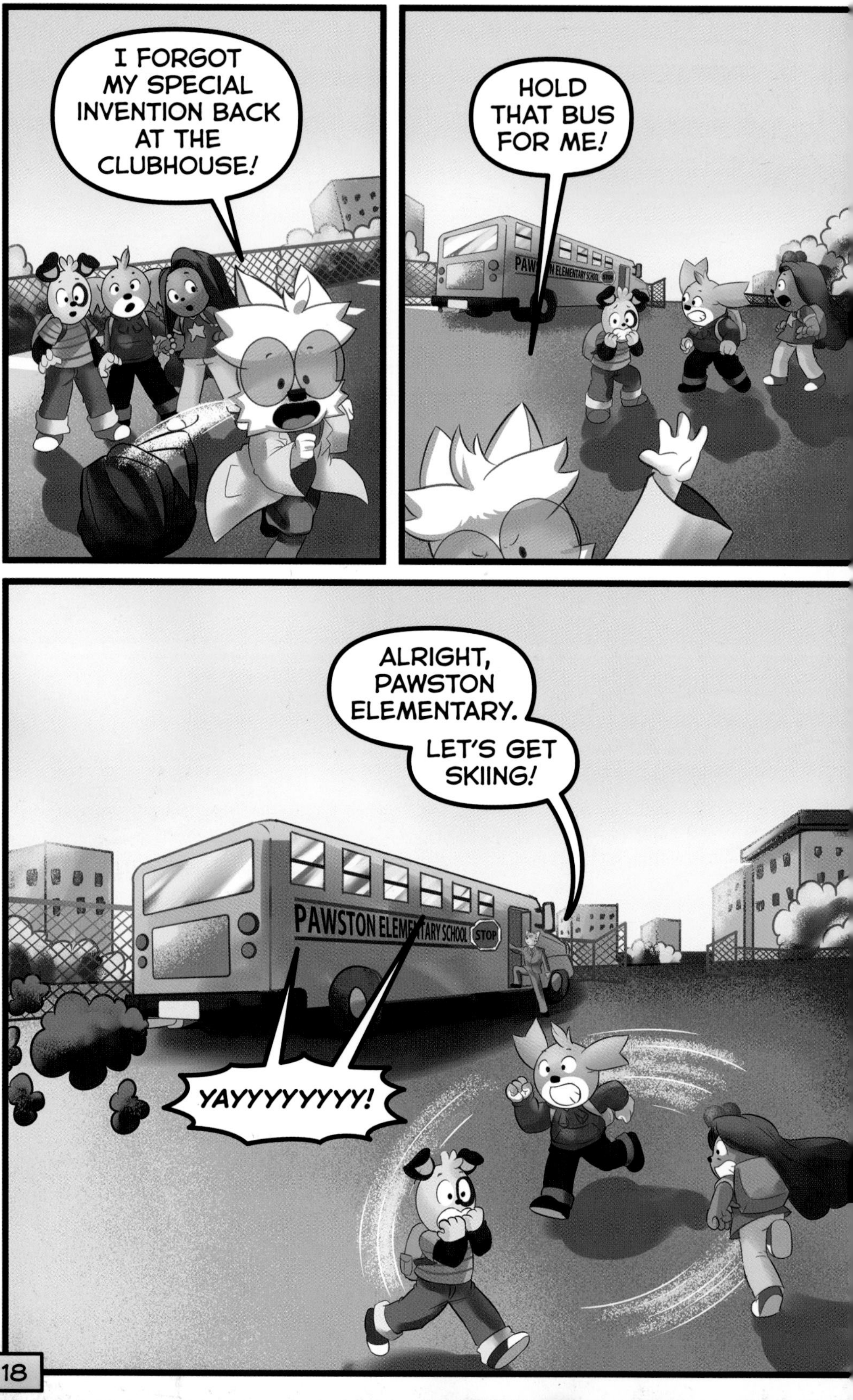
I FORGOT MY SPECIAL INVENTION BACK AT THE CLUBHOUSE!
HOLD THAT BUS FOR ME!
ALRIGHT, PAWSTON ELEMENTARY.
LET'S GET SKIING!
PAWSTON ELEMENTARY SCHOOL
STOP
YAYYYYYYYYY!

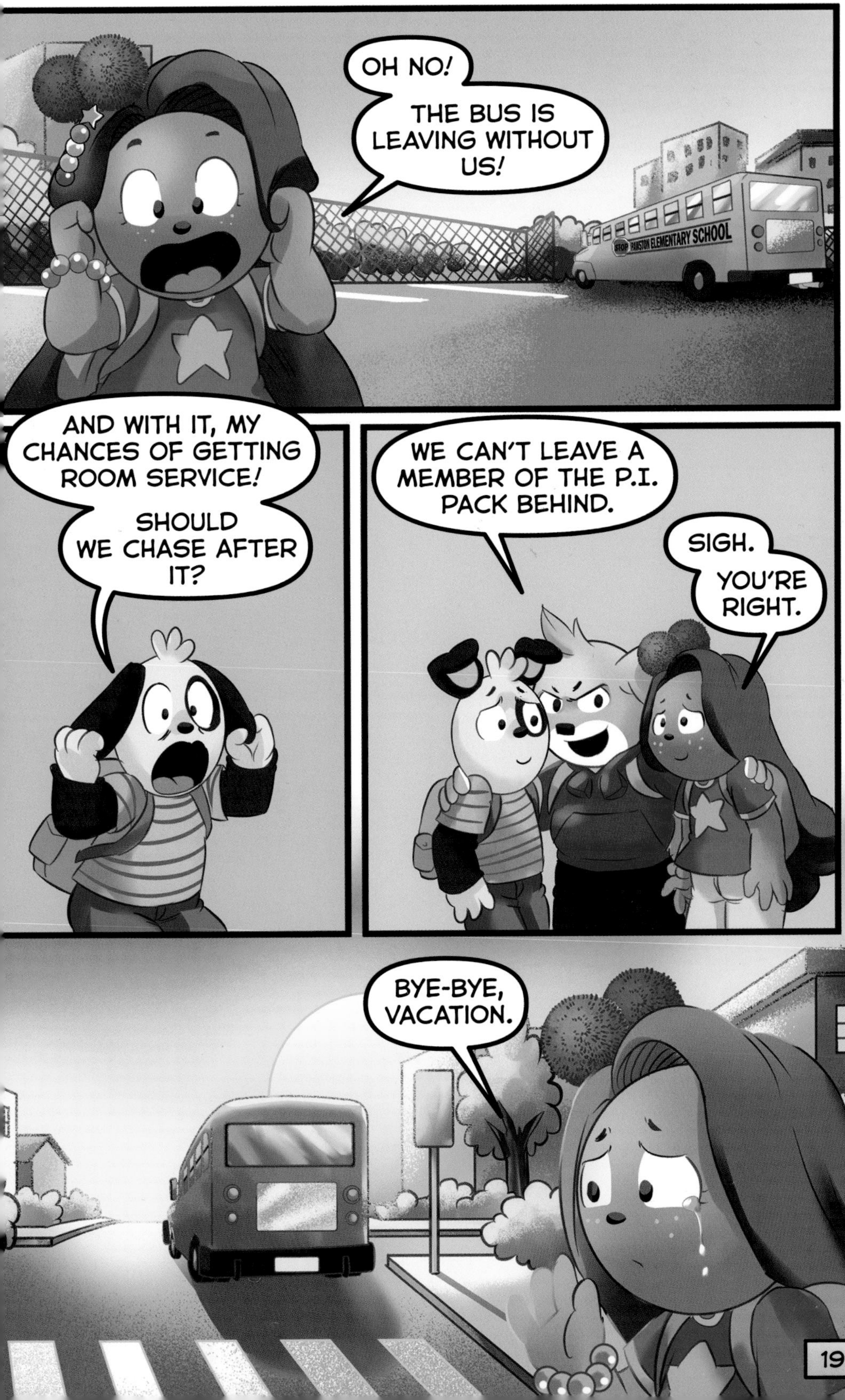
OH NO!
THE BUS IS LEAVING WITHOUT US!
PAWSTON ELEMENTARY SCHOOL
AND WITH IT, MY CHANCES OF GETTING ROOM SERVICE!
SHOULD WE CHASE AFTER IT?
WE CAN'T LEAVE A MEMBER OF THE P.I. PACK BEHIND.
SIGH.
YOU'RE RIGHT.
BYE-BYE, VACATION.

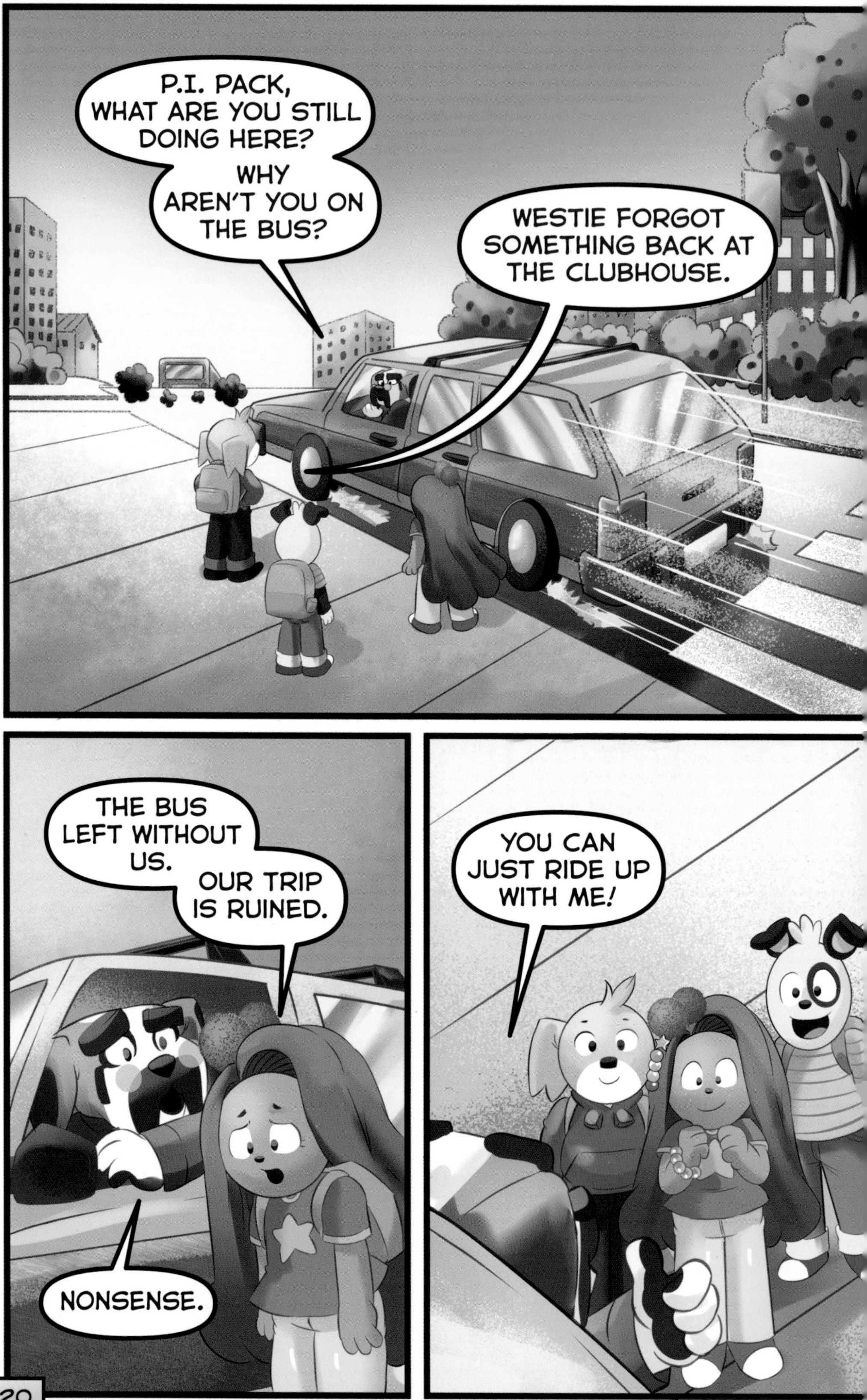
P.I. PACK, WHAT ARE YOU STILL DOING HERE?
WHY AREN'T YOU ON THE BUS?
WESTIE FORGOT SOMETHING BACK AT THE CLUBHOUSE.
THE BUS LEFT WITHOUT US.
OUR TRIP IS RUINED.
NONSENSE.
YOU CAN JUST RIDE UP WITH ME!

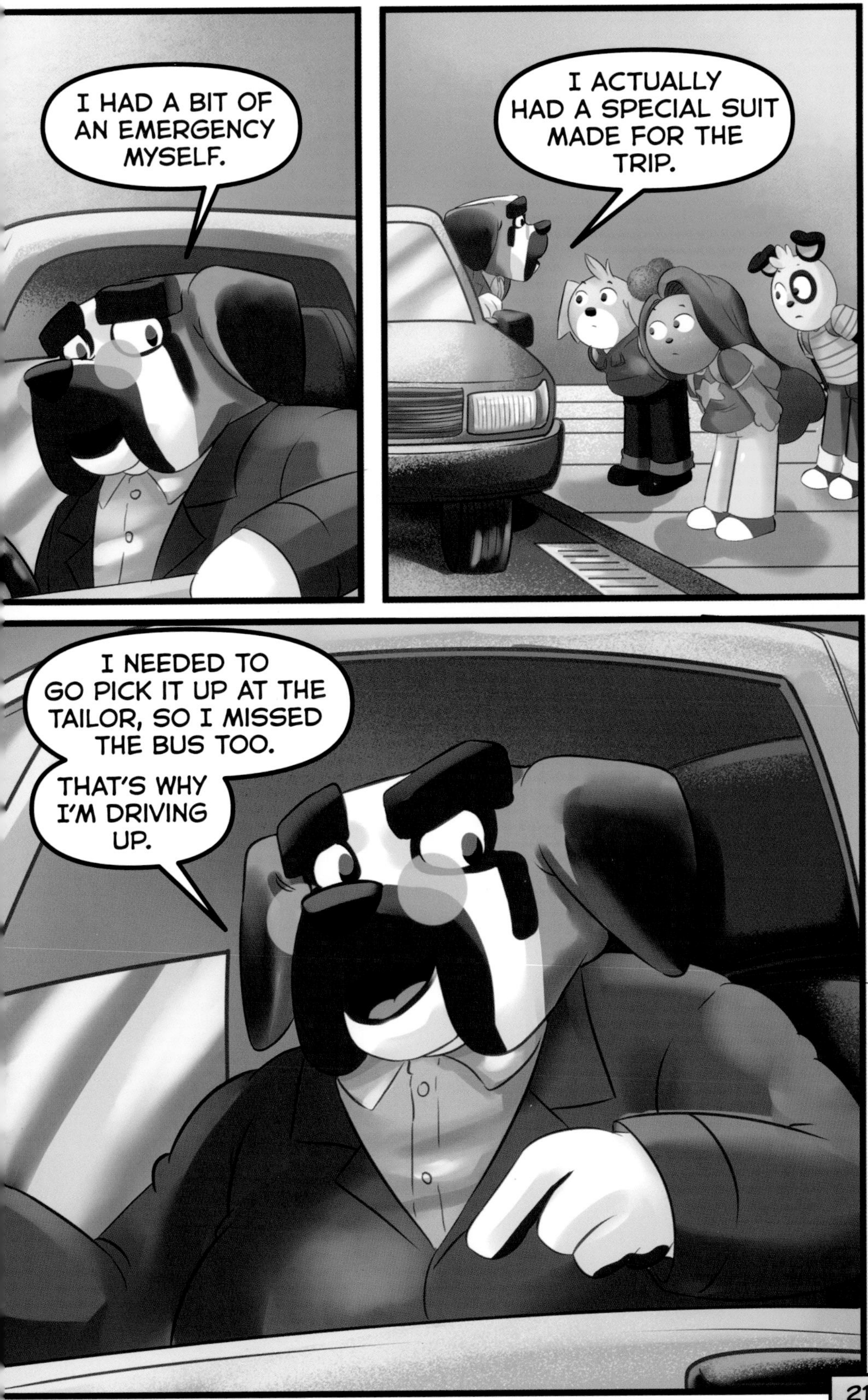
I HAD A BIT OF AN EMERGENCY MYSELF.
I ACTUALLY HAD A SPECIAL SUIT MADE FOR THE TRIP.
I NEEDED TO GO PICK IT UP AT THE TAILOR, SO I MISSED THE BUS TOO.
THAT'S WHY I'M DRIVING UP.

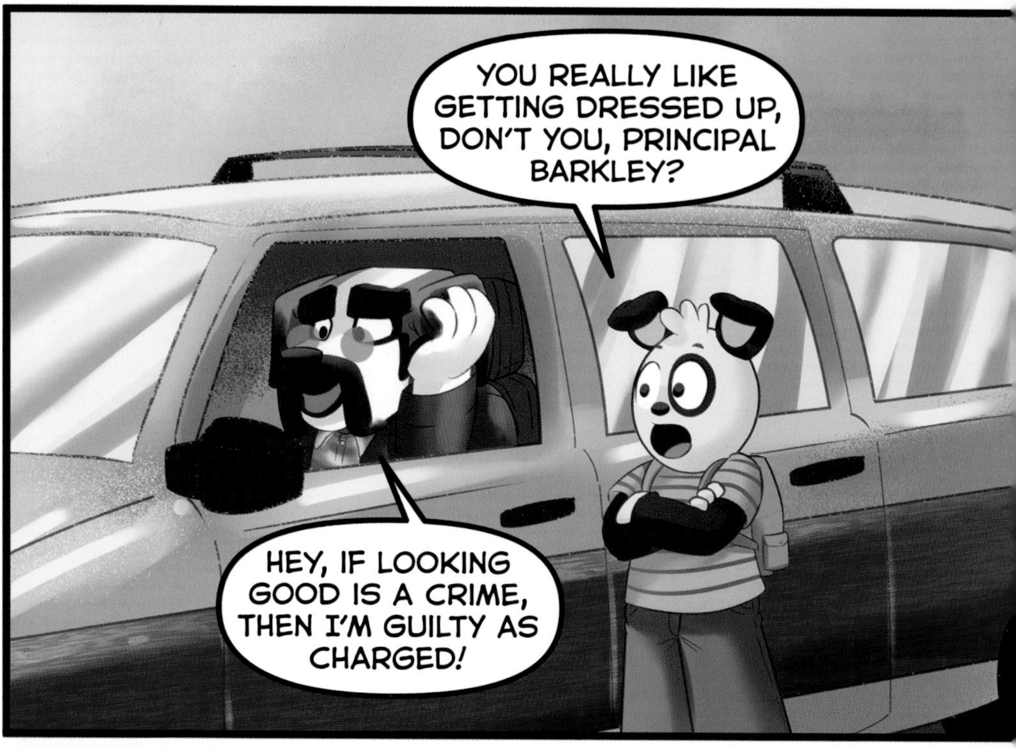
YOU REALLY LIKE GETTING DRESSED UP, DON'T YOU, PRINCIPAL BARKLEY?
HEY, IF LOOKING GOOD IS A CRIME, THEN I'M GUILTY AS CHARGED!

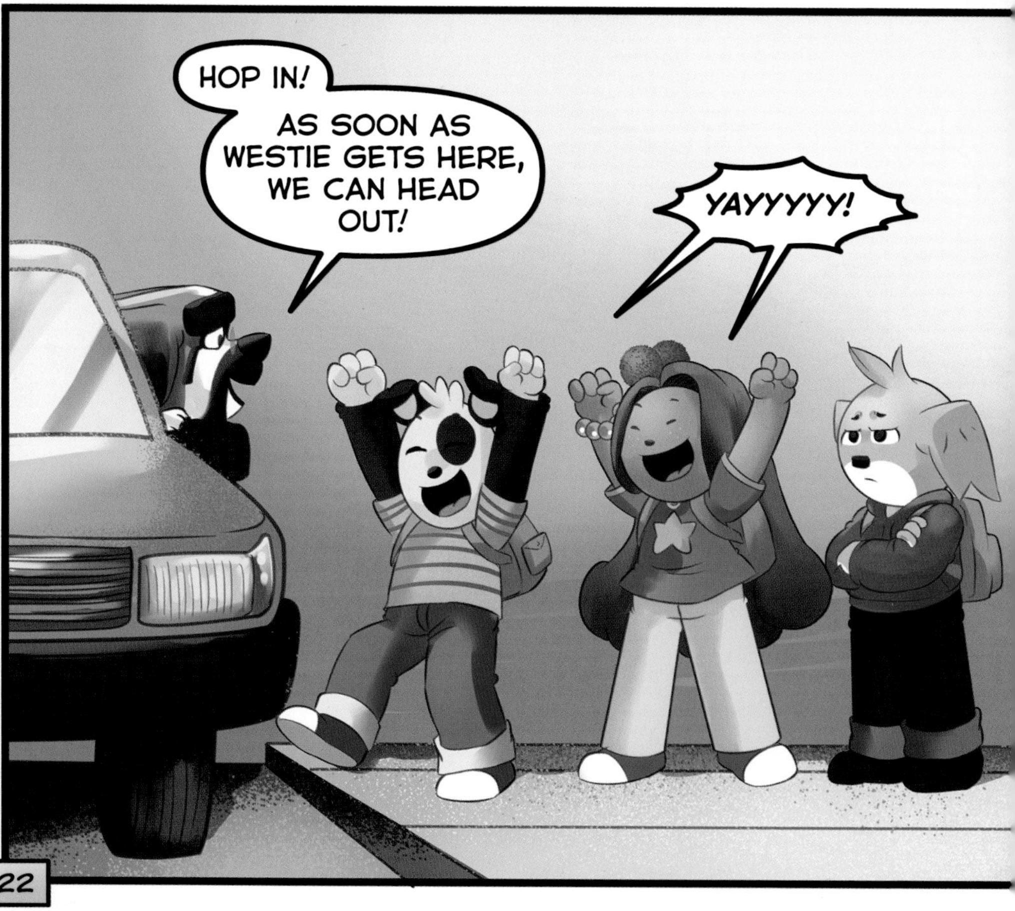
HOP IN!
AS SOON AS WESTIE GETS HERE, WE CAN HEAD OUT!
YAYYYYY!

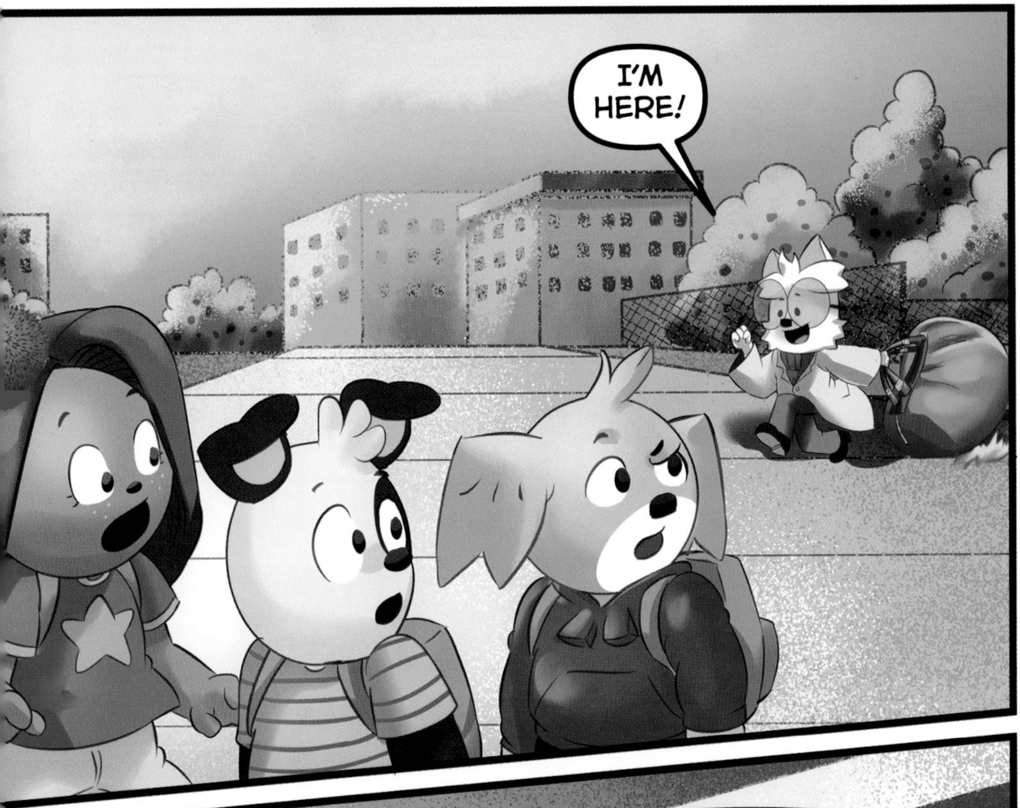
I'M HERE!

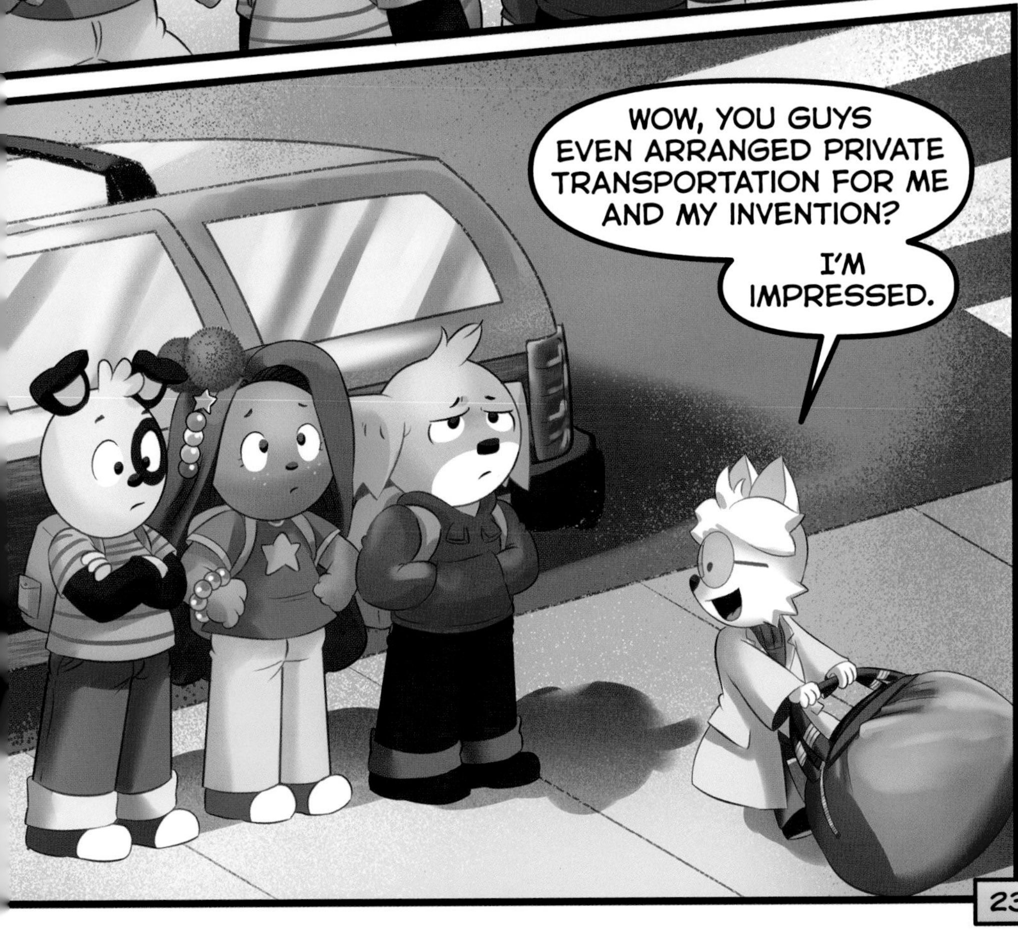
WOW, YOU GUYS EVEN ARRANGED PRIVATE TRANSPORTATION FOR ME AND MY INVENTION?
I'M IMPRESSED.

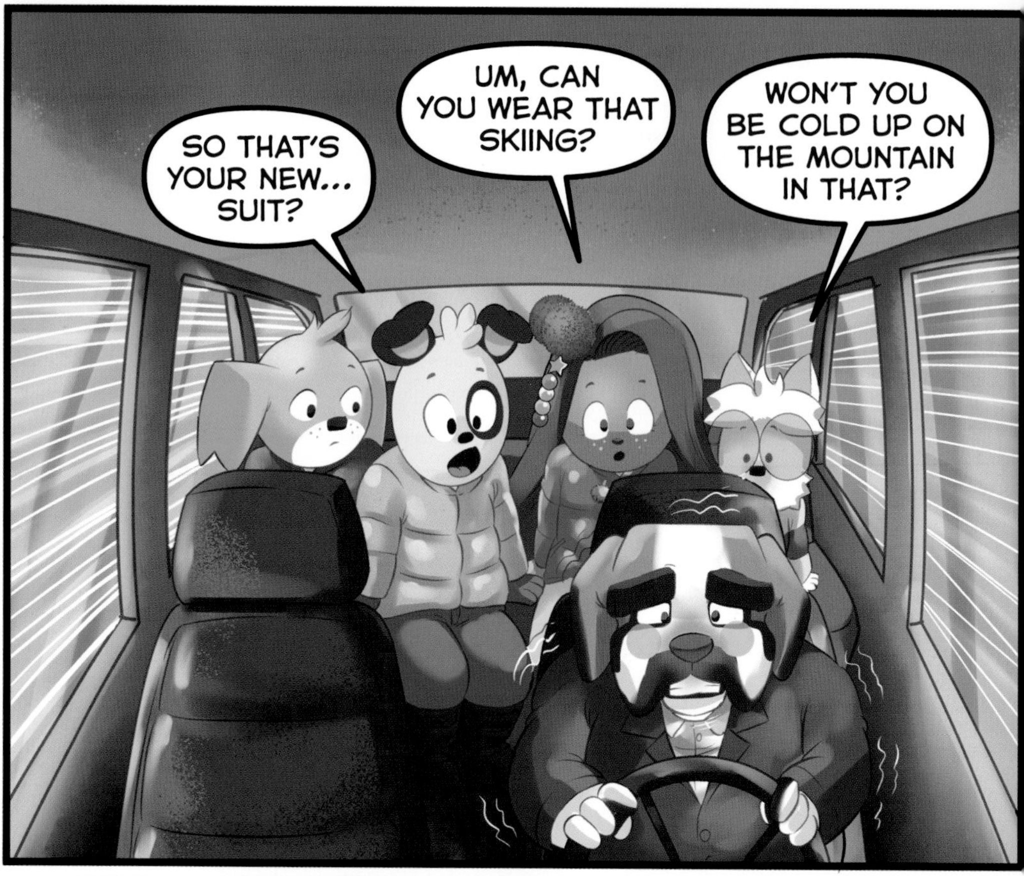
SO THAT'S YOUR NEW... SUIT?
UM, CAN YOU WEAR THAT SKIING?
WON'T YOU BE COLD UP ON THE MOUNTAIN IN THAT?

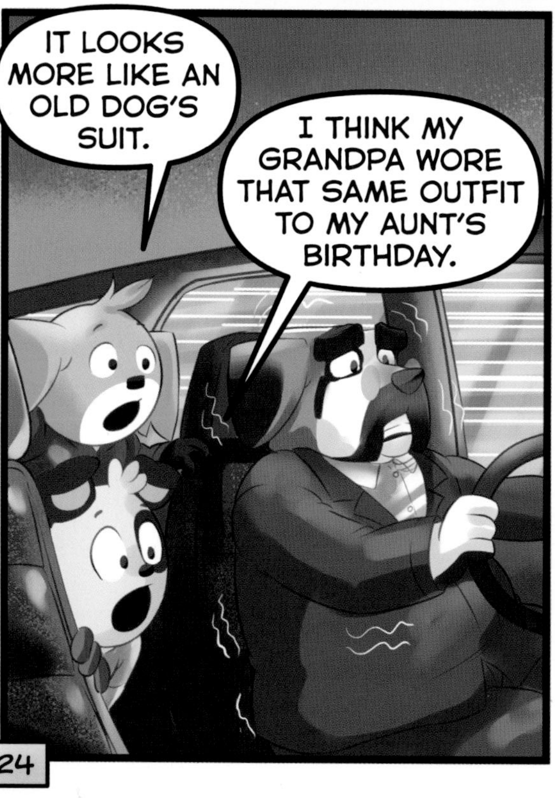
IT LOOKS MORE LIKE AN OLD DOG'S SUIT.
I THINK MY GRANDPA WORE THAT SAME OUTFIT TO MY AUNT'S BIRTHDAY.

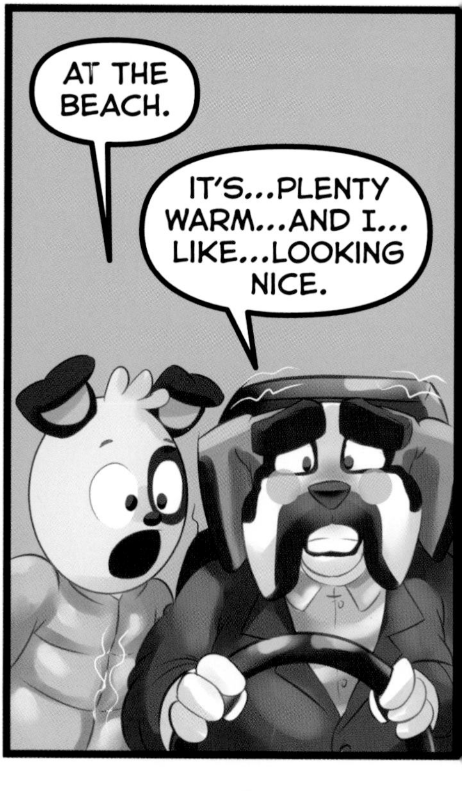
AT THE BEACH.
IT'S...PLENTY WARM...AND I... LIKE...LOOKING NICE.

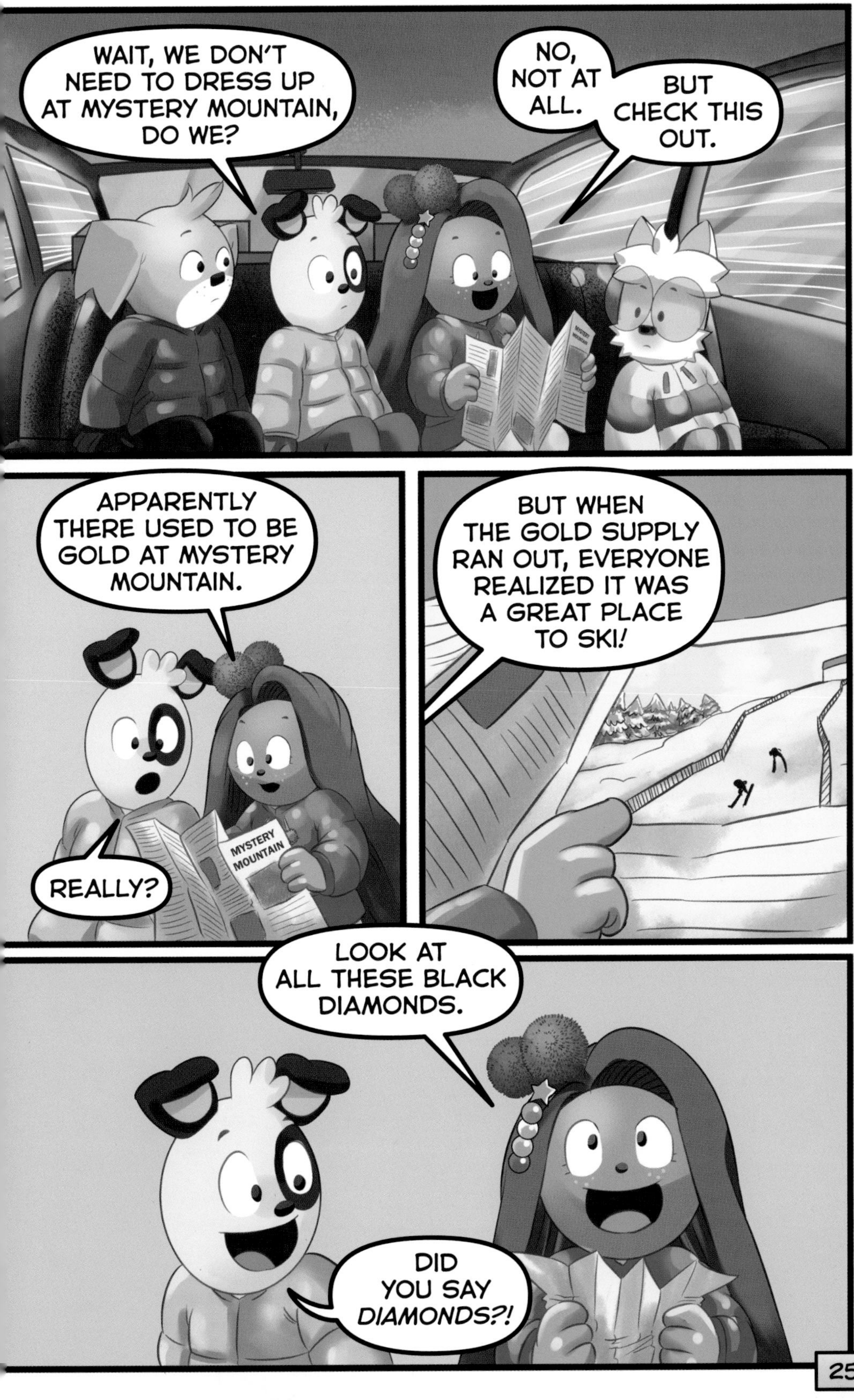
WAIT, WE DON'T NEED TO DRESS UP AT MYSTERY MOUNTAIN, DO WE?
NO, NOT AT ALL.
BUT CHECK THIS OUT.
MYSTERY MOUNTAIN
APPARENTLY THERE USED TO BE GOLD AT MYSTERY MOUNTAIN.
REALLY?
MYSTERY MOUNTAIN
BUT WHEN THE GOLD SUPPLY RAN OUT, EVERYONE REALIZED IT WAS A GREAT PLACE TO SKI!
LOOK AT ALL THESE BLACK DIAMONDS.
DID YOU SAY *DIAMONDS*?!

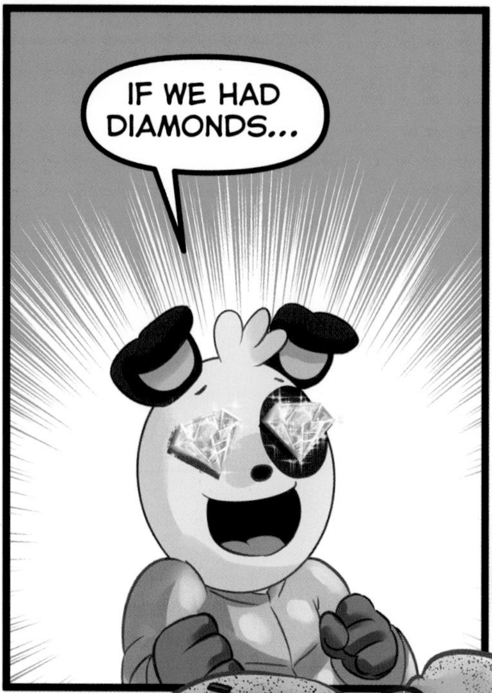
IF WE HAD DIAMONDS...

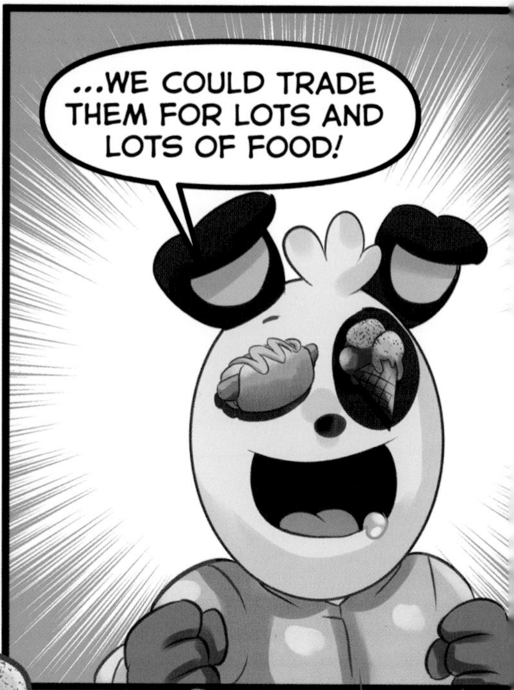
...WE COULD TRADE THEM FOR LOTS AND LOTS OF FOOD!

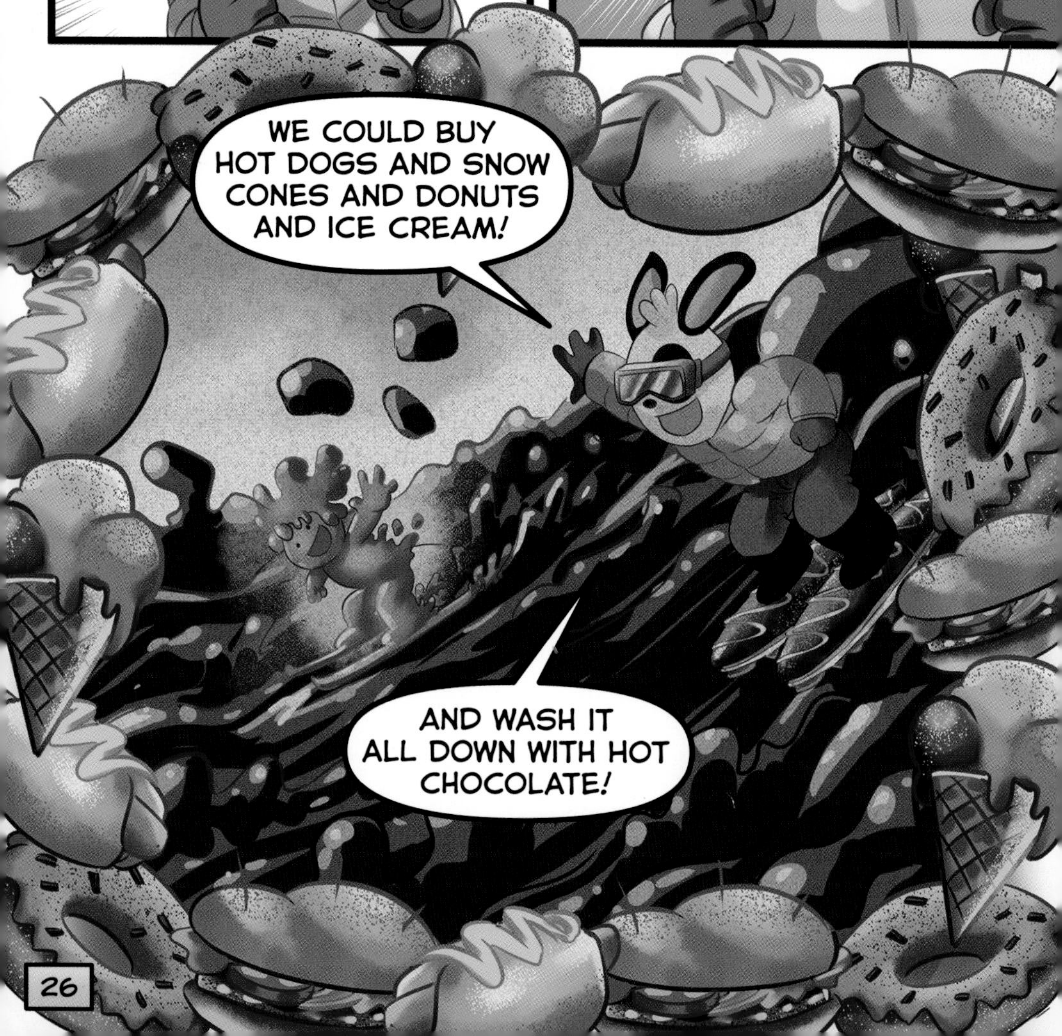
WE COULD BUY HOT DOGS AND SNOW CONES AND DONUTS AND ICE CREAM!
AND WASH IT ALL DOWN WITH HOT CHOCOLATE!

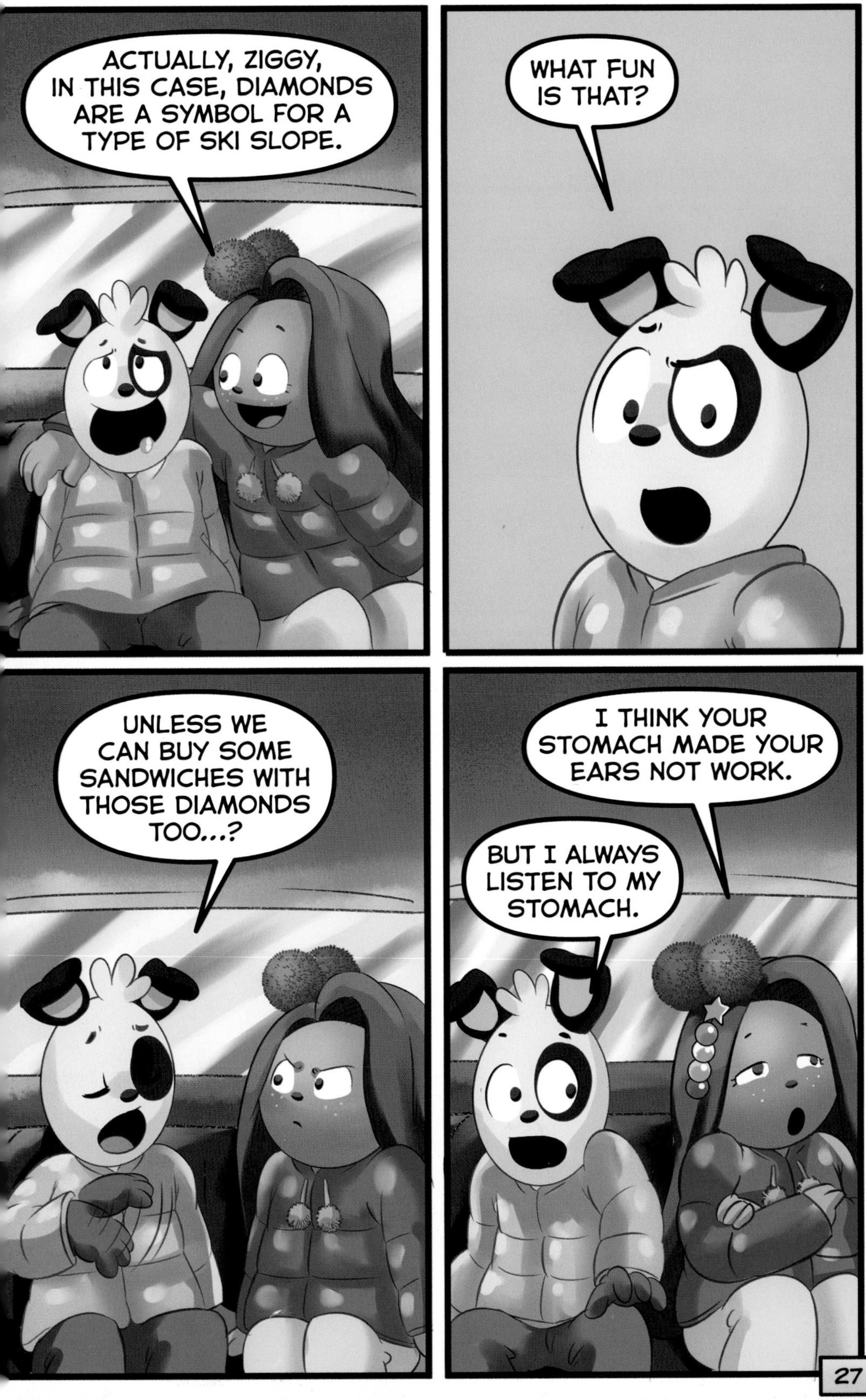
ACTUALLY, ZIGGY, IN THIS CASE, DIAMONDS ARE A SYMBOL FOR A TYPE OF SKI SLOPE.
WHAT FUN IS THAT?
UNLESS WE CAN BUY SOME SANDWICHES WITH THOSE DIAMONDS TOO...?
I THINK YOUR STOMACH MADE YOUR EARS NOT WORK.
BUT I ALWAYS LISTEN TO MY STOMACH.

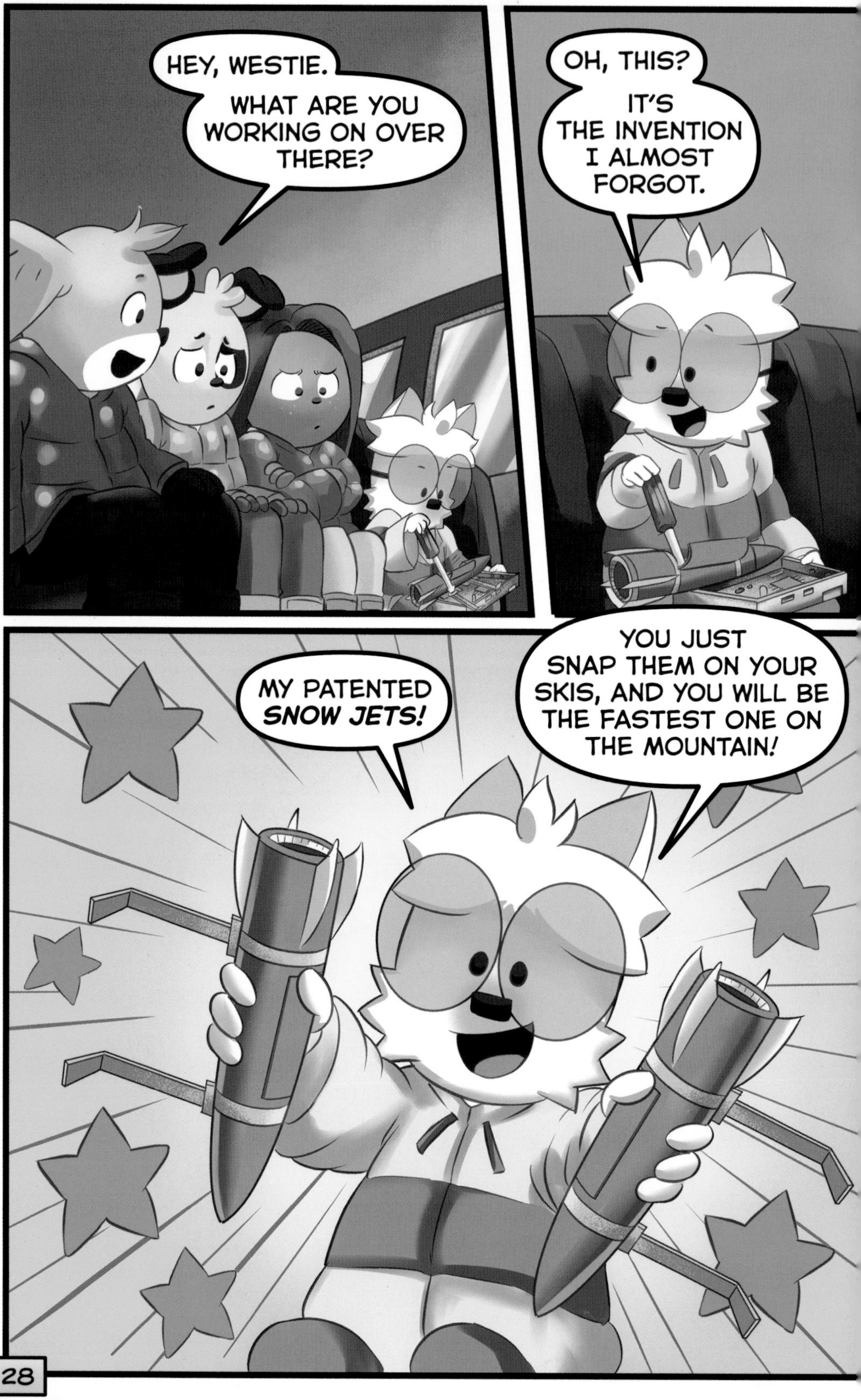
HEY, WESTIE.
WHAT ARE YOU WORKING ON OVER THERE?
OH, THIS?
IT'S THE INVENTION I ALMOST FORGOT.
MY PATENTED *SNOW JETS!*
YOU JUST SNAP THEM ON YOUR SKIS, AND YOU WILL BE THE FASTEST ONE ON THE MOUNTAIN!

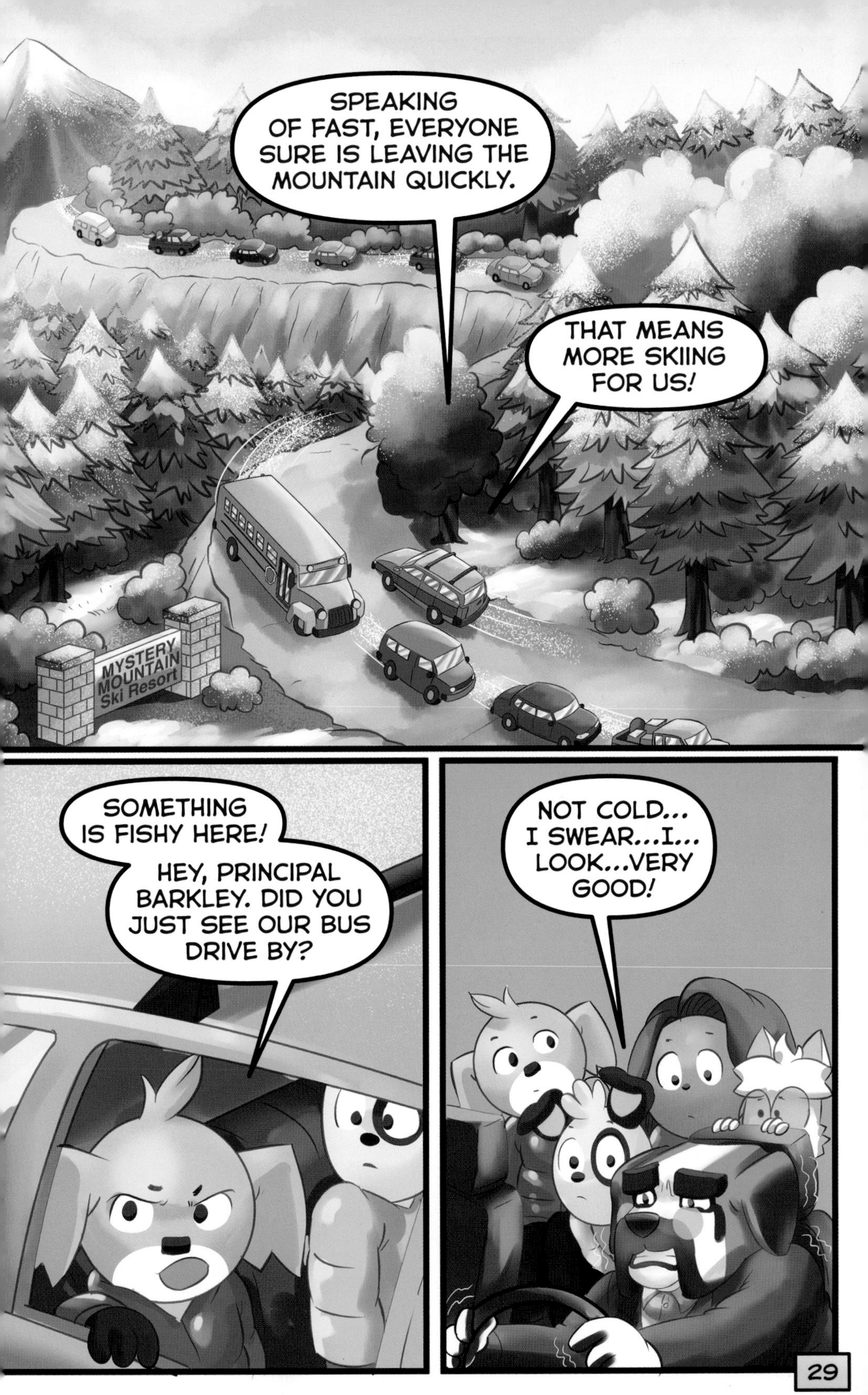
SPEAKING OF FAST, EVERYONE SURE IS LEAVING THE MOUNTAIN QUICKLY.
THAT MEANS MORE SKIING FOR US!
MYSTERY MOUNTAIN Ski Resort
SOMETHING IS FISHY HERE!
HEY, PRINCIPAL BARKLEY. DID YOU JUST SEE OUR BUS DRIVE BY?
NOT COLD... I SWEAR...I... LOOK...VERY GOOD!

CHAPTER 3

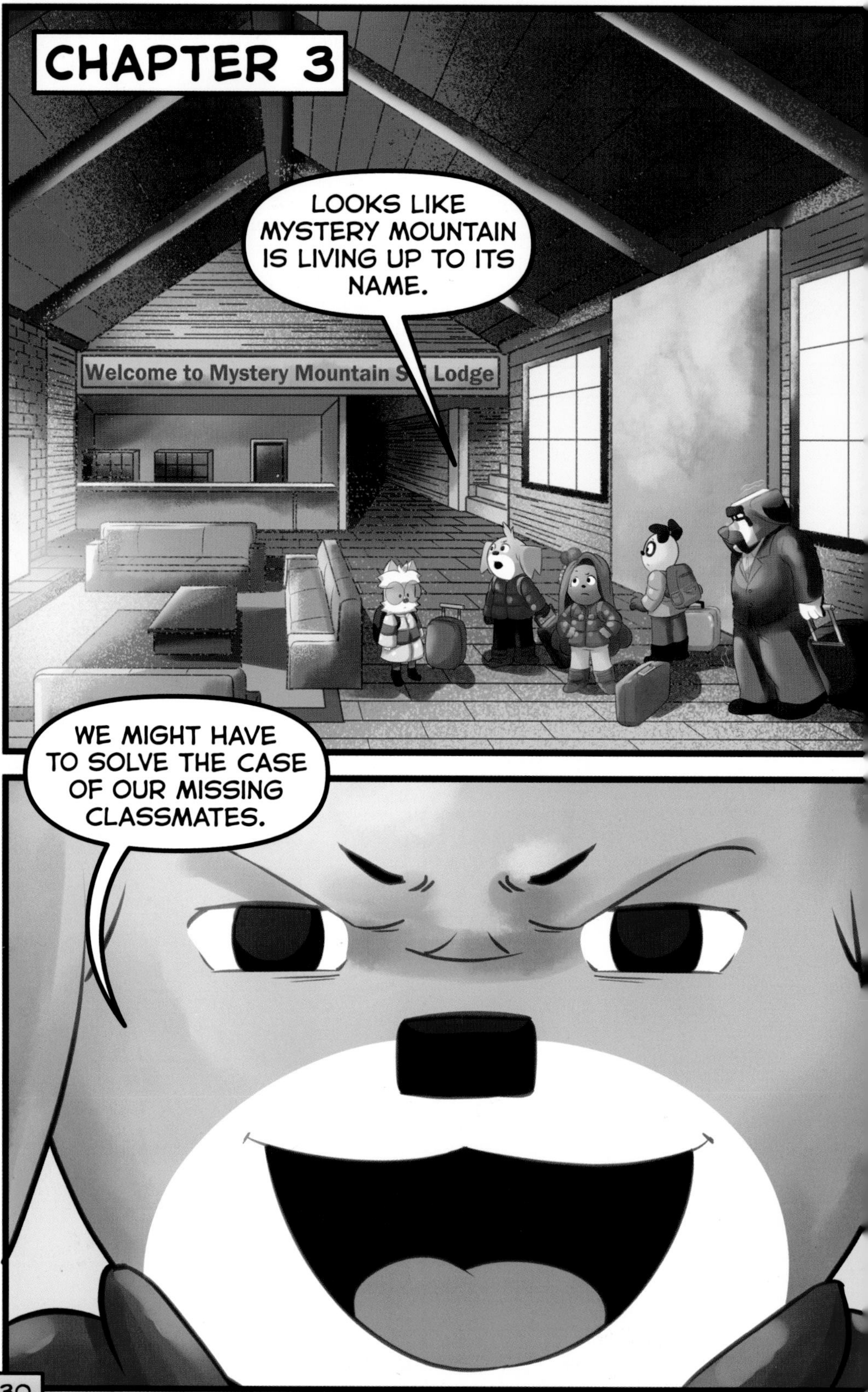
LOOKS LIKE MYSTERY MOUNTAIN IS LIVING UP TO ITS NAME.
Welcome to Mystery Mountain
Lodge
WE MIGHT HAVE TO SOLVE THE CASE OF OUR MISSING CLASSMATES.

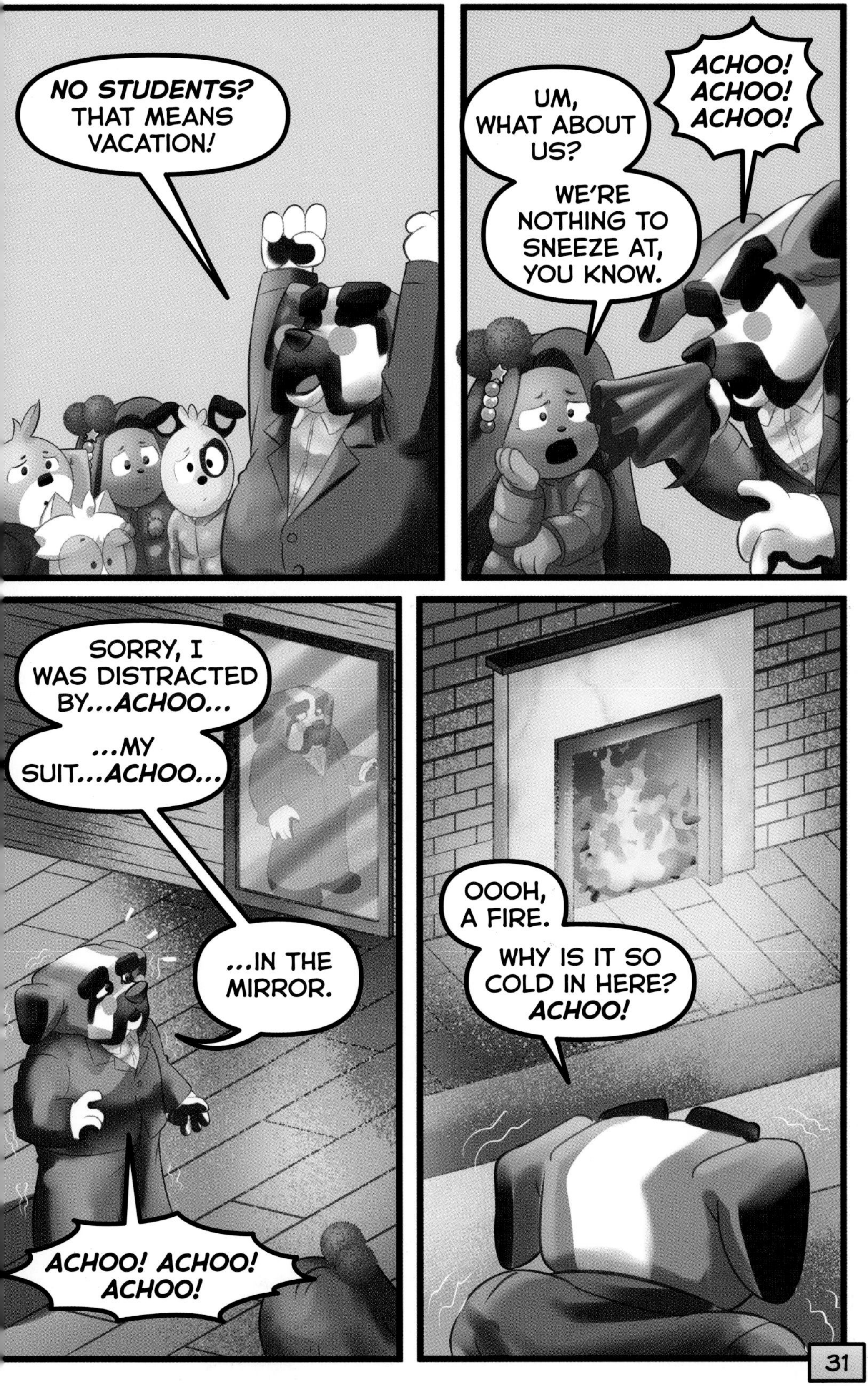
NO STUDENTS? THAT MEANS VACATION!
UM, WHAT ABOUT US?
WE'RE NOTHING TO SNEEZE AT, YOU KNOW.
ACHOO! ACHOO! ACHOO!
SORRY, I WAS DISTRACTED BY...ACHOO...
...MY SUIT...ACHOO...
...IN THE MIRROR.
ACHOO! ACHOO! ACHOO!
OOOH, A FIRE.
WHY IS IT SO COLD IN HERE? ACHOO!

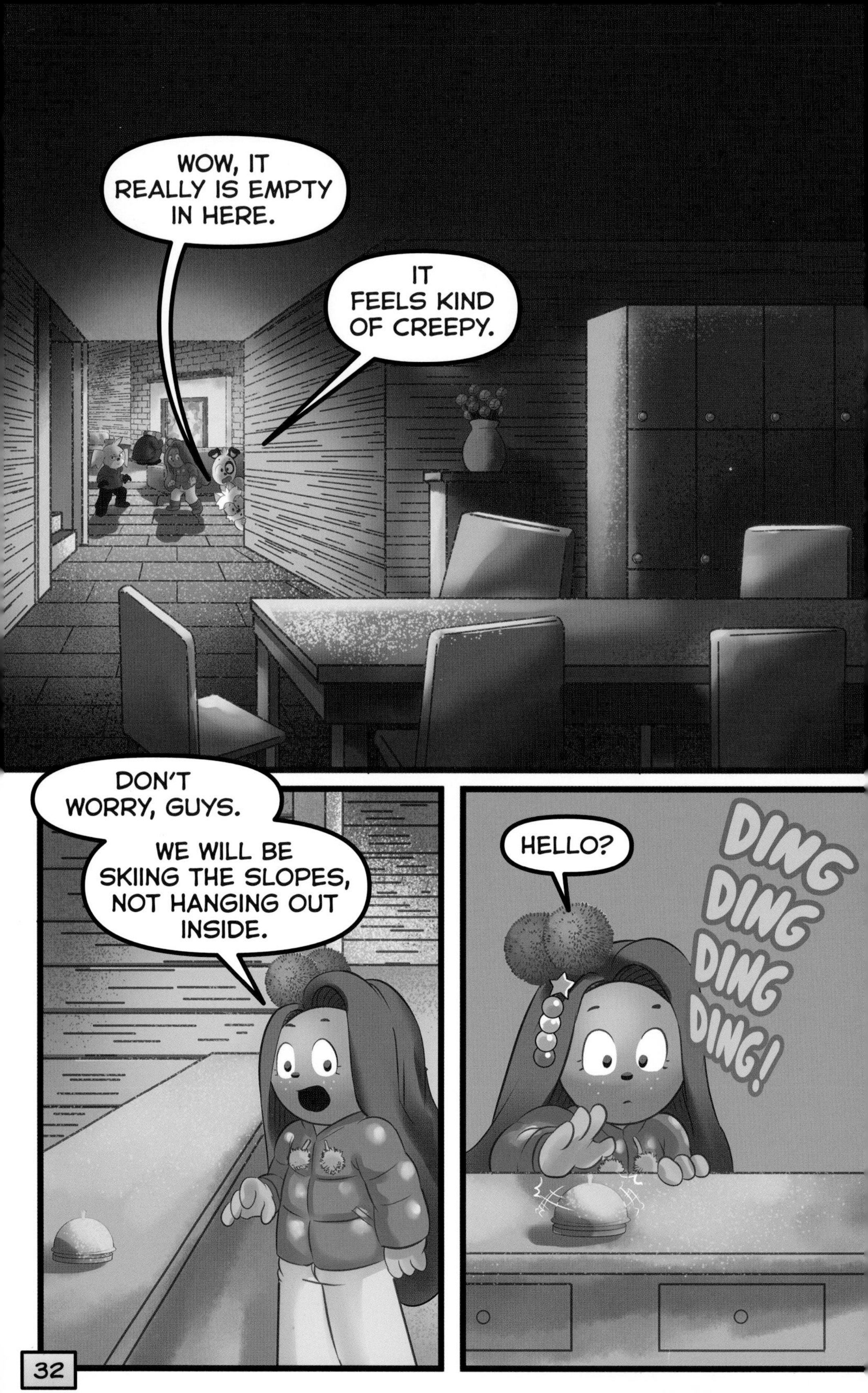
WOW, IT REALLY IS EMPTY IN HERE.
IT FEELS KIND OF CREEPY.
DON'T WORRY, GUYS.
WE WILL BE SKIING THE SLOPES, NOT HANGING OUT INSIDE.
HELLO?
DING DING DING DING!

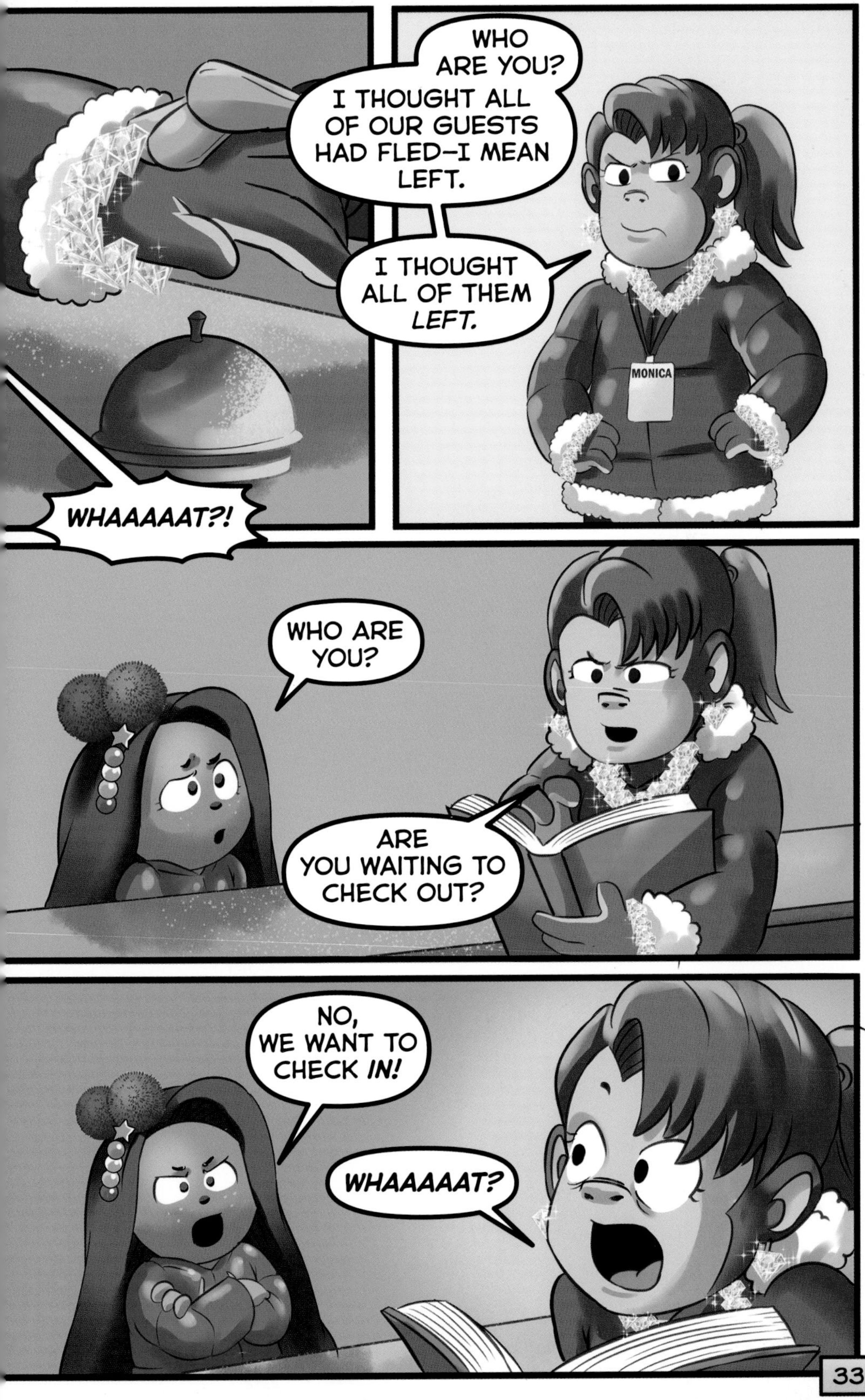
WHO ARE YOU?
I THOUGHT ALL OF OUR GUESTS HAD FLED—I MEAN LEFT.
I THOUGHT ALL OF THEM *LEFT.*
MONICA
WHAAAAAT?!
WHO ARE YOU?
ARE YOU WAITING TO CHECK OUT?
NO, WE WANT TO CHECK *IN!*
WHAAAAAT?

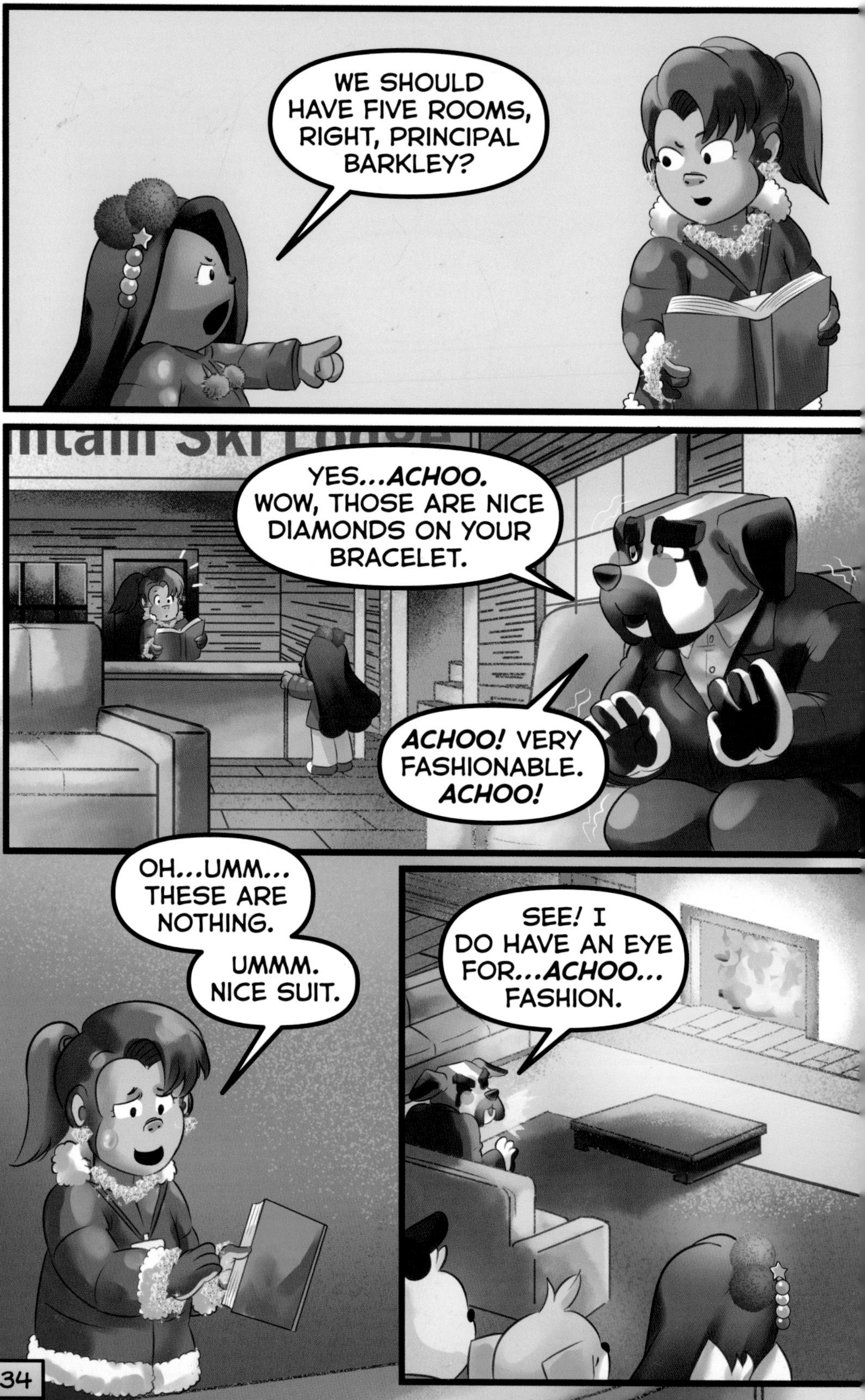
WE SHOULD HAVE FIVE ROOMS, RIGHT, PRINCIPAL BARKLEY?
ntain Ski Lodge
YES...ACHOO. WOW, THOSE ARE NICE DIAMONDS ON YOUR BRACELET.
ACHOO! VERY FASHIONABLE. ACHOO!
OH...UMM... THESE ARE NOTHING.
UMMM. NICE SUIT.
SEE! I DO HAVE AN EYE FOR...ACHOO... FASHION.

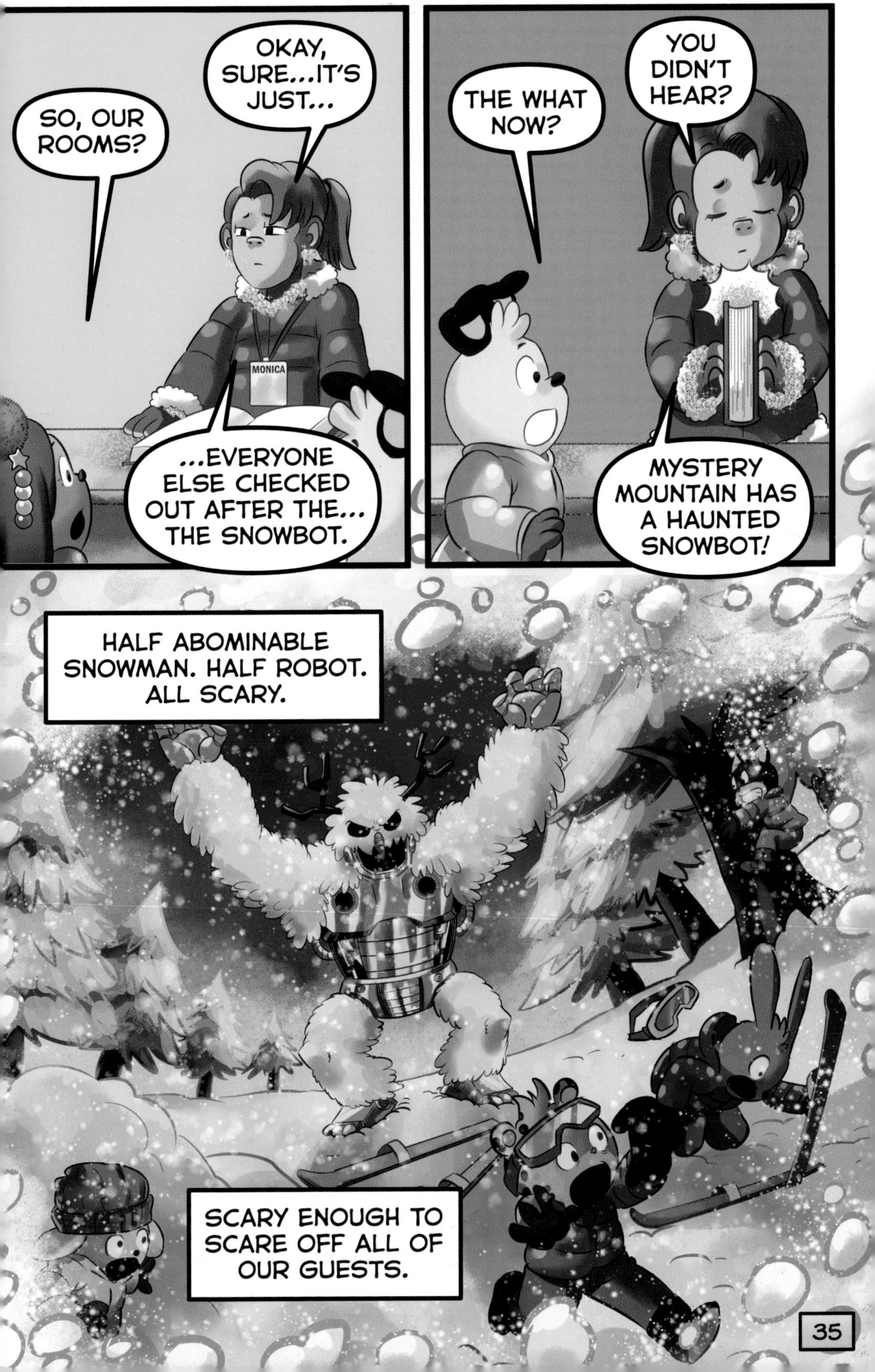
SO, OUR ROOMS?
OKAY, SURE...IT'S JUST...
...EVERYONE ELSE CHECKED OUT AFTER THE... THE SNOWBOT.
MONICA
THE WHAT NOW?
YOU DIDN'T HEAR?
MYSTERY MOUNTAIN HAS A HAUNTED SNOWBOT!
HALF ABOMINABLE SNOWMAN. HALF ROBOT. ALL SCARY.
SCARY ENOUGH TO SCARE OFF ALL OF OUR GUESTS.

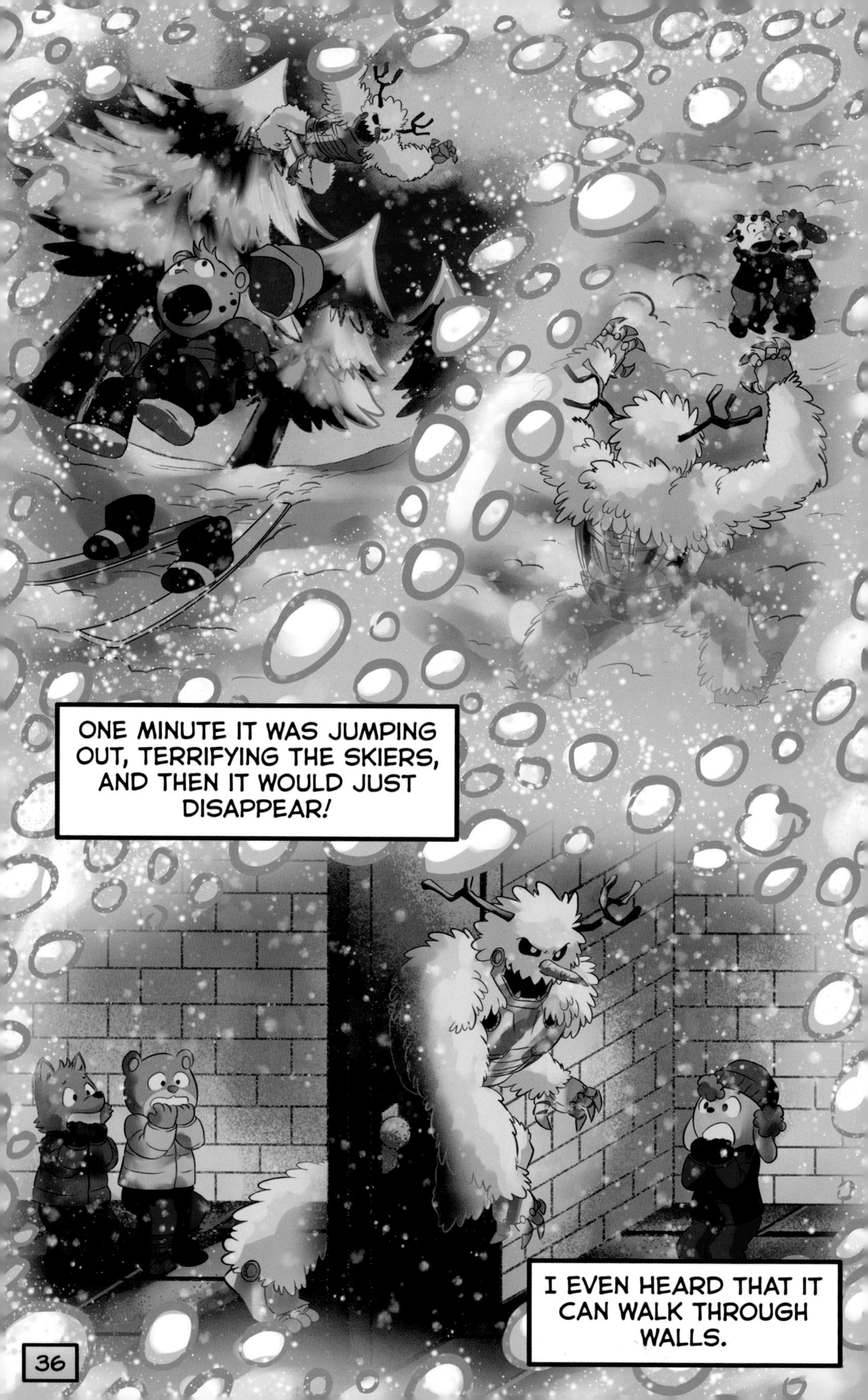
ONE MINUTE IT WAS JUMPING OUT, TERRIFYING THE SKIERS, AND THEN IT WOULD JUST DISAPPEAR!
I EVEN HEARD THAT IT CAN WALK THROUGH WALLS.

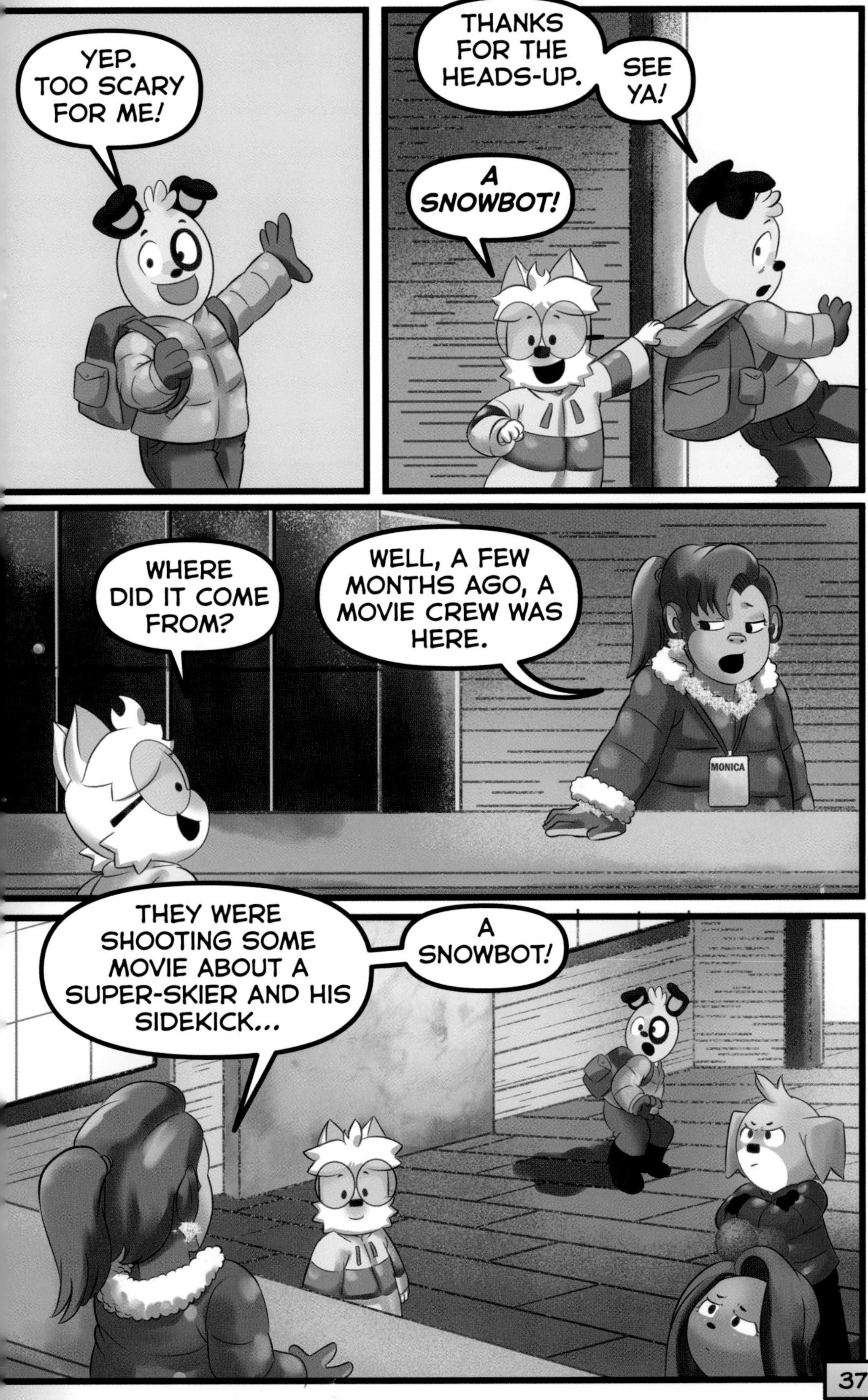

YEP. TOO SCARY FOR ME!
THANKS FOR THE HEADS-UP.
SEE YA!
A SNOWBOT!
WHERE DID IT COME FROM?
WELL, A FEW MONTHS AGO, A MOVIE CREW WAS HERE.
MONICA
THEY WERE SHOOTING SOME MOVIE ABOUT A SUPER-SKIER AND HIS SIDEKICK...
A SNOWBOT!

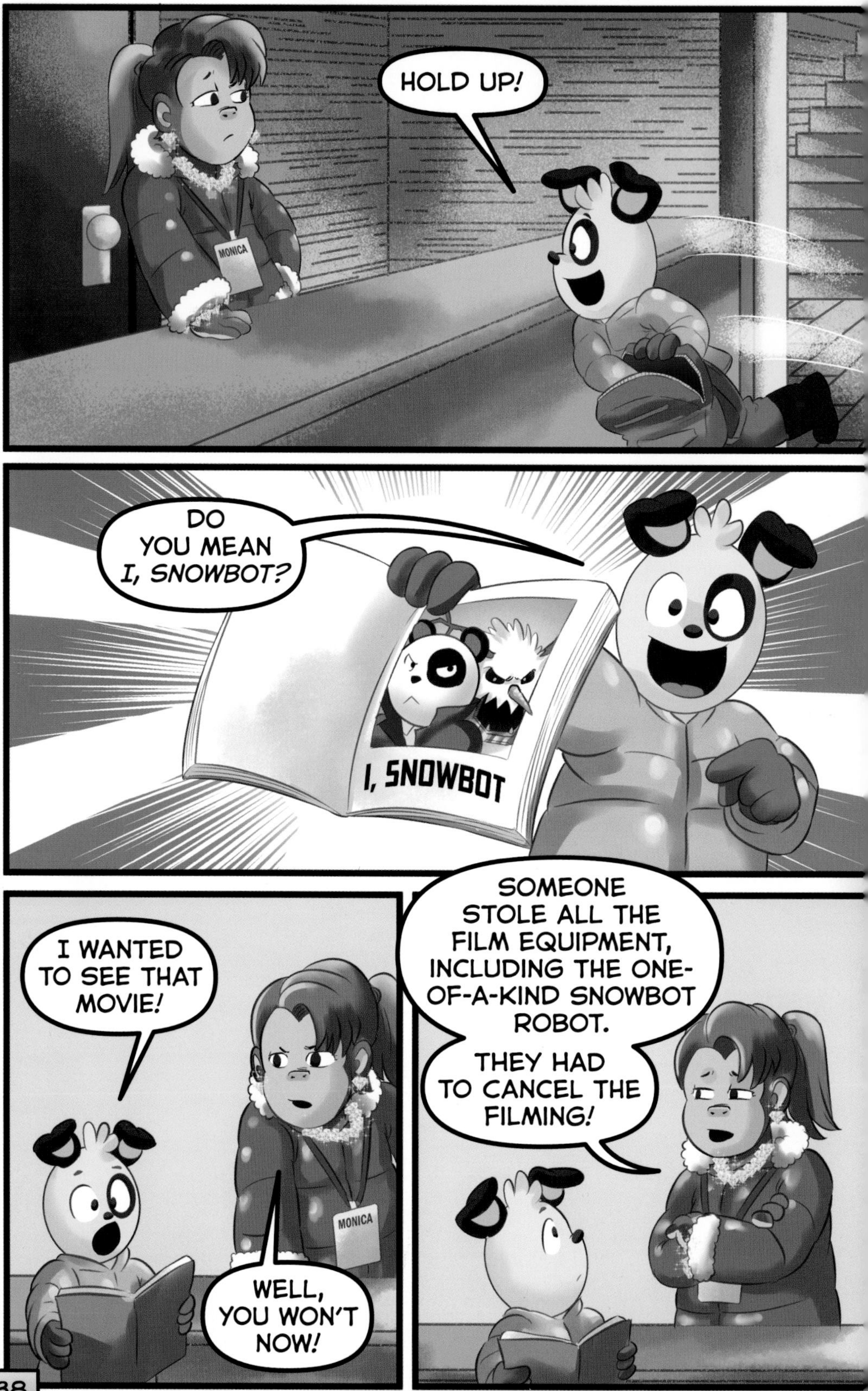
HOLD UP!
DO YOU MEAN I, SNOWBOT?
I, SNOWBOT
I WANTED TO SEE THAT MOVIE!
WELL, YOU WON'T NOW!
MONICA
SOMEONE STOLE ALL THE FILM EQUIPMENT, INCLUDING THE ONE-OF-A-KIND SNOWBOT ROBOT.
THEY HAD TO CANCEL THE FILMING!

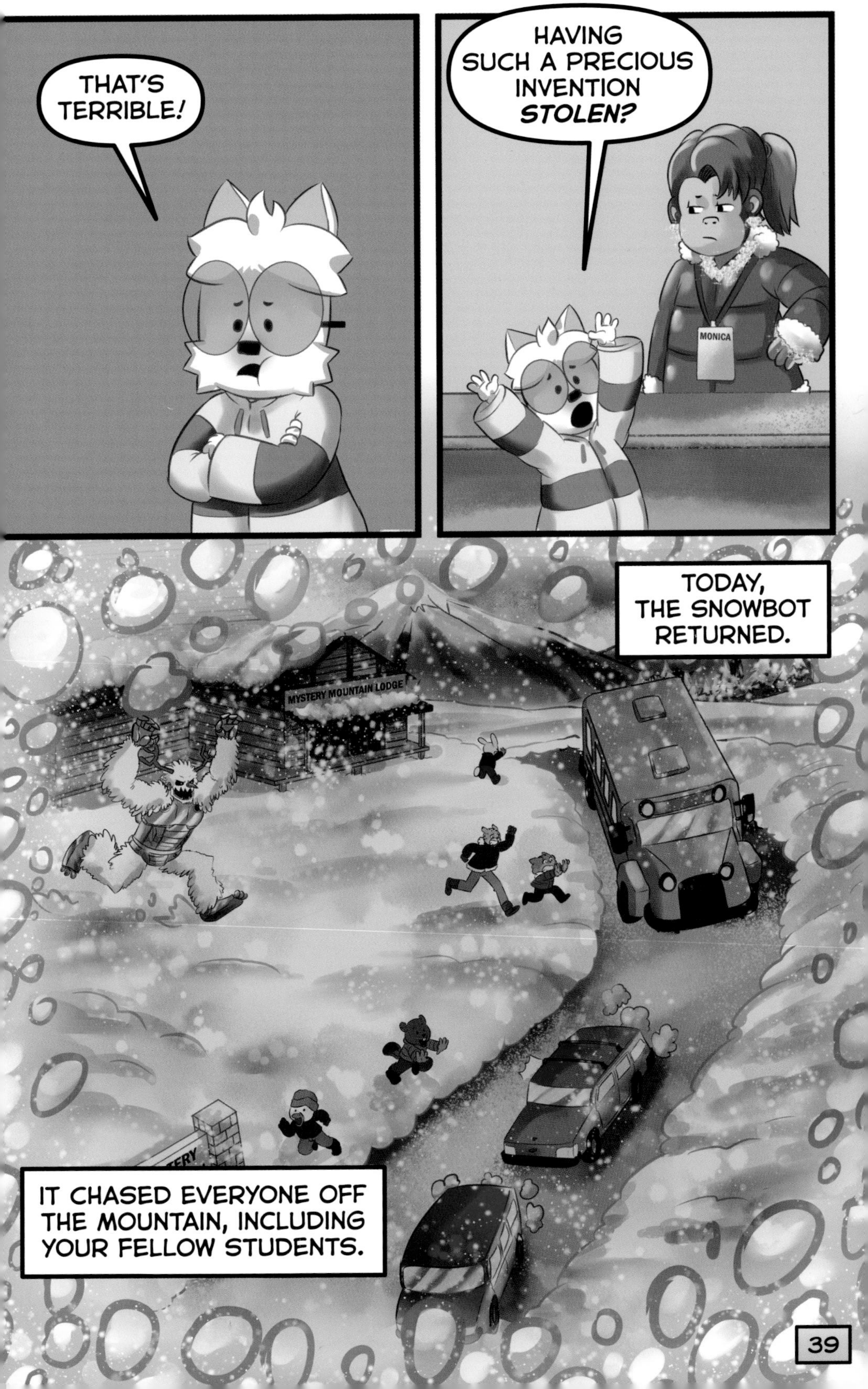
THAT'S TERRIBLE!
HAVING SUCH A PRECIOUS INVENTION STOLEN?
MONICA
TODAY, THE SNOWBOT RETURNED.
MYSTERY MOUNTAIN LODGE
IT CHASED EVERYONE OFF THE MOUNTAIN, INCLUDING YOUR FELLOW STUDENTS.

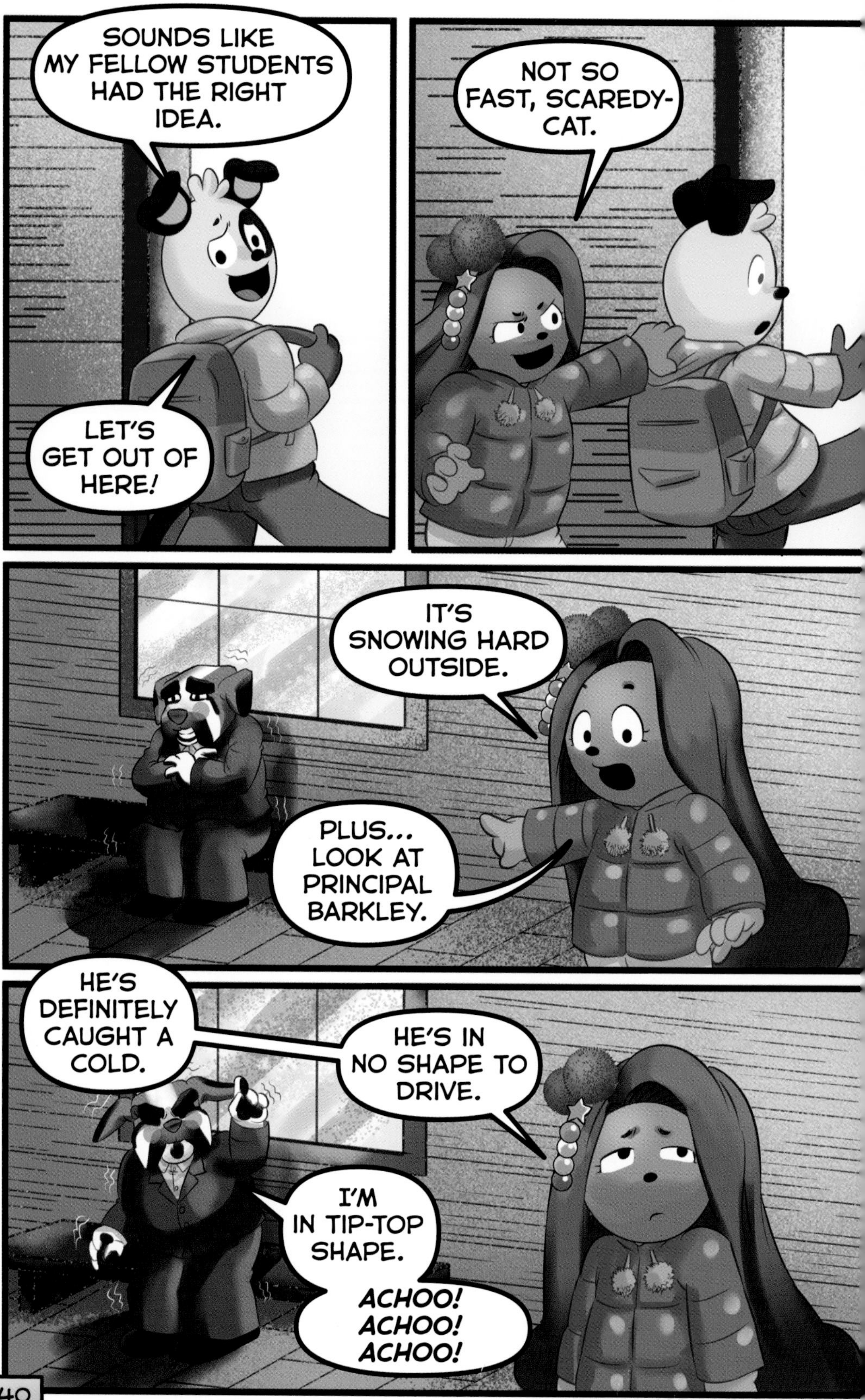
SOUNDS LIKE MY FELLOW STUDENTS HAD THE RIGHT IDEA.
LET'S GET OUT OF HERE!
NOT SO FAST, SCAREDY-CAT.
IT'S SNOWING HARD OUTSIDE.
PLUS... LOOK AT PRINCIPAL BARKLEY.
HE'S DEFINITELY CAUGHT A COLD.
HE'S IN NO SHAPE TO DRIVE.
I'M IN TIP-TOP SHAPE.
ACHOO! ACHOO! ACHOO!

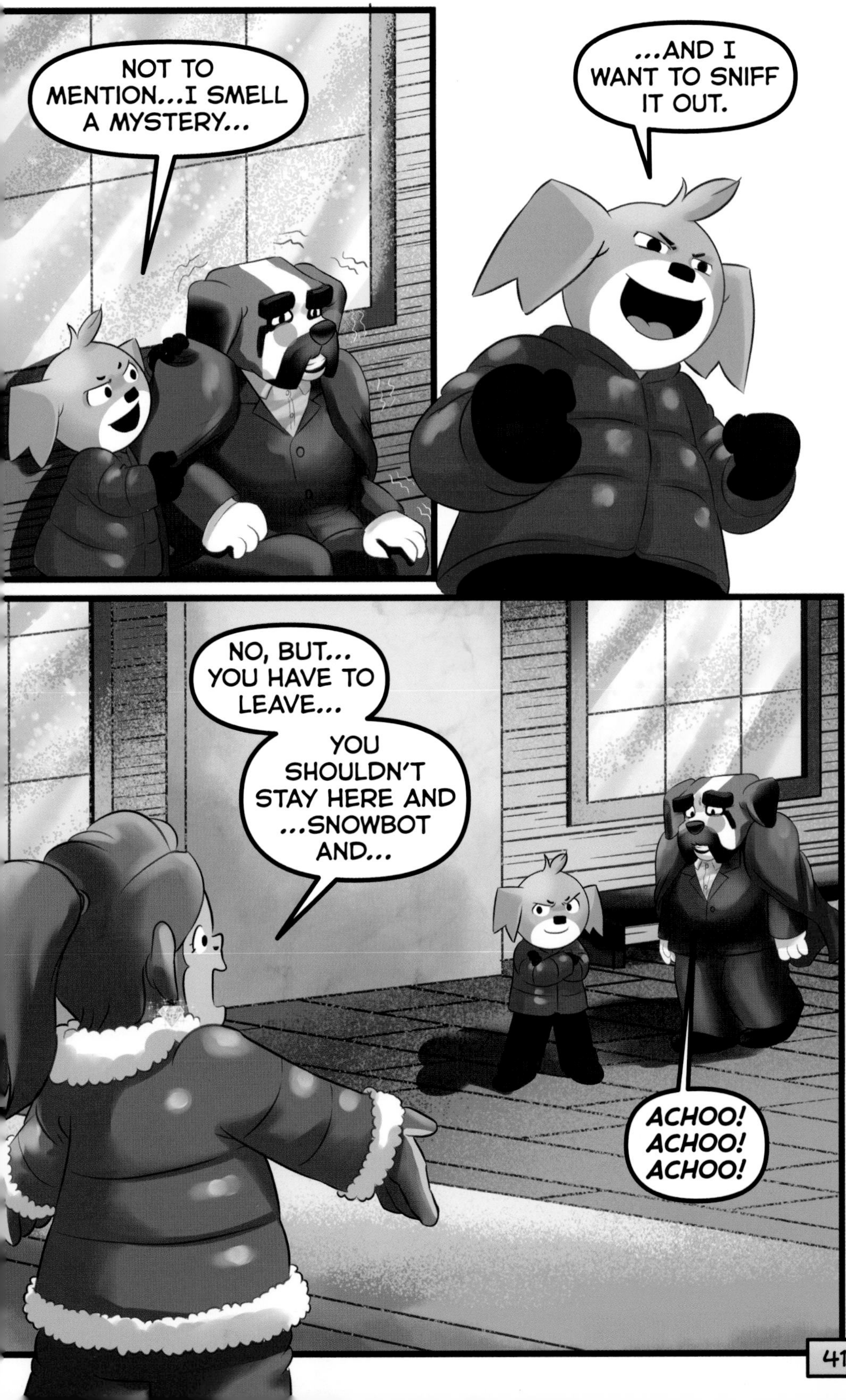
NOT TO MENTION...I SMELL A MYSTERY...
...AND I WANT TO SNIFF IT OUT.
NO, BUT... YOU HAVE TO LEAVE...
YOU SHOULDN'T STAY HERE AND ...SNOWBOT AND...
ACHOO! ACHOO! ACHOO!

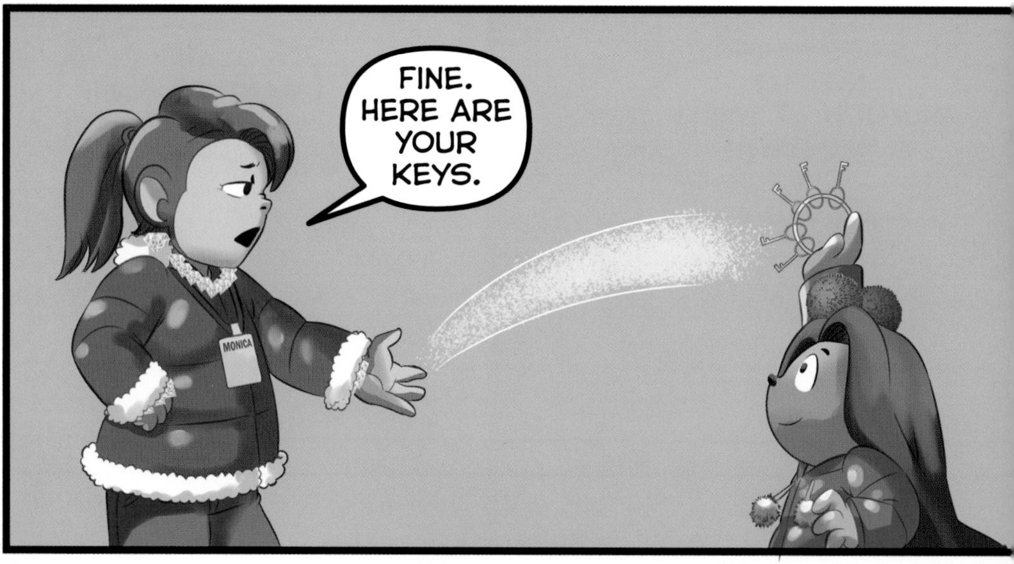
FINE. HERE ARE YOUR KEYS.
MONICA

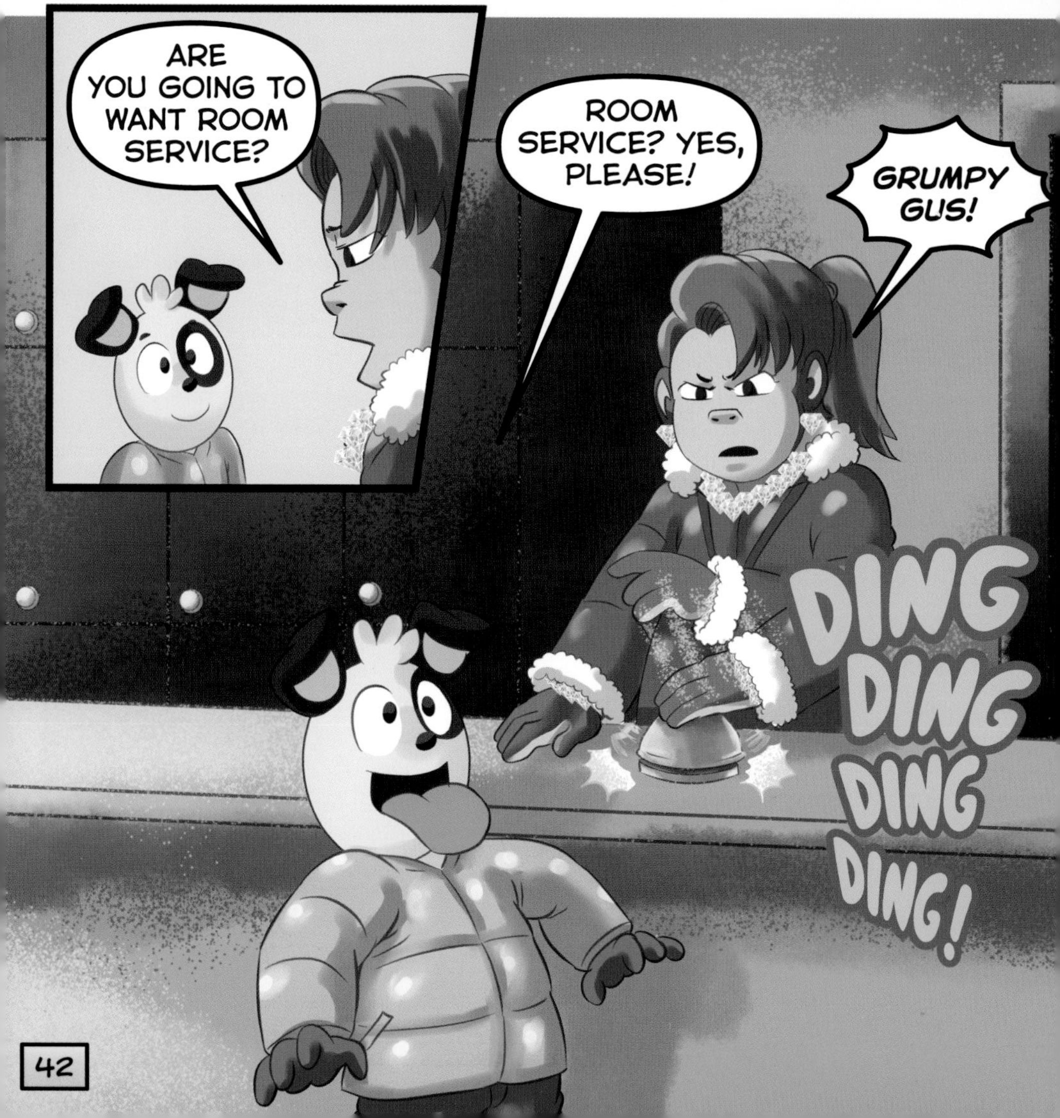
ARE YOU GOING TO WANT ROOM SERVICE?
ROOM SERVICE? YES, PLEASE!
GRUMPY GUS!
DING DING DING DING!

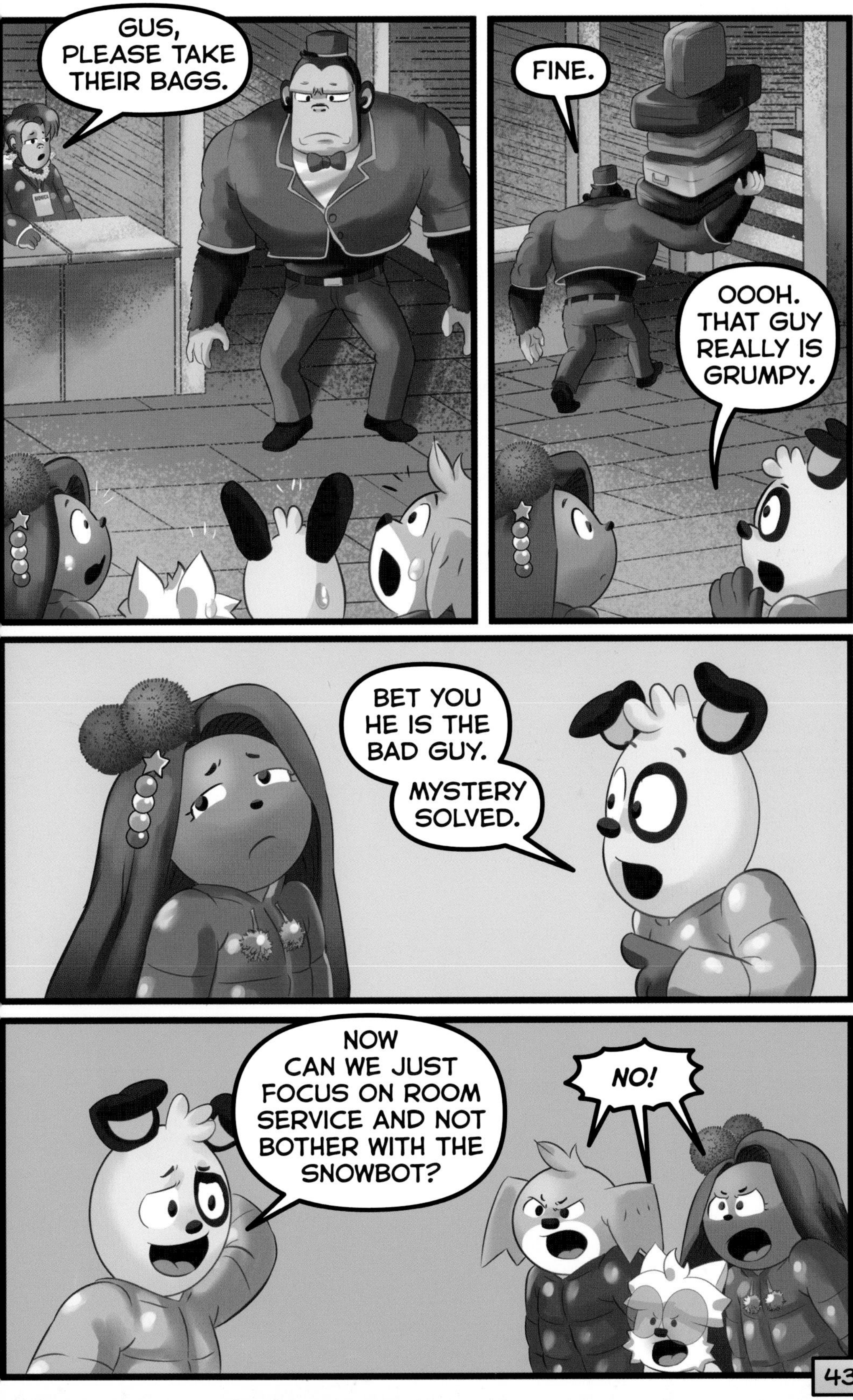
GUS, PLEASE TAKE THEIR BAGS.
FINE.
OOOH. THAT GUY REALLY IS GRUMPY.
BET YOU HE IS THE BAD GUY.
MYSTERY SOLVED.
NOW CAN WE JUST FOCUS ON ROOM SERVICE AND NOT BOTHER WITH THE SNOWBOT?
NO!

CHAPTER 4

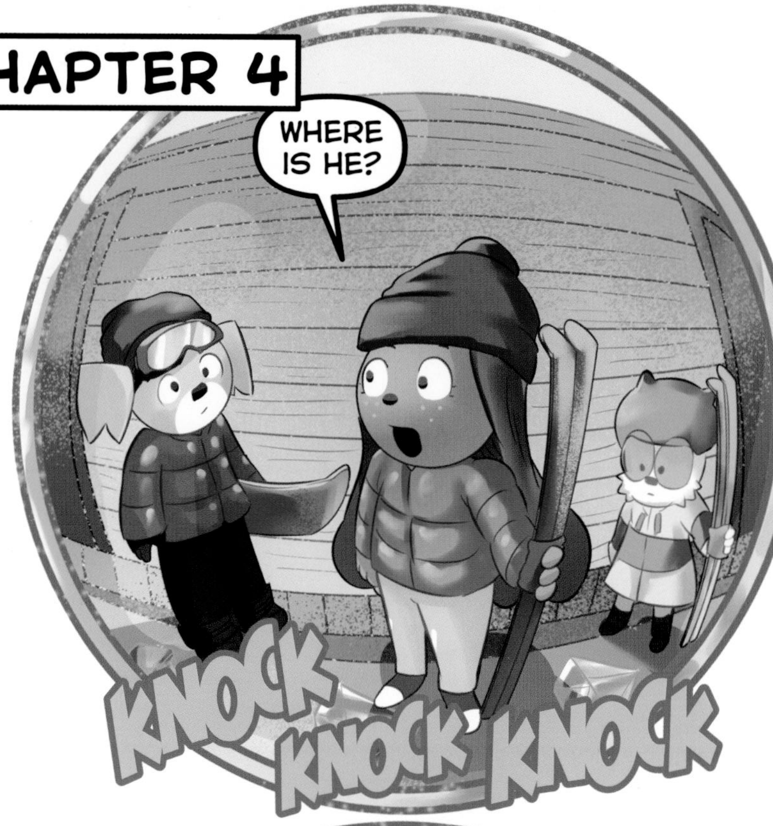
WHERE IS HE?
KNOCK KNOCK KNOCK

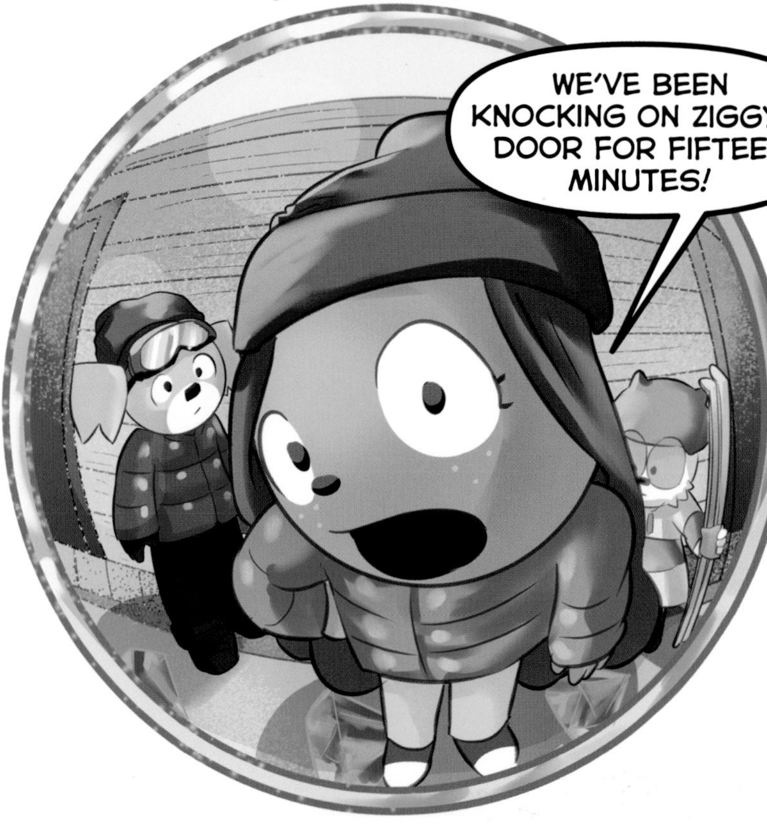
WE'VE BEEN KNOCKING ON ZIGGY'S DOOR FOR FIFTEEN MINUTES!

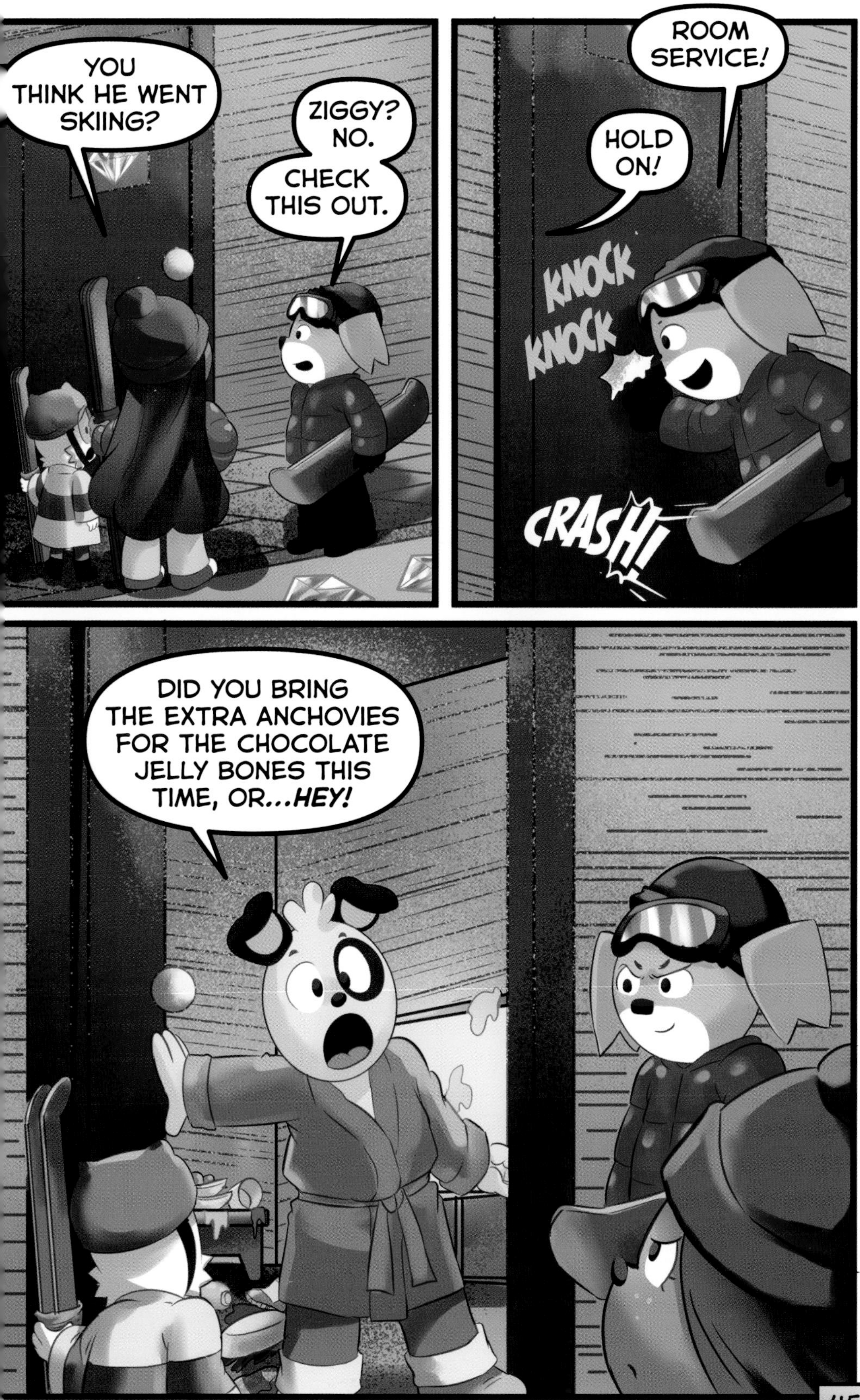
YOU THINK HE WENT SKIING?
ZIGGY? NO.
CHECK THIS OUT.
KNOCK KNOCK
HOLD ON!
ROOM SERVICE!
CRASH!
DID YOU BRING THE EXTRA ANCHOVIES FOR THE CHOCOLATE JELLY BONES THIS TIME, OR...*HEY!*

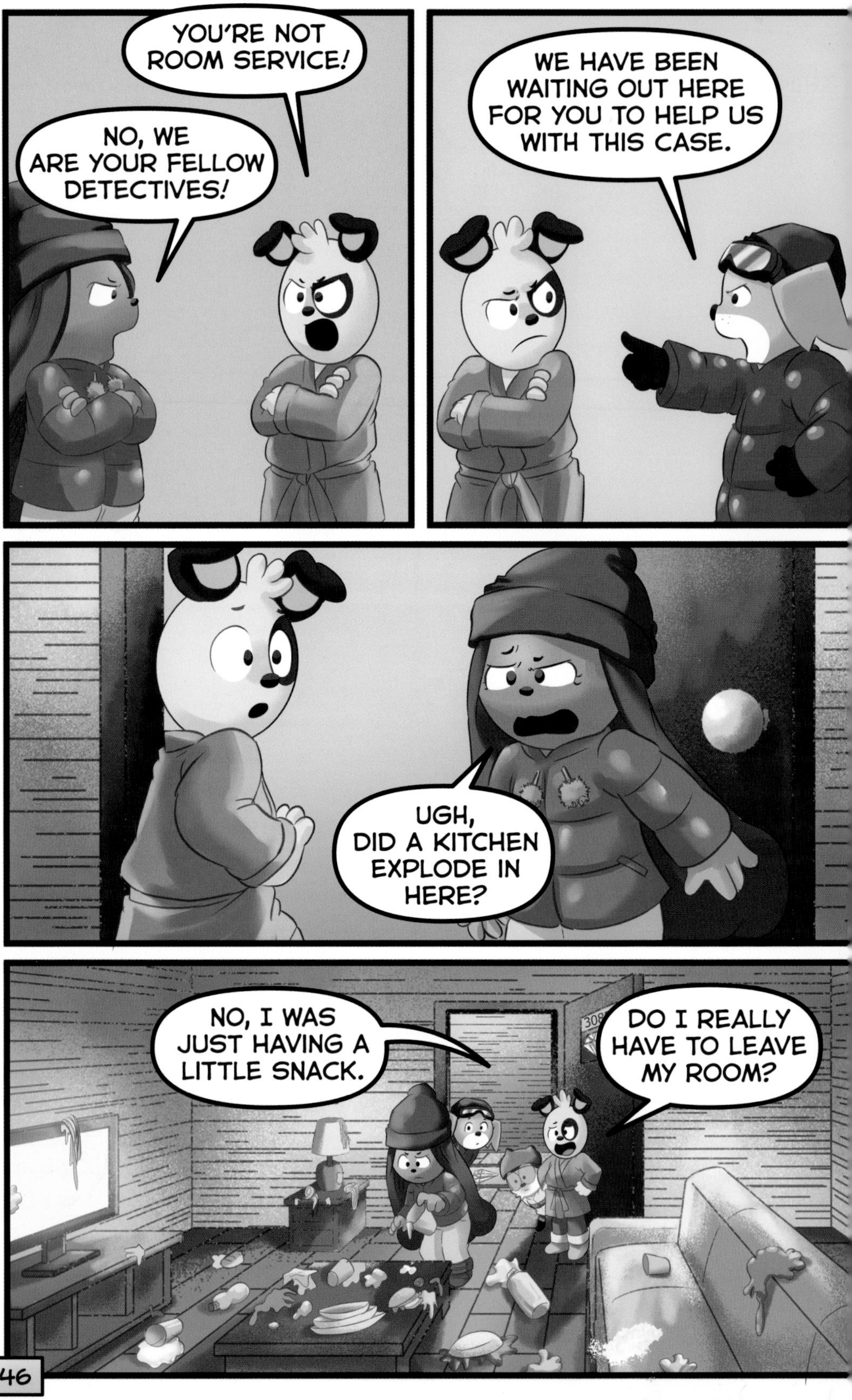
NO, WE ARE YOUR FELLOW DETECTIVES!
YOU'RE NOT ROOM SERVICE!
WE HAVE BEEN WAITING OUT HERE FOR YOU TO HELP US WITH THIS CASE.
UGH, DID A KITCHEN EXPLODE IN HERE?
NO, I WAS JUST HAVING A LITTLE SNACK.
DO I REALLY HAVE TO LEAVE MY ROOM?
308

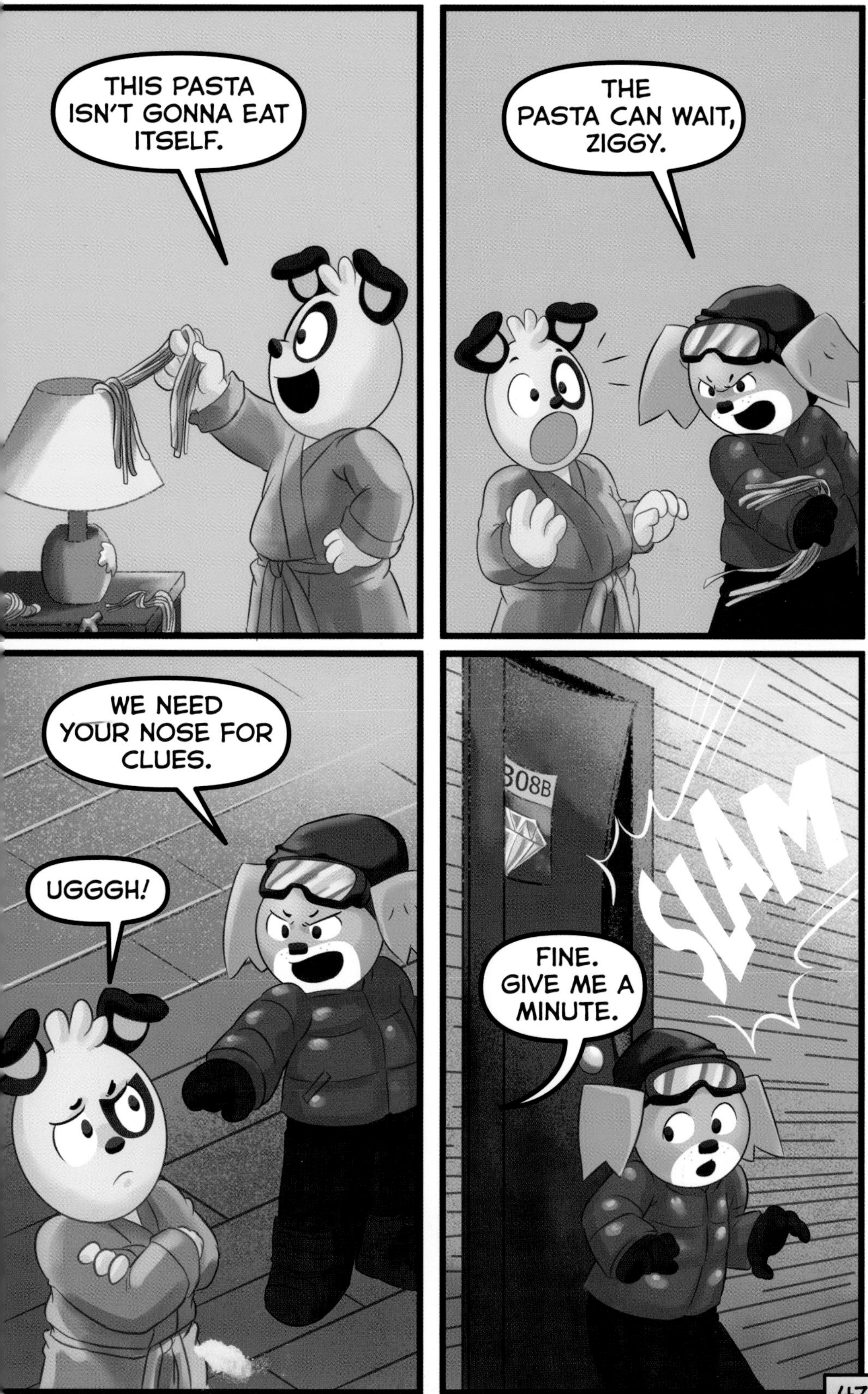
THIS PASTA ISN'T GONNA EAT ITSELF.
THE PASTA CAN WAIT, ZIGGY.
WE NEED YOUR NOSE FOR CLUES.
UGGGH!
308B
SLAM
FINE. GIVE ME A MINUTE.

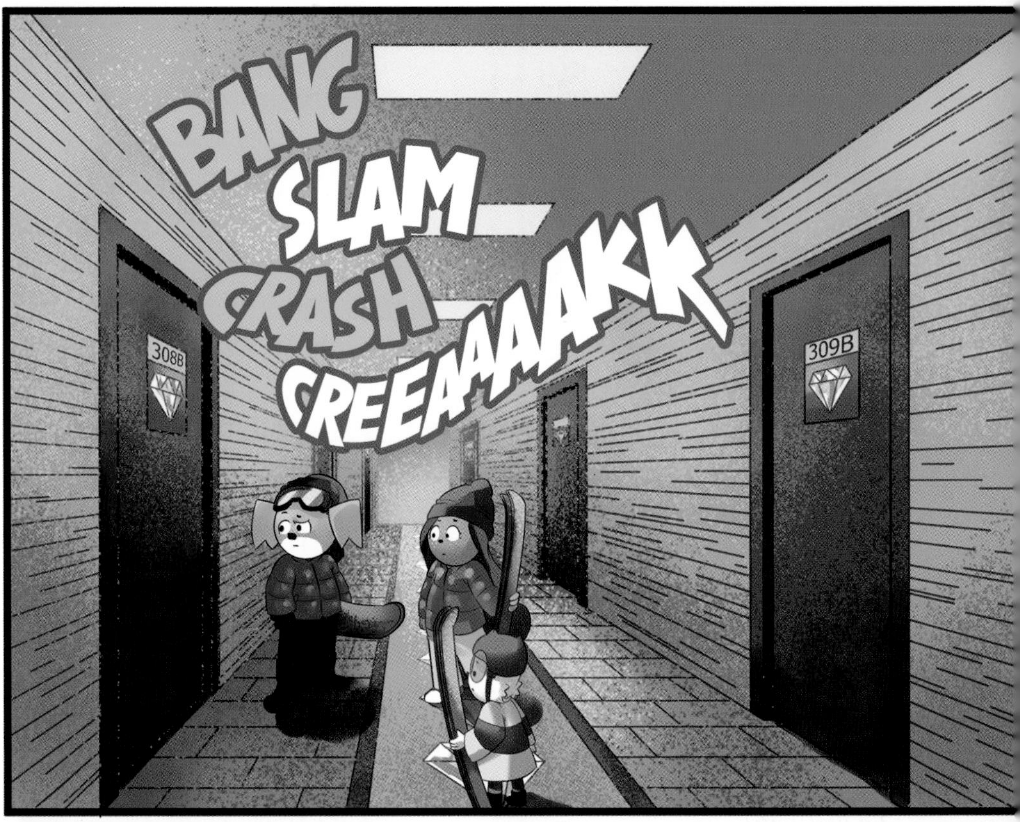
BANG
SLAM
CRASH
CREEAAAAKK
308B
309B

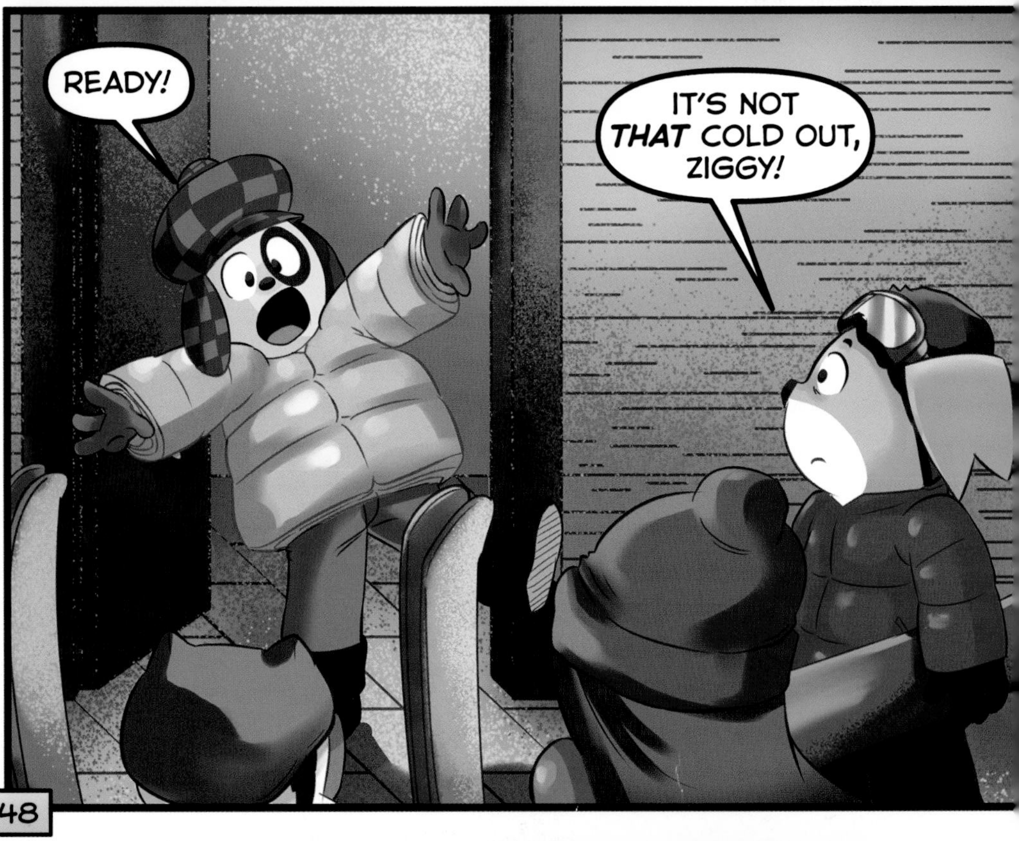
READY!
IT'S NOT *THAT* COLD OUT, ZIGGY!

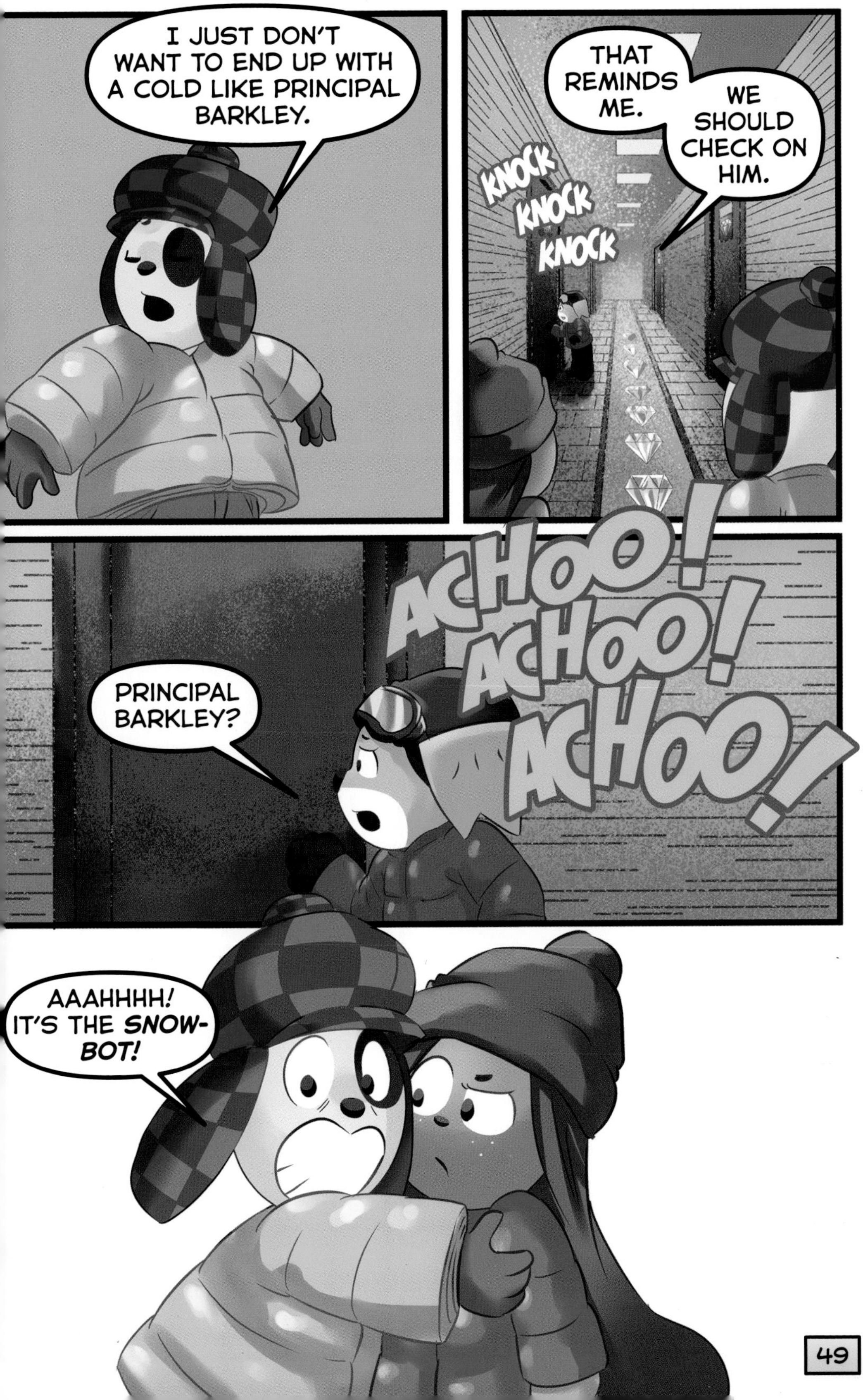
I JUST DON'T WANT TO END UP WITH A COLD LIKE PRINCIPAL BARKLEY.
THAT REMINDS ME.
WE SHOULD CHECK ON HIM.
KNOCK KNOCK KNOCK
ACHOO! ACHOO! ACHOO!
PRINCIPAL BARKLEY?
AAAHHHH! IT'S THE *SNOW-BOT!*

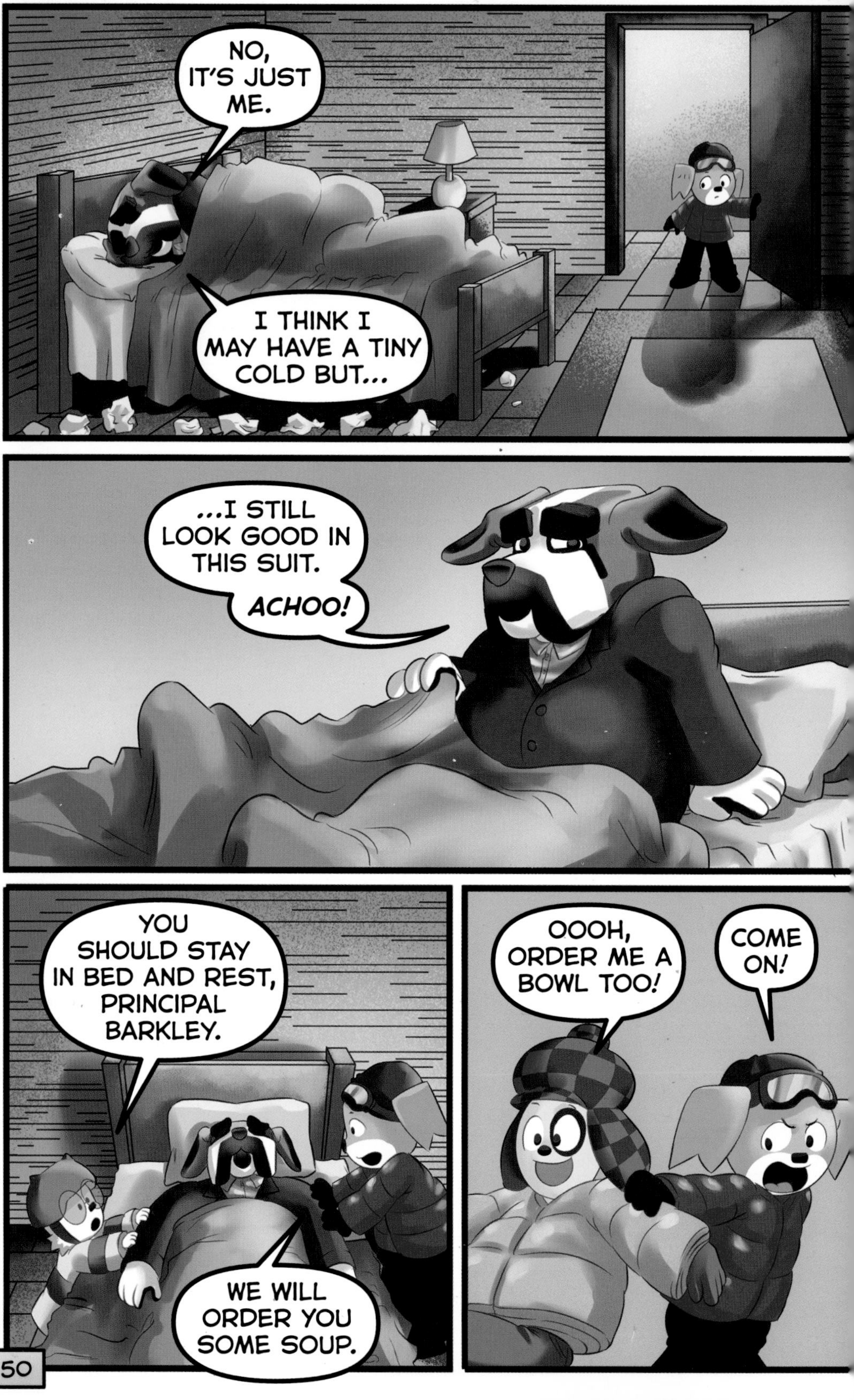
NO, IT'S JUST ME.
I THINK I MAY HAVE A TINY COLD BUT...
...I STILL LOOK GOOD IN THIS SUIT.
ACHOO!
YOU SHOULD STAY IN BED AND REST, PRINCIPAL BARKLEY.
WE WILL ORDER YOU SOME SOUP.
OOOH, ORDER ME A BOWL TOO!
COME ON!

OKAY, THIS DOES *NOT* SEEM SAFE AT ALL!

OH, IT'S VERY SAFE.

LOOK!

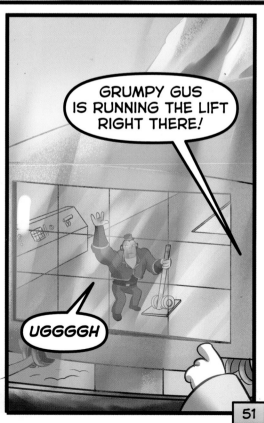

GRUMPY GUS IS RUNNING THE LIFT RIGHT THERE!

UGGGGH

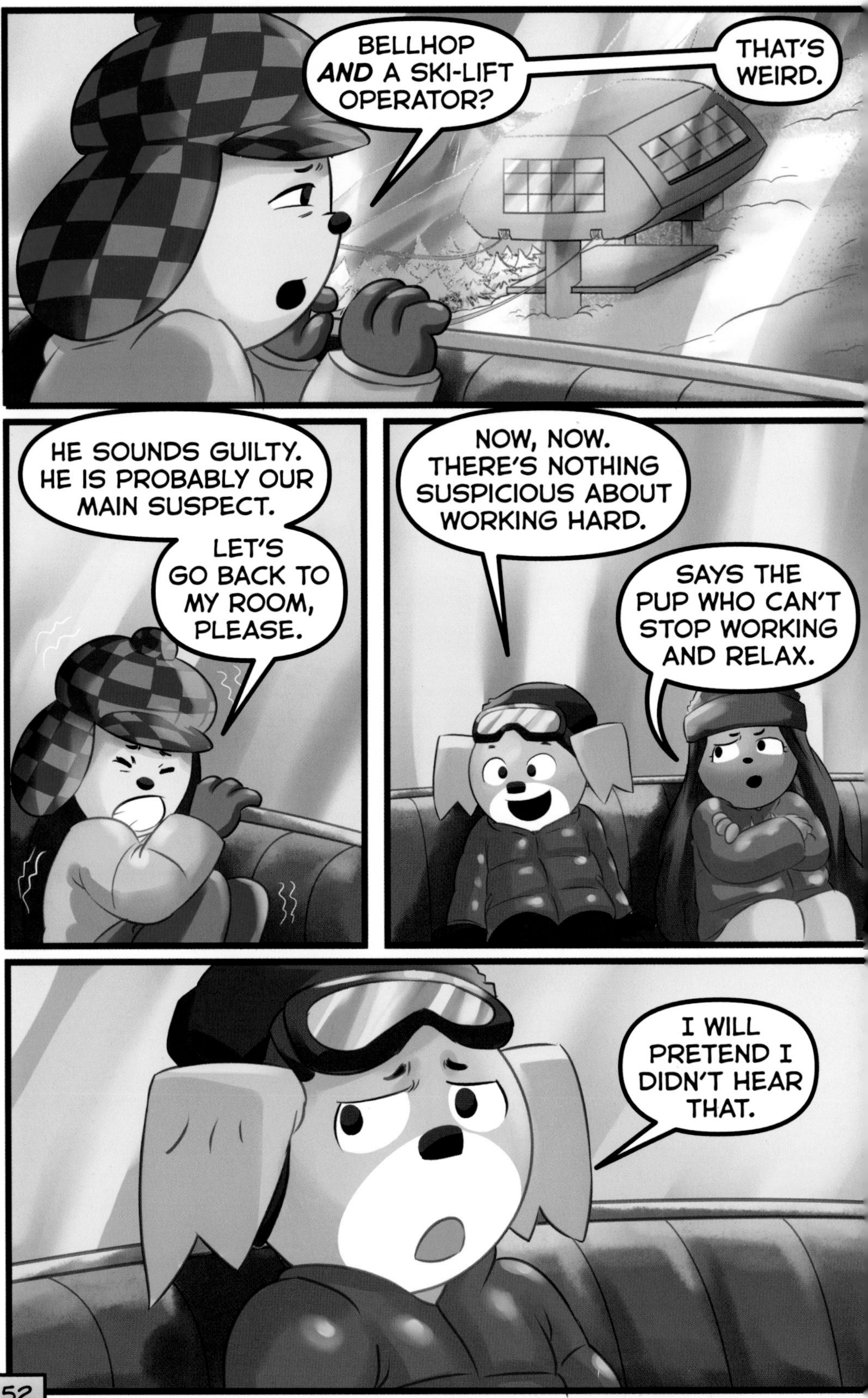
BELLHOP AND A SKI-LIFT OPERATOR?
THAT'S WEIRD.
HE SOUNDS GUILTY. HE IS PROBABLY OUR MAIN SUSPECT.
LET'S GO BACK TO MY ROOM, PLEASE.
NOW, NOW. THERE'S NOTHING SUSPICIOUS ABOUT WORKING HARD.
SAYS THE PUP WHO CAN'T STOP WORKING AND RELAX.
I WILL PRETEND I DIDN'T HEAR THAT.

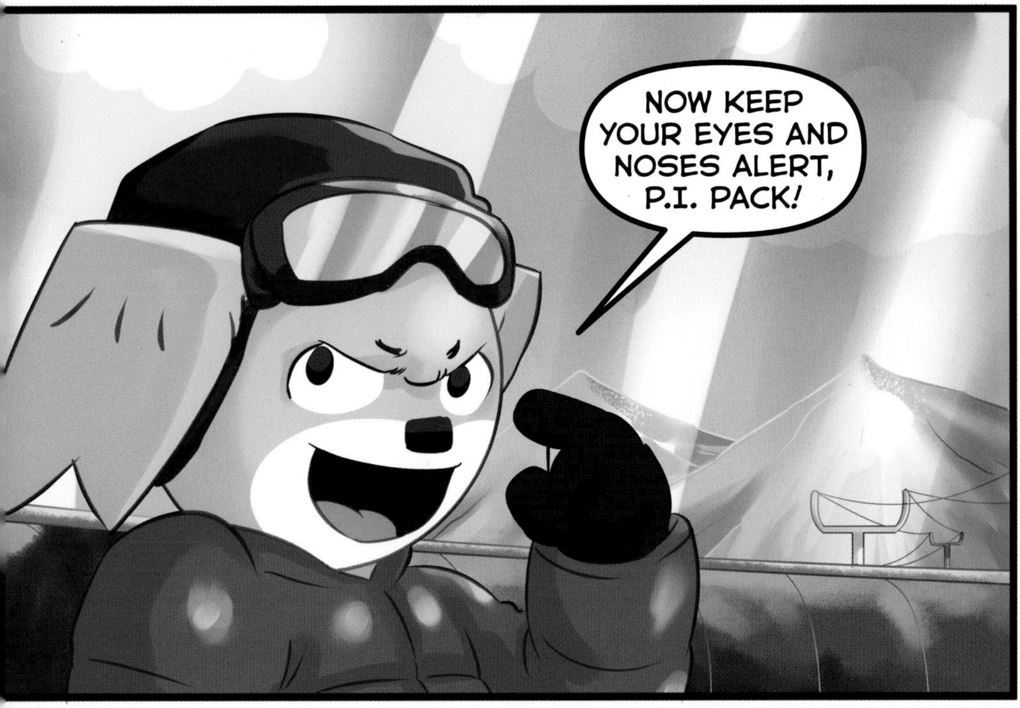
NOW KEEP YOUR EYES AND NOSES ALERT, P.I. PACK!

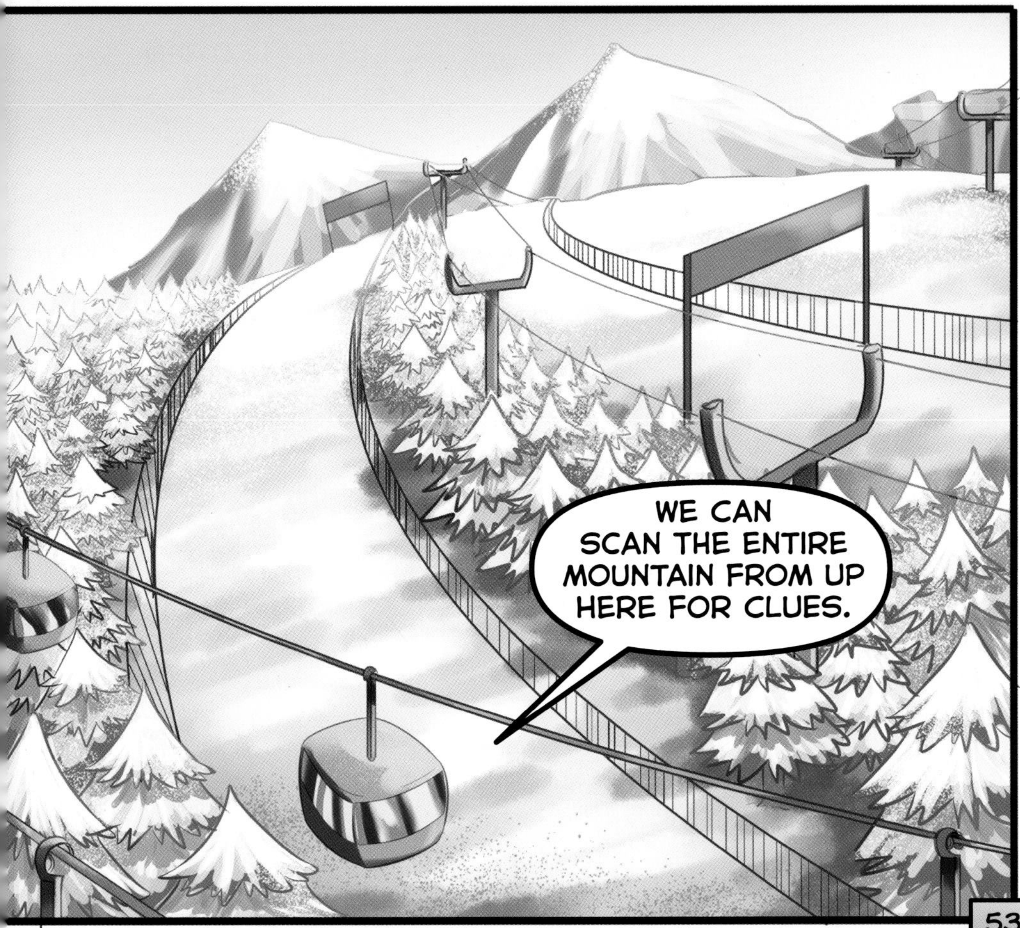
WE CAN SCAN THE ENTIRE MOUNTAIN FROM UP HERE FOR CLUES.

I CAN'T SEE *ANYTHING* FROM UP HERE.

IT'S SO BRIGHT.

THAT'S BECAUSE THE SUN IS REFLECTING OFF THE SNOW.

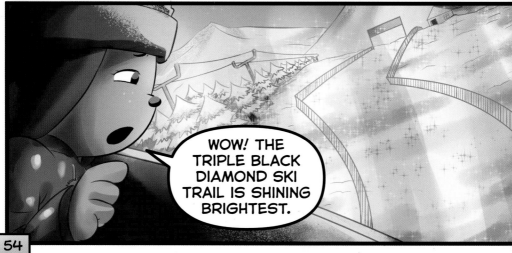

WOW! THE TRIPLE BLACK DIAMOND SKI TRAIL IS SHINING BRIGHTEST.

THAT'S WAY TOO HARD FOR ME.

I'LL STICK TO THE BUNNY SLOPE.

WOW, A SPECIAL SLOPE JUST FOR BUNNIES?

THIS MOUNTAIN HAS EVERYTHING.

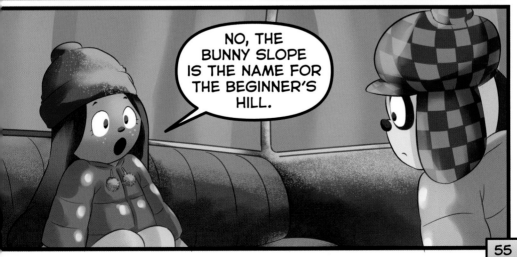

NO, THE BUNNY SLOPE IS THE NAME FOR THE BEGINNER'S HILL.

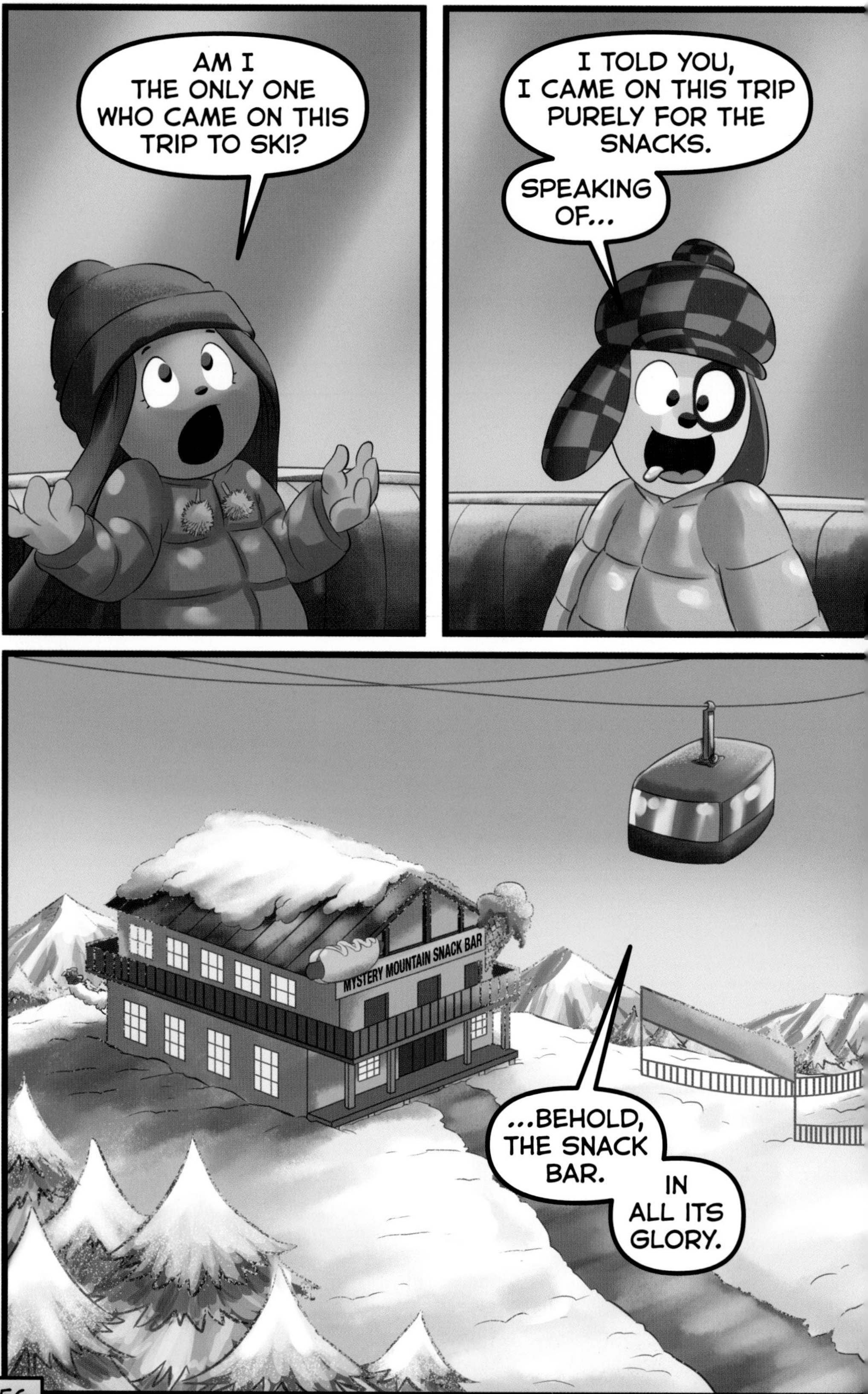
AM I THE ONLY ONE WHO CAME ON THIS TRIP TO SKI?
I TOLD YOU, I CAME ON THIS TRIP PURELY FOR THE SNACKS.
SPEAKING OF...
MYSTERY MOUNTAIN SNACK BAR
...BEHOLD, THE SNACK BAR.
IN ALL ITS GLORY.

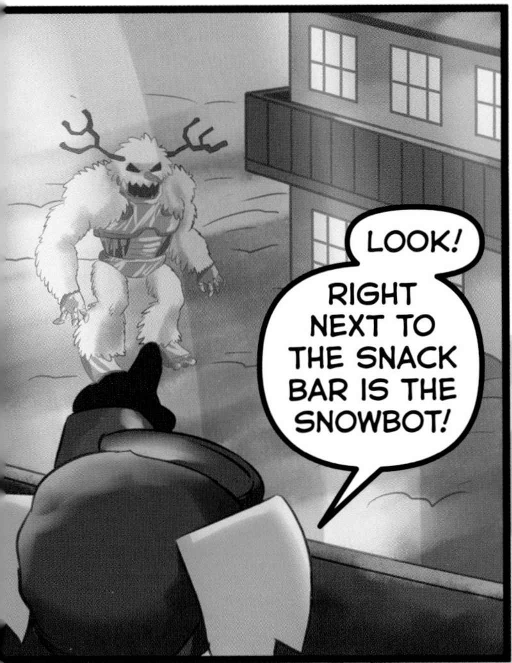
LOOK!
RIGHT NEXT TO THE SNACK BAR IS THE SNOWBOT!

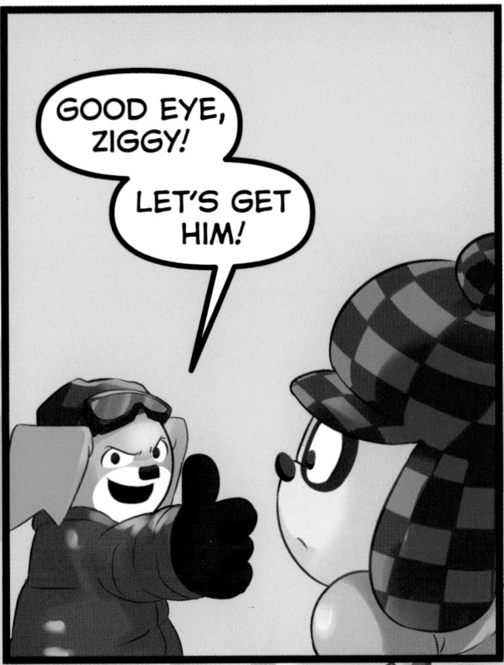
GOOD EYE, ZIGGY!
LET'S GET HIM!

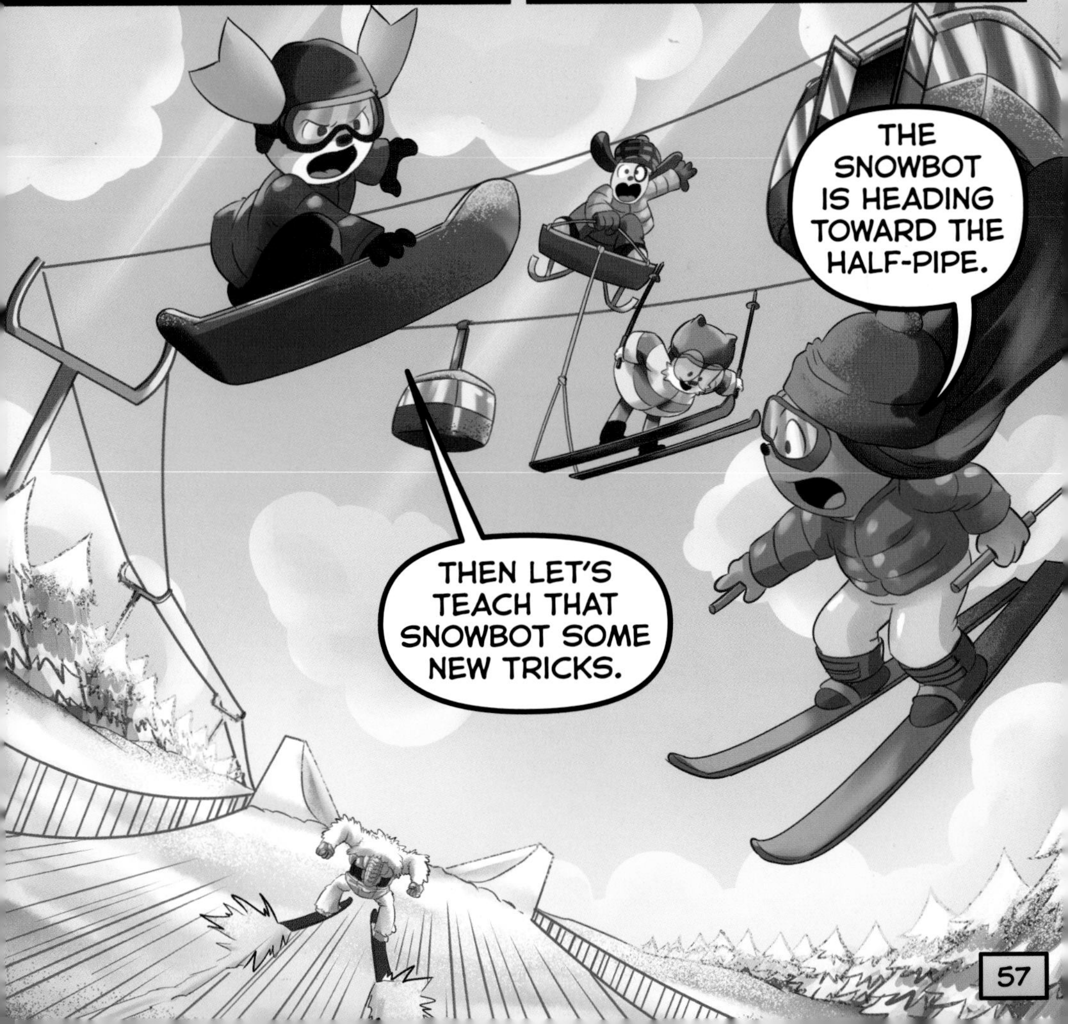
THE SNOWBOT IS HEADING TOWARD THE HALF-PIPE.
THEN LET'S TEACH THAT SNOWBOT SOME NEW TRICKS.

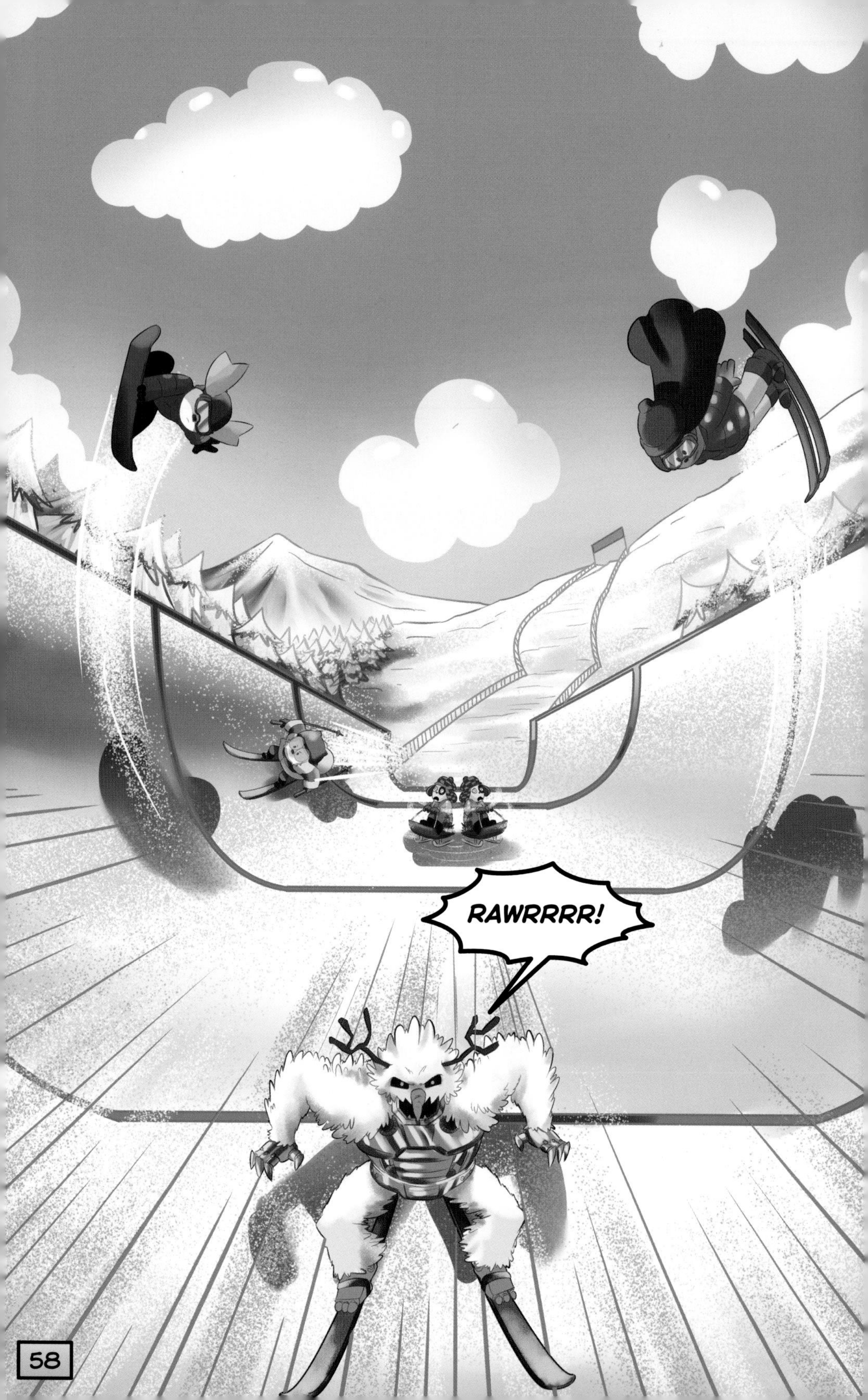
RAWRRRR!

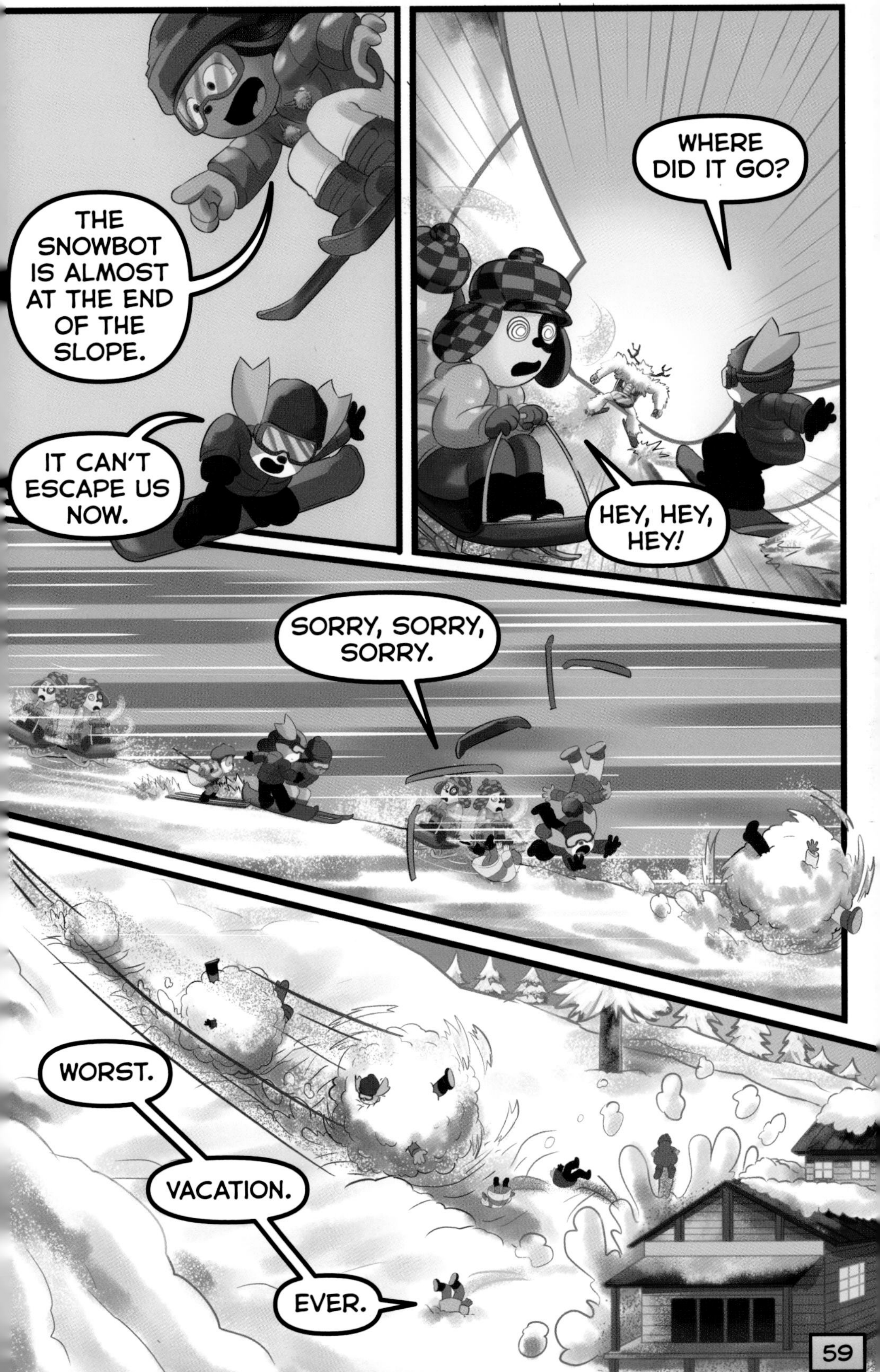
THE SNOWBOT IS ALMOST AT THE END OF THE SLOPE.
IT CAN'T ESCAPE US NOW.
WHERE DID IT GO?
HEY, HEY, HEY!
SORRY, SORRY, SORRY.
WORST.
VACATION.
EVER.

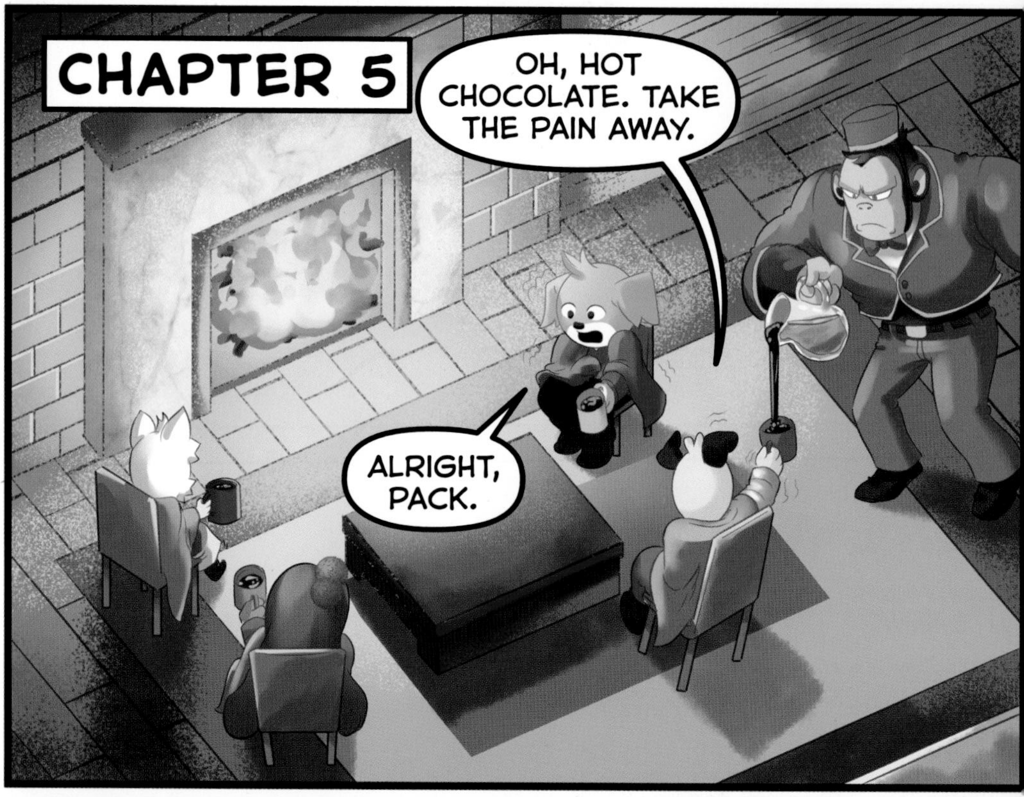
CHAPTER 5
OH, HOT CHOCOLATE. TAKE THE PAIN AWAY.
ALRIGHT, PACK.

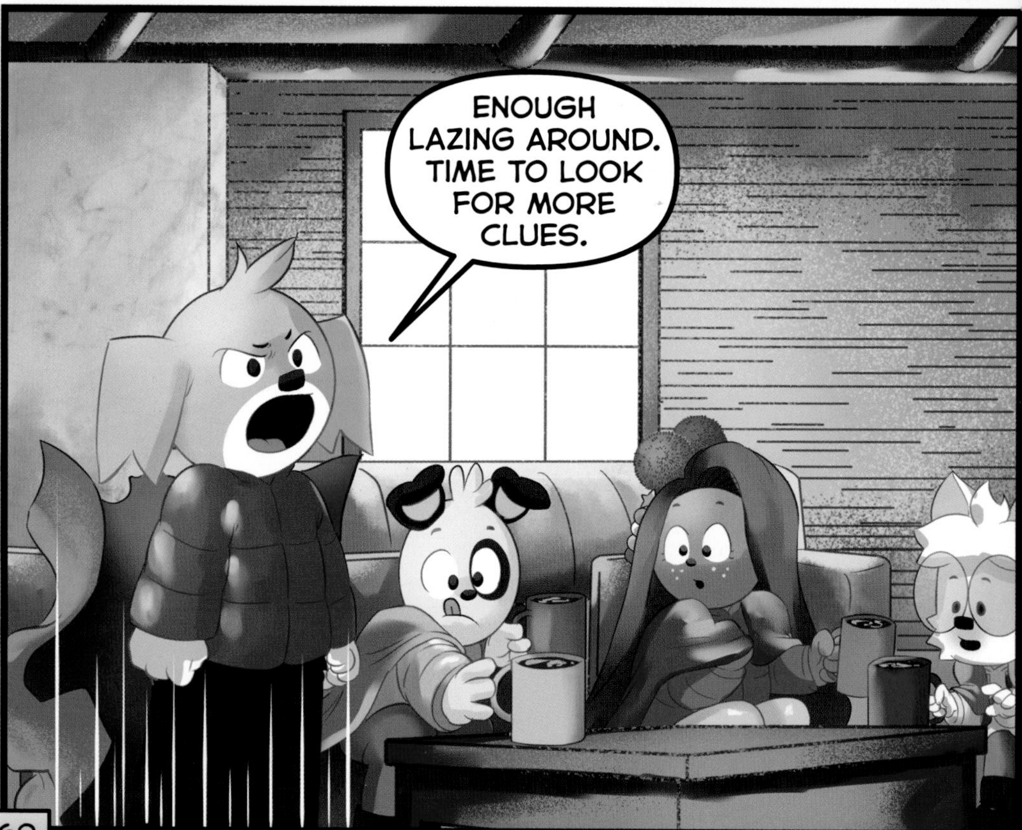
ENOUGH LAZING AROUND. TIME TO LOOK FOR MORE CLUES.

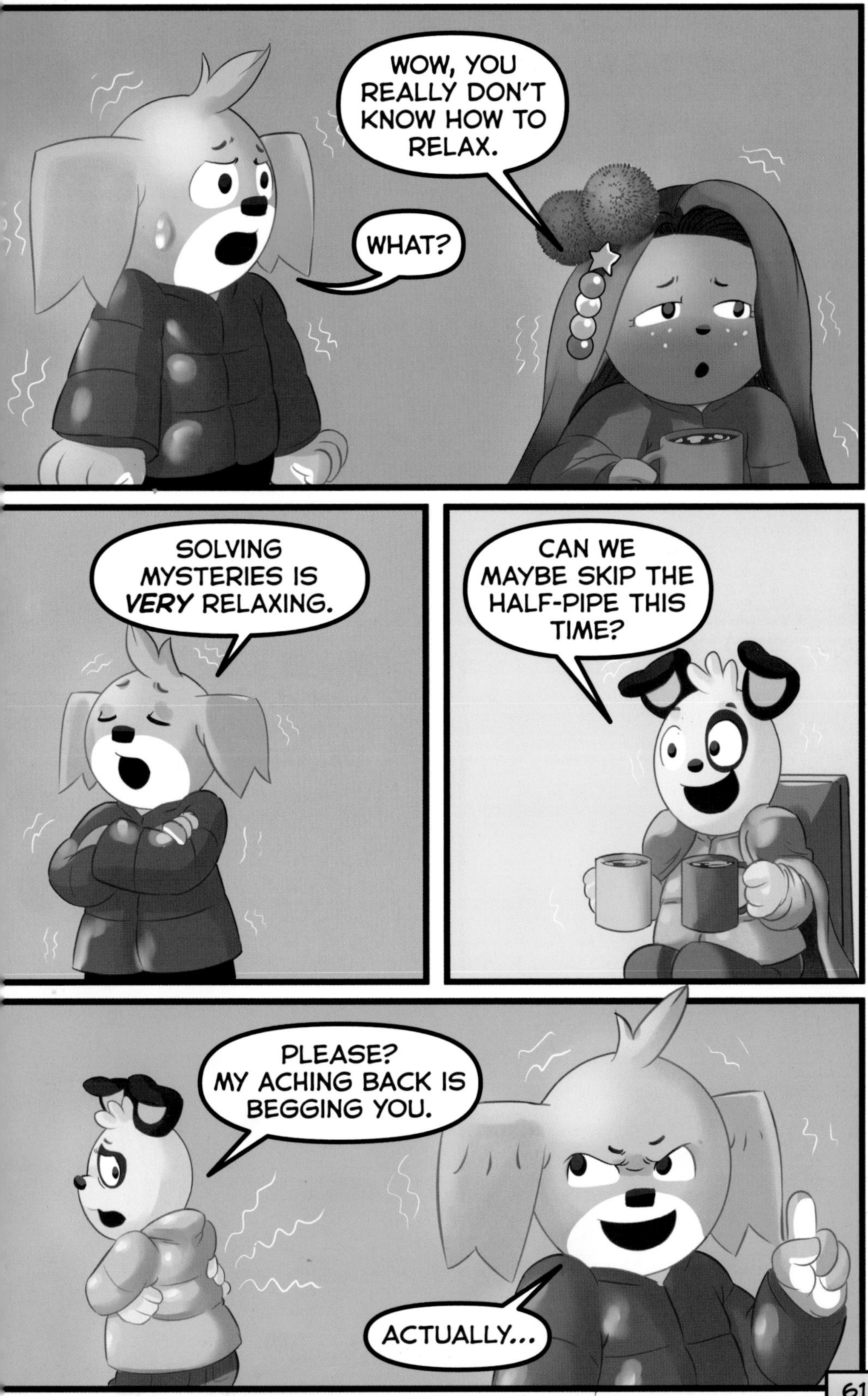
WOW, YOU REALLY DON'T KNOW HOW TO RELAX.
WHAT?
SOLVING MYSTERIES IS *VERY* RELAXING.
CAN WE MAYBE SKIP THE HALF-PIPE THIS TIME?
PLEASE? MY ACHING BACK IS BEGGING YOU.
ACTUALLY...

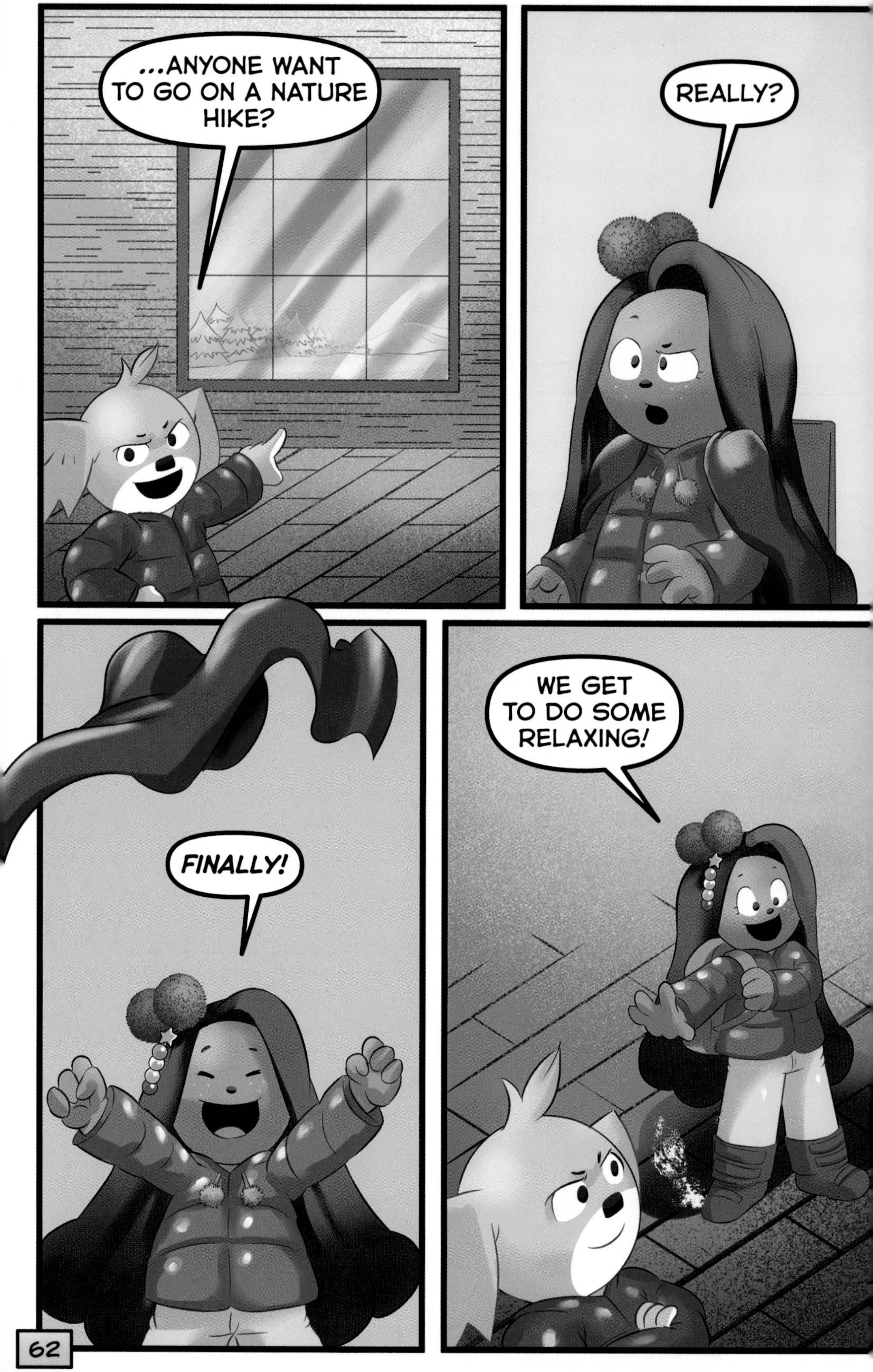
...ANYONE WANT TO GO ON A NATURE HIKE?
REALLY?
FINALLY!
WE GET TO DO SOME RELAXING!

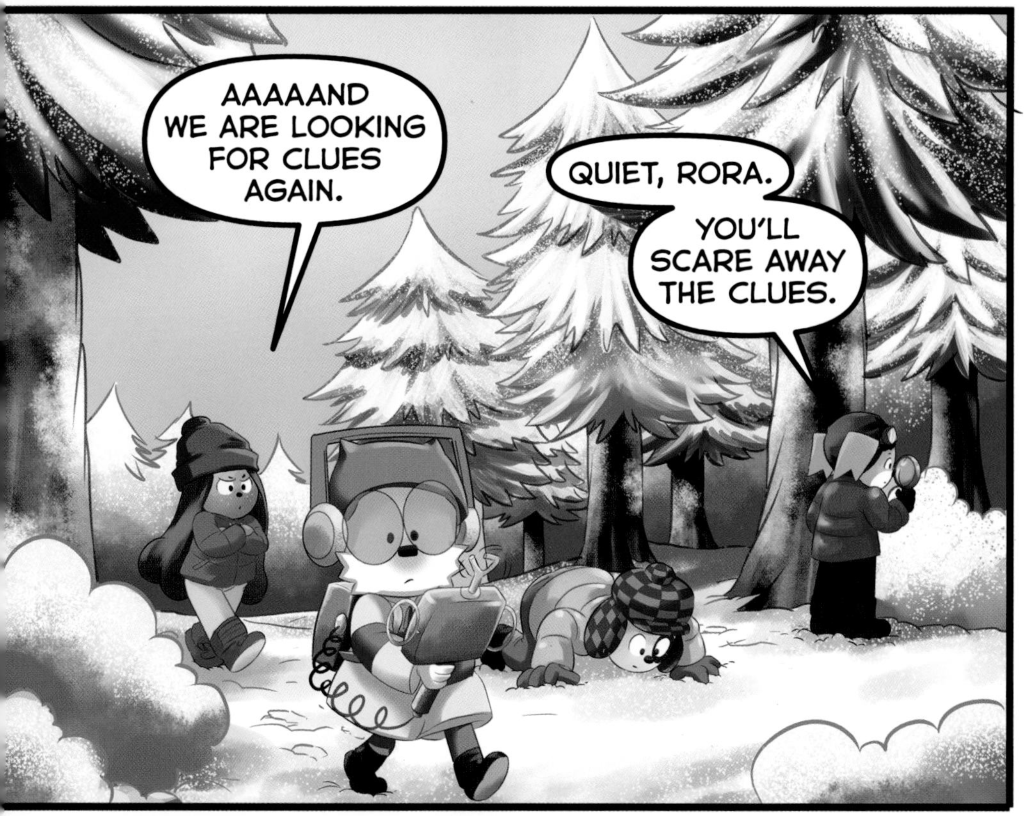
AAAAAND WE ARE LOOKING FOR CLUES AGAIN.
QUIET, RORA.
YOU'LL SCARE AWAY THE CLUES.

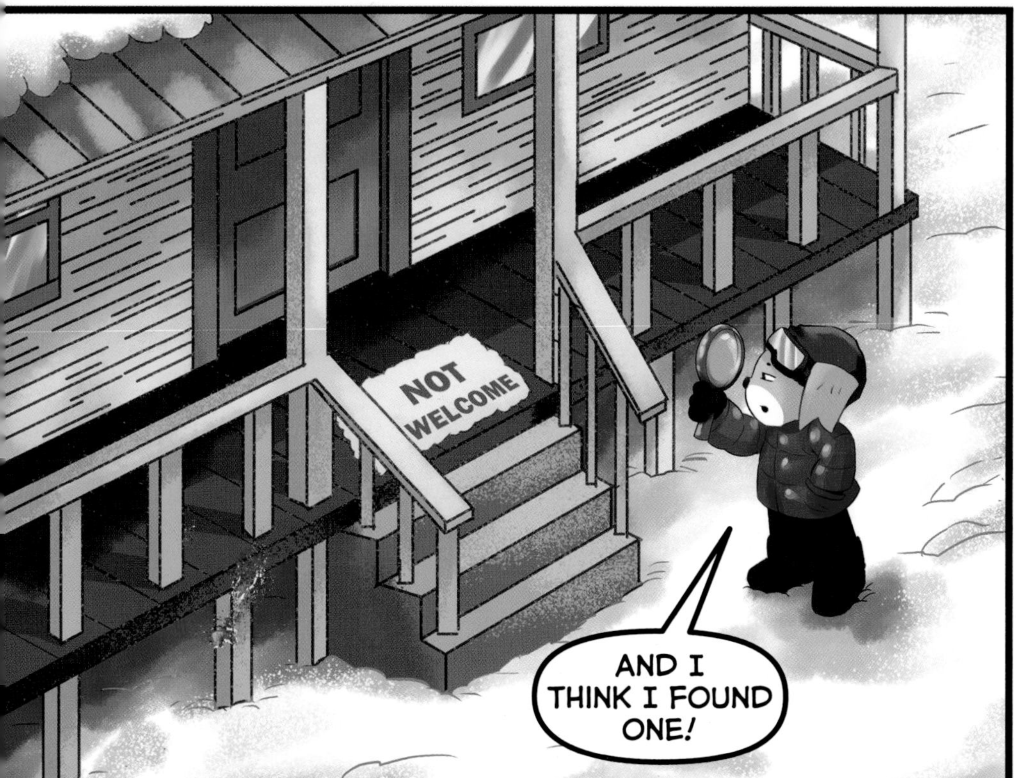
NOT WELCOME
AND I THINK I FOUND ONE!

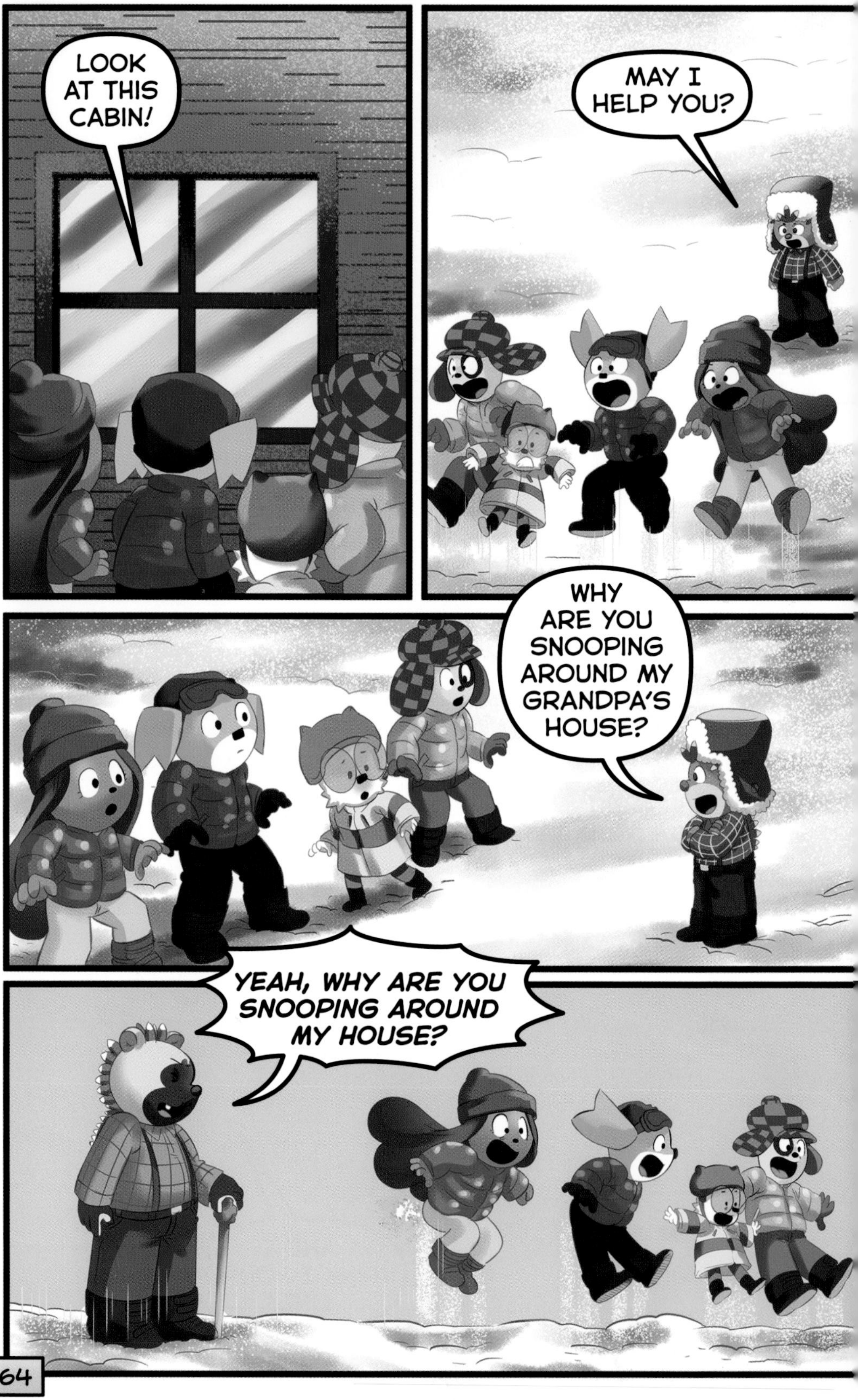
LOOK AT THIS CABIN!
MAY I HELP YOU?
WHY ARE YOU SNOOPING AROUND MY GRANDPA'S HOUSE?
YEAH, WHY ARE YOU SNOOPING AROUND MY HOUSE?

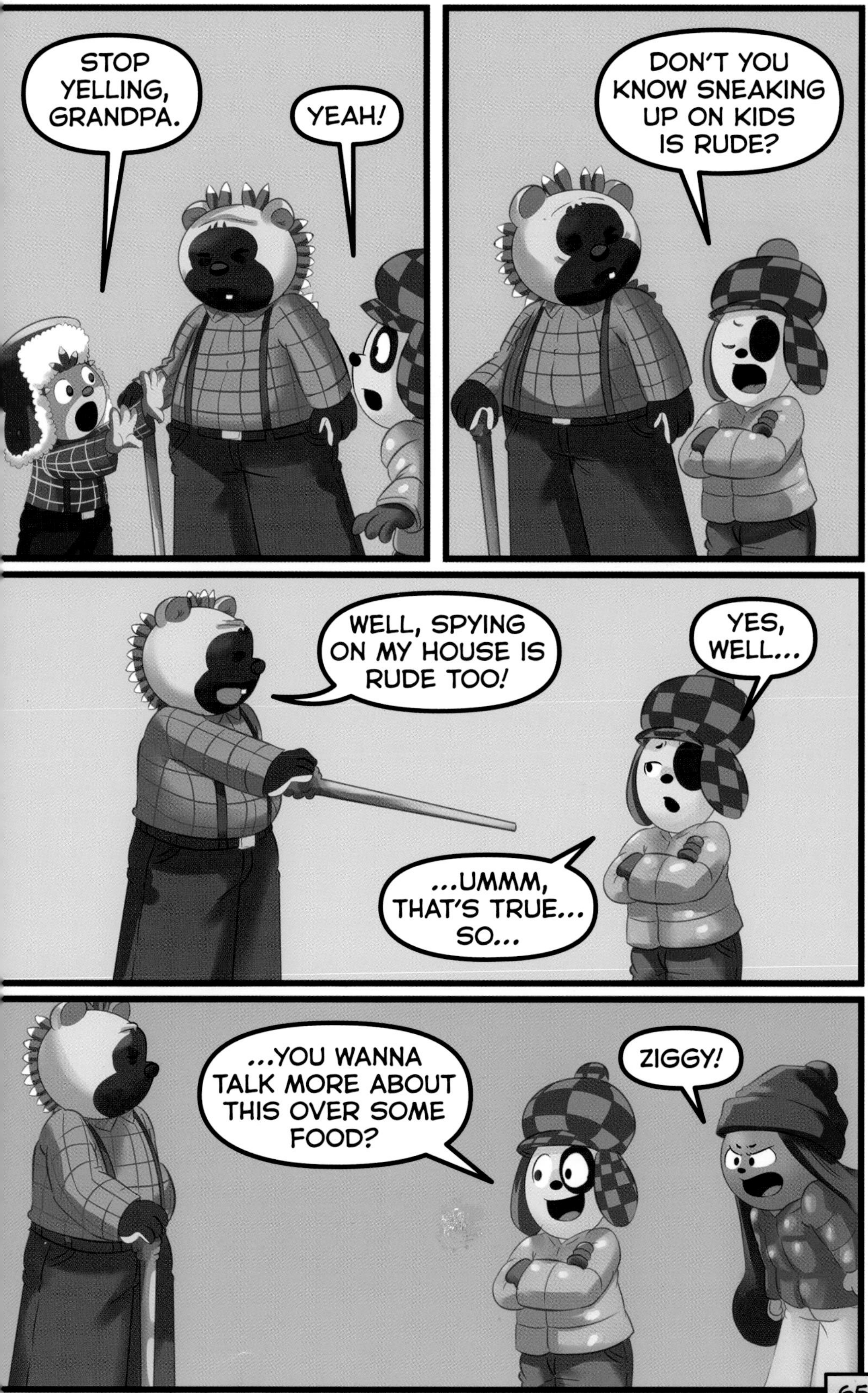
STOP YELLING, GRANDPA.
YEAH!
DON'T YOU KNOW SNEAKING UP ON KIDS IS RUDE?
WELL, SPYING ON MY HOUSE IS RUDE TOO!
YES, WELL...
...UMMM, THAT'S TRUE... SO...
...YOU WANNA TALK MORE ABOUT THIS OVER SOME FOOD?
ZIGGY!

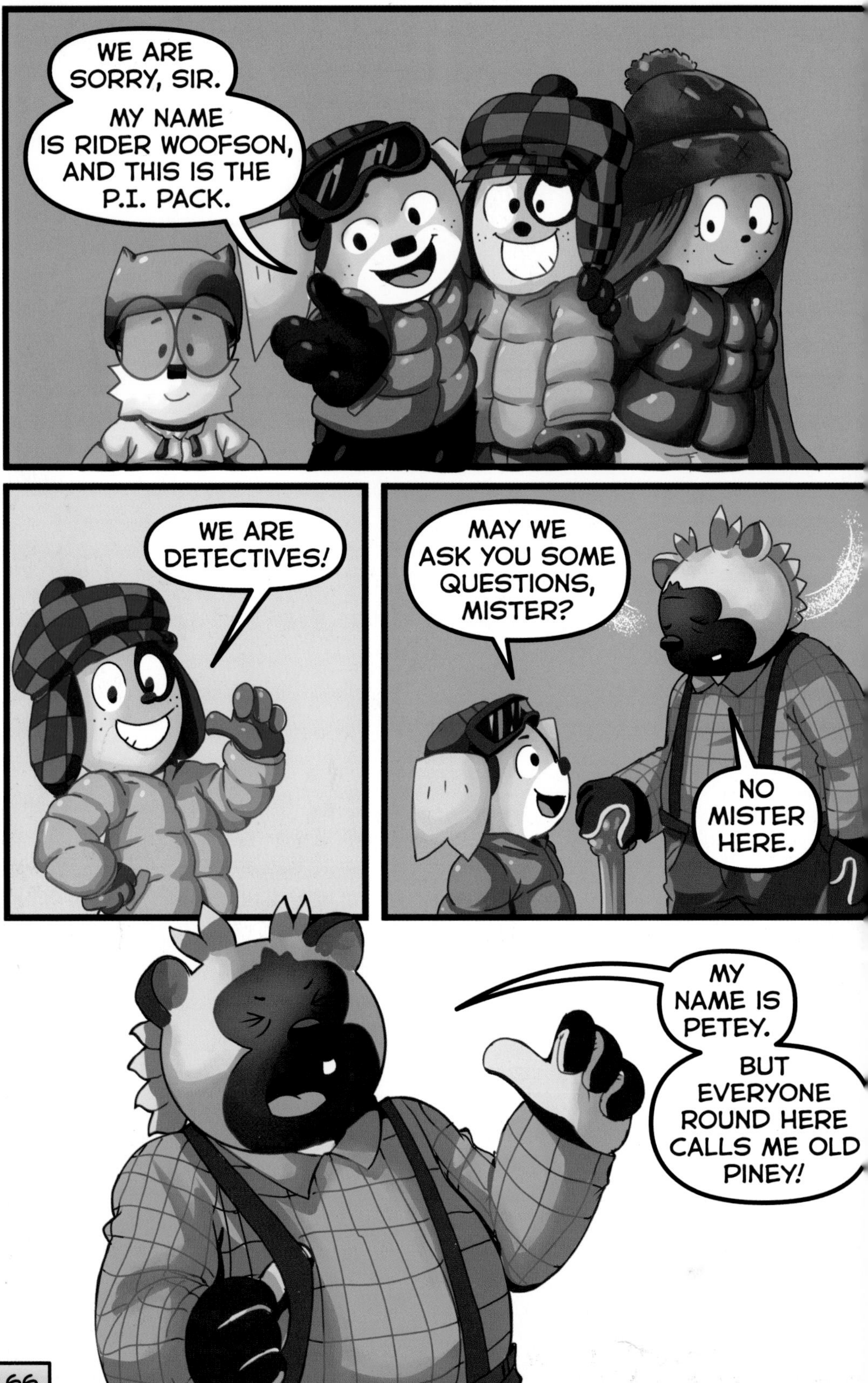
WE ARE SORRY, SIR.
MY NAME IS RIDER WOOFSON, AND THIS IS THE P.I. PACK.
WE ARE DETECTIVES!
MAY WE ASK YOU SOME QUESTIONS, MISTER?
NO MISTER HERE.
MY NAME IS PETEY.
BUT EVERYONE ROUND HERE CALLS ME OLD PINEY!

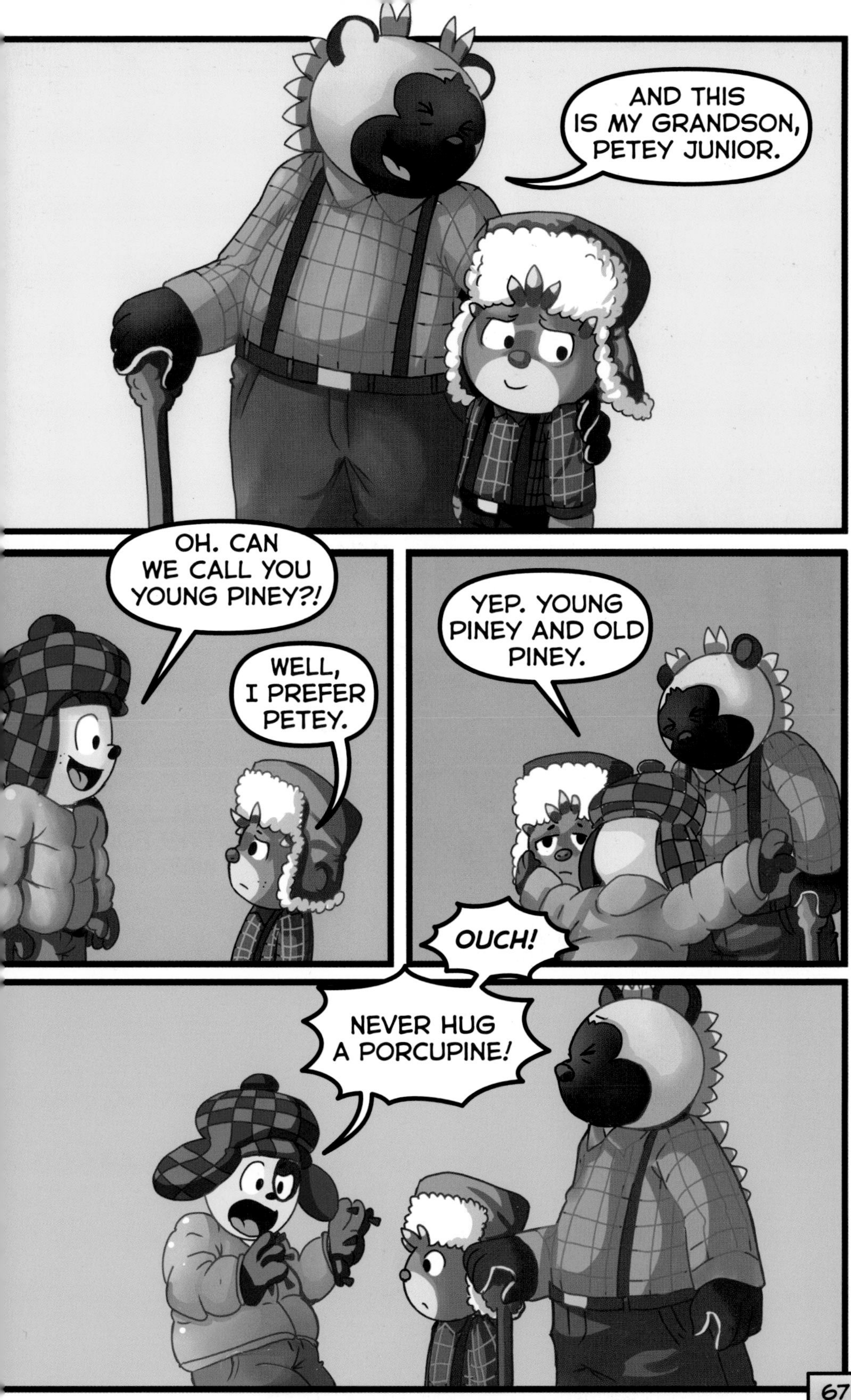
AND THIS IS MY GRANDSON, PETEY JUNIOR.
OH. CAN WE CALL YOU YOUNG PINEY?!
WELL, I PREFER PETEY.
YEP. YOUNG PINEY AND OLD PINEY.
OUCH!
NEVER HUG A PORCUPINE!

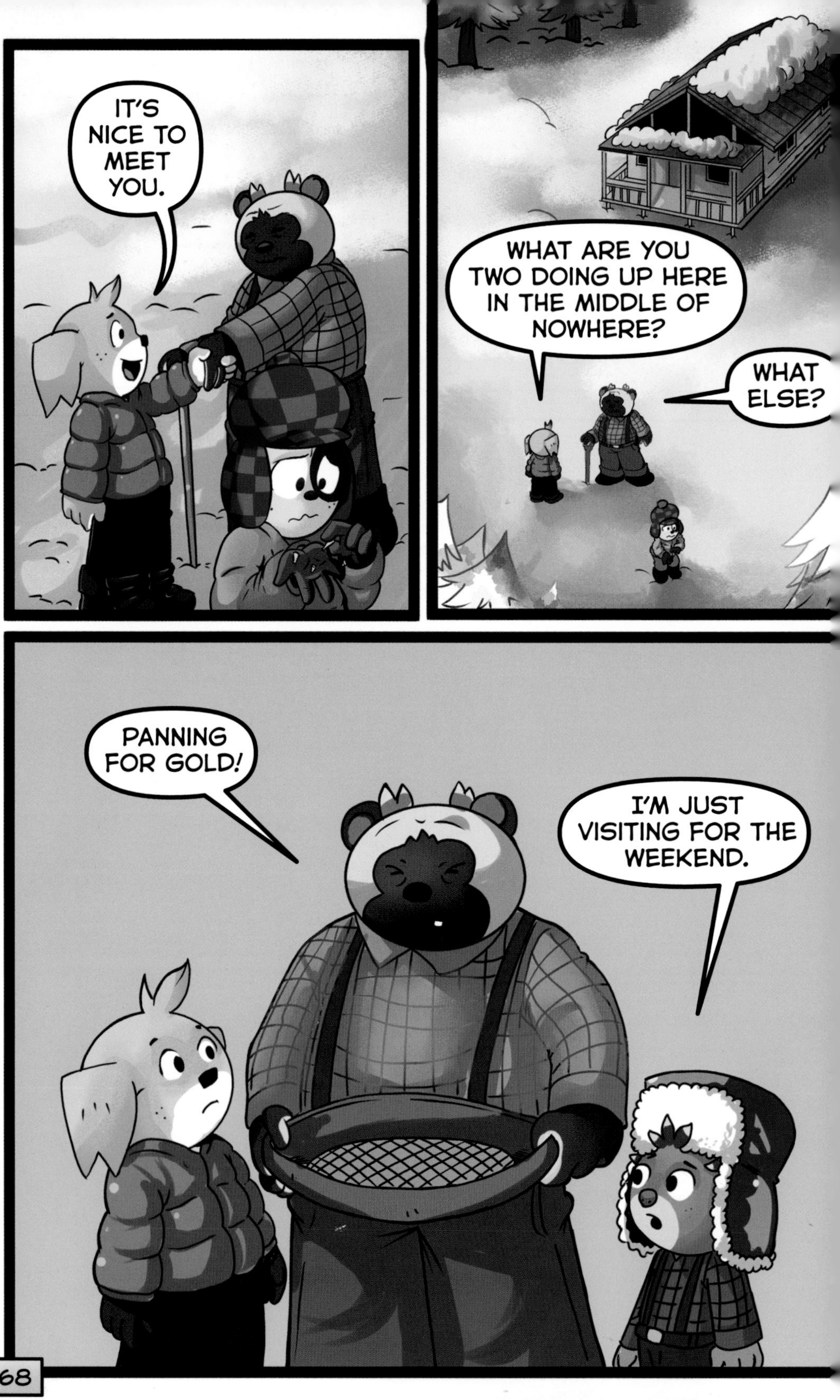

IT'S NICE TO MEET YOU.
WHAT ARE YOU TWO DOING UP HERE IN THE MIDDLE OF NOWHERE?
WHAT ELSE?
PANNING FOR GOLD!
I'M JUST VISITING FOR THE WEEKEND.

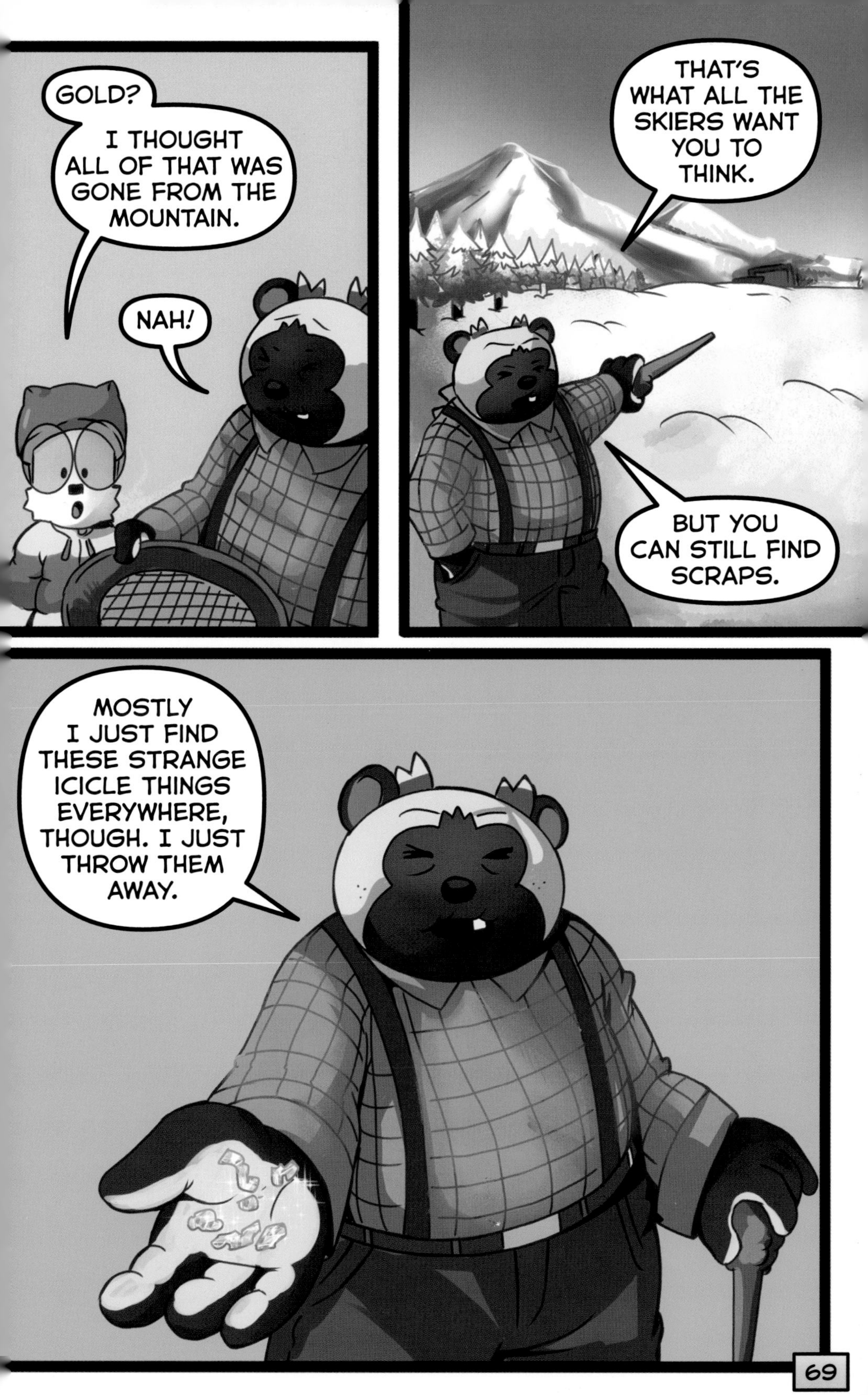
GOLD?
I THOUGHT ALL OF THAT WAS GONE FROM THE MOUNTAIN.
NAH!
THAT'S WHAT ALL THE SKIERS WANT YOU TO THINK.
BUT YOU CAN STILL FIND SCRAPS.
MOSTLY I JUST FIND THESE STRANGE ICICLE THINGS EVERYWHERE, THOUGH. I JUST THROW THEM AWAY.

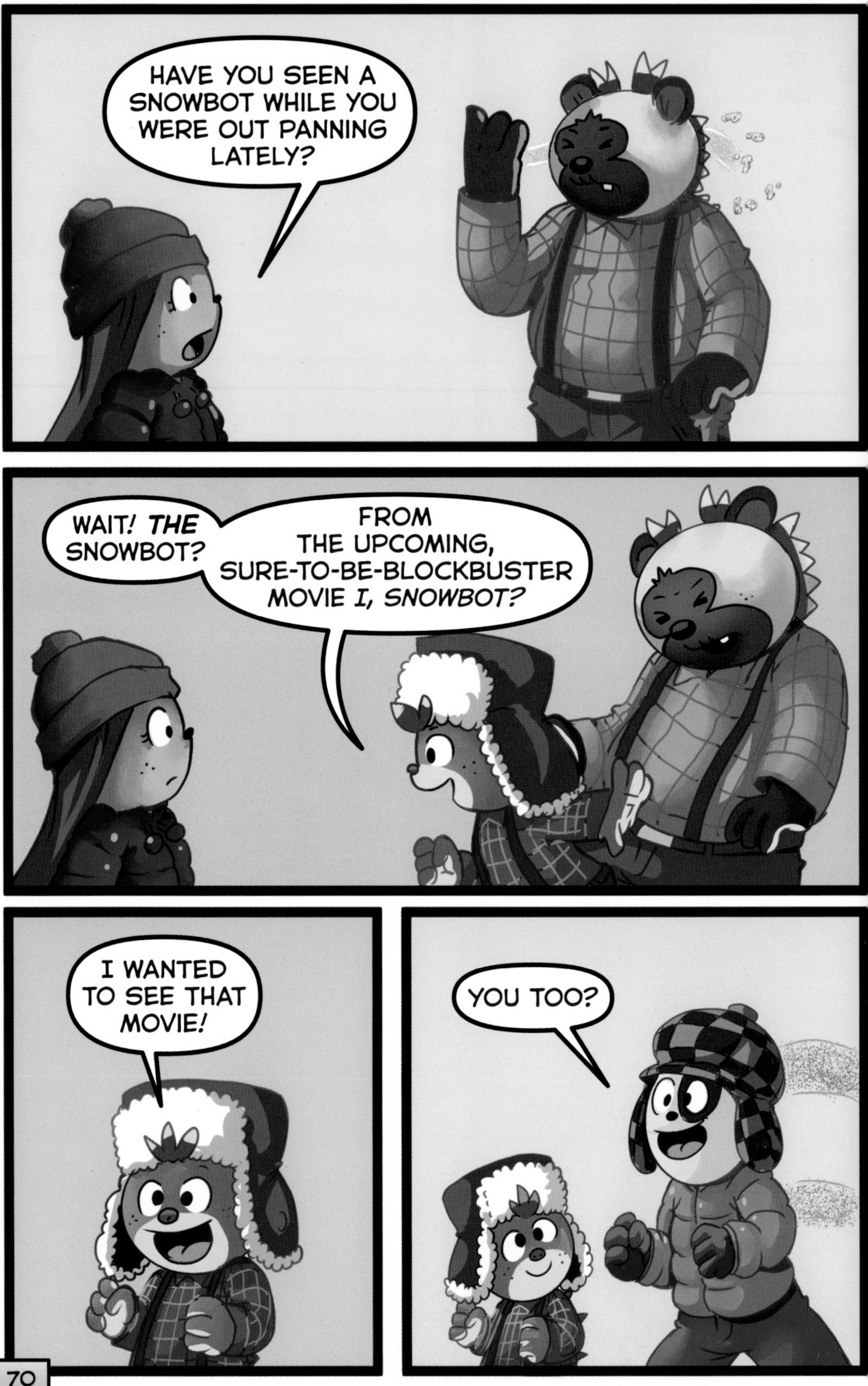
HAVE YOU SEEN A SNOWBOT WHILE YOU WERE OUT PANNING LATELY?
WAIT! THE SNOWBOT?
FROM THE UPCOMING, SURE-TO-BE-BLOCKBUSTER MOVIE I, SNOWBOT?
I WANTED TO SEE THAT MOVIE!
YOU TOO?

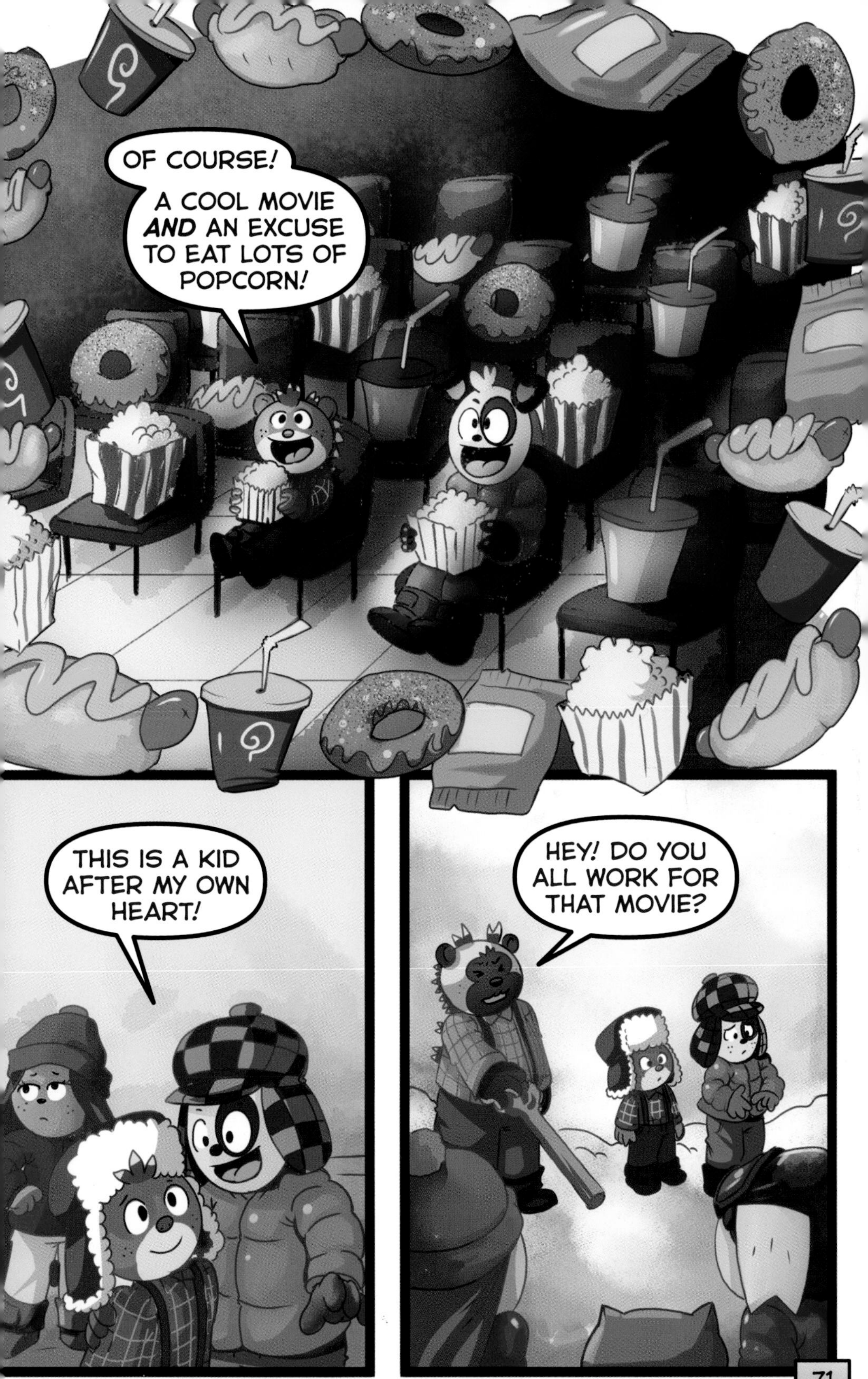
OF COURSE!
A COOL MOVIE *AND* AN EXCUSE TO EAT LOTS OF POPCORN!
THIS IS A KID AFTER MY OWN HEART!
HEY! DO YOU ALL WORK FOR THAT MOVIE?

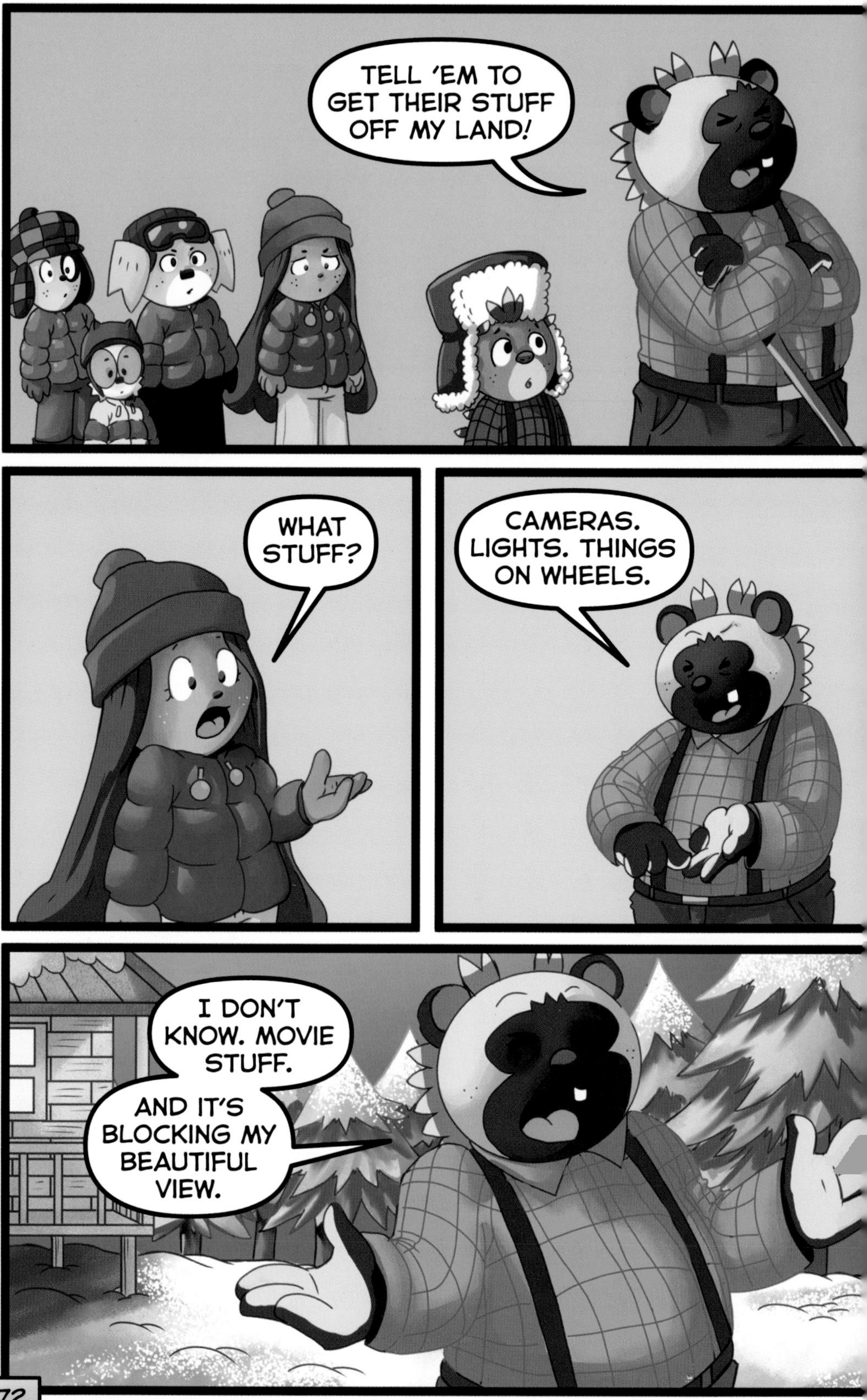
TELL 'EM TO GET THEIR STUFF OFF MY LAND!
WHAT STUFF?
CAMERAS. LIGHTS. THINGS ON WHEELS.
I DON'T KNOW. MOVIE STUFF.
AND IT'S BLOCKING MY BEAUTIFUL VIEW.

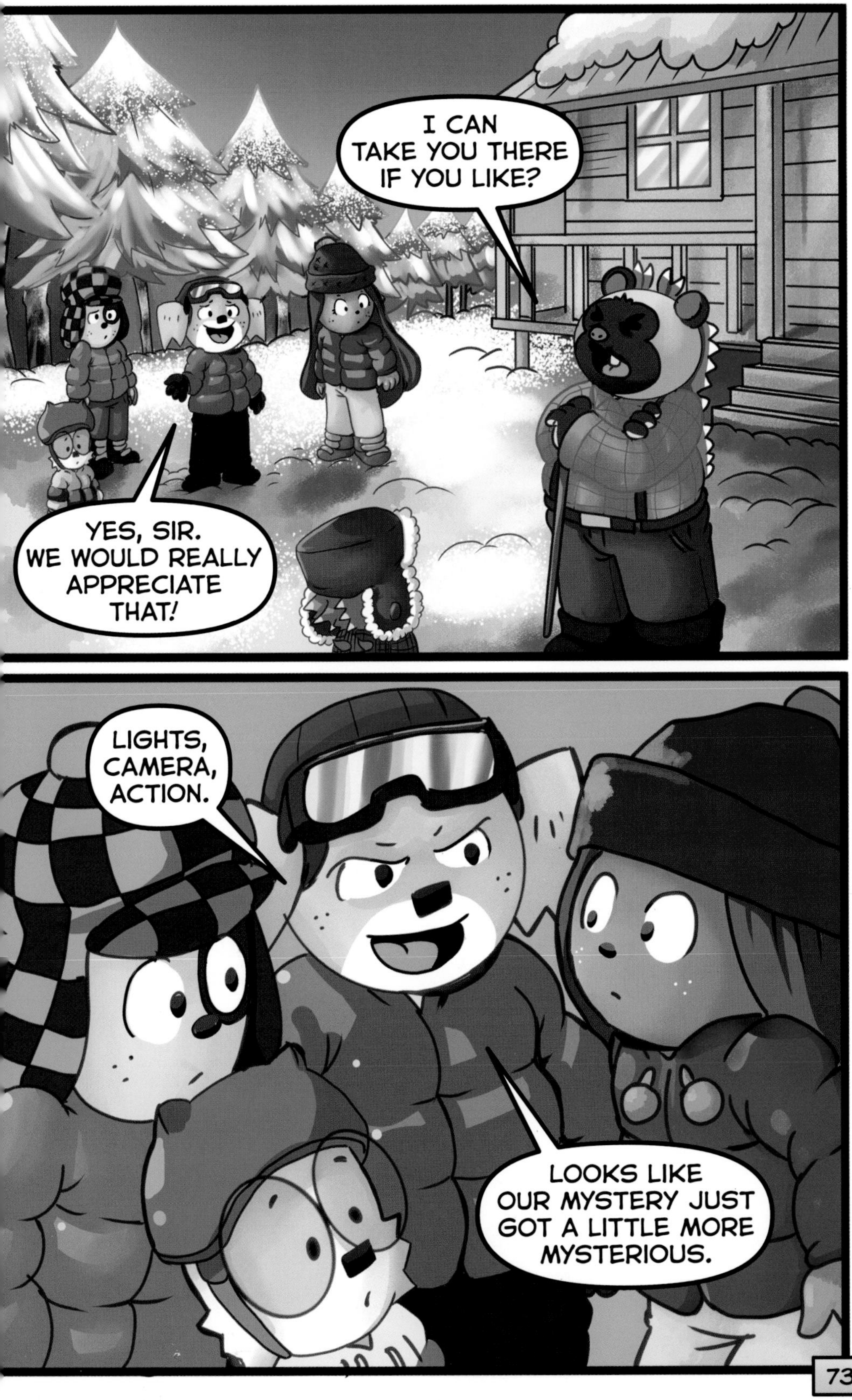
I CAN TAKE YOU THERE IF YOU LIKE?
YES, SIR. WE WOULD REALLY APPRECIATE THAT!
LIGHTS, CAMERA, ACTION.
LOOKS LIKE OUR MYSTERY JUST GOT A LITTLE MORE MYSTERIOUS.

CHAPTER 6

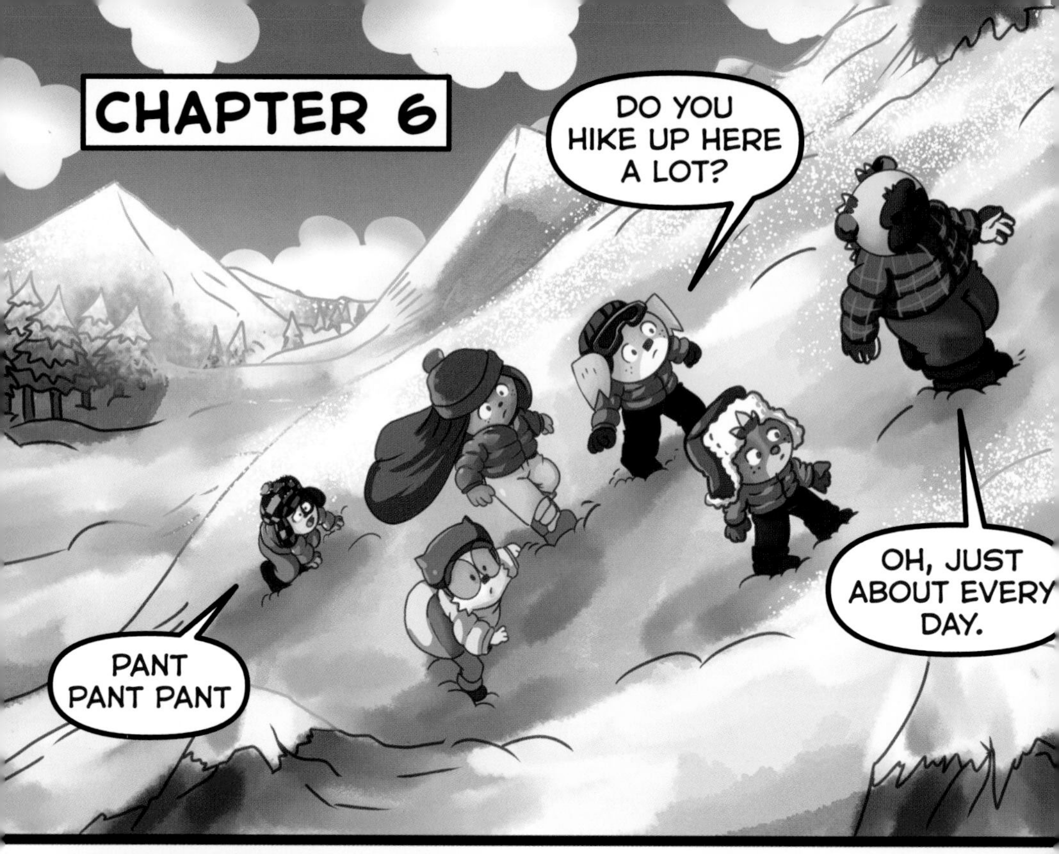
DO YOU HIKE UP HERE A LOT?
OH, JUST ABOUT EVERY DAY.
PANT PANT PANT

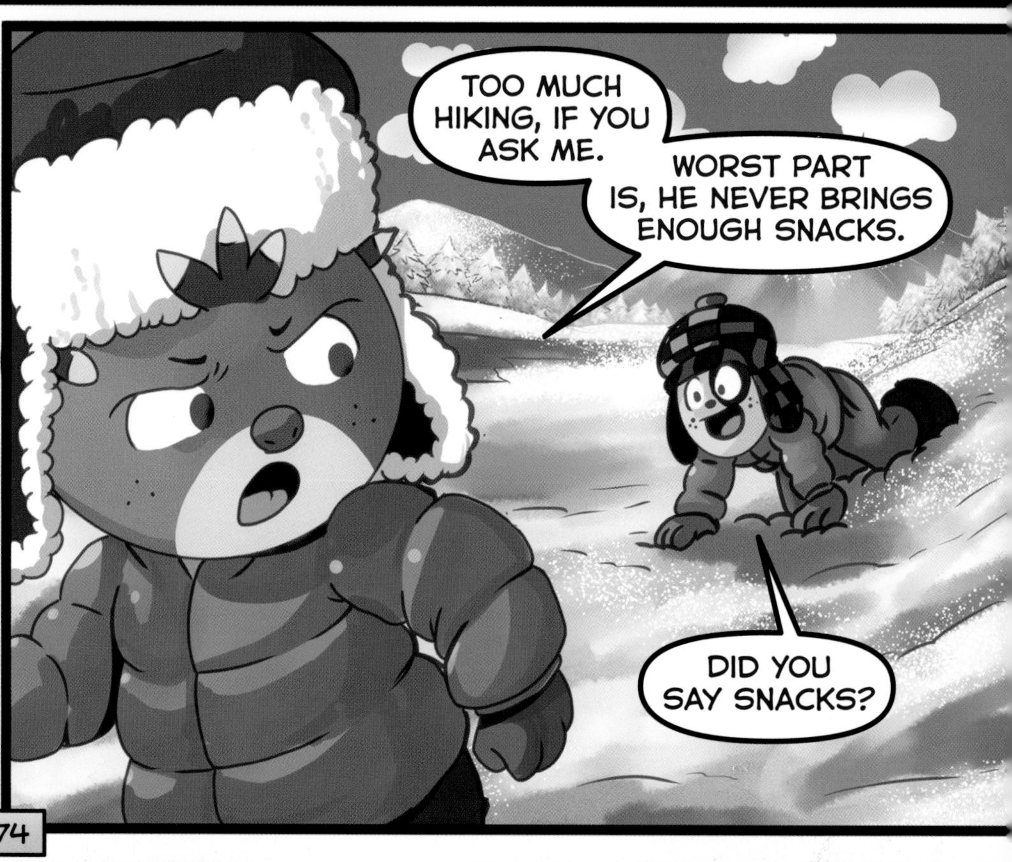
TOO MUCH HIKING, IF YOU ASK ME.
WORST PART IS, HE NEVER BRINGS ENOUGH SNACKS.
DID YOU SAY SNACKS?

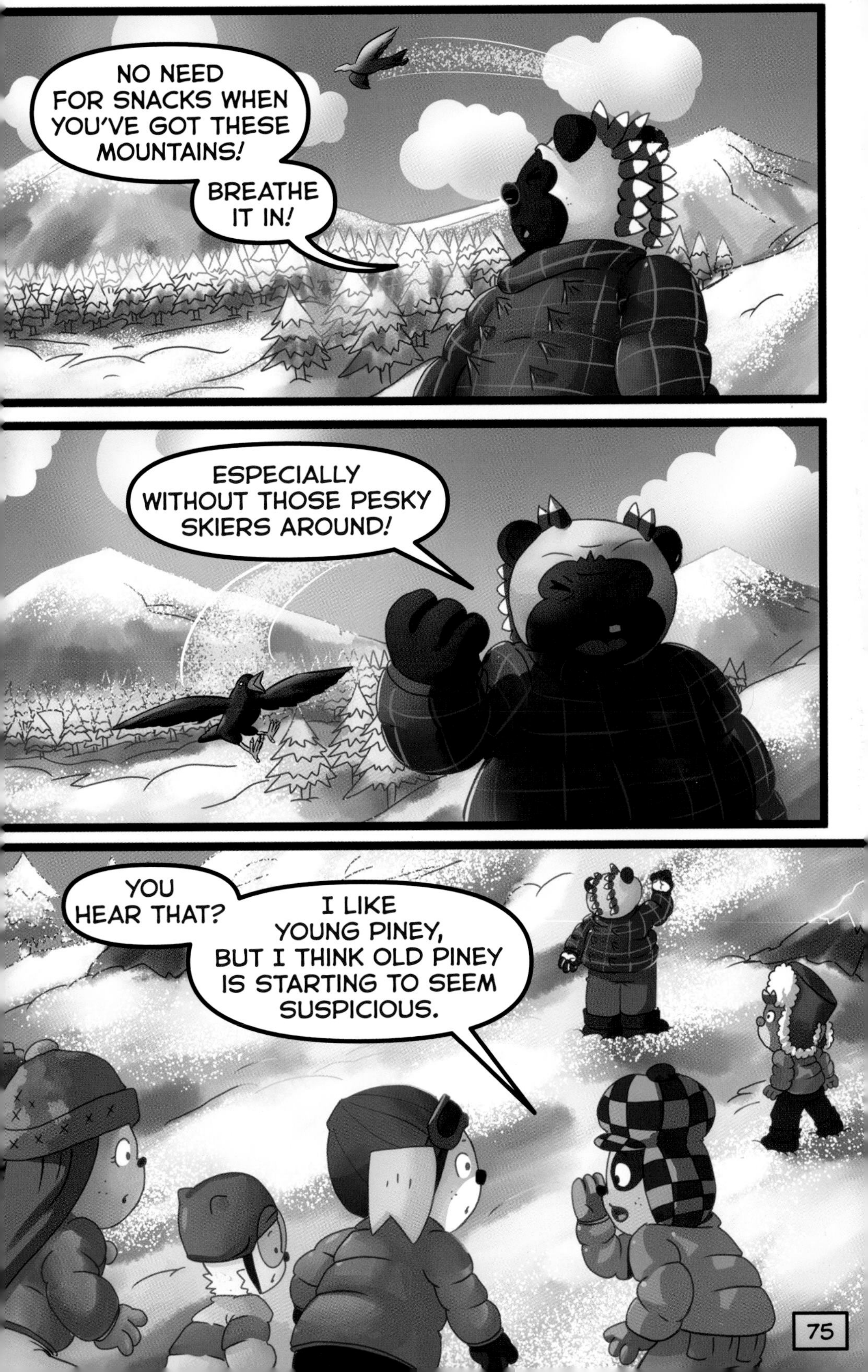
NO NEED FOR SNACKS WHEN YOU'VE GOT THESE MOUNTAINS!
BREATHE IT IN!
ESPECIALLY WITHOUT THOSE PESKY SKIERS AROUND!
YOU HEAR THAT?
I LIKE YOUNG PINEY, BUT I THINK OLD PINEY IS STARTING TO SEEM SUSPICIOUS.

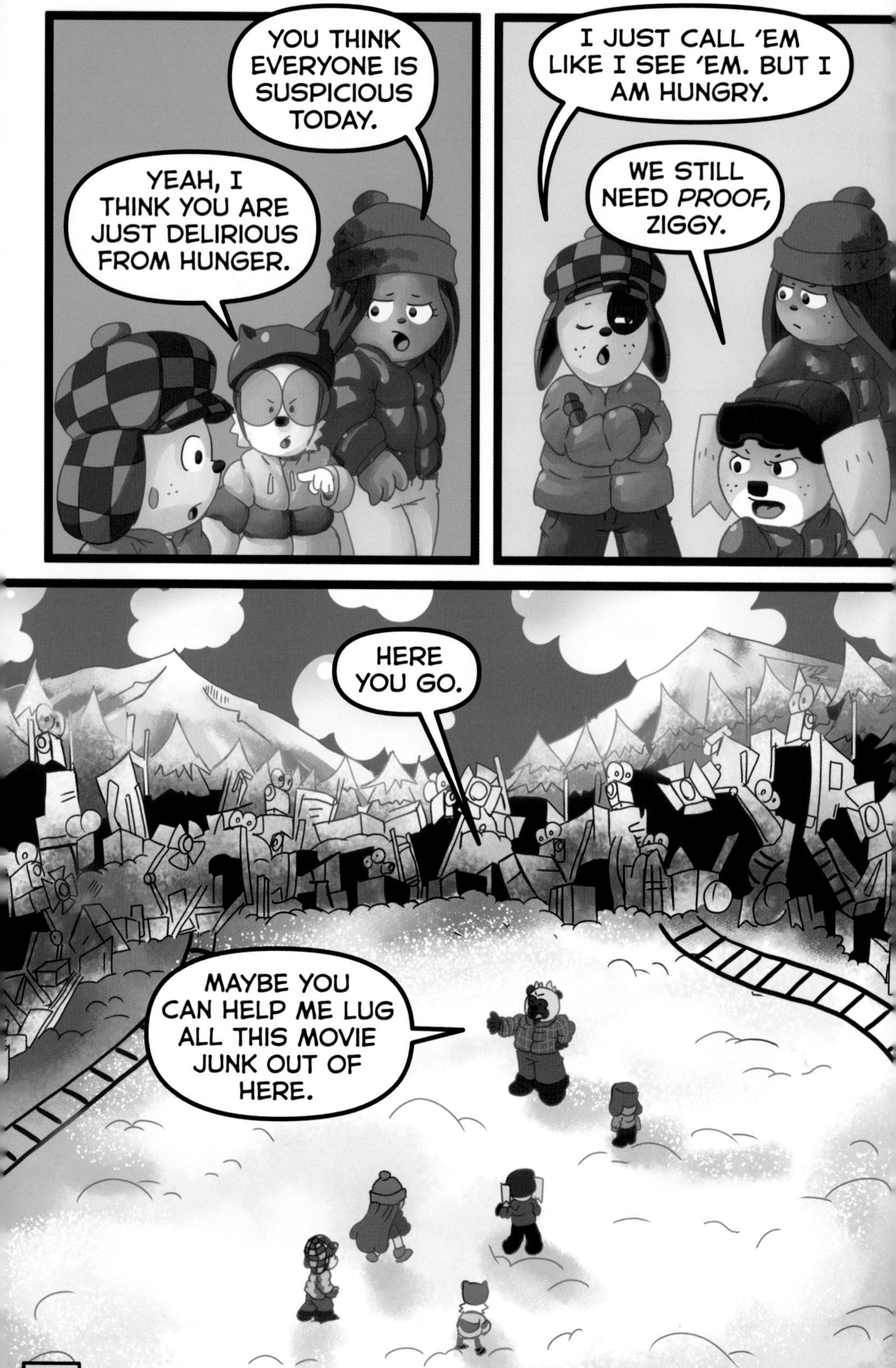
YOU THINK EVERYONE IS SUSPICIOUS TODAY.
YEAH, I THINK YOU ARE JUST DELIRIOUS FROM HUNGER.
I JUST CALL 'EM LIKE I SEE 'EM. BUT I AM HUNGRY.
WE STILL NEED *PROOF*, ZIGGY.
HERE YOU GO.
MAYBE YOU CAN HELP ME LUG ALL THIS MOVIE JUNK OUT OF HERE.

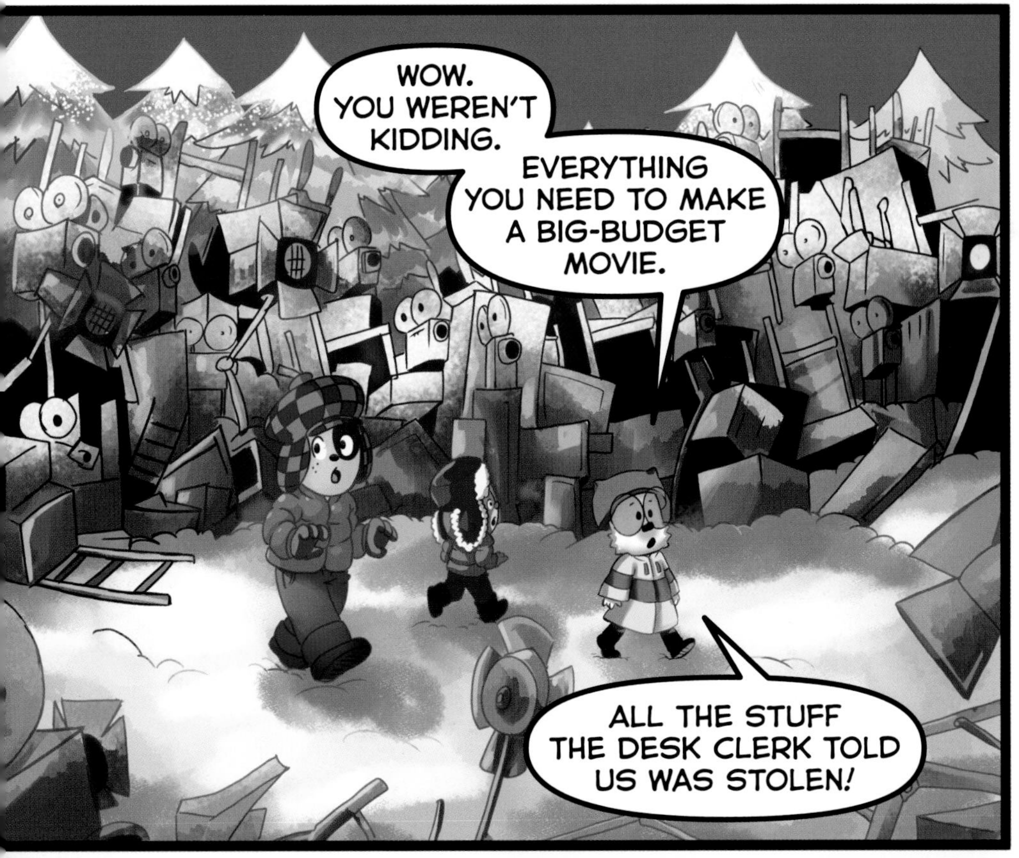
WOW. YOU WEREN'T KIDDING.
EVERYTHING YOU NEED TO MAKE A BIG-BUDGET MOVIE.
ALL THE STUFF THE DESK CLERK TOLD US WAS STOLEN!

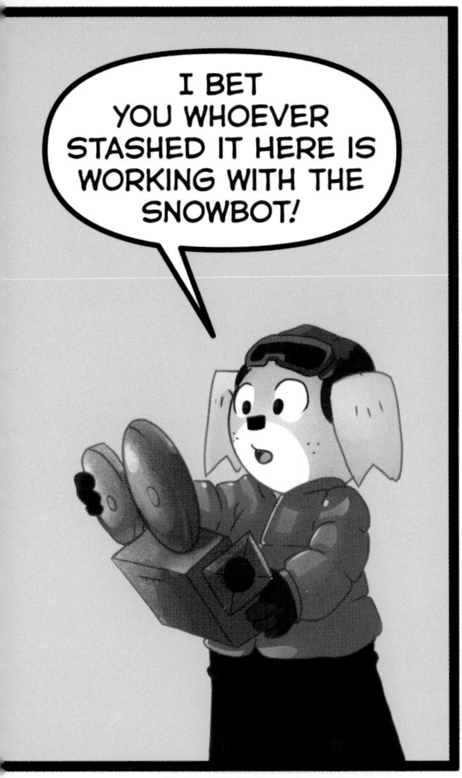
I BET YOU WHOEVER STASHED IT HERE IS WORKING WITH THE SNOWBOT!

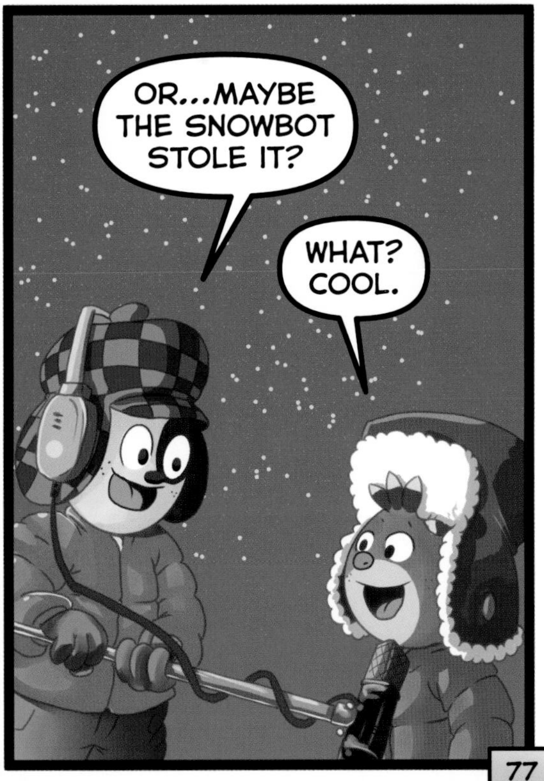
OR...MAYBE THE SNOWBOT STOLE IT?
WHAT? COOL.

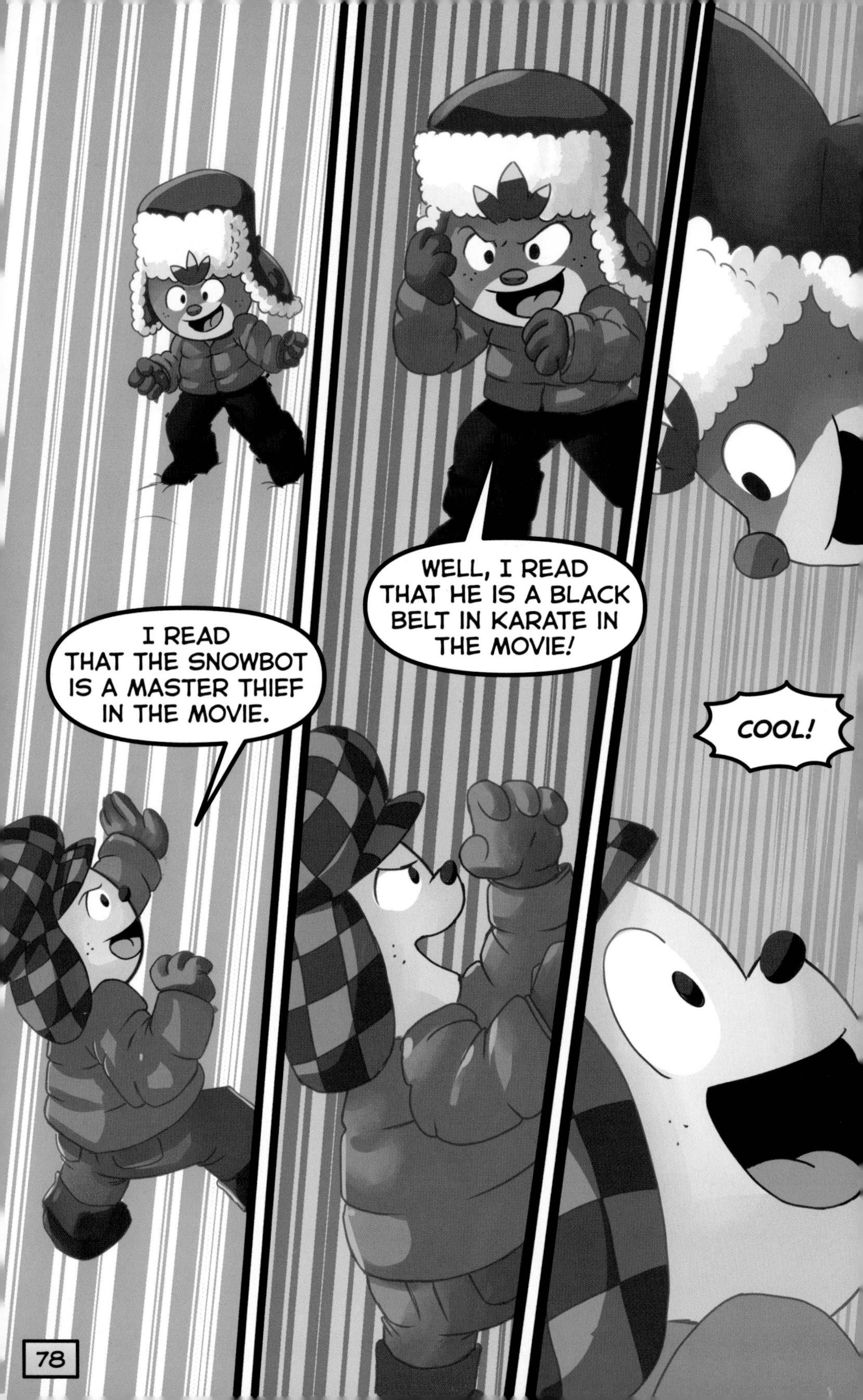
I READ
THAT THE SNOWBOT
IS A MASTER THIEF
IN THE MOVIE.
WELL, I READ
THAT HE IS A BLACK
BELT IN KARATE IN
THE MOVIE!
COOL!

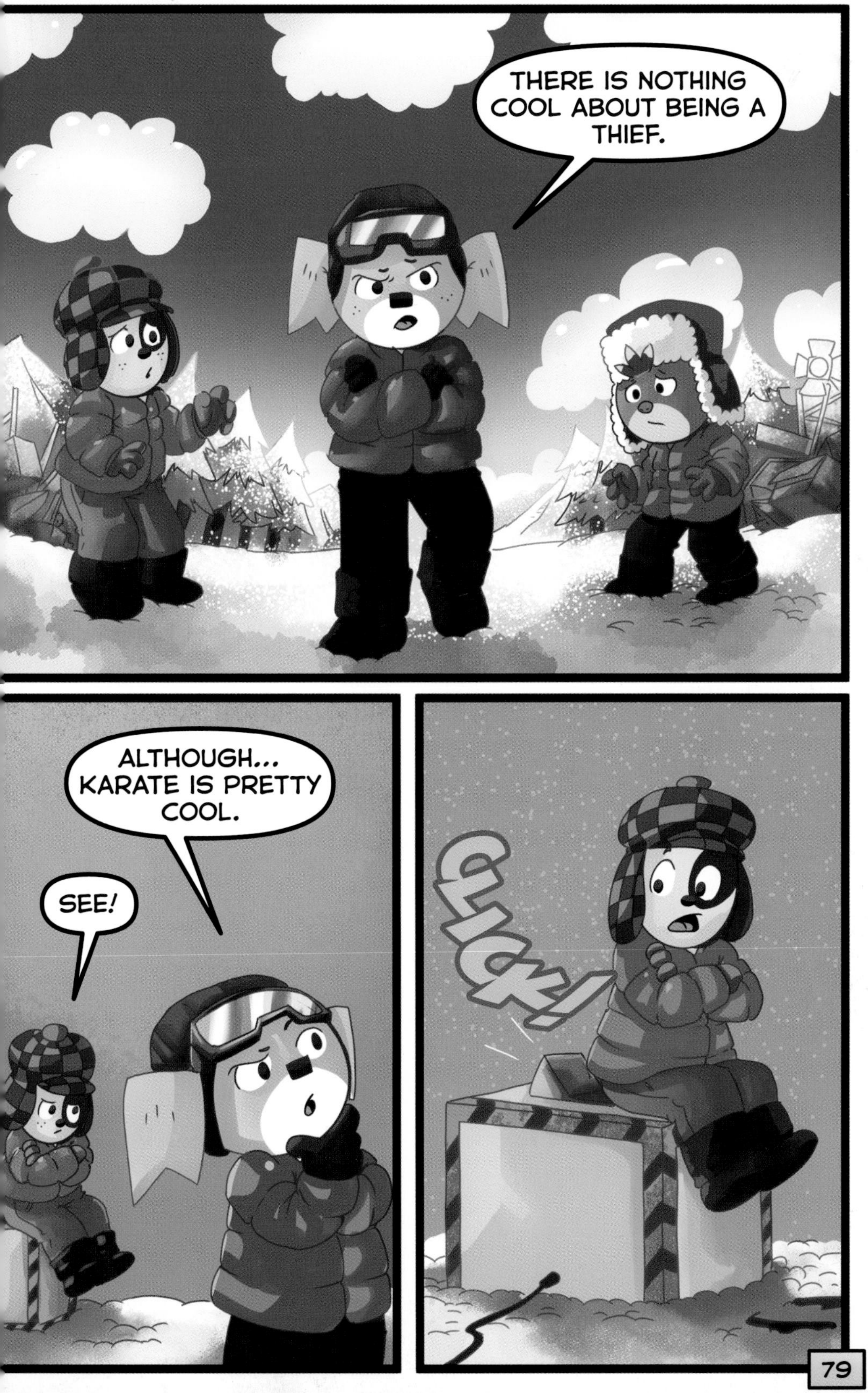
THERE IS NOTHING COOL ABOUT BEING A THIEF.
ALTHOUGH... KARATE IS PRETTY COOL.
SEE!
CLICK!

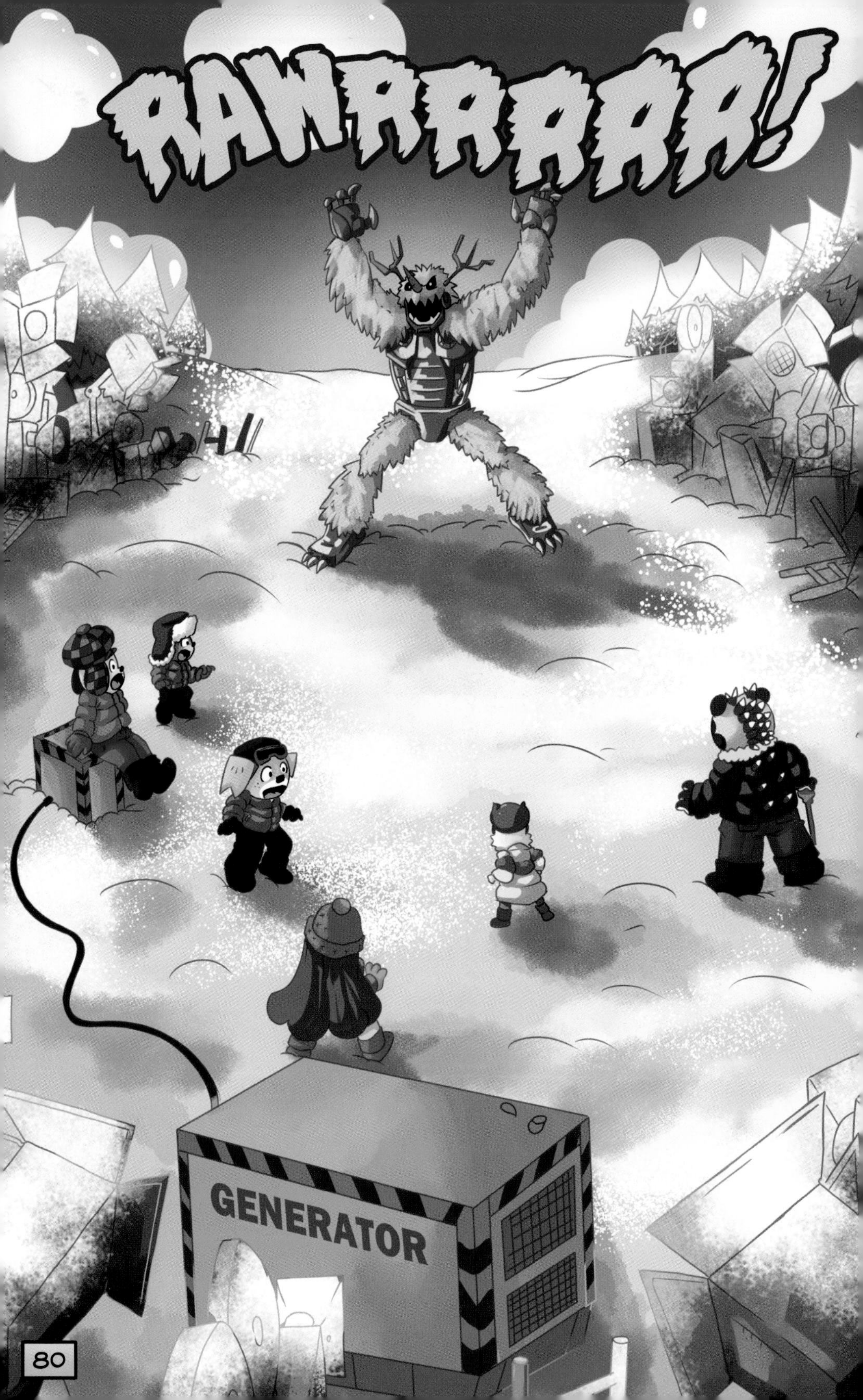
RAWRRRRR!
GENERATOR

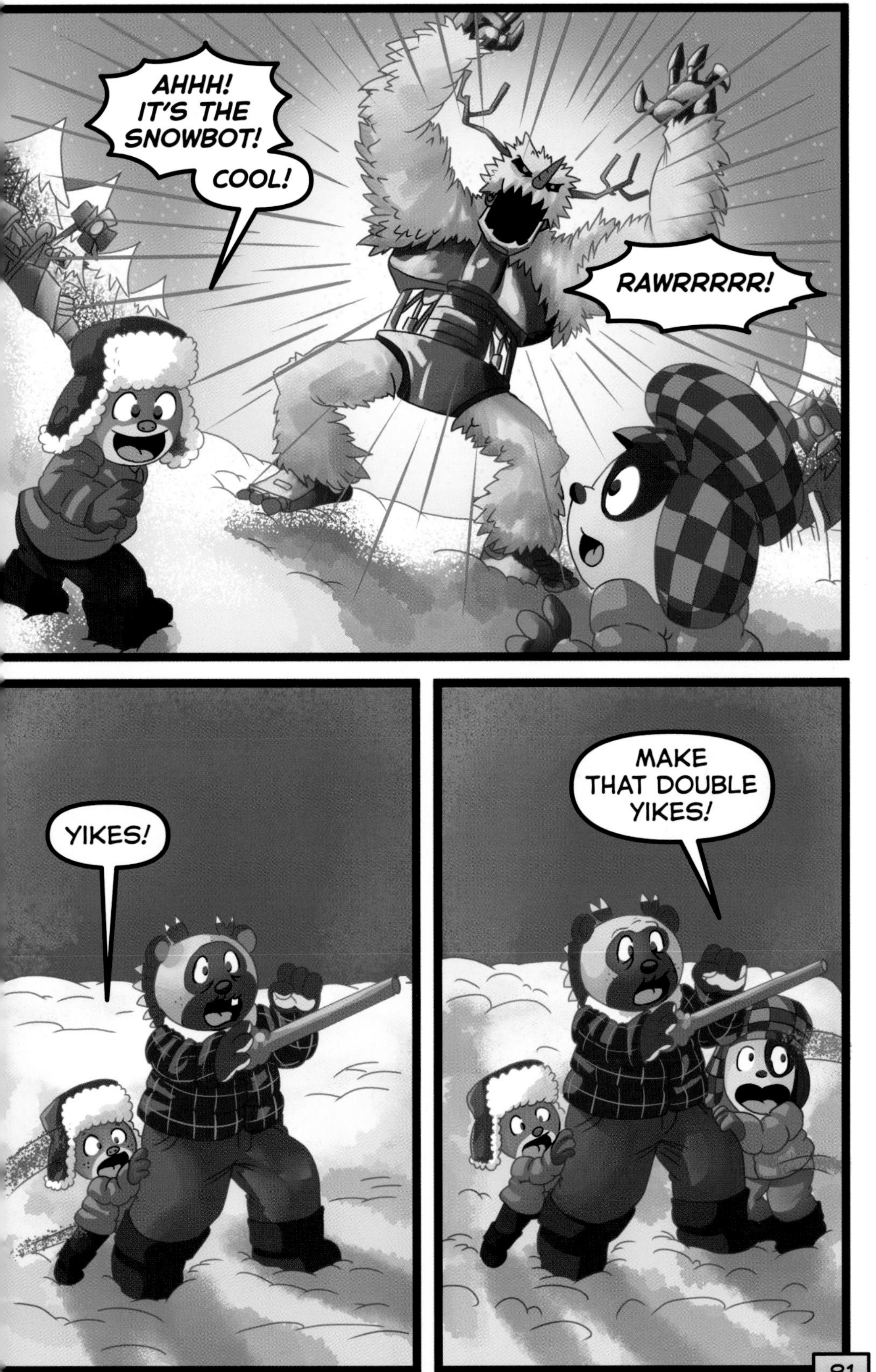
AHHH! IT'S THE SNOWBOT!
COOL!
RAWRRRRR!
YIKES!
MAKE THAT DOUBLE YIKES!

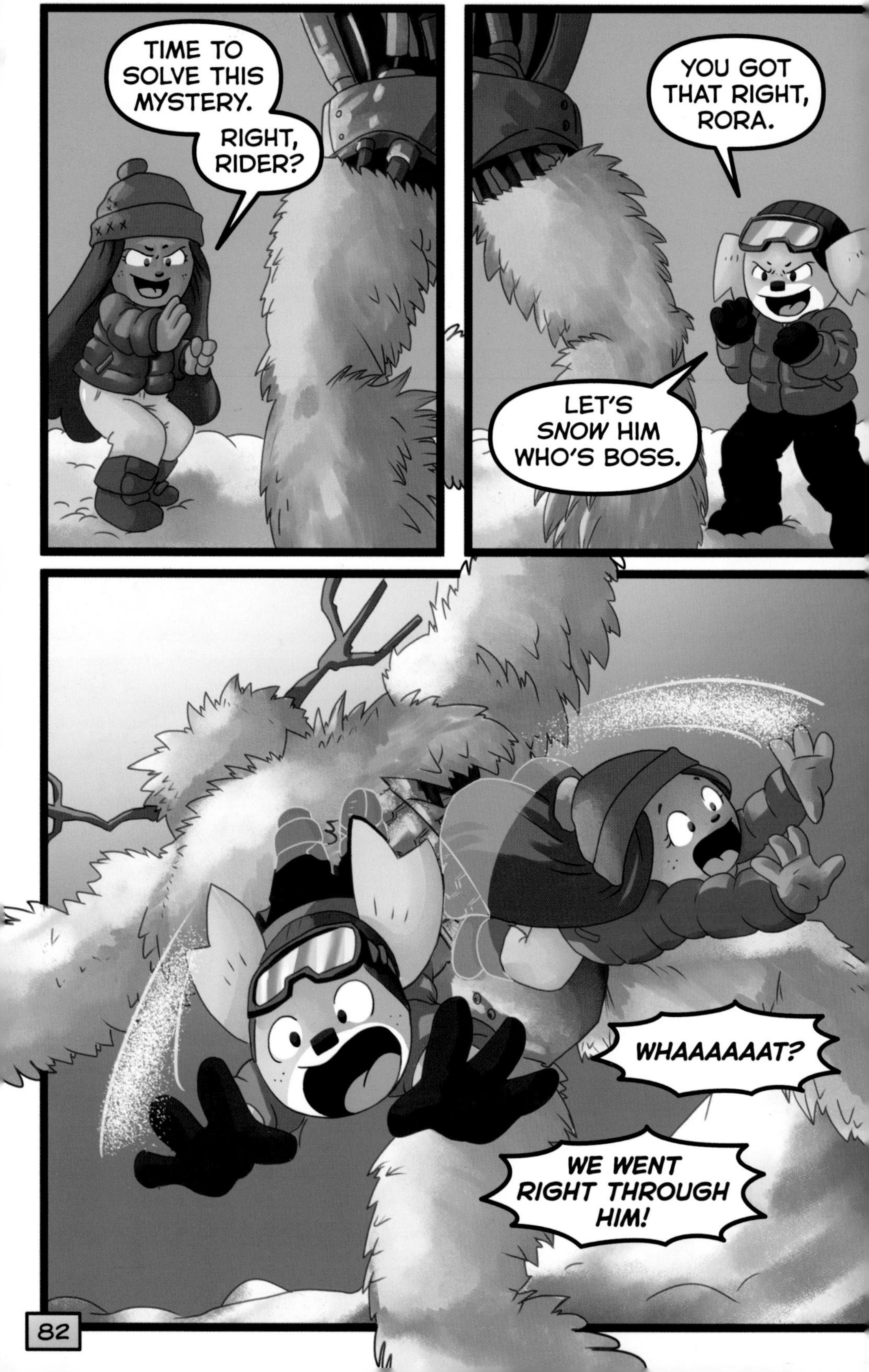
TIME TO SOLVE THIS MYSTERY.
RIGHT, RIDER?
YOU GOT THAT RIGHT, RORA.
LET'S *SNOW* HIM WHO'S BOSS.
WHAAAAAAT?
WE WENT RIGHT THROUGH HIM!

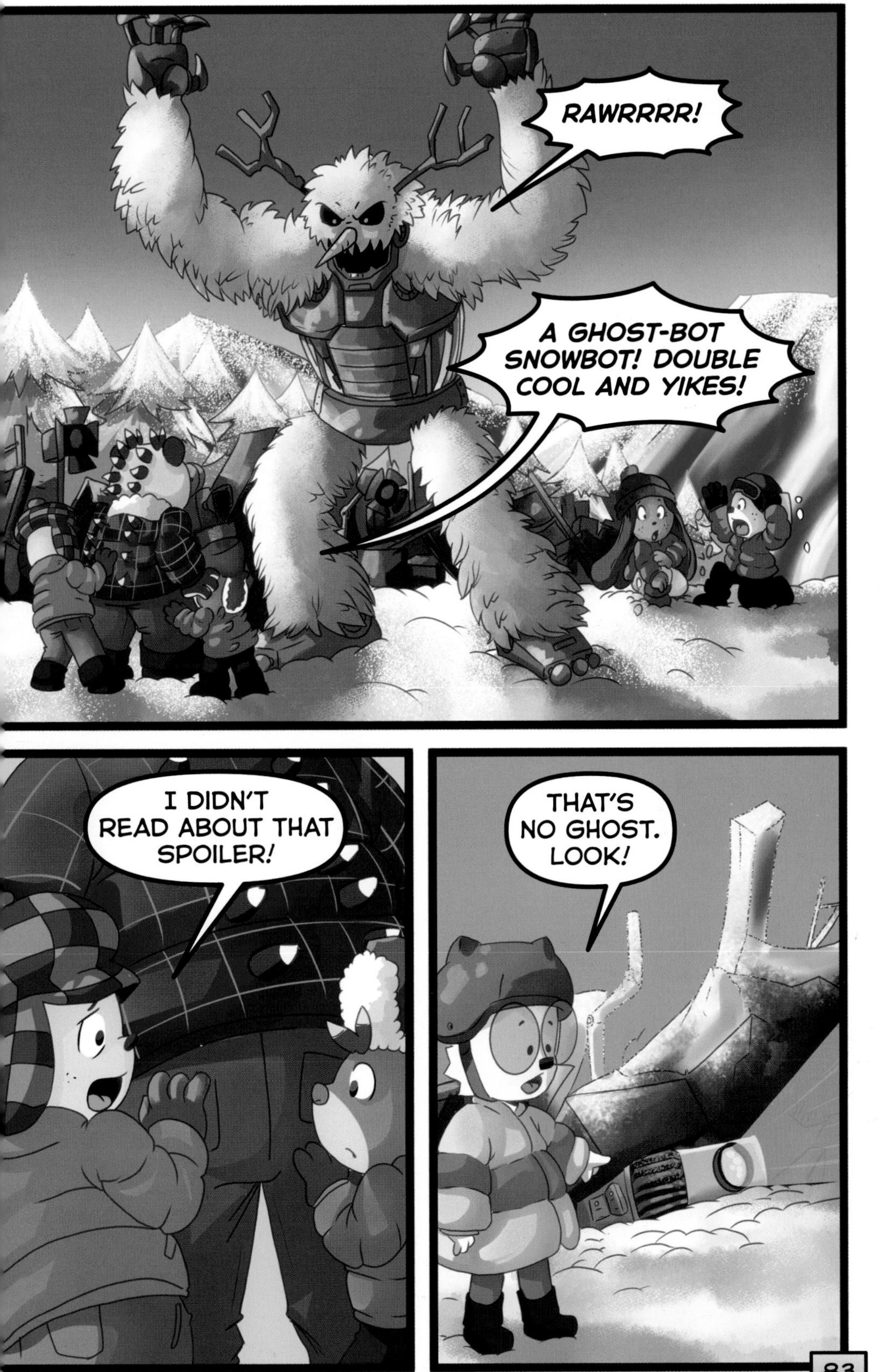
RAWRRRR!
A GHOST-BOT SNOWBOT! DOUBLE COOL AND YIKES!
I DIDN'T READ ABOUT THAT SPOILER!
THAT'S NO GHOST. LOOK!

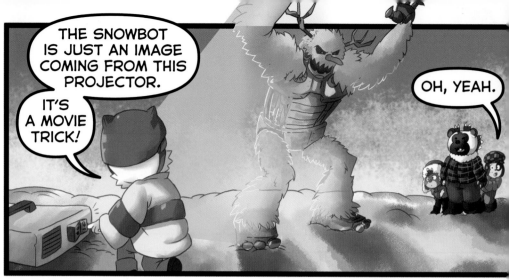

THE SNOWBOT IS JUST AN IMAGE COMING FROM THIS PROJECTOR.

IT'S A MOVIE TRICK!

OH, YEAH.

WE KNEW THAT WAS FAKE THE WHOLE TIME.

JUST MOVIE MAGIC.

LIKE THIS SNOWBOT RUBBER MASK OVER HERE.

MOVIE MAGIC!

I READ ABOUT THAT ONLINE TOO!

DITTO.

UMMMMM, GUYS? THAT'S REAL!

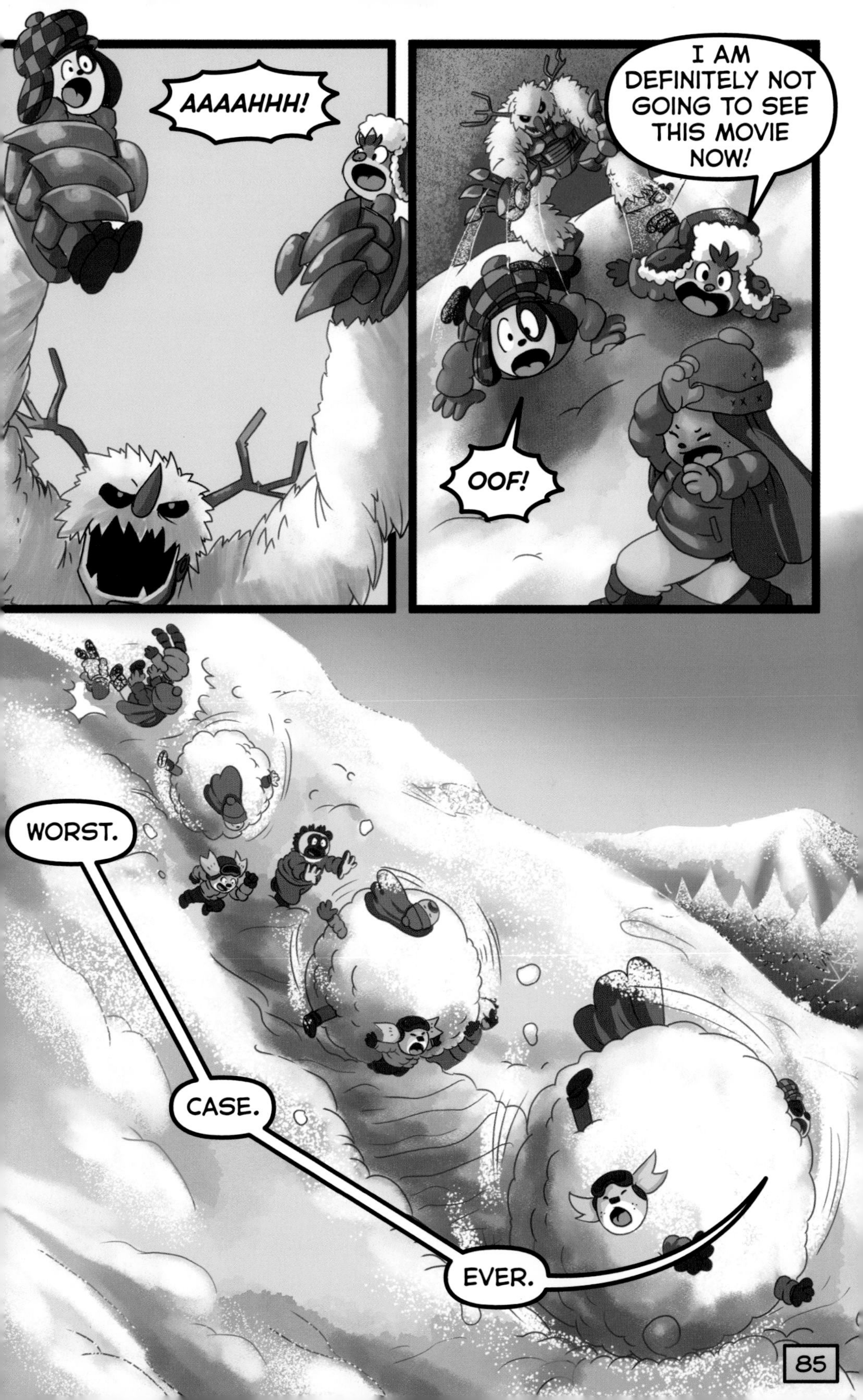
AAAAHHH!
I AM DEFINITELY NOT GOING TO SEE THIS MOVIE NOW!
OOF!
WORST.
CASE.
EVER.

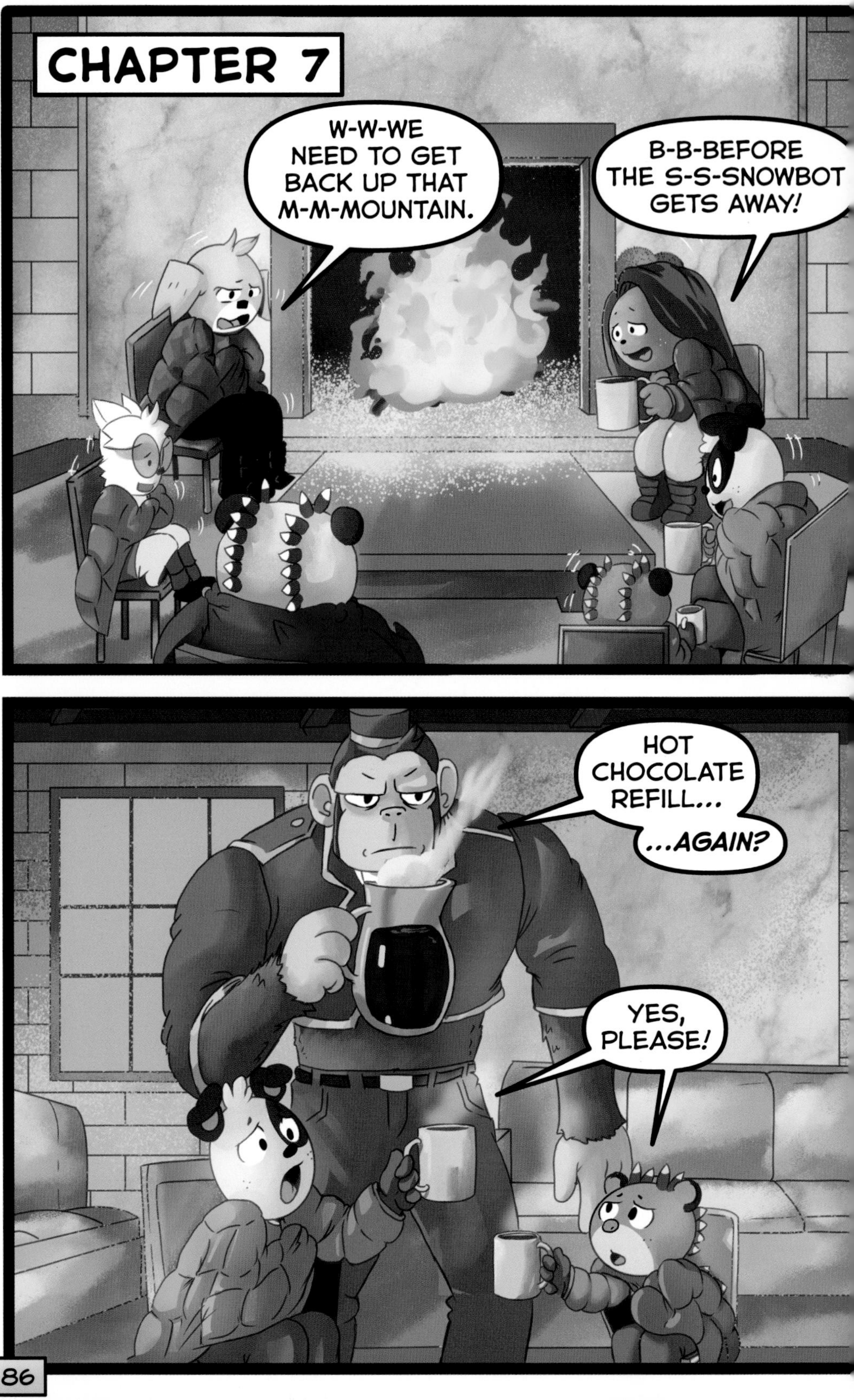
CHAPTER 7
W-W-WE NEED TO GET BACK UP THAT M-M-MOUNTAIN.
B-B-BEFORE THE S-S-SNOWBOT GETS AWAY!
HOT CHOCOLATE REFILL...
...AGAIN?
YES, PLEASE!

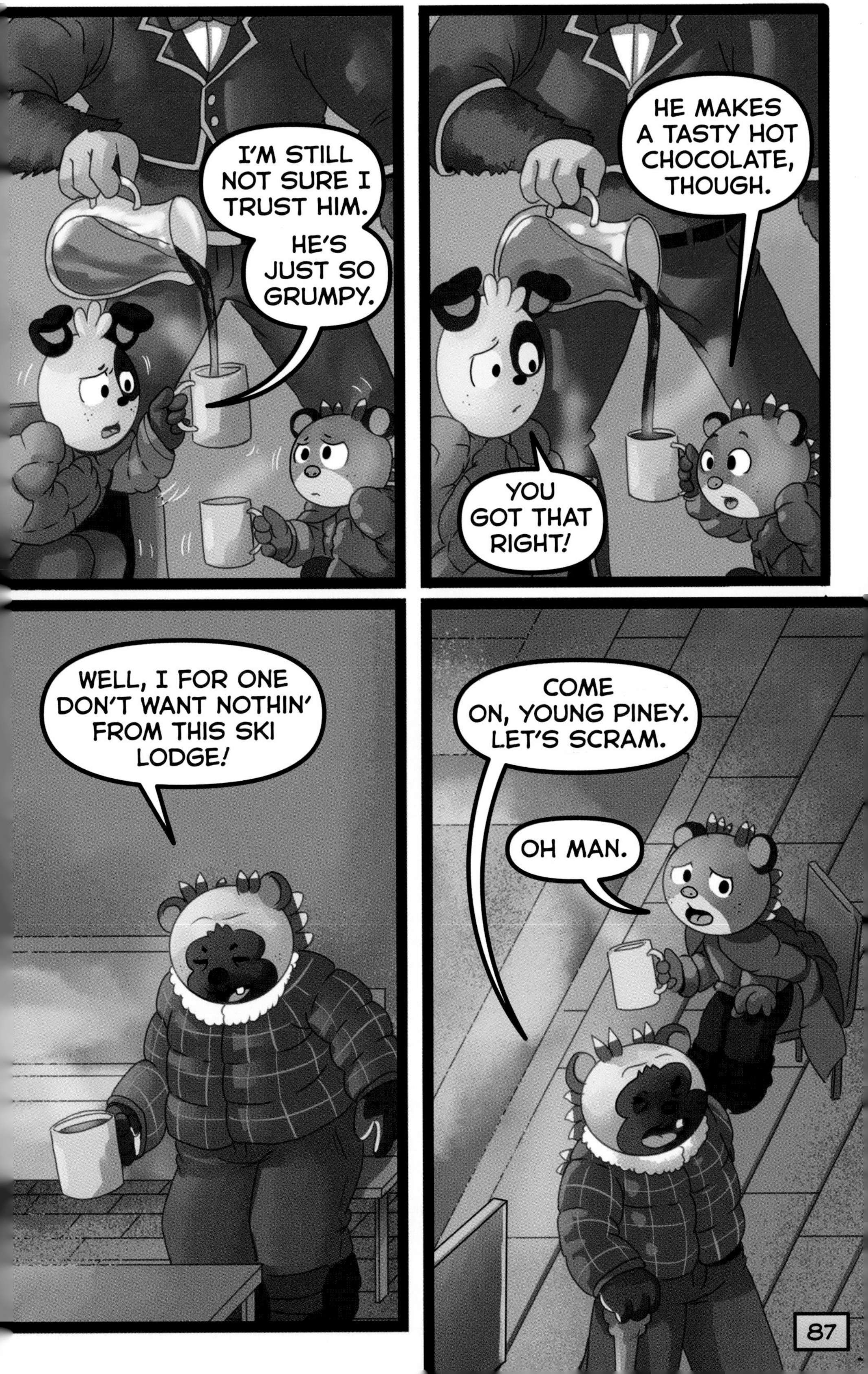
I'M STILL NOT SURE I TRUST HIM.
HE'S JUST SO GRUMPY.
HE MAKES A TASTY HOT CHOCOLATE, THOUGH.
YOU GOT THAT RIGHT!
WELL, I FOR ONE DON'T WANT NOTHIN' FROM THIS SKI LODGE!
COME ON, YOUNG PINEY. LET'S SCRAM.
OH MAN.

CAN I GET THIS IN A TO-GO CUP?

I REALLY NEED TO GO.

UGH. YES, FINE.

DON'T WANT TO CATCH A COLD LIKE THAT PRINCIPAL.

OH, RIGHT! HOW IS HE?

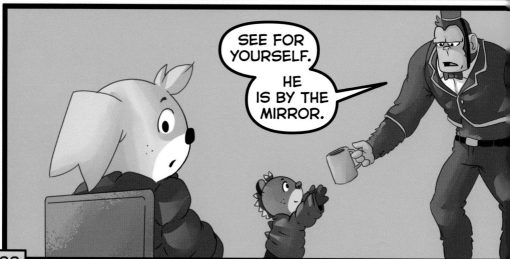

SEE FOR YOURSELF.

HE IS BY THE MIRROR.

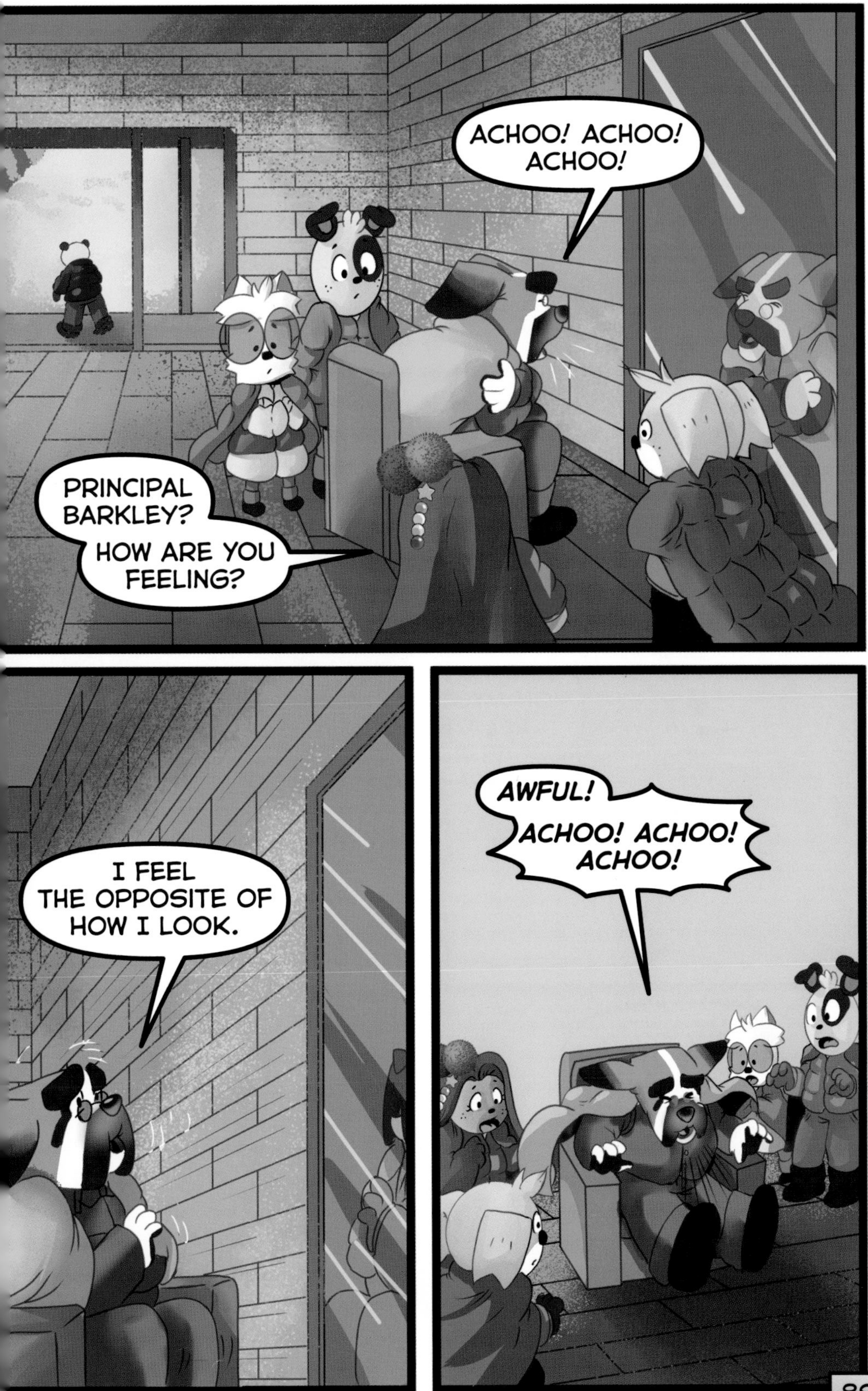
ACHOO! ACHOO! ACHOO!
PRINCIPAL BARKLEY?
HOW ARE YOU FEELING?
I FEEL THE OPPOSITE OF HOW I LOOK.
AWFUL!
ACHOO! ACHOO! ACHOO!

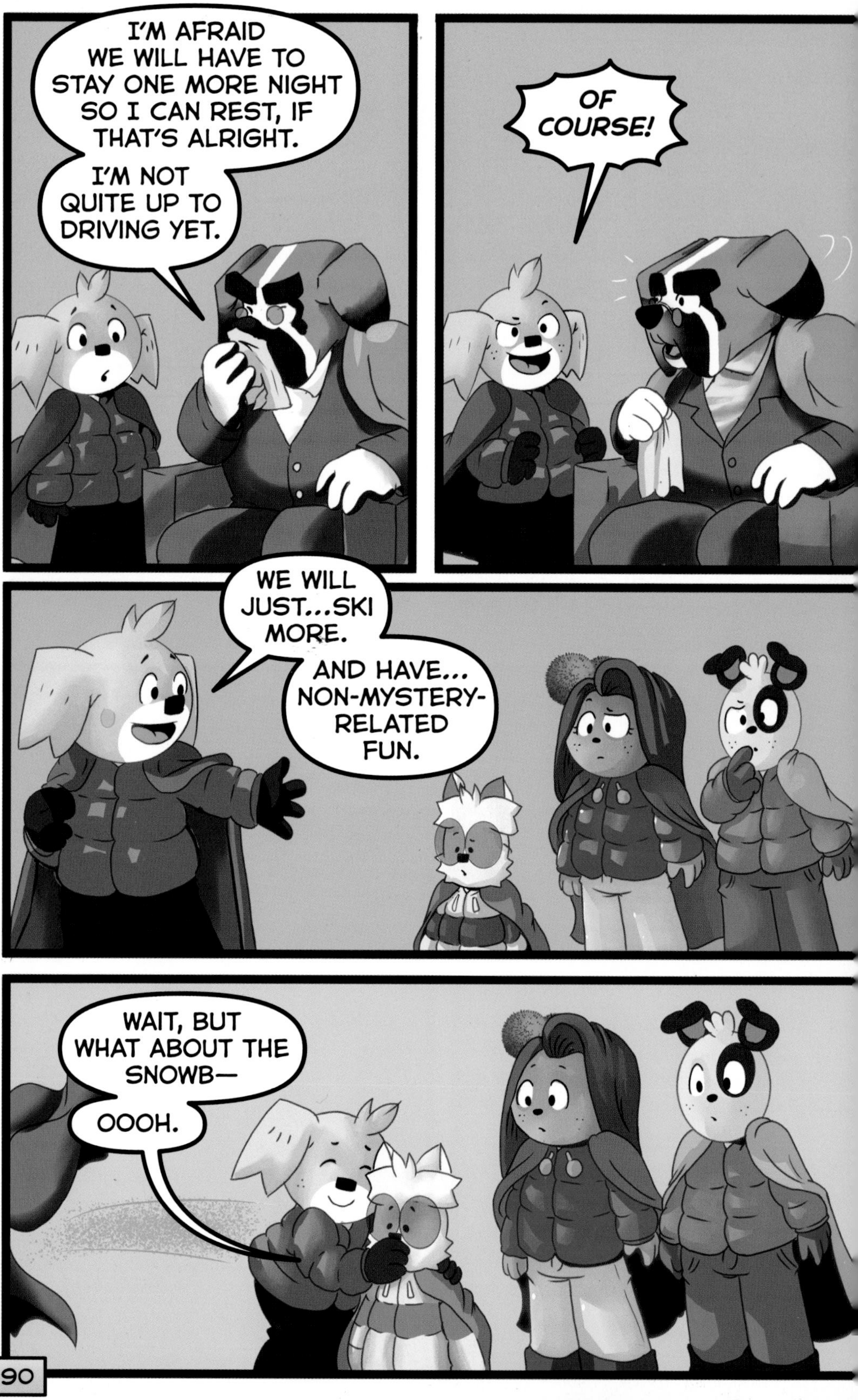
I'M AFRAID WE WILL HAVE TO STAY ONE MORE NIGHT SO I CAN REST, IF THAT'S ALRIGHT.
I'M NOT QUITE UP TO DRIVING YET.
OF COURSE!
WE WILL JUST...SKI MORE.
AND HAVE... NON-MYSTERY-RELATED FUN.
WAIT, BUT WHAT ABOUT THE SNOWB—
OOOH.

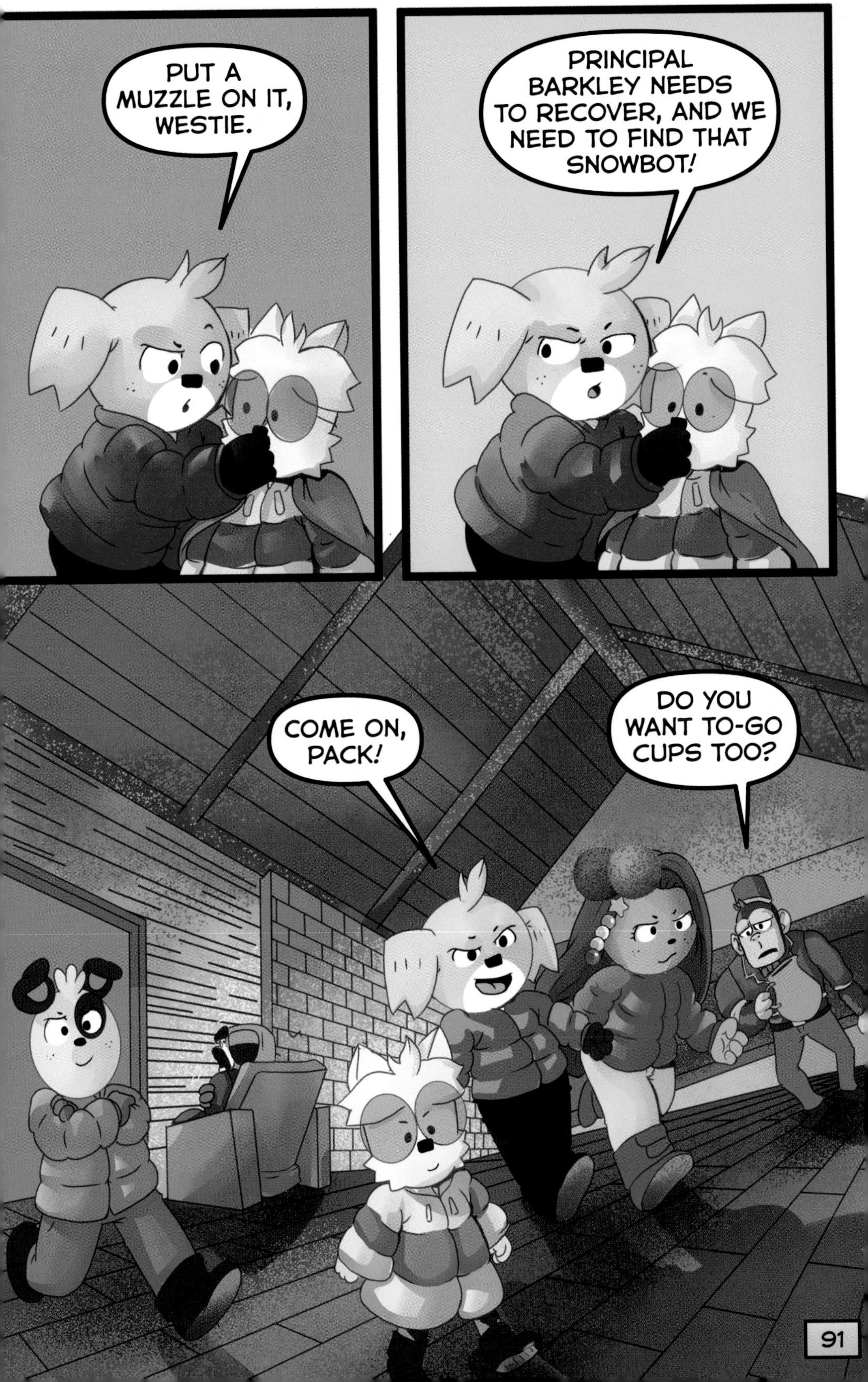
PUT A MUZZLE ON IT, WESTIE.
PRINCIPAL BARKLEY NEEDS TO RECOVER, AND WE NEED TO FIND THAT SNOWBOT!
COME ON, PACK!
DO YOU WANT TO-GO CUPS TOO?

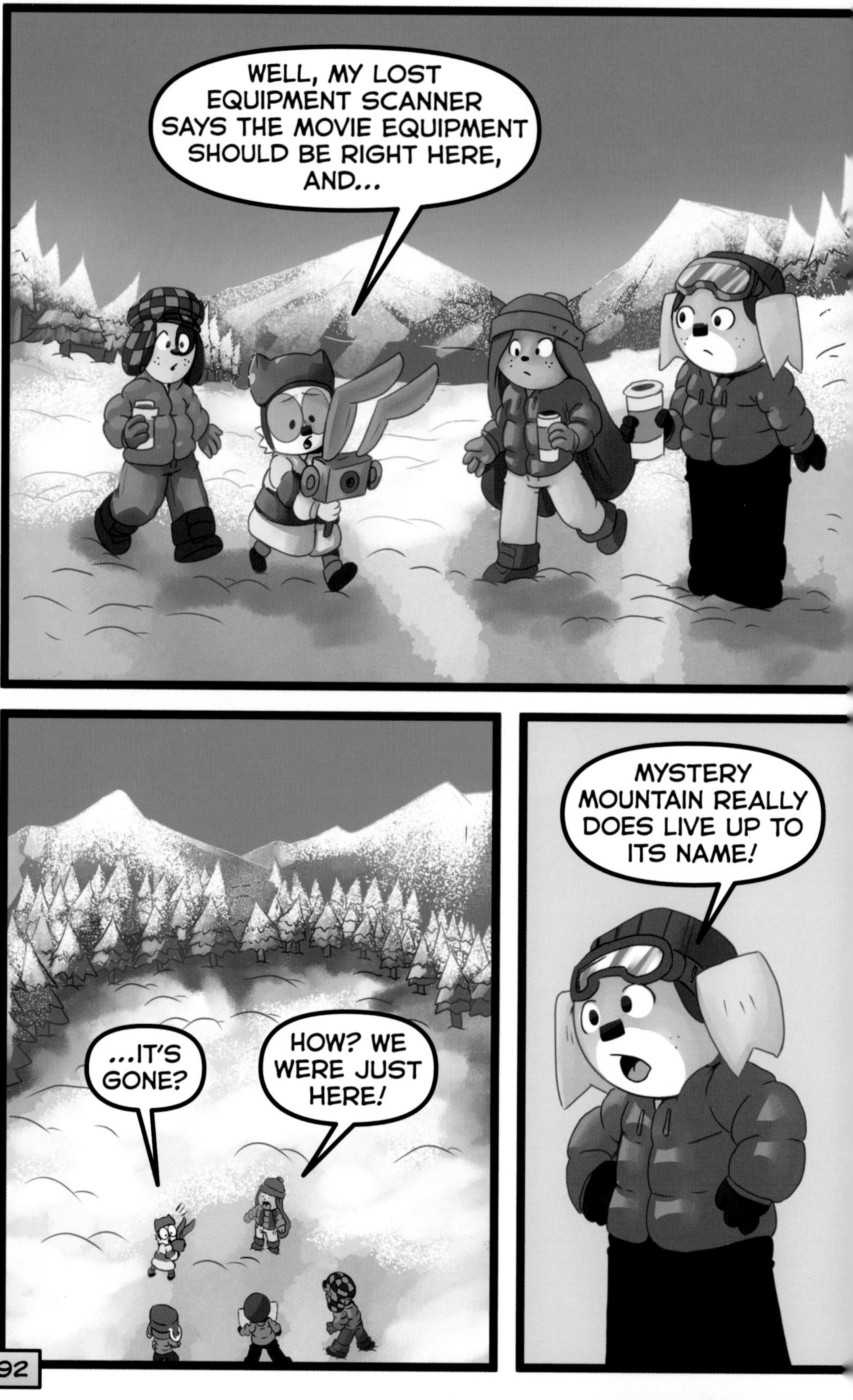
WELL, MY LOST EQUIPMENT SCANNER SAYS THE MOVIE EQUIPMENT SHOULD BE RIGHT HERE, AND...
...IT'S GONE?
HOW? WE WERE JUST HERE!
MYSTERY MOUNTAIN REALLY DOES LIVE UP TO ITS NAME!

I'LL SAY. BACK AT THE LODGE I WAS RESEARCHING THIS PLACE...

...AND THERE'S LOTS OF INFORMATION ONLINE!

LOOK AT ALL THESE MONSTERS PEOPLE HAVE REPORTED, AND...

MONSTERS ATTACK MYSTERY MOUNTAIN

SKI RESORT RUINED BY RISKY REINDEER

EVIL ELF ENDS ENJOYMENT (of skiing)

PRICKLY PORCUPINE POPS PLANS FOR POTENTIAL S...

...ONE OF THEM APPARENTLY LOOKED LIKE A PORCUPINE.

(of skiing)

PRICKLY PORCUPINE POPS PLANS FOR POTENTIAL PAR...

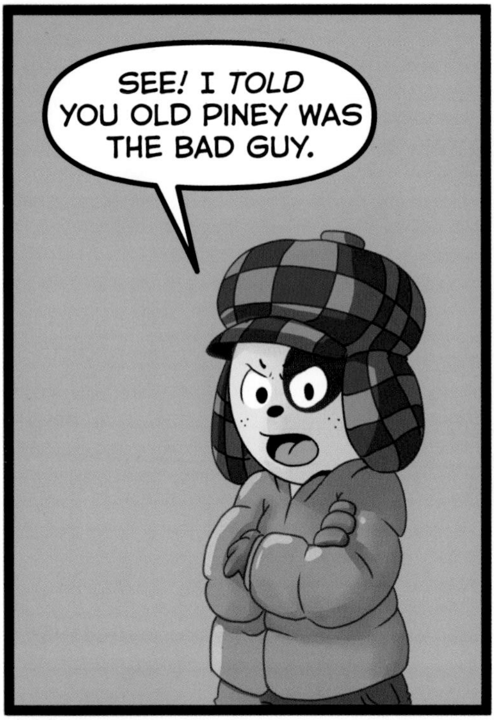
SEE! I TOLD YOU OLD PINEY WAS THE BAD GUY.

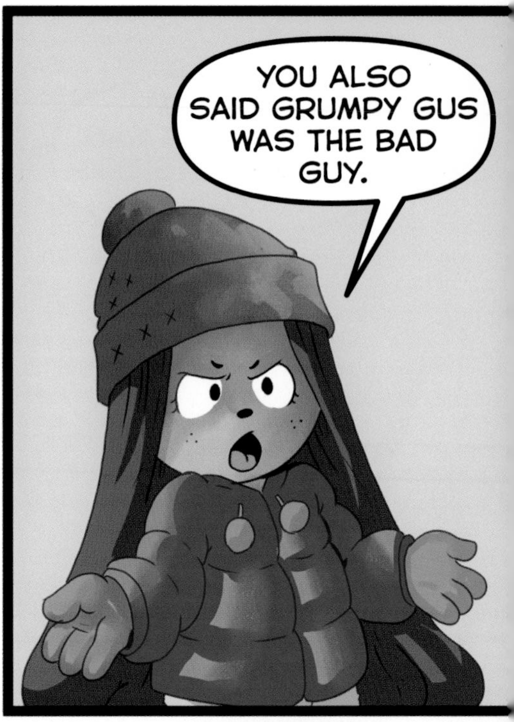
YOU ALSO SAID GRUMPY GUS WAS THE BAD GUY.

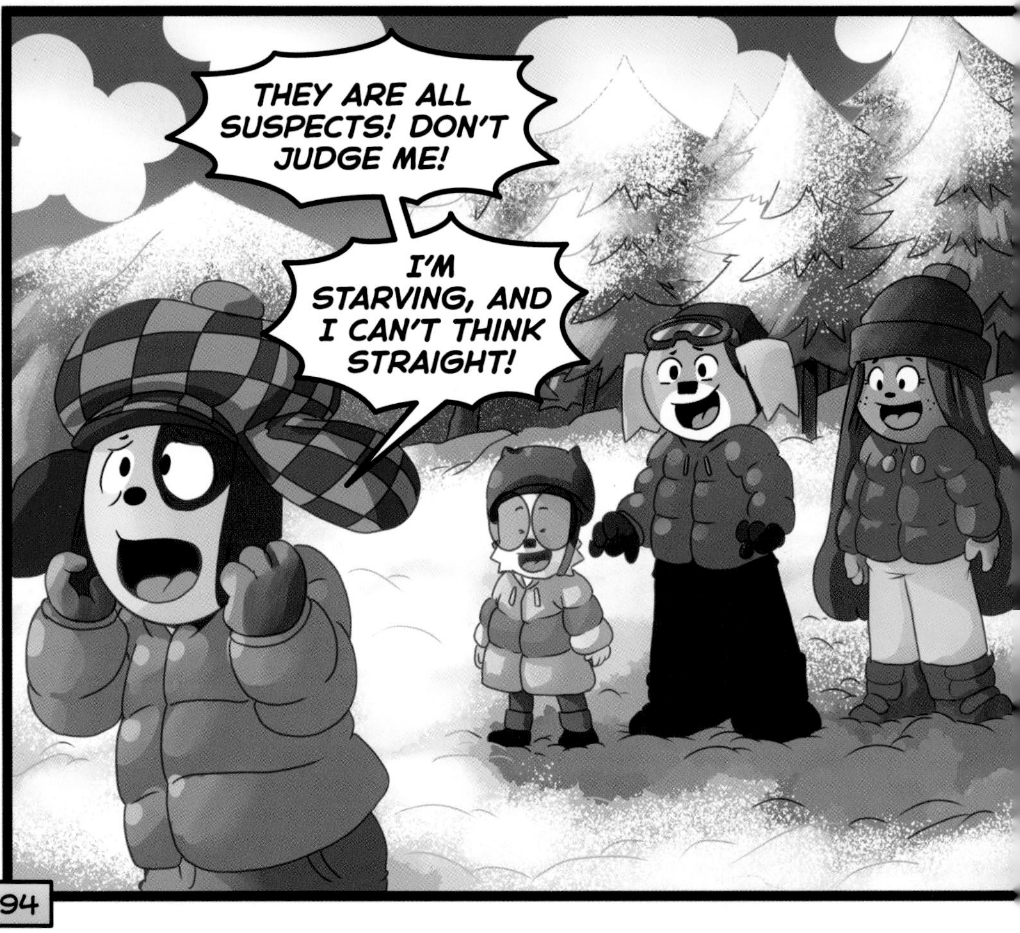
THEY ARE ALL SUSPECTS! DON'T JUDGE ME!
I'M STARVING, AND I CAN'T THINK STRAIGHT!

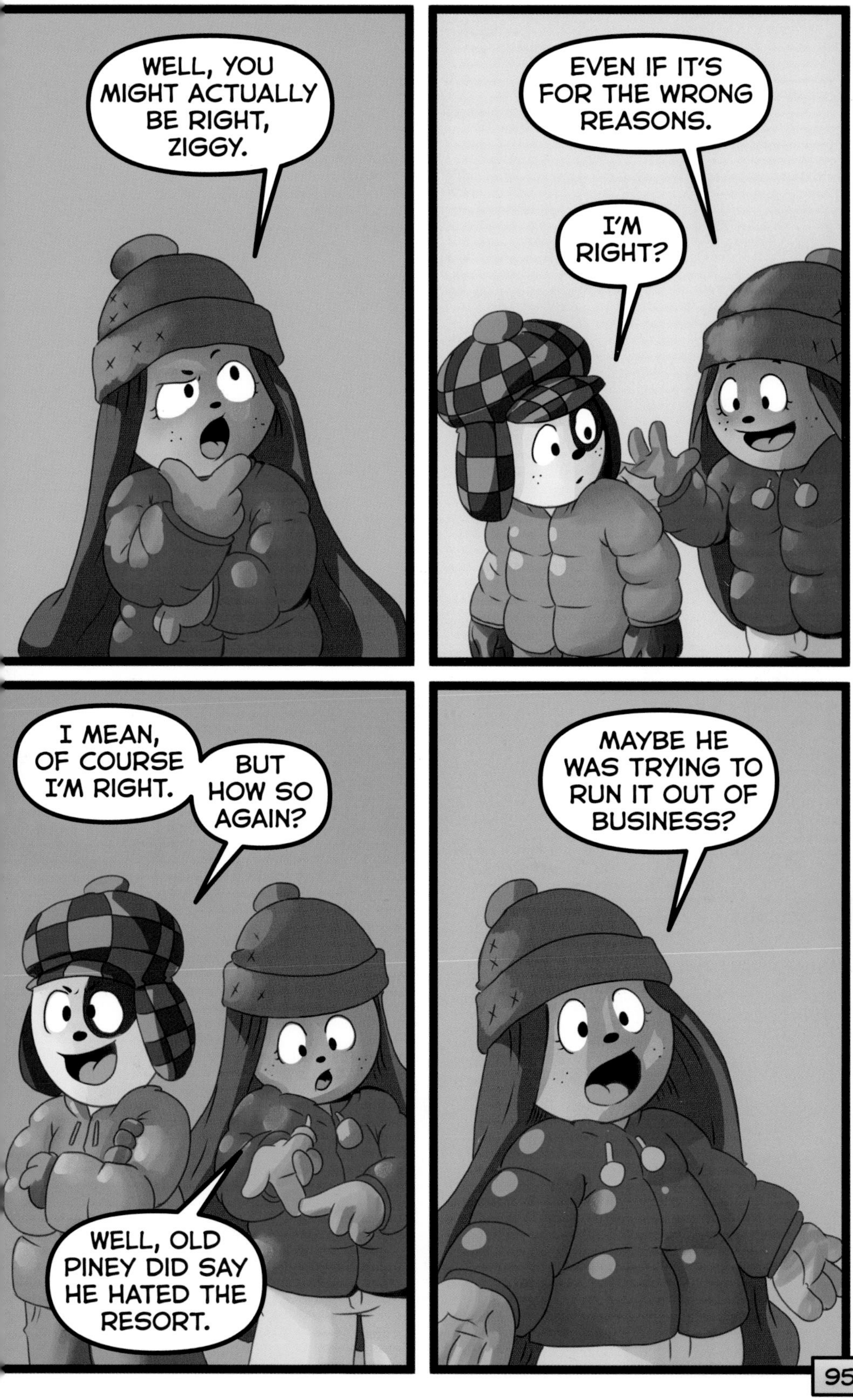
WELL, YOU MIGHT ACTUALLY BE RIGHT, ZIGGY.
EVEN IF IT'S FOR THE WRONG REASONS.
I'M RIGHT?
I MEAN, OF COURSE I'M RIGHT.
BUT HOW SO AGAIN?
WELL, OLD PINEY DID SAY HE HATED THE RESORT.
MAYBE HE WAS TRYING TO RUN IT OUT OF BUSINESS?

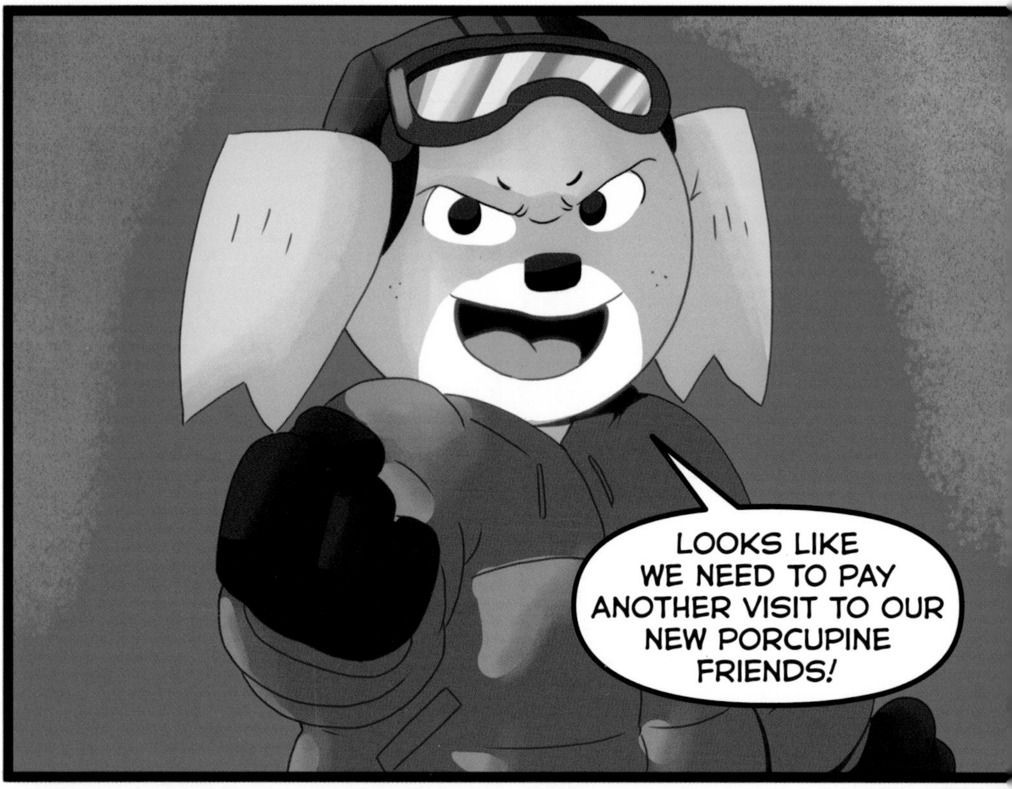
LOOKS LIKE WE NEED TO PAY ANOTHER VISIT TO OUR NEW PORCUPINE FRIENDS!

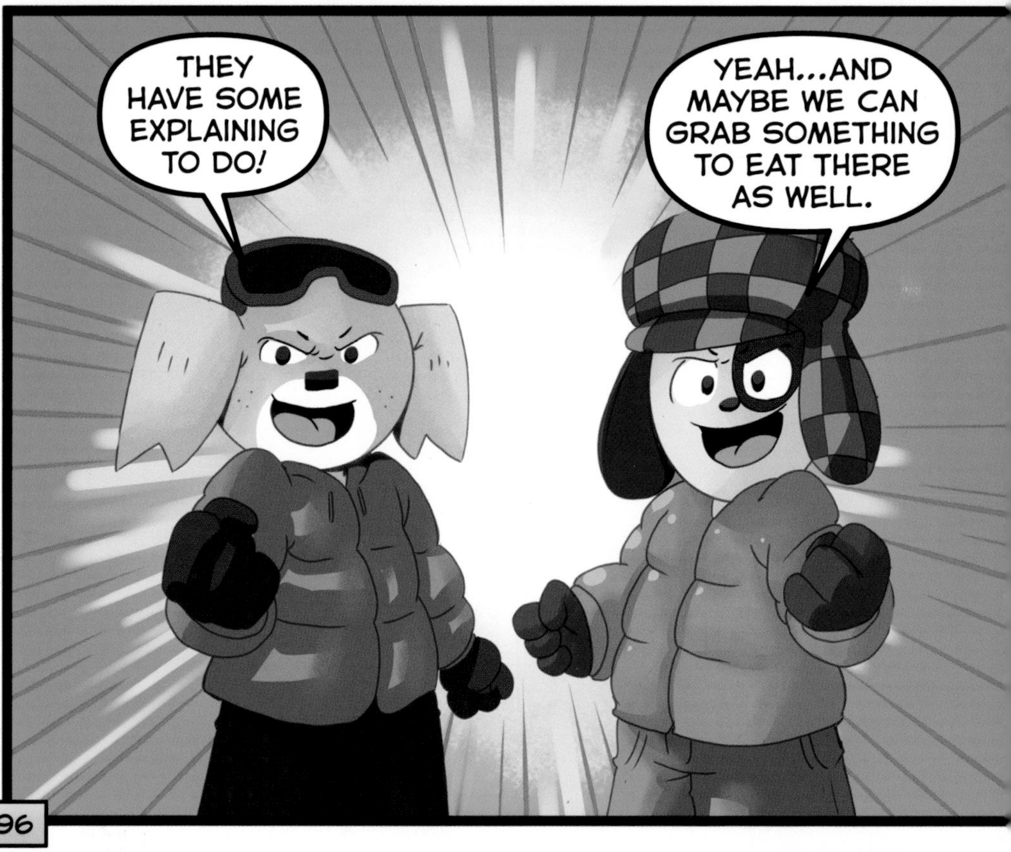
THEY HAVE SOME EXPLAINING TO DO!
YEAH...AND MAYBE WE CAN GRAB SOMETHING TO EAT THERE AS WELL.

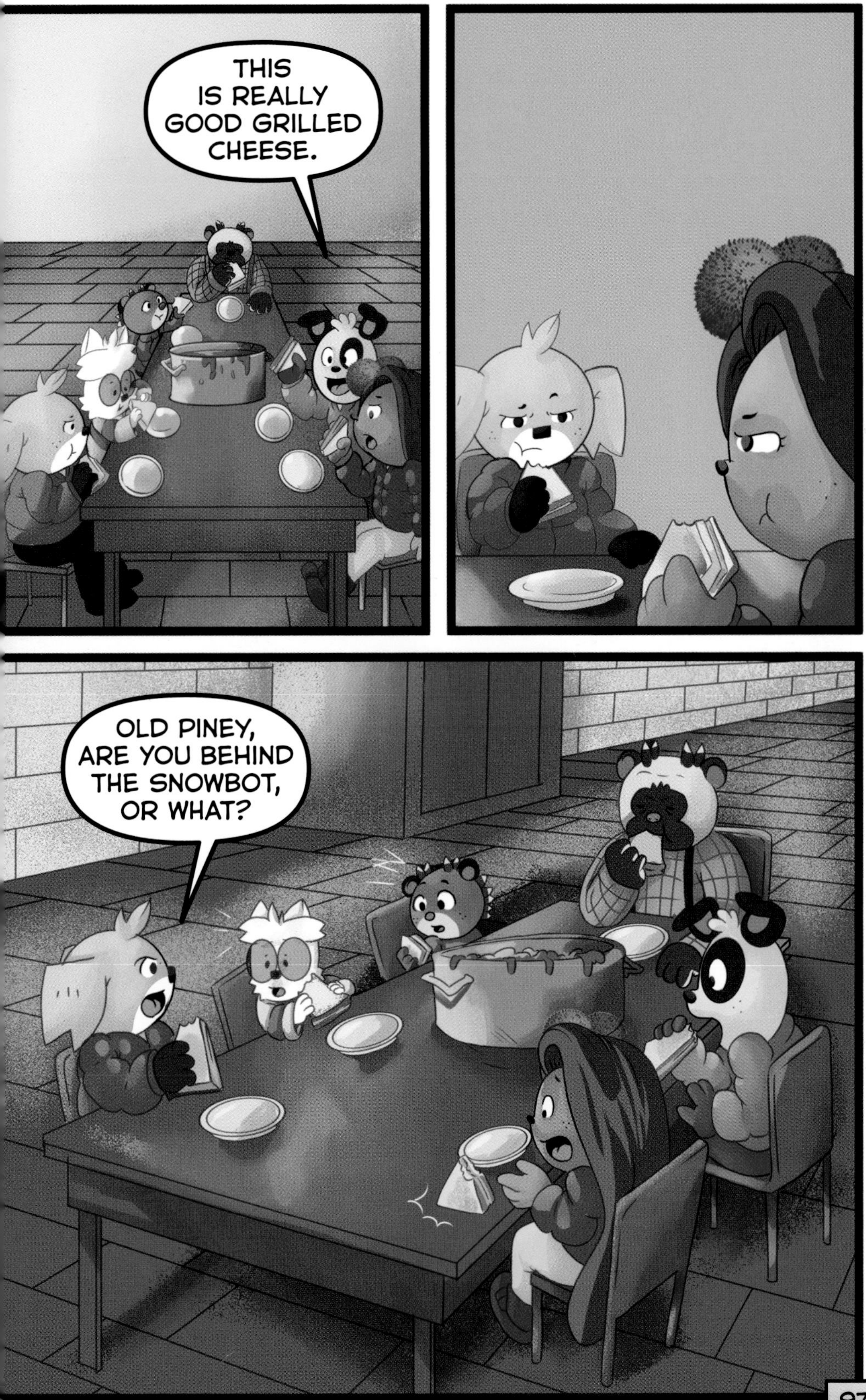
THIS IS REALLY GOOD GRILLED CHEESE.
OLD PINEY, ARE YOU BEHIND THE SNOWBOT, OR WHAT?

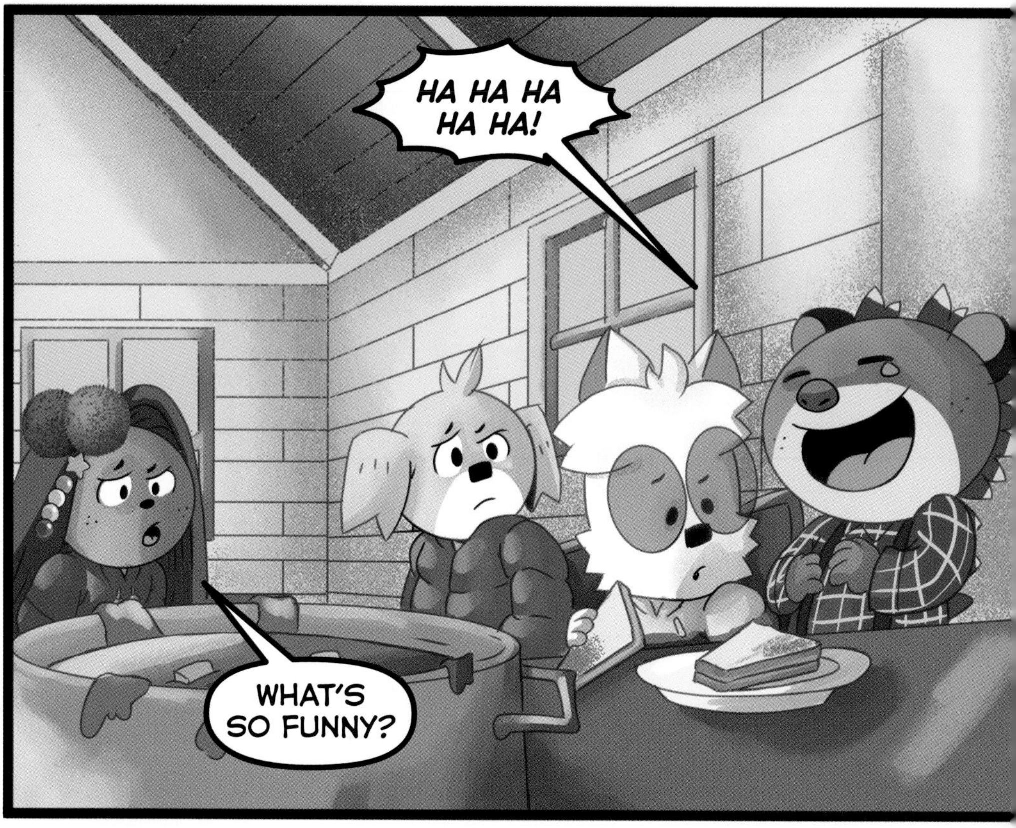
HA HA HA
HA HA!
WHAT'S SO FUNNY?

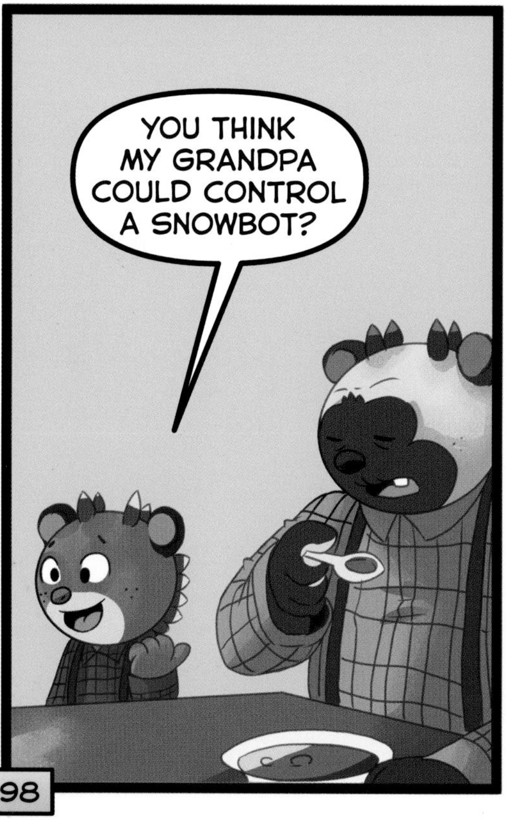
YOU THINK MY GRANDPA COULD CONTROL A SNOWBOT?

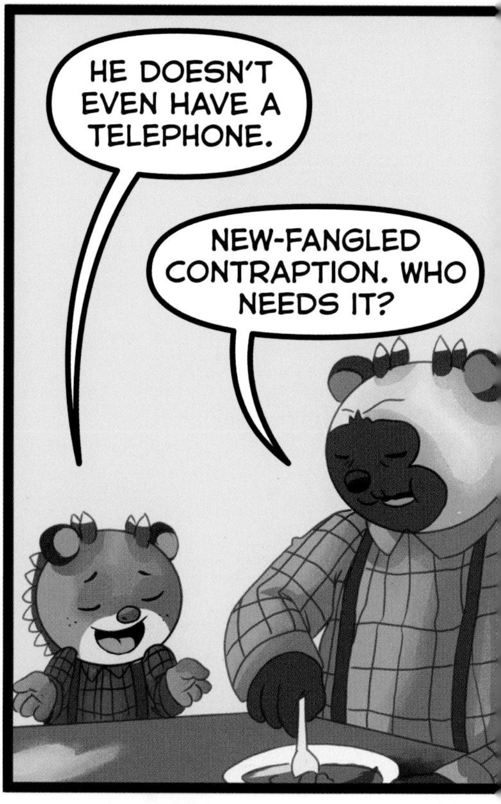
HE DOESN'T EVEN HAVE A TELEPHONE.
NEW-FANGLED CONTRAPTION. WHO NEEDS IT?

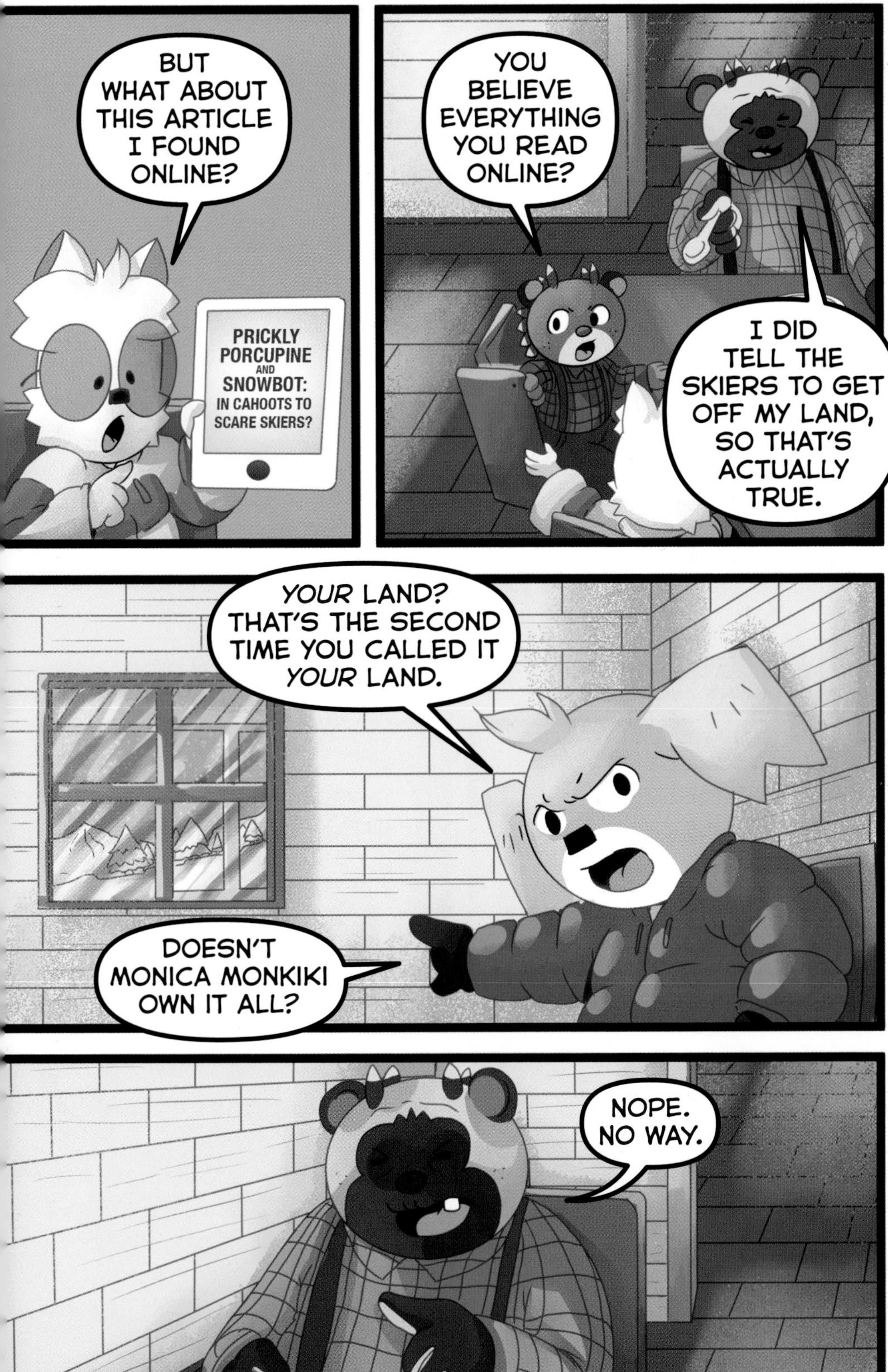
BUT WHAT ABOUT THIS ARTICLE I FOUND ONLINE?
PRICKLY PORCUPINE AND SNOWBOT: IN CAHOOTS TO SCARE SKIERS?
YOU BELIEVE EVERYTHING YOU READ ONLINE?
I DID TELL THE SKIERS TO GET OFF MY LAND, SO THAT'S ACTUALLY TRUE.
YOUR LAND? THAT'S THE SECOND TIME YOU CALLED IT *YOUR* LAND.
DOESN'T MONICA MONKIKI OWN IT ALL?
NOPE. NO WAY.

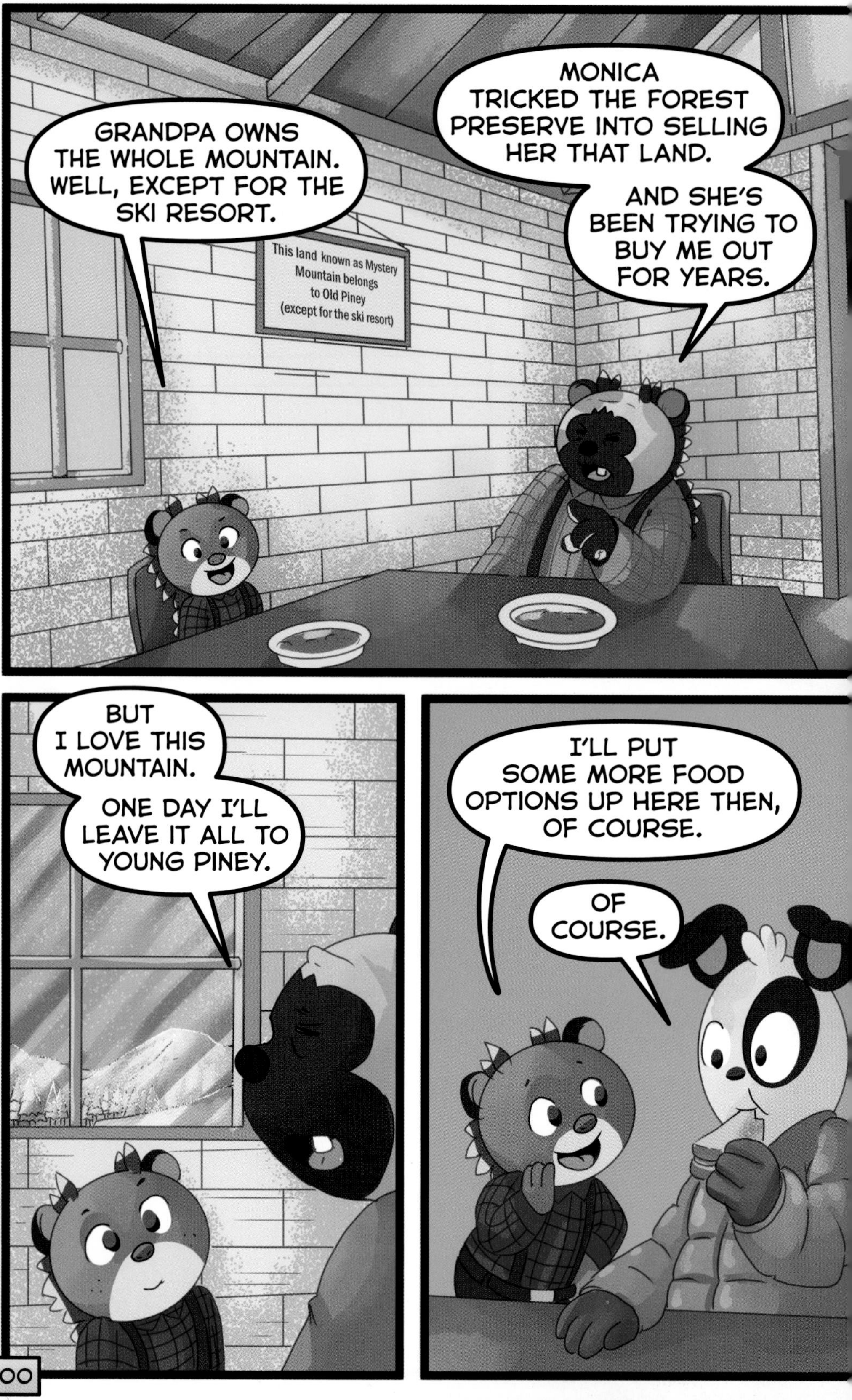
GRANDPA OWNS THE WHOLE MOUNTAIN. WELL, EXCEPT FOR THE SKI RESORT.
This land known as Mystery Mountain belongs to Old Piney (except for the ski resort)
MONICA TRICKED THE FOREST PRESERVE INTO SELLING HER THAT LAND.
AND SHE'S BEEN TRYING TO BUY ME OUT FOR YEARS.
BUT I LOVE THIS MOUNTAIN.
ONE DAY I'LL LEAVE IT ALL TO YOUNG PINEY.
I'LL PUT SOME MORE FOOD OPTIONS UP HERE THEN, OF COURSE.
OF COURSE.

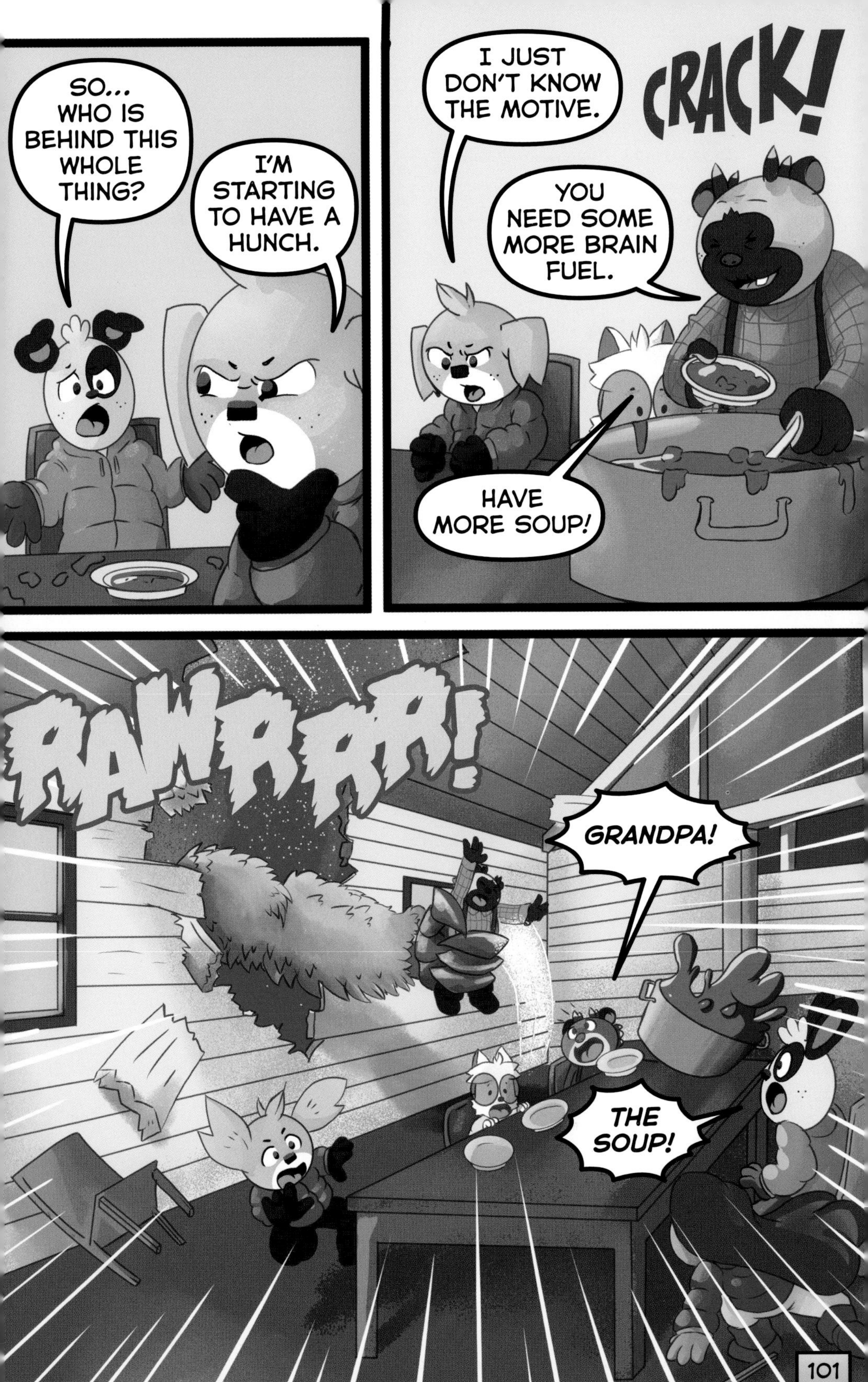
SO... WHO IS BEHIND THIS WHOLE THING?
I'M STARTING TO HAVE A HUNCH.
I JUST DON'T KNOW THE MOTIVE.
CRACK!
YOU NEED SOME MORE BRAIN FUEL.
HAVE MORE SOUP!
RAWRRR!
GRANDPA!
THE SOUP!

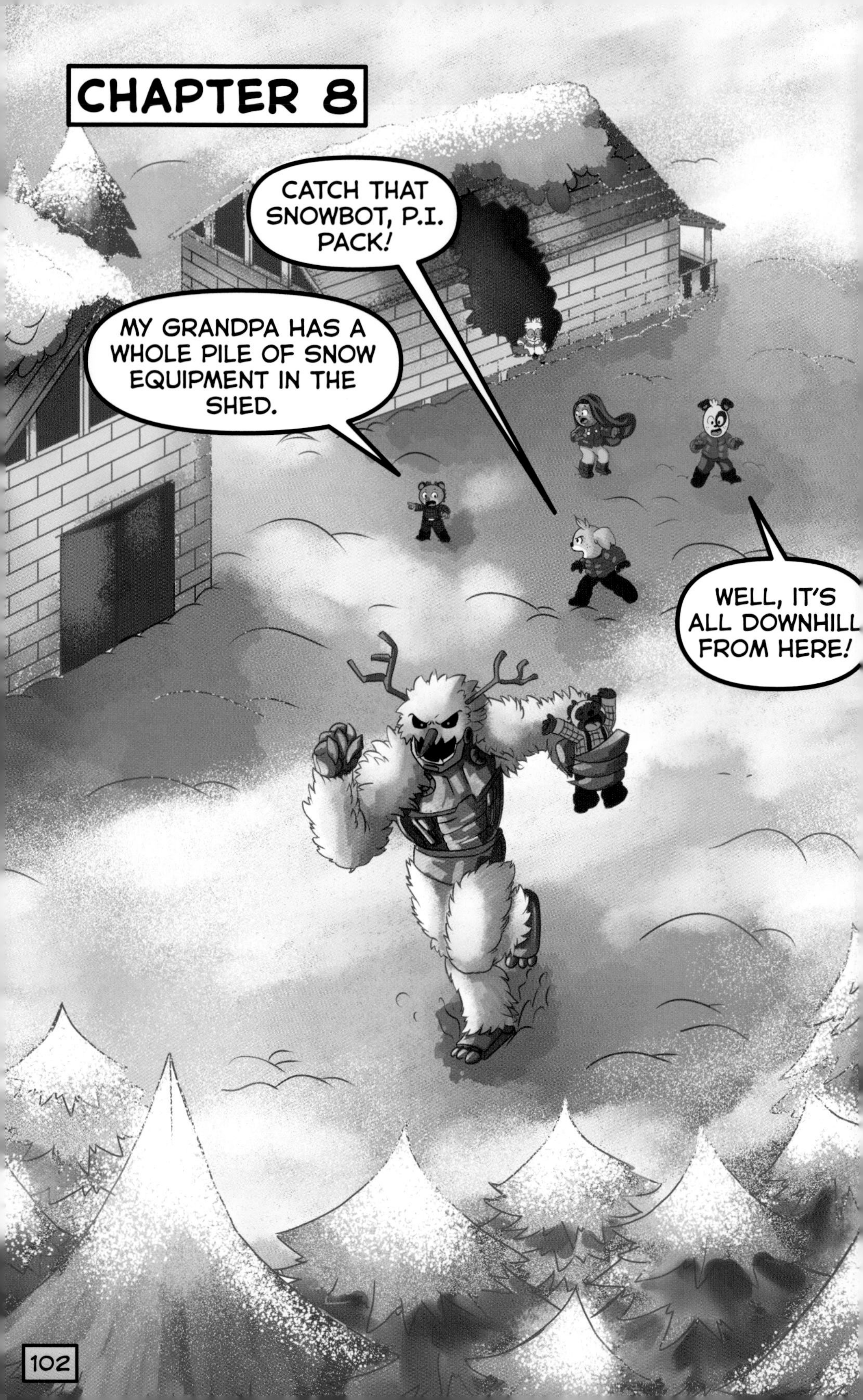
CHAPTER 8
CATCH THAT SNOWBOT, P.I. PACK!
MY GRANDPA HAS A WHOLE PILE OF SNOW EQUIPMENT IN THE SHED.
WELL, IT'S ALL DOWNHILL FROM HERE!

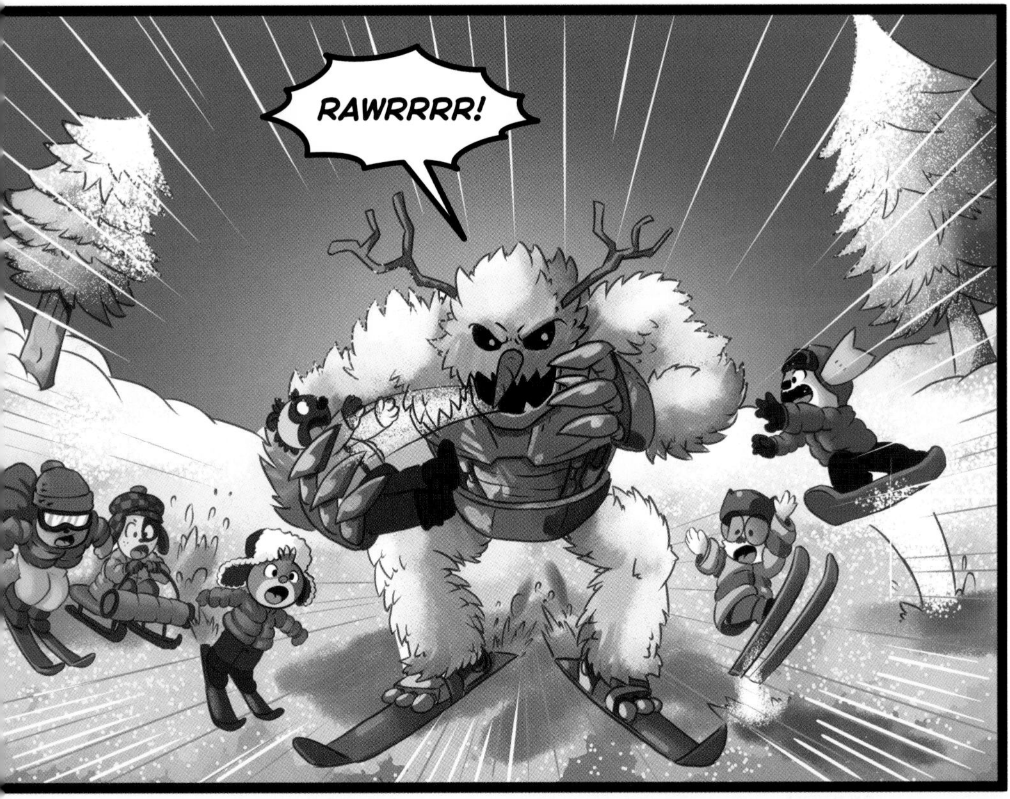
RAWRRRR!

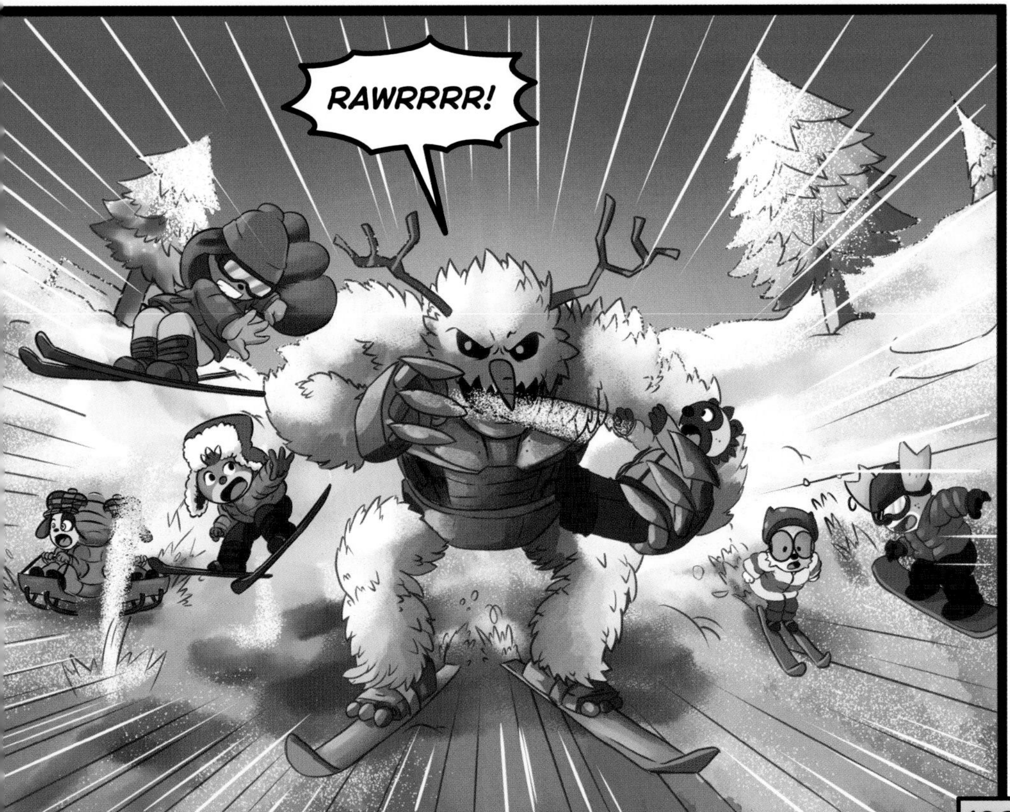
RAWRRRR!

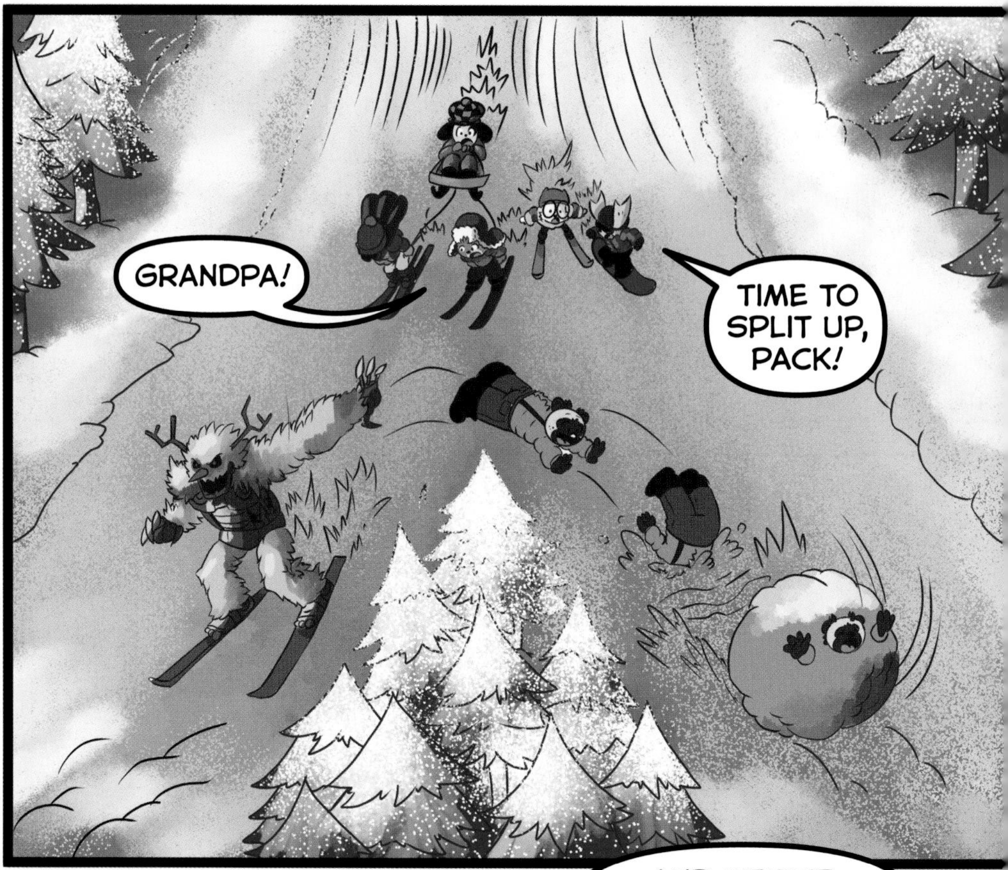
GRANDPA!
TIME TO SPLIT UP, PACK!

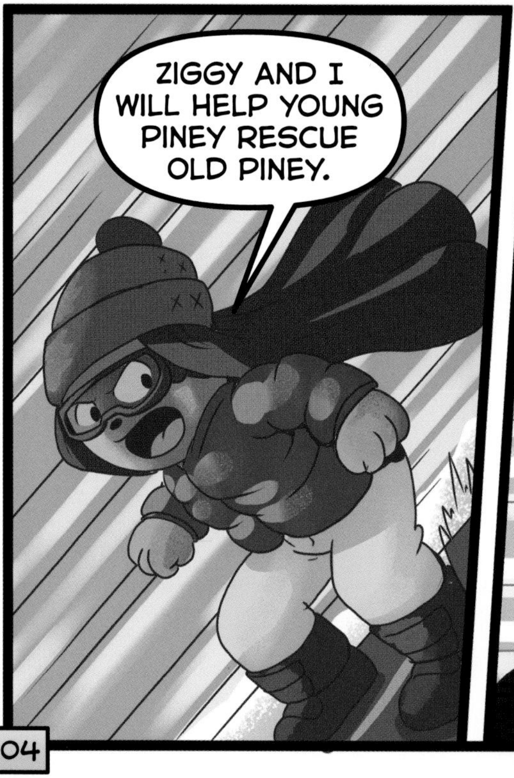
ZIGGY AND I WILL HELP YOUNG PINEY RESCUE OLD PINEY.

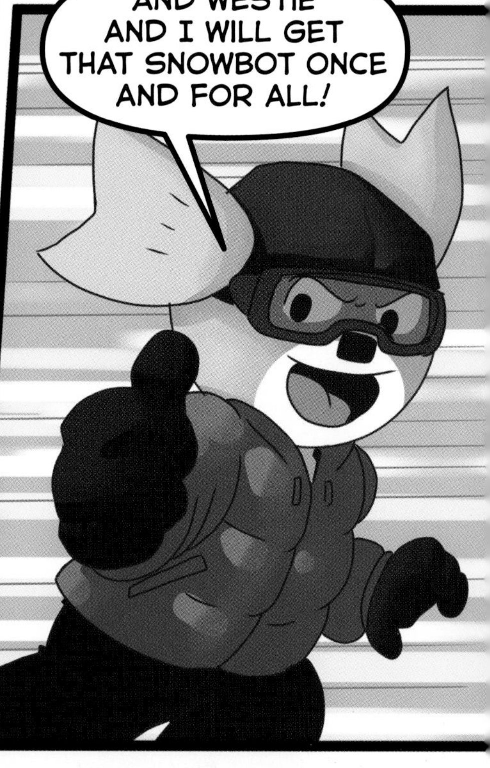
AND WESTIE AND I WILL GET THAT SNOWBOT ONCE AND FOR ALL!

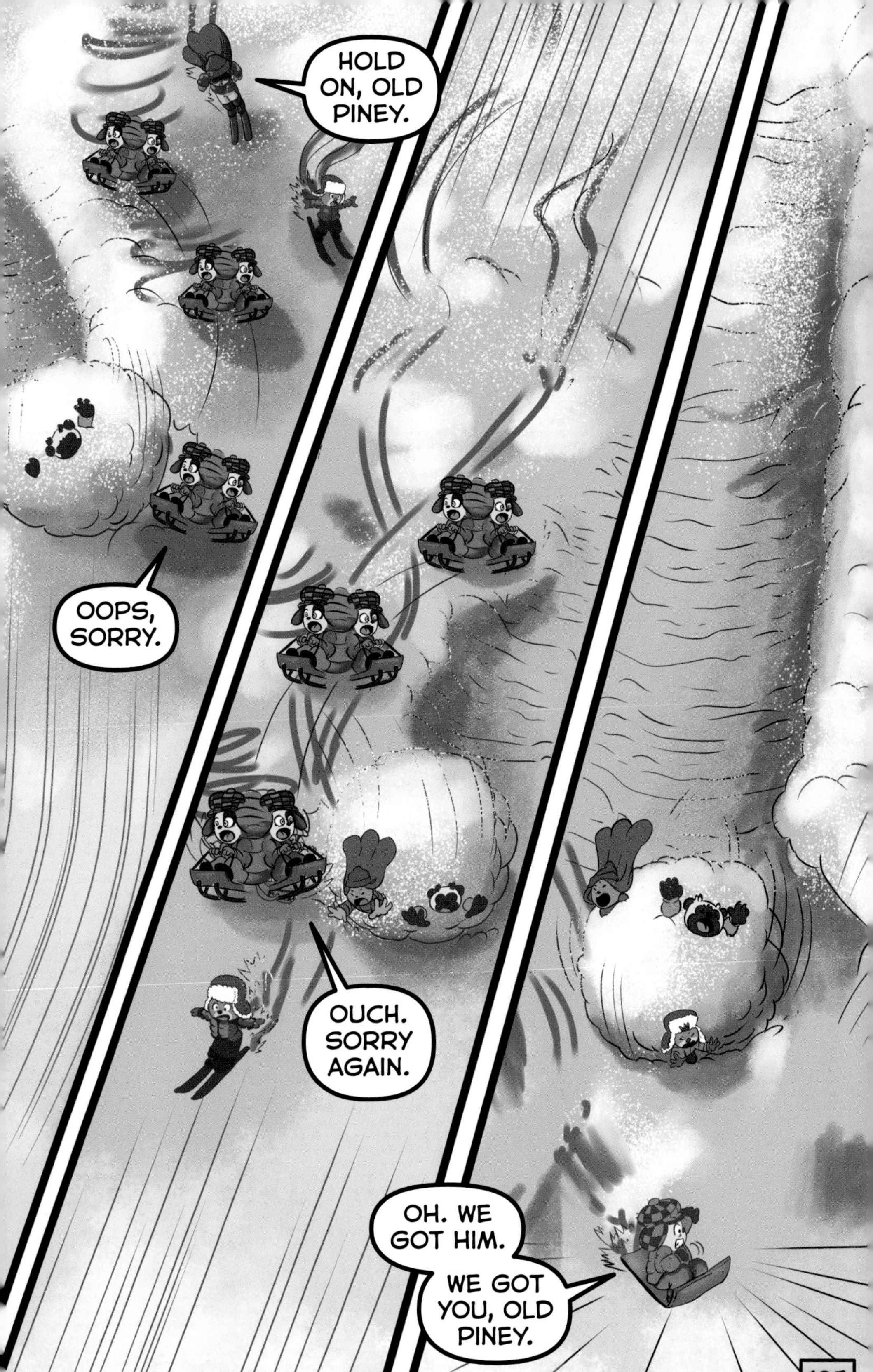
HOLD ON, OLD PINEY.
OOPS, SORRY.
OUCH. SORRY AGAIN.
OH. WE GOT HIM.
WE GOT YOU, OLD PINEY.

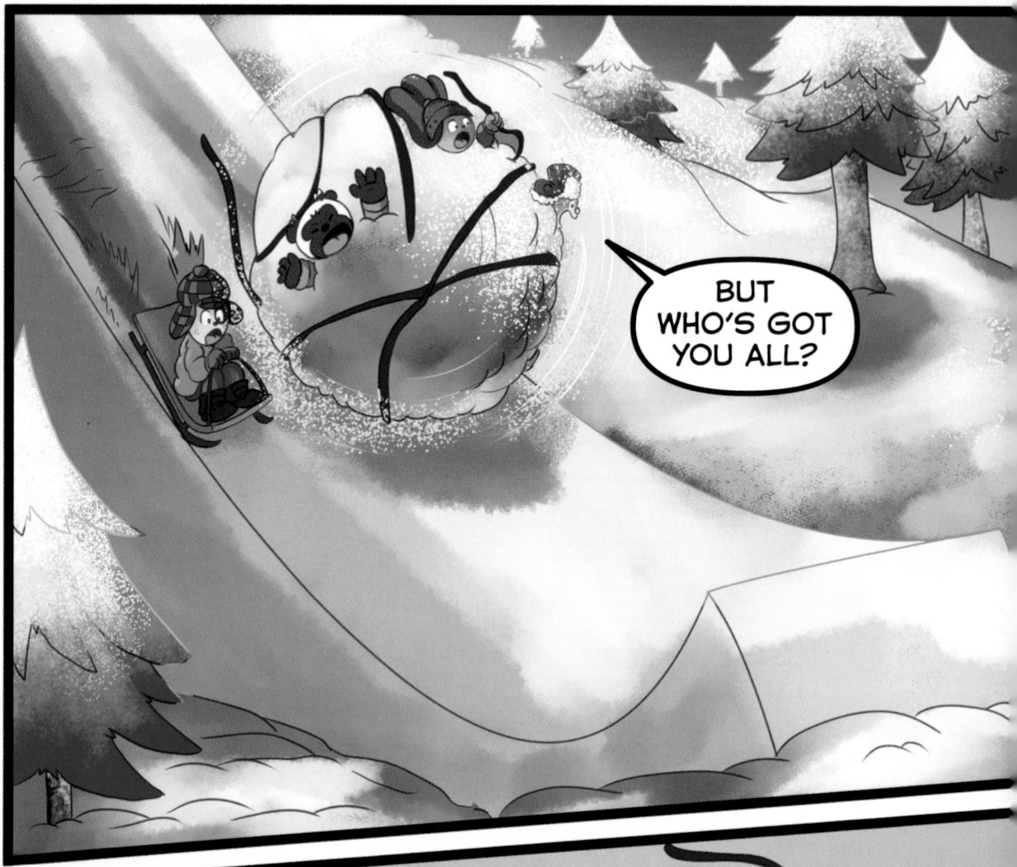
BUT WHO'S GOT YOU ALL?

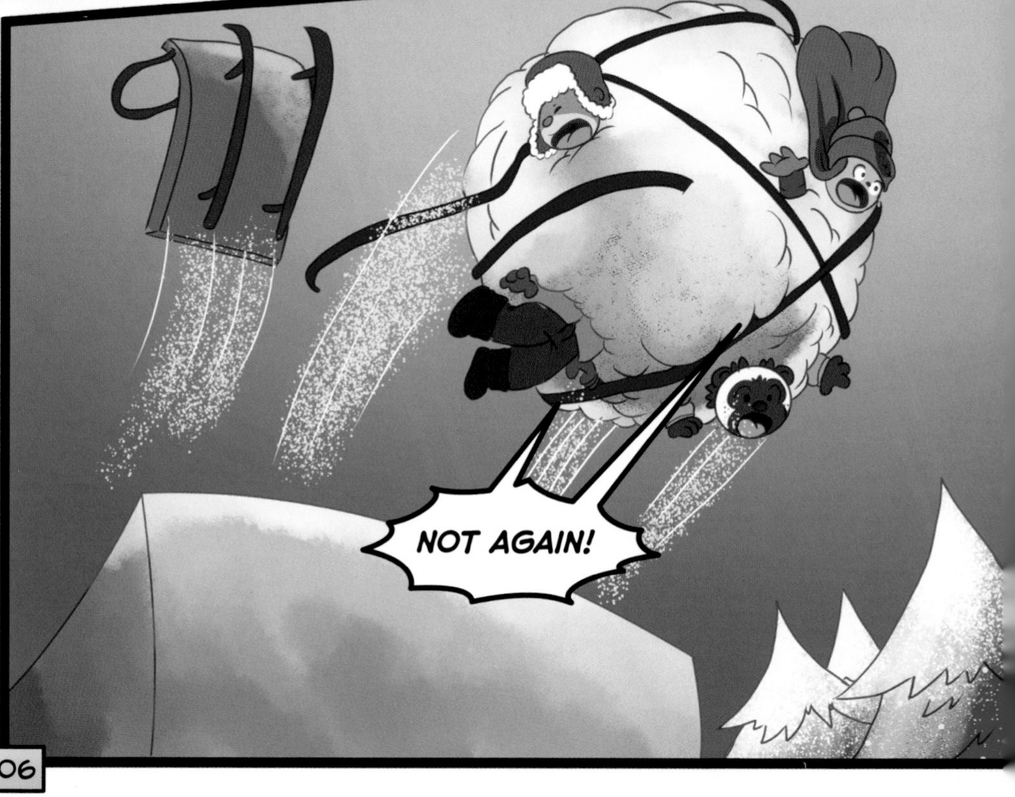
NOT AGAIN!

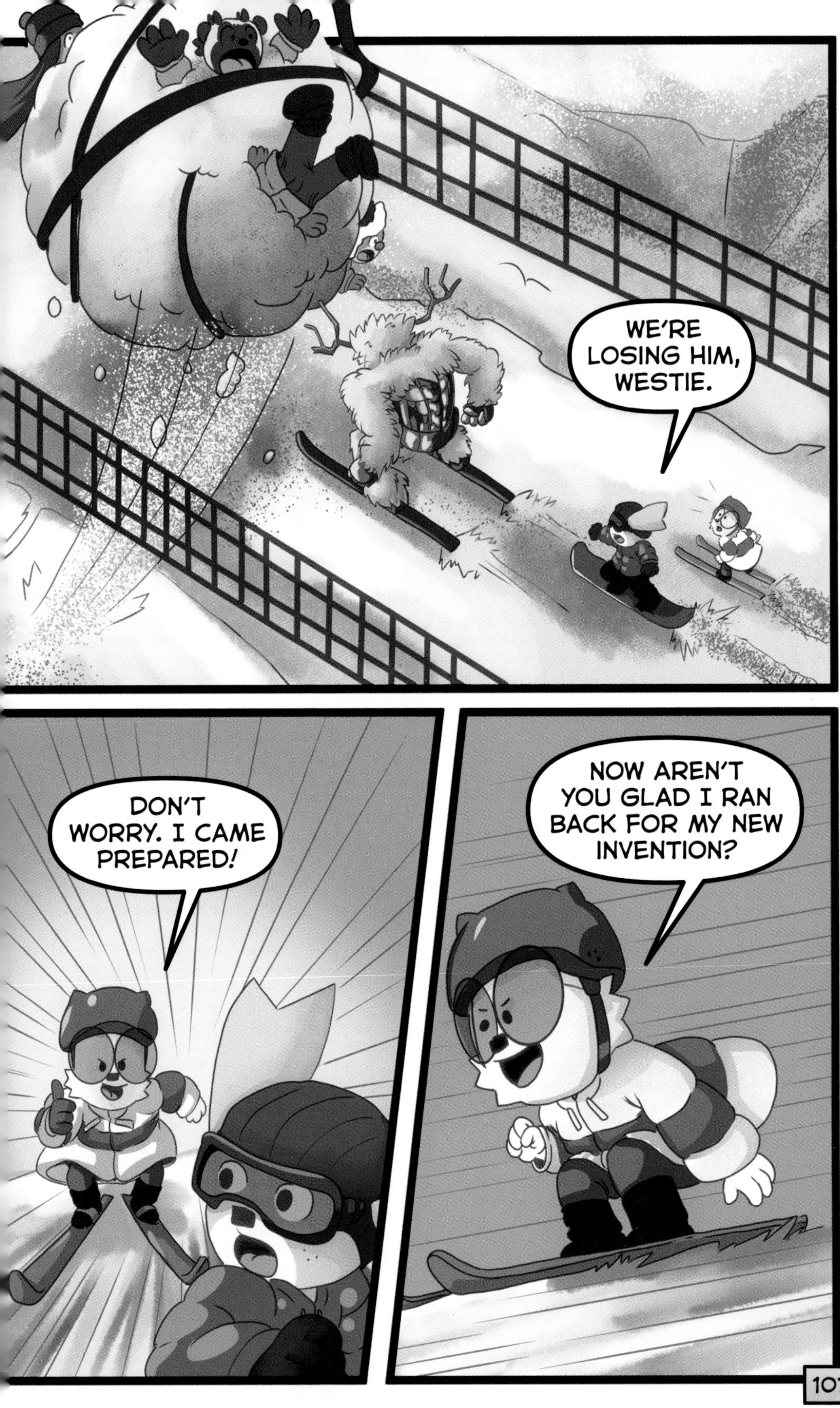
WE'RE LOSING HIM, WESTIE.
DON'T WORRY. I CAME PREPARED!
NOW AREN'T YOU GLAD I RAN BACK FOR MY NEW INVENTION?

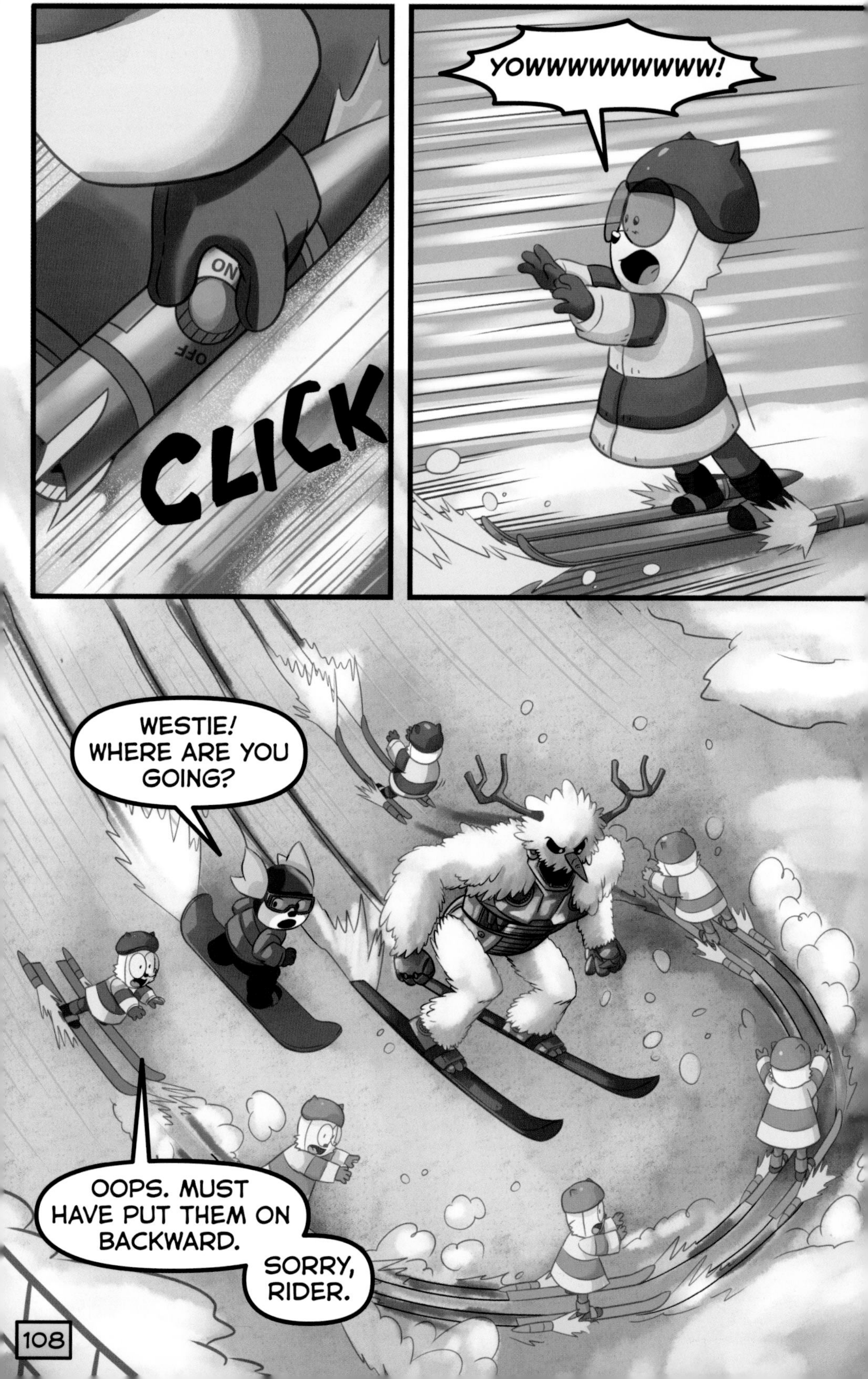
ON
OFF
CLICK
YOWWWWWWWWW!
WESTIE! WHERE ARE YOU GOING?
OOPS. MUST HAVE PUT THEM ON BACKWARD.
SORRY, RIDER.

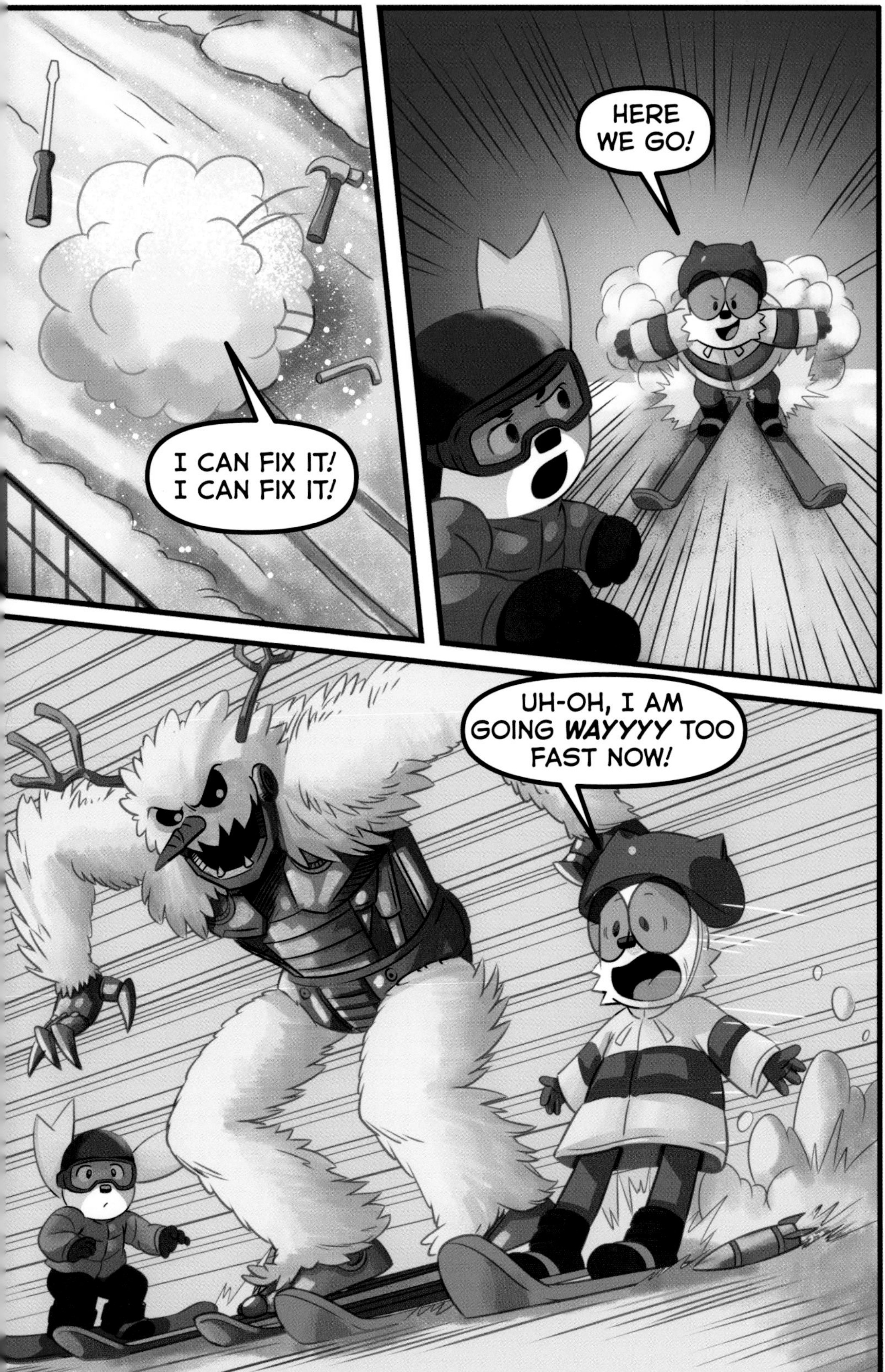
I CAN FIX IT! I CAN FIX IT!
HERE WE GO!
UH-OH, I AM GOING *WAYYYY* TOO FAST NOW!

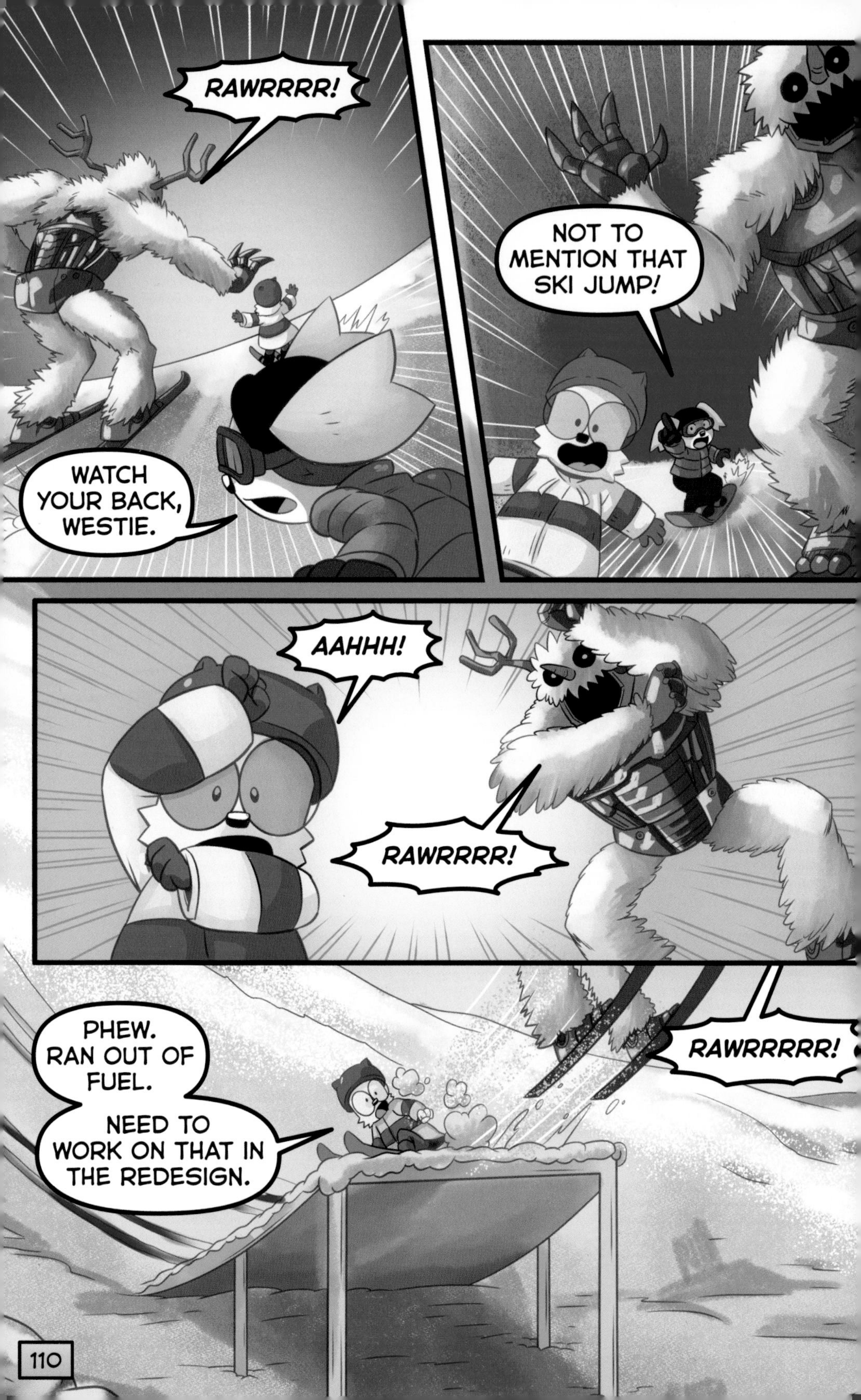
RAWRRRR!
WATCH YOUR BACK, WESTIE.
NOT TO MENTION THAT SKI JUMP!
AAHHH!
RAWRRRR!
PHEW. RAN OUT OF FUEL.
NEED TO WORK ON THAT IN THE REDESIGN.
RAWRRRRR!

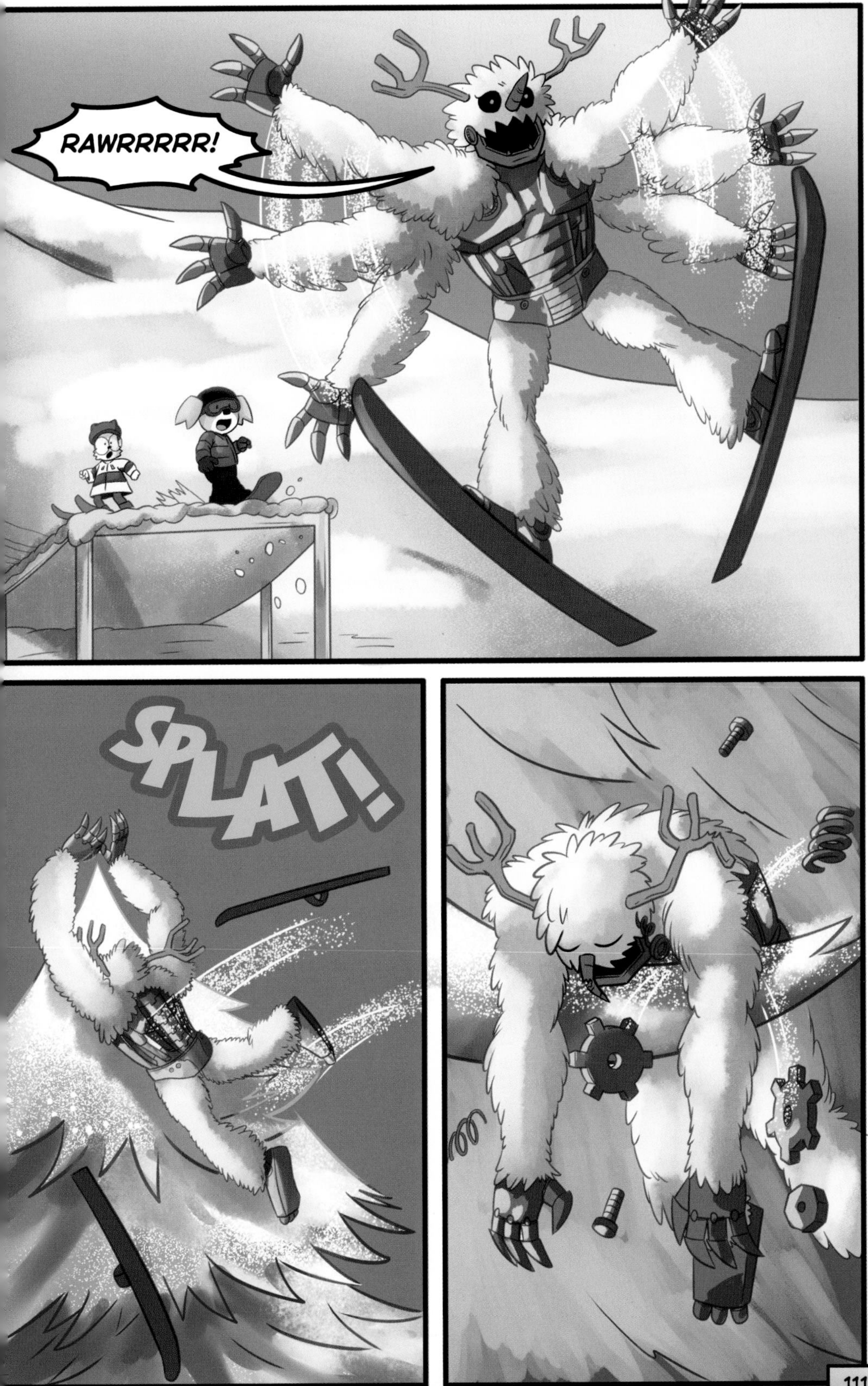
RAWRRRRR!
SPLAT!

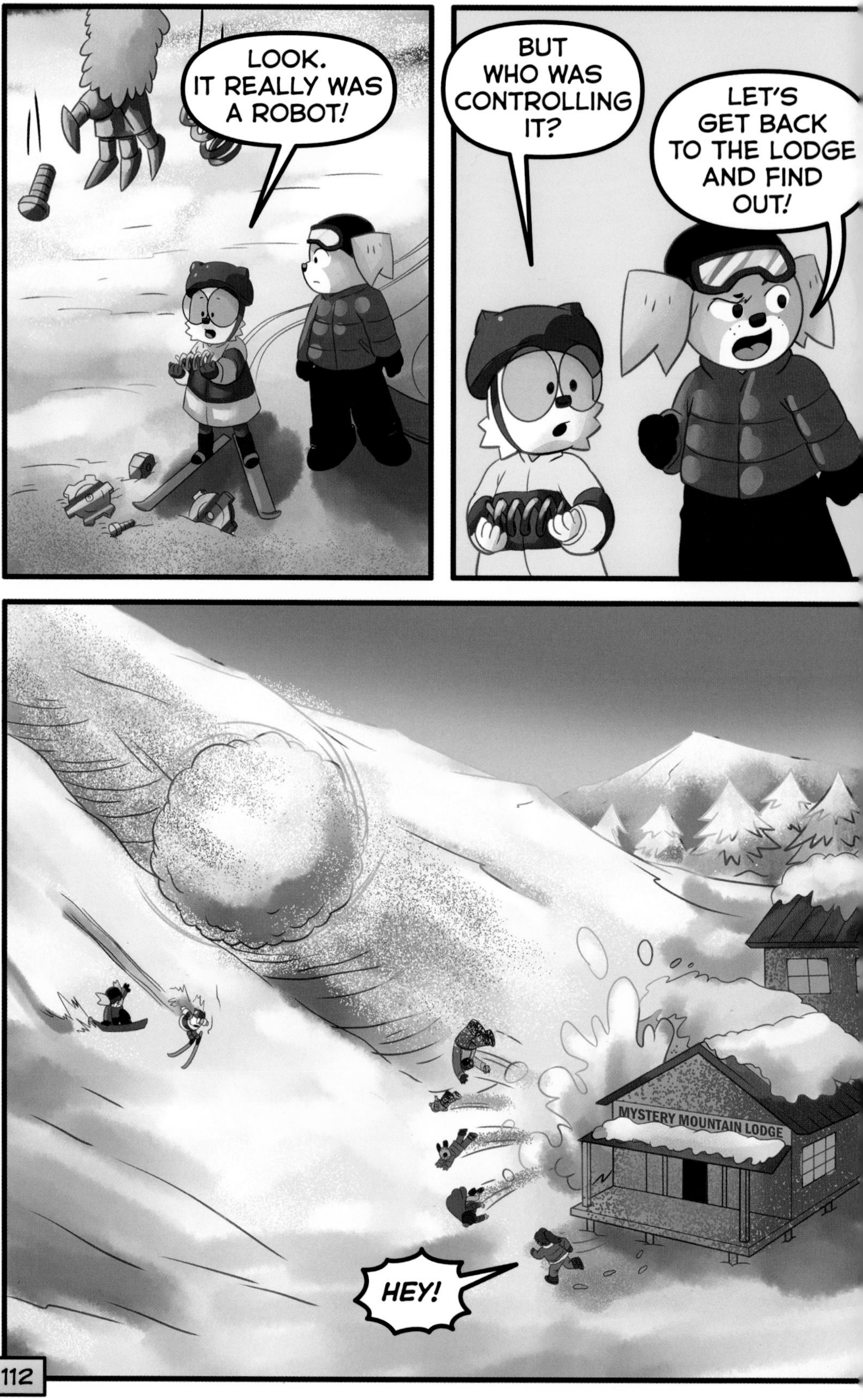
LOOK. IT REALLY WAS A ROBOT!
BUT WHO WAS CONTROLLING IT?
LET'S GET BACK TO THE LODGE AND FIND OUT!
MYSTERY MOUNTAIN LODGE
HEY!

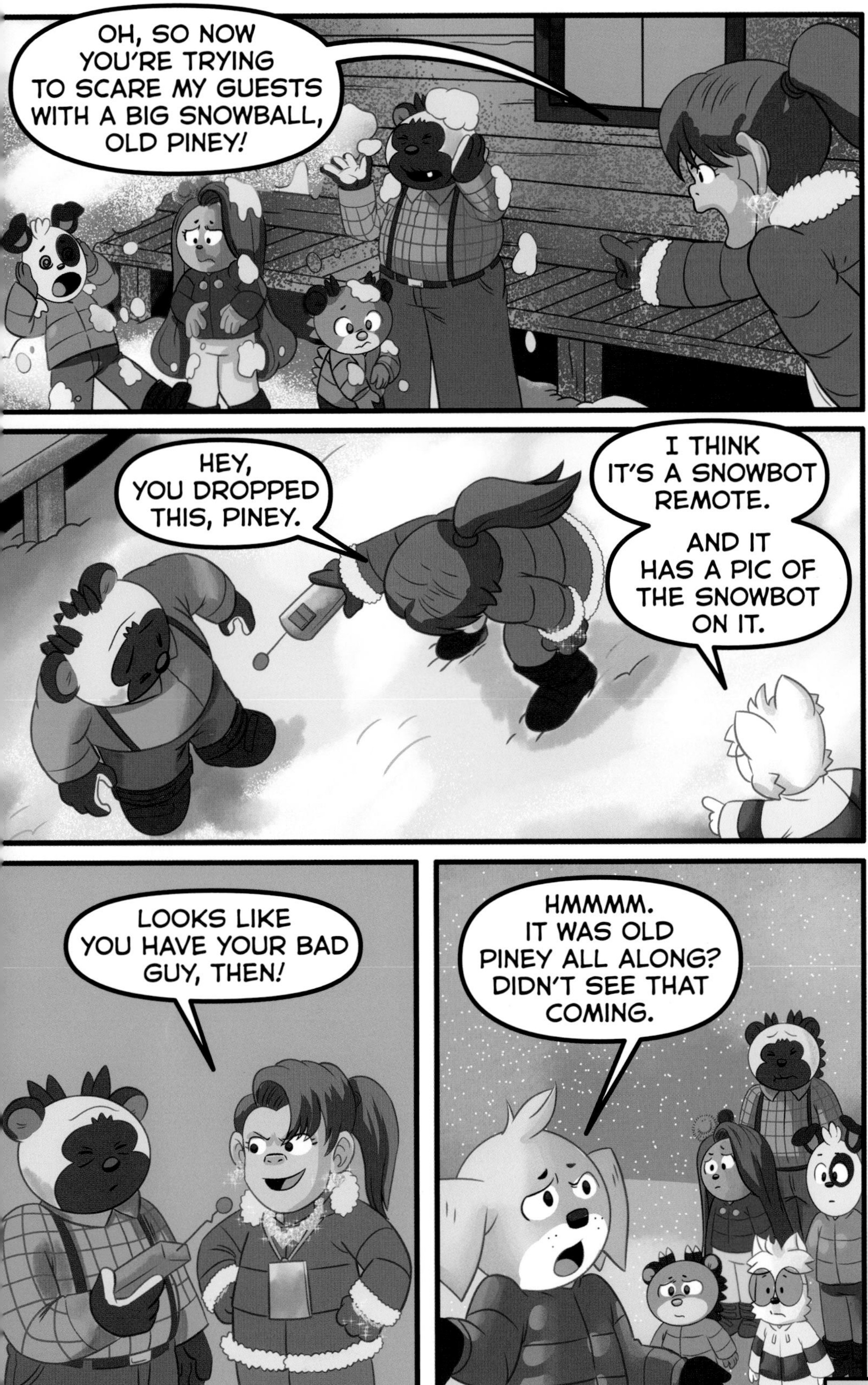
OH, SO NOW YOU'RE TRYING TO SCARE MY GUESTS WITH A BIG SNOWBALL, OLD PINEY!
HEY, YOU DROPPED THIS, PINEY.
I THINK IT'S A SNOWBOT REMOTE.
AND IT HAS A PIC OF THE SNOWBOT ON IT.
LOOKS LIKE YOU HAVE YOUR BAD GUY, THEN!
HMMMM. IT WAS OLD PINEY ALL ALONG? DIDN'T SEE THAT COMING.

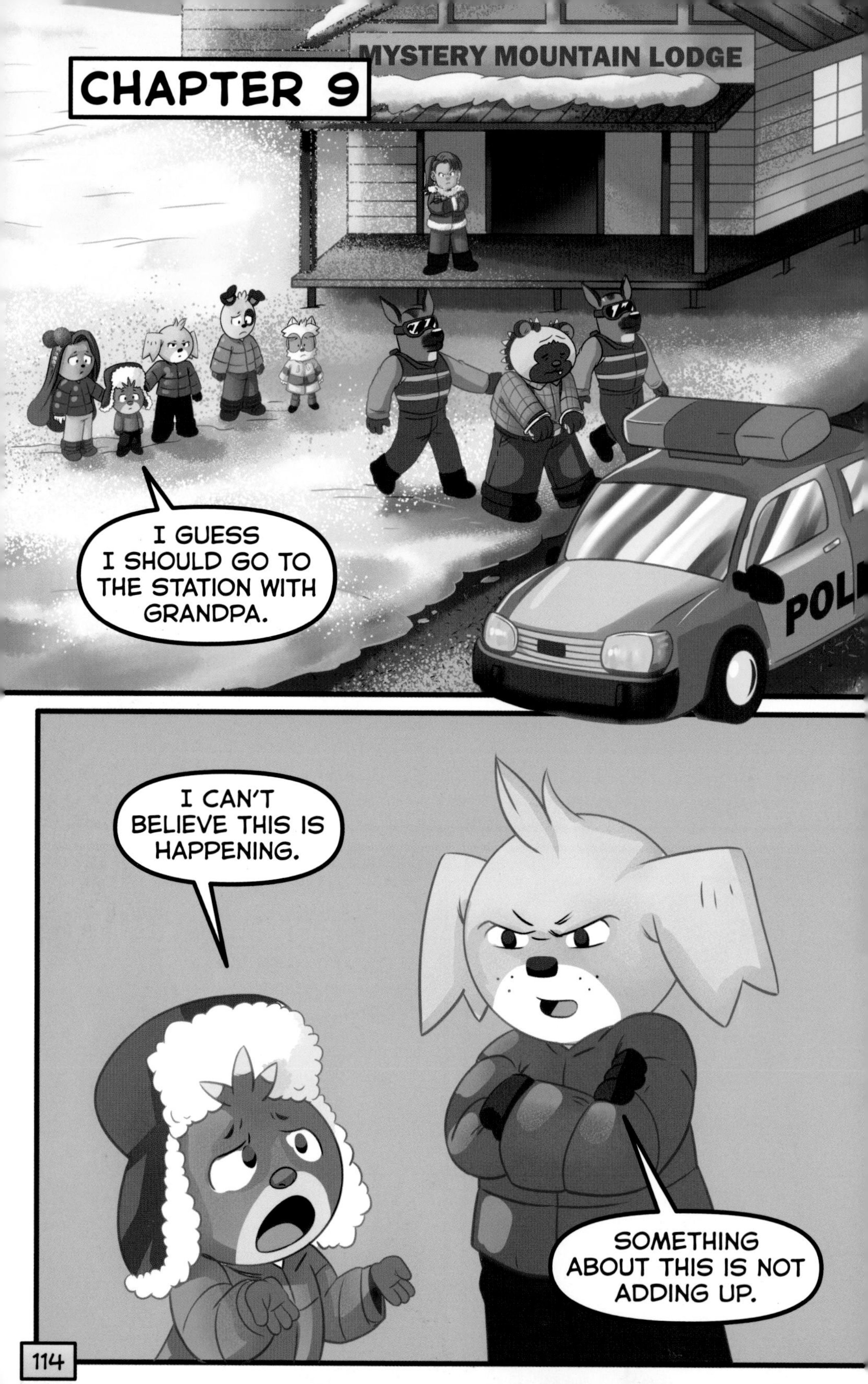
CHAPTER 9
MYSTERY MOUNTAIN LODGE
I GUESS I SHOULD GO TO THE STATION WITH GRANDPA.
POL
I CAN'T BELIEVE THIS IS HAPPENING.
SOMETHING ABOUT THIS IS NOT ADDING UP.

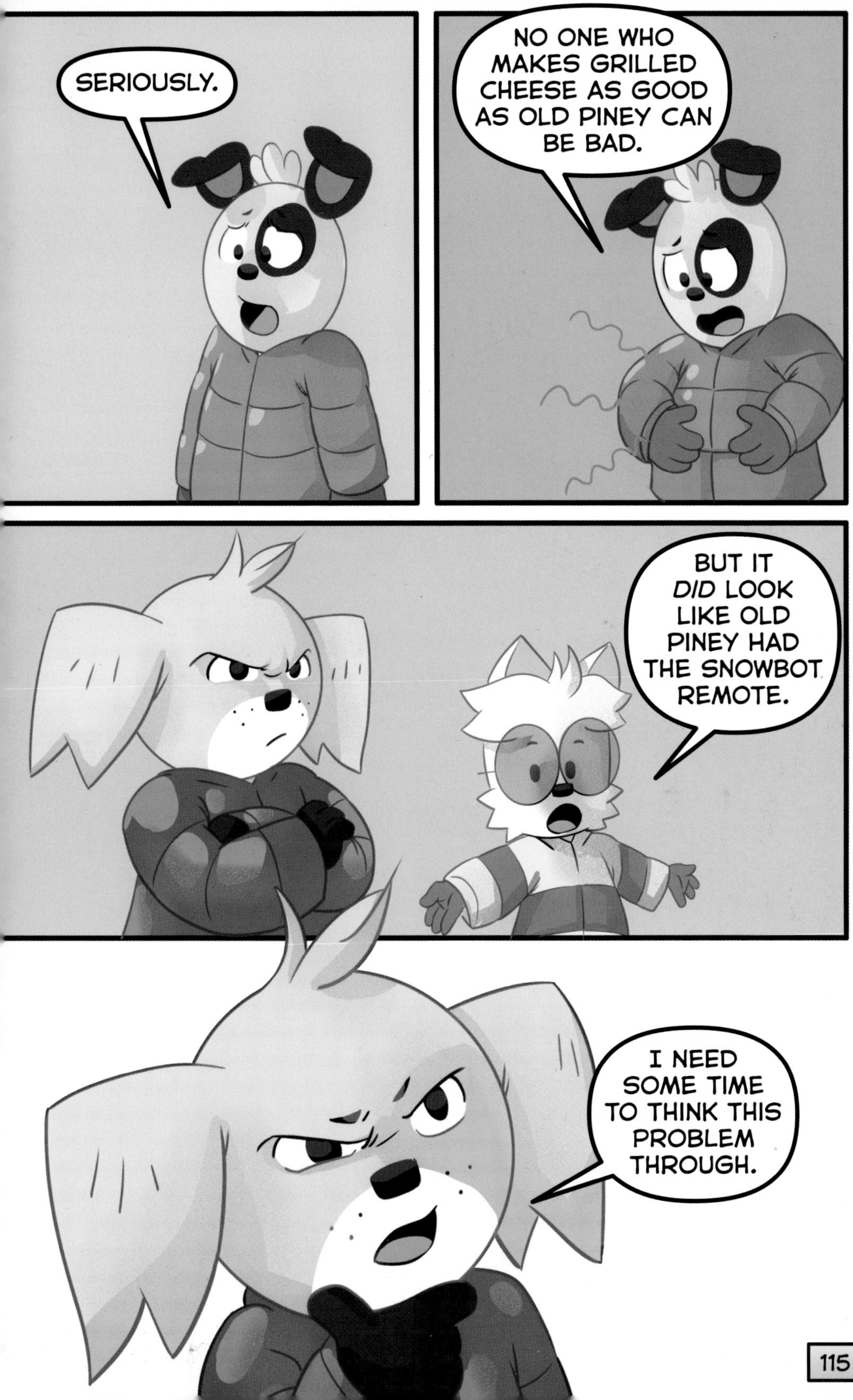
SERIOUSLY.
NO ONE WHO MAKES GRILLED CHEESE AS GOOD AS OLD PINEY CAN BE BAD.
BUT IT *DID* LOOK LIKE OLD PINEY HAD THE SNOWBOT REMOTE.
I NEED SOME TIME TO THINK THIS PROBLEM THROUGH.

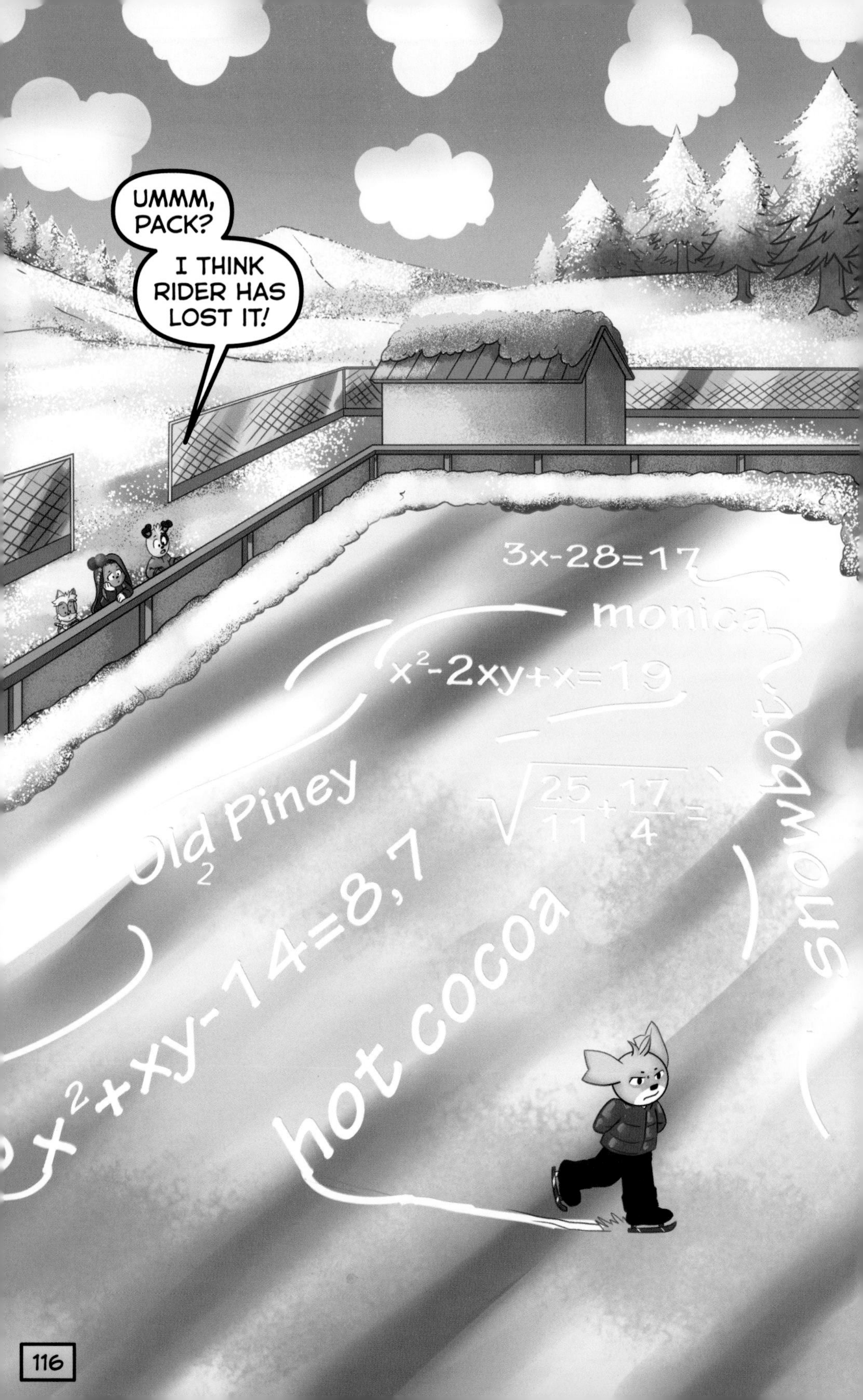
UMMM, PACK?
I THINK RIDER HAS LOST IT!
3x-28=17
monica
x²-2xy+x=19
Old Piney
√(25/11 + 17/4) =
snowbot
x²+xy-14=8,7
hot cocoa

BUT HE'S...

REALLY GOOD AT SKATING? WHO KNEW?

NO, ZIGGY, RIDER IS JUST DOING SOME ICE-RINK THINKING.

IF ANYONE CAN FIGURE THIS OUT, IT'S RIDER.

I HOPE.

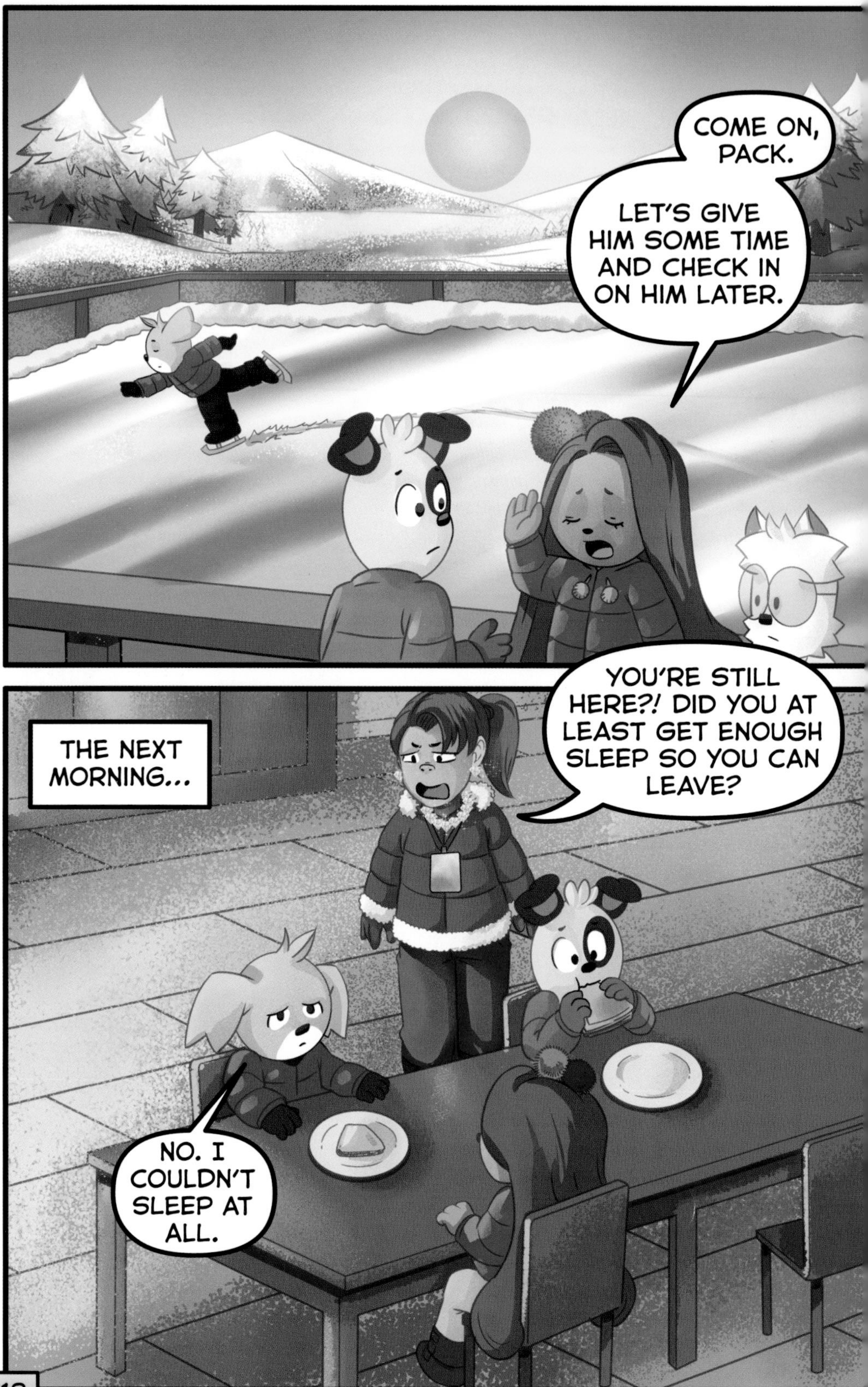
COME ON, PACK.
LET'S GIVE HIM SOME TIME AND CHECK IN ON HIM LATER.
THE NEXT MORNING...
YOU'RE STILL HERE?! DID YOU AT LEAST GET ENOUGH SLEEP SO YOU CAN LEAVE?
NO. I COULDN'T SLEEP AT ALL.

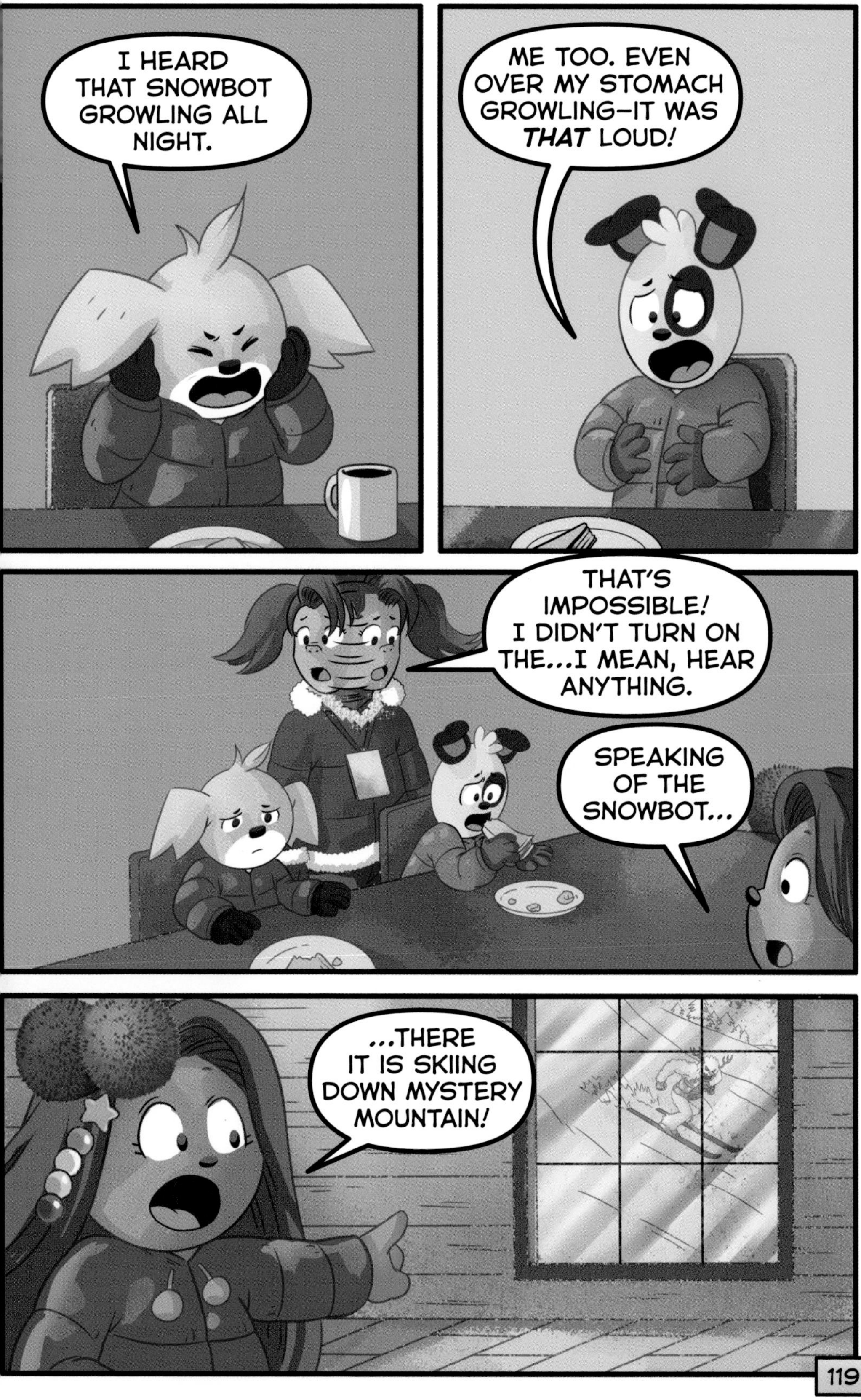
I HEARD THAT SNOWBOT GROWLING ALL NIGHT.
ME TOO. EVEN OVER MY STOMACH GROWLING—IT WAS *THAT* LOUD!
THAT'S IMPOSSIBLE! I DIDN'T TURN ON THE...I MEAN, HEAR ANYTHING.
SPEAKING OF THE SNOWBOT...
...THERE IT IS SKIING DOWN MYSTERY MOUNTAIN!

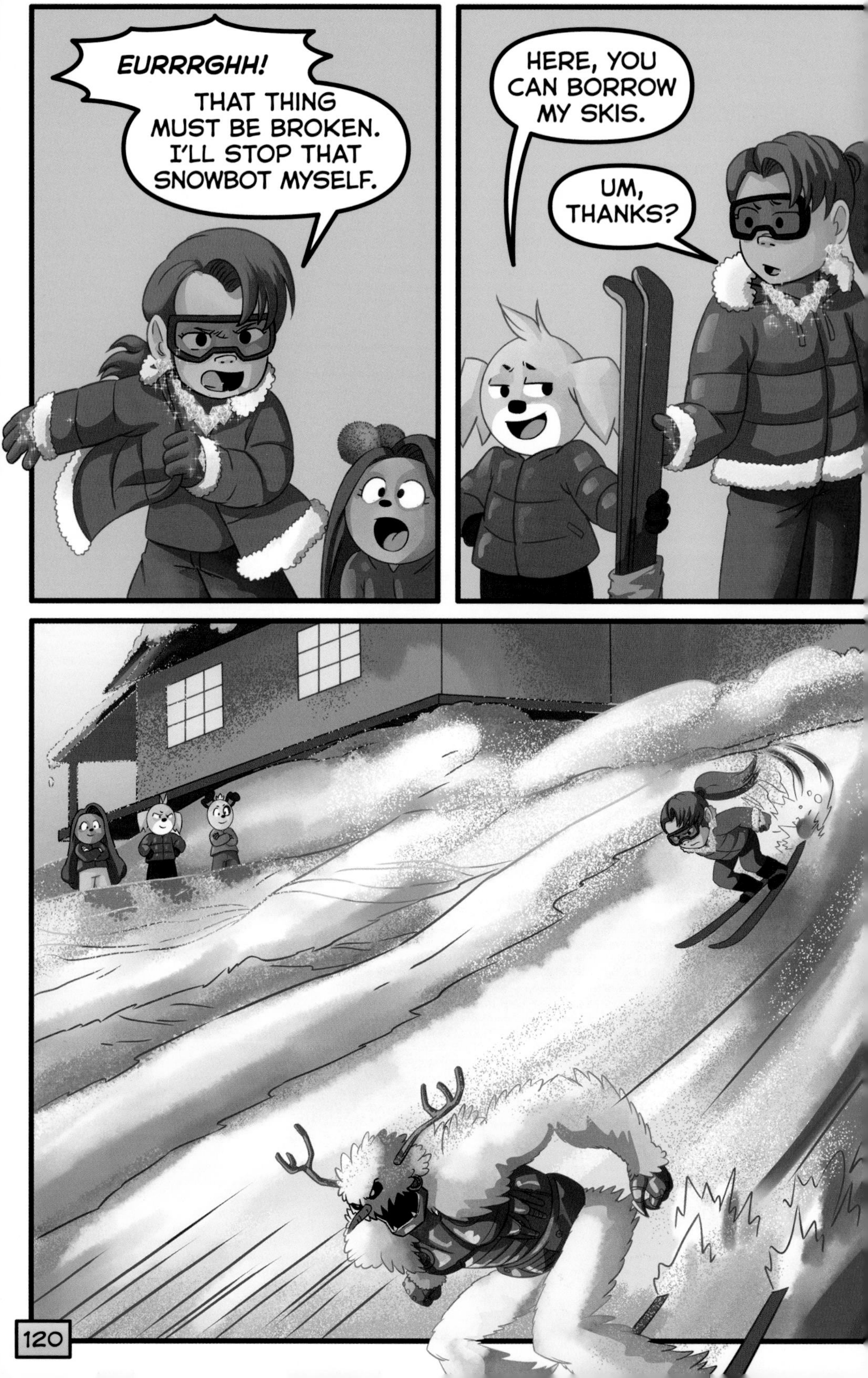
EURRRGHH!
THAT THING MUST BE BROKEN. I'LL STOP THAT SNOWBOT MYSELF.
HERE, YOU CAN BORROW MY SKIS.
UM, THANKS?

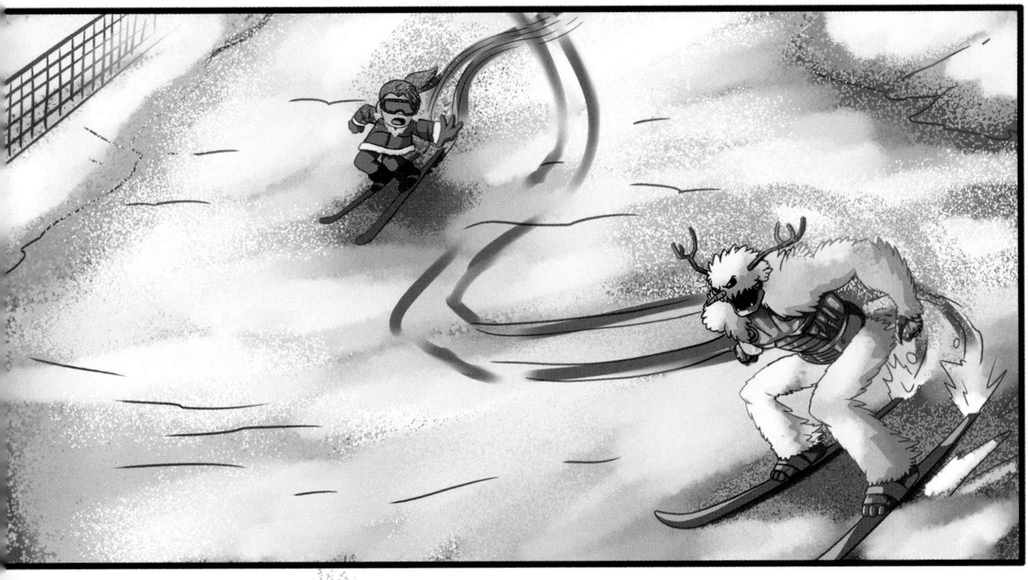

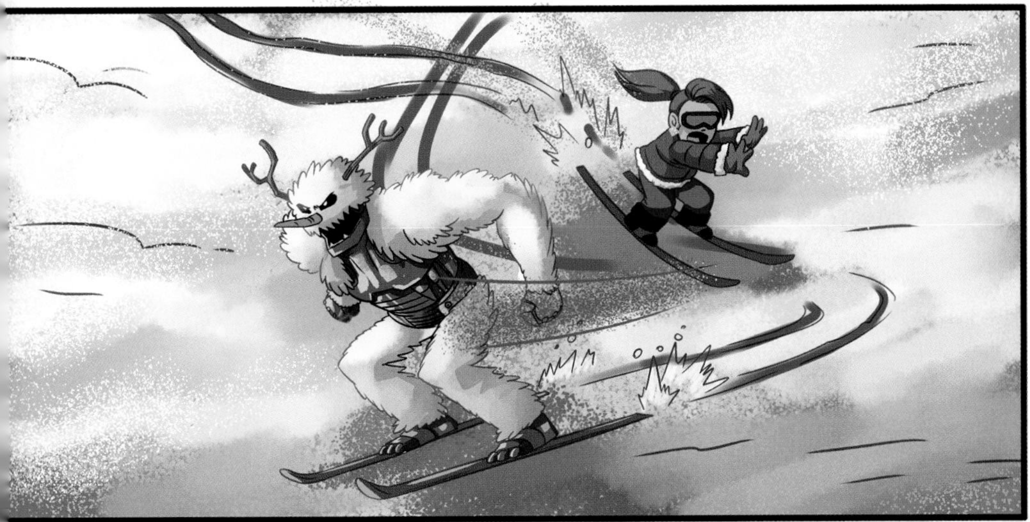

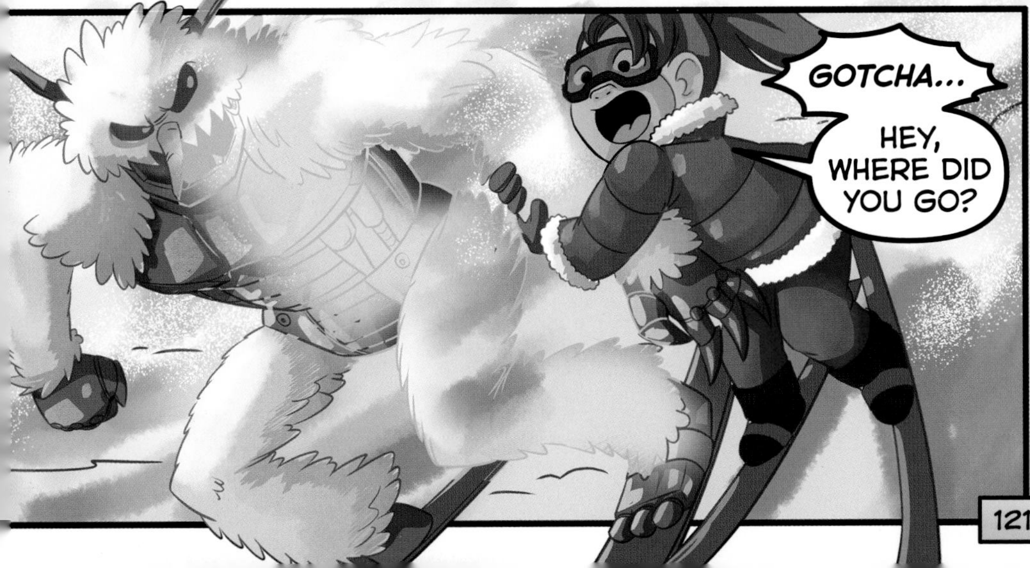
GOTCHA...
HEY, WHERE DID YOU GO?

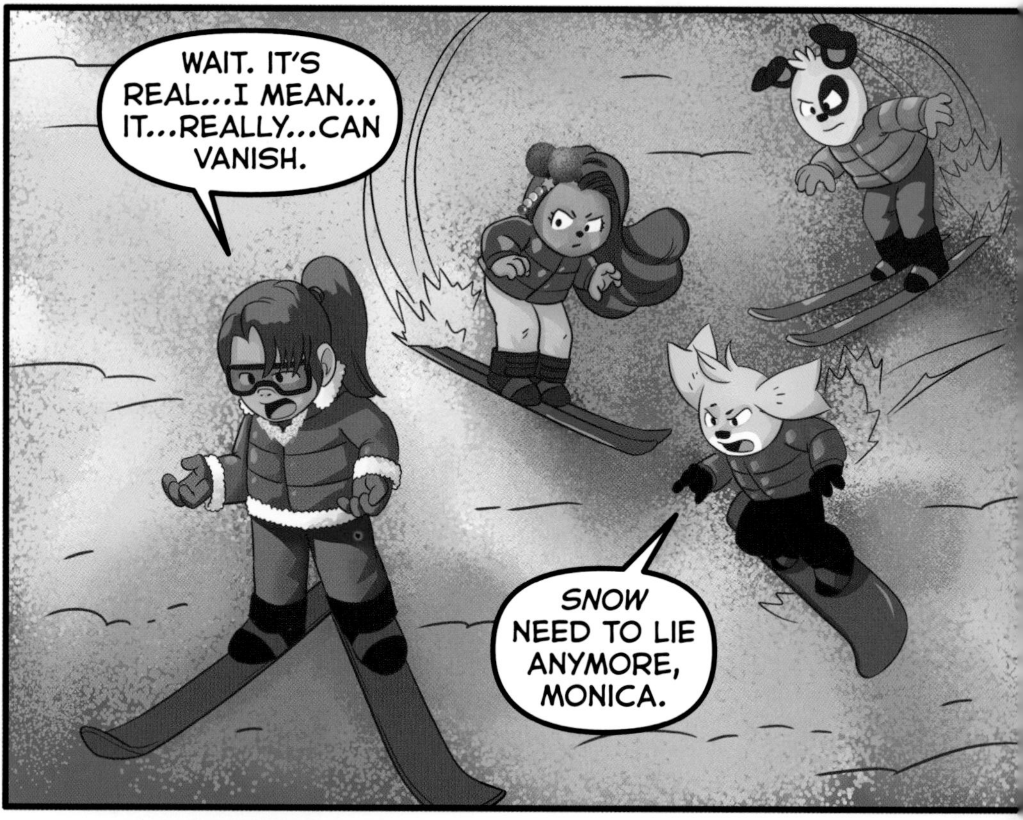
WAIT. IT'S REAL...I MEAN... IT...REALLY...CAN VANISH.
SNOW NEED TO LIE ANYMORE, MONICA.

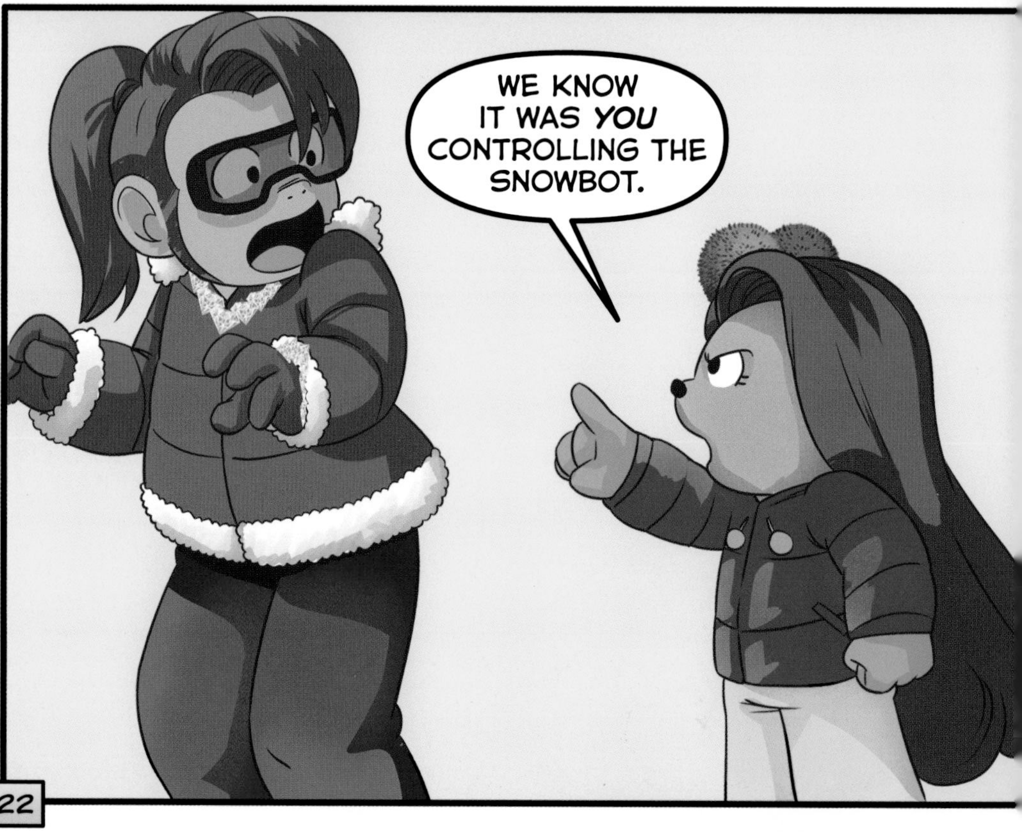
WE KNOW IT WAS *YOU* CONTROLLING THE SNOWBOT.

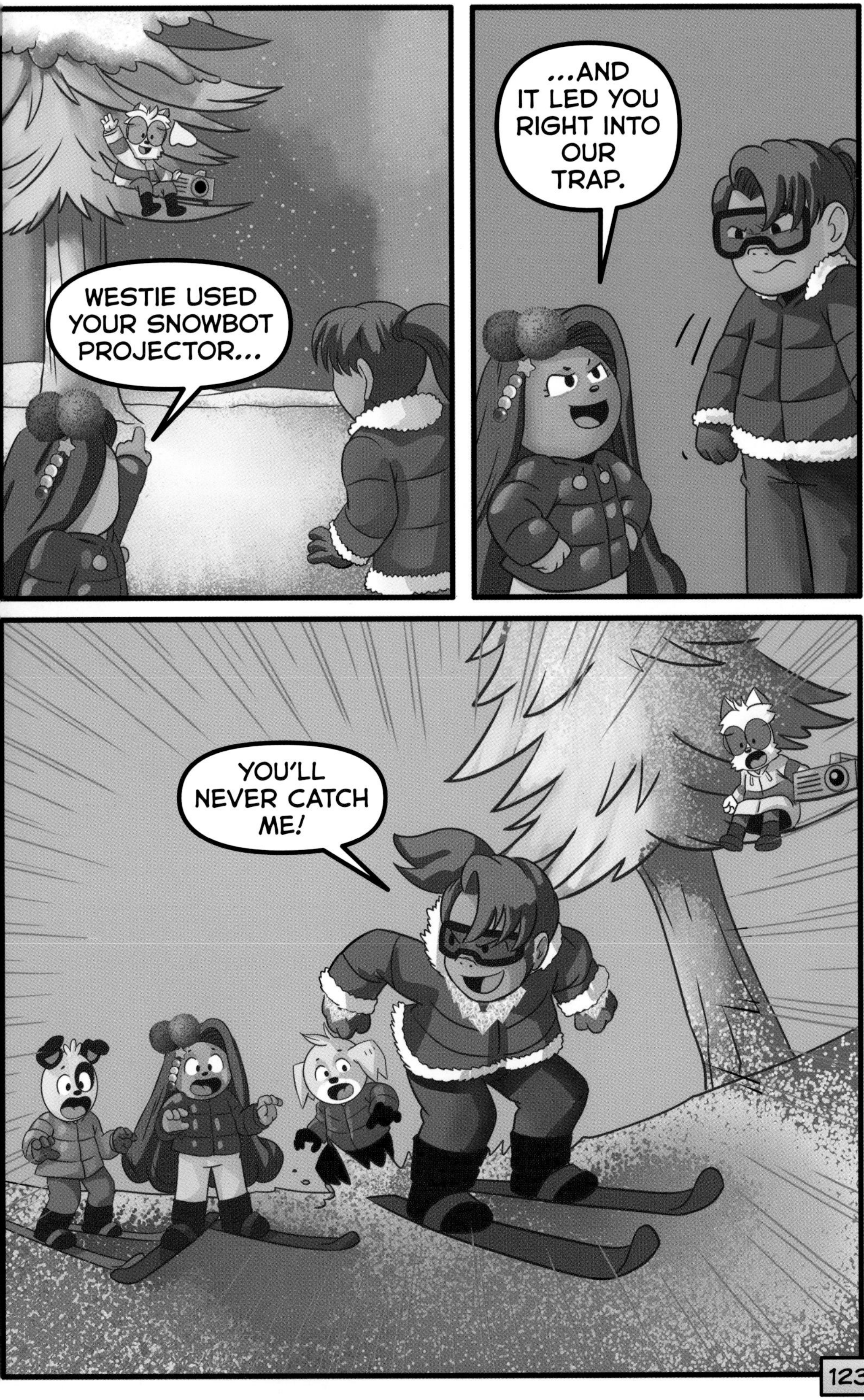
WESTIE USED YOUR SNOWBOT PROJECTOR...
...AND IT LED YOU RIGHT INTO OUR TRAP.
YOU'LL NEVER CATCH ME!

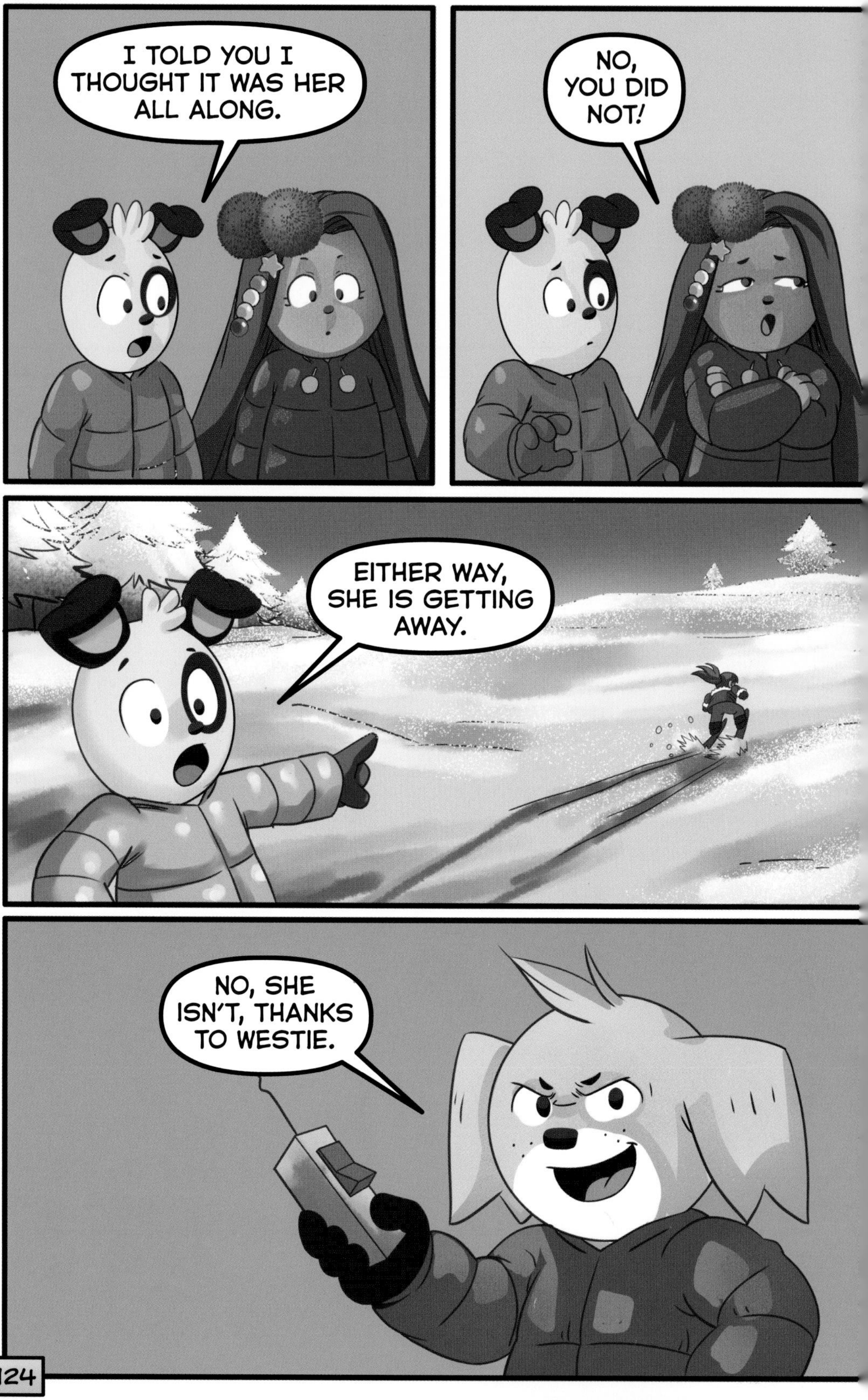
I TOLD YOU I THOUGHT IT WAS HER ALL ALONG.
NO, YOU DID NOT!
EITHER WAY, SHE IS GETTING AWAY.
NO, SHE ISN'T, THANKS TO WESTIE.

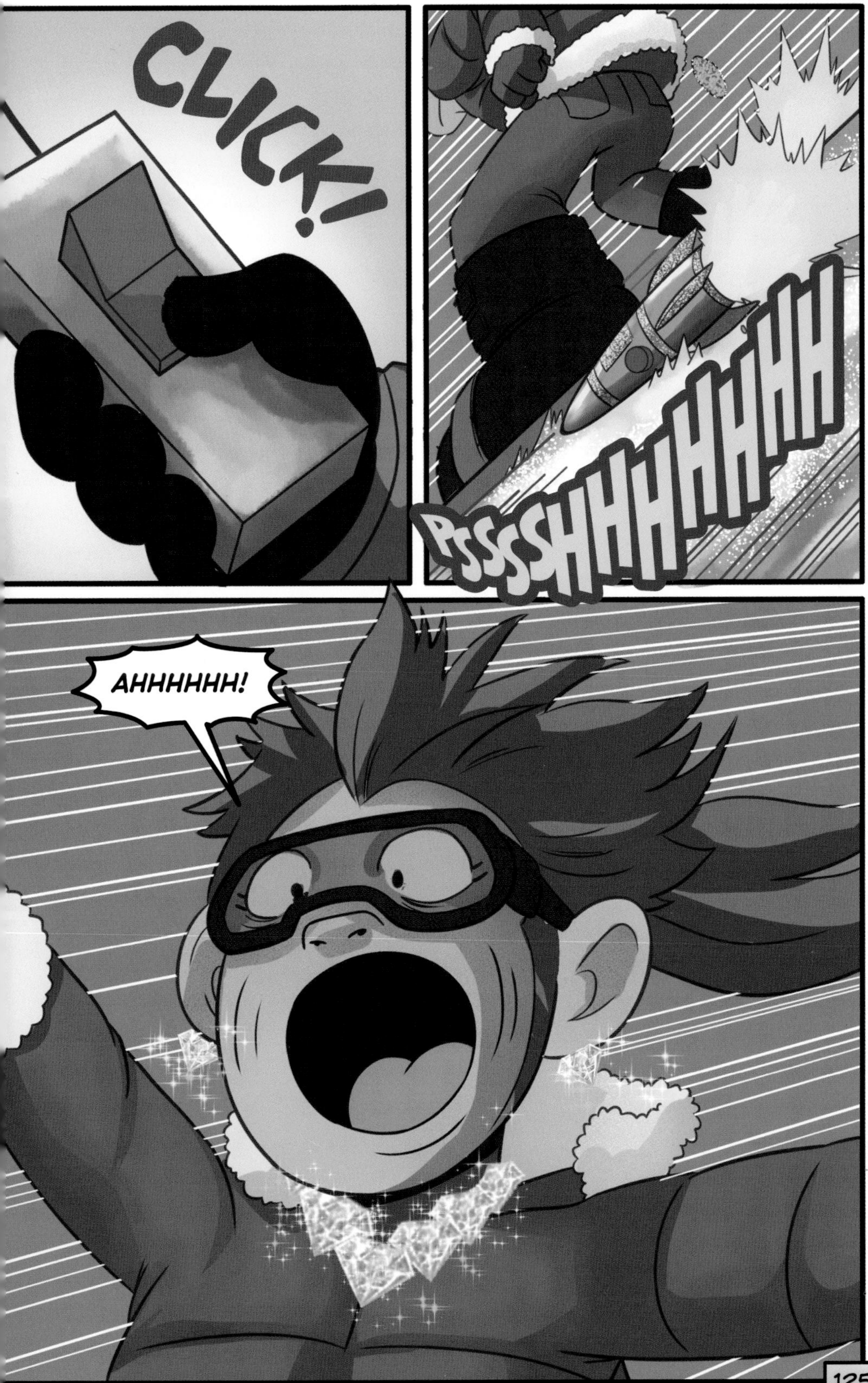
CLICK!
PSSSSHHHHHHHHHHHHH
AHHHHHH!

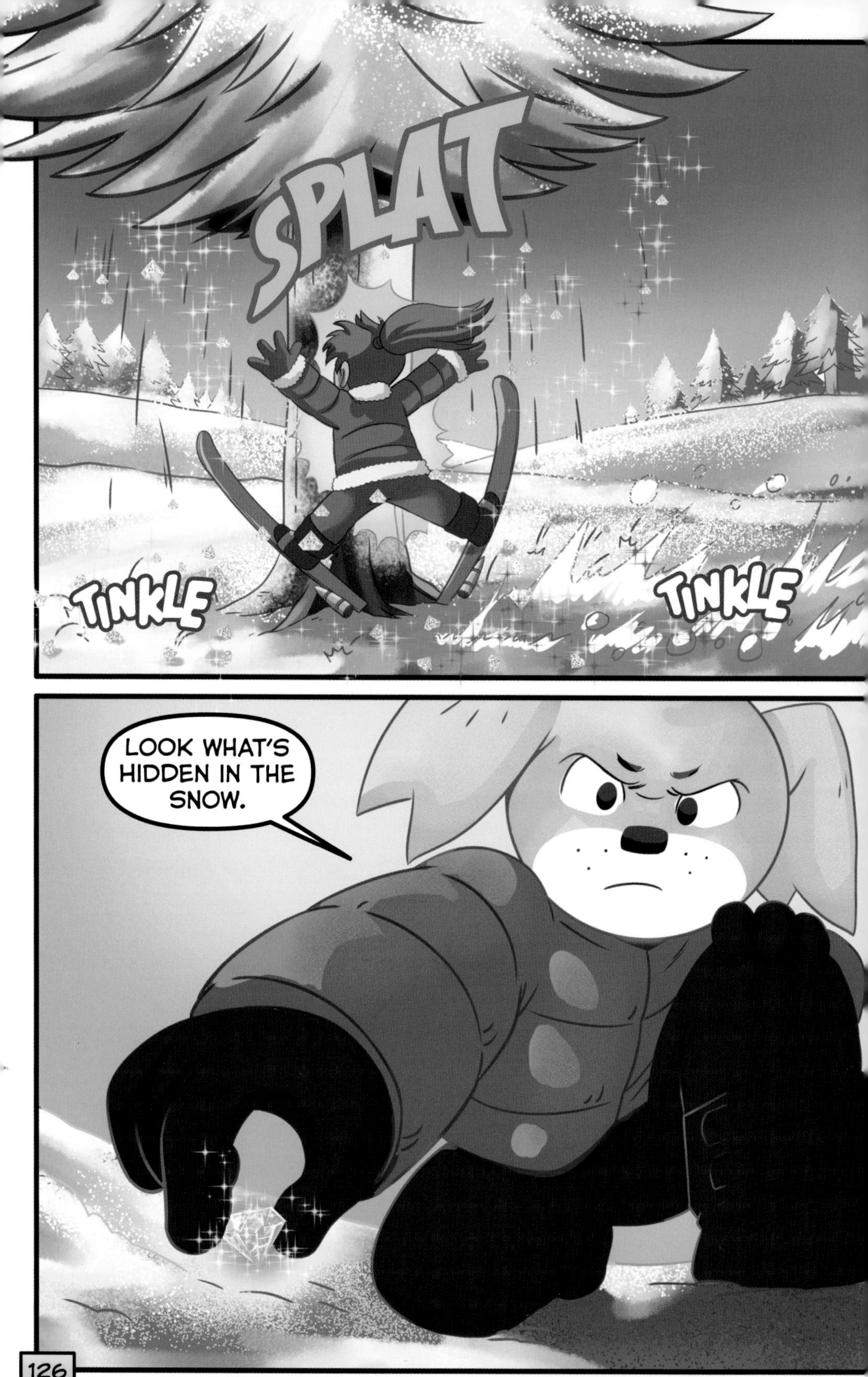
SPLAT
TINKLE
TINKLE
LOOK WHAT'S HIDDEN IN THE SNOW.

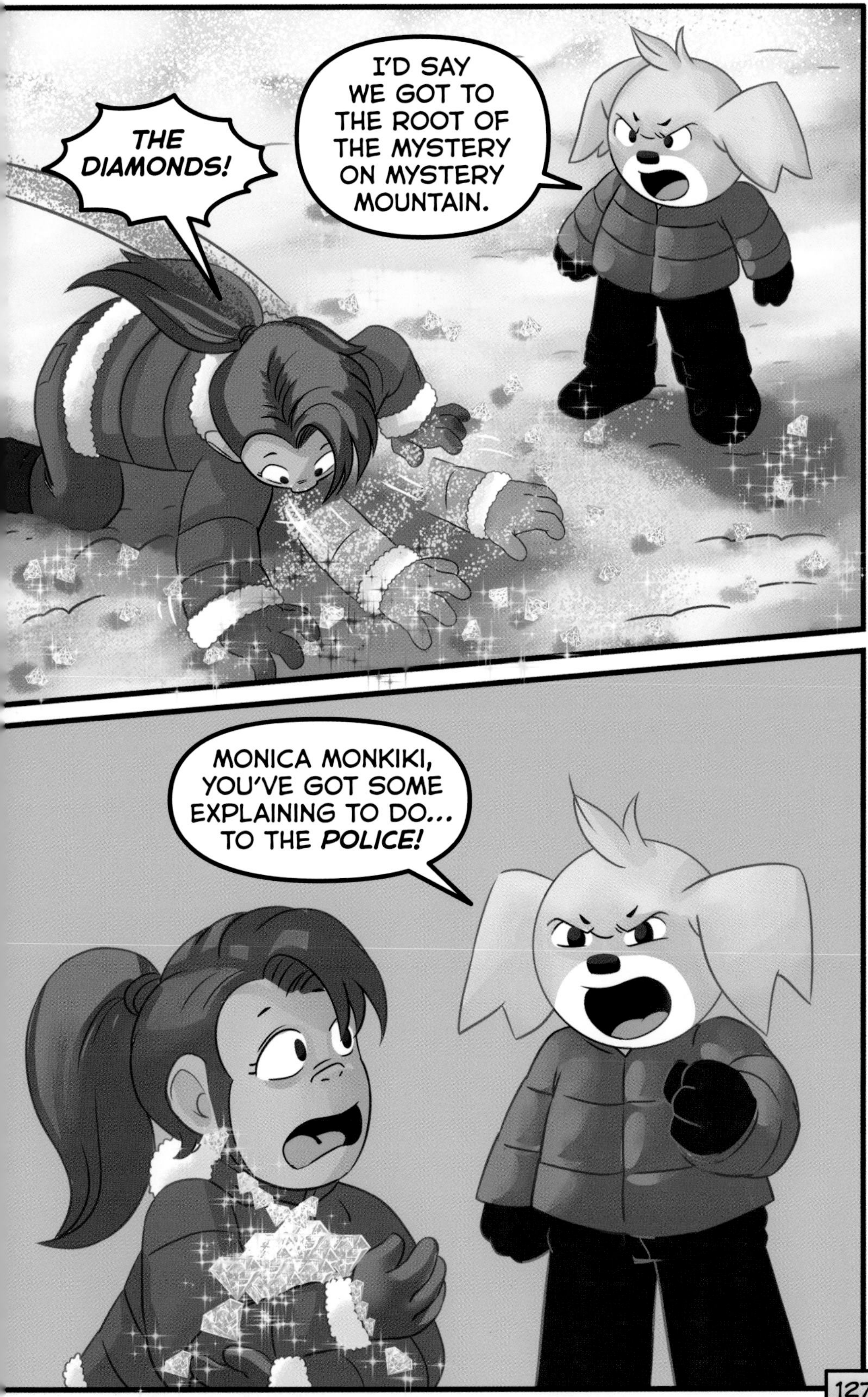
THE DIAMONDS!
I'D SAY WE GOT TO THE ROOT OF THE MYSTERY ON MYSTERY MOUNTAIN.
MONICA MONKIKI, YOU'VE GOT SOME EXPLAINING TO DO... TO THE POLICE!

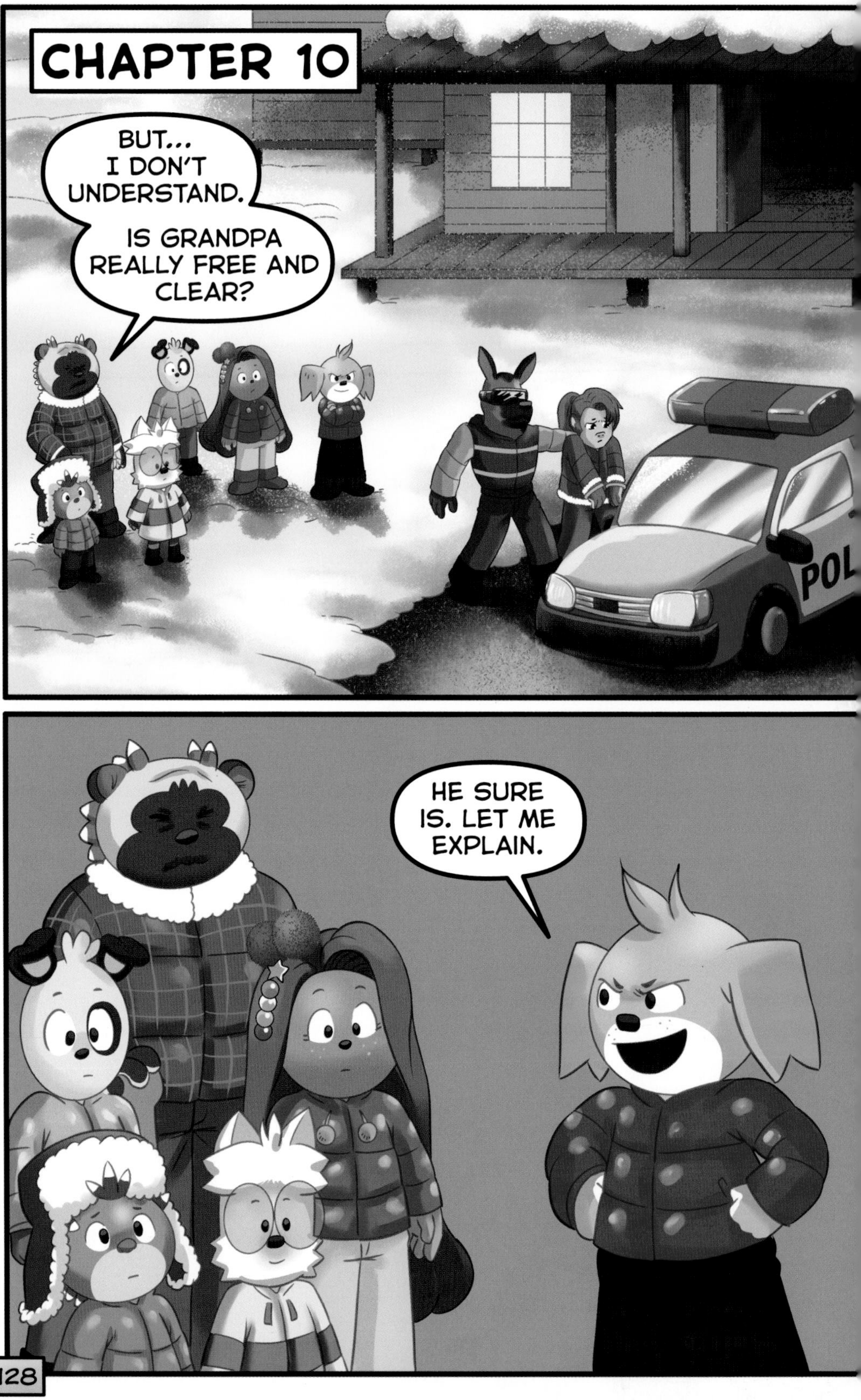
CHAPTER 10
BUT... I DON'T UNDERSTAND.
IS GRANDPA REALLY FREE AND CLEAR?
HE SURE IS. LET ME EXPLAIN.

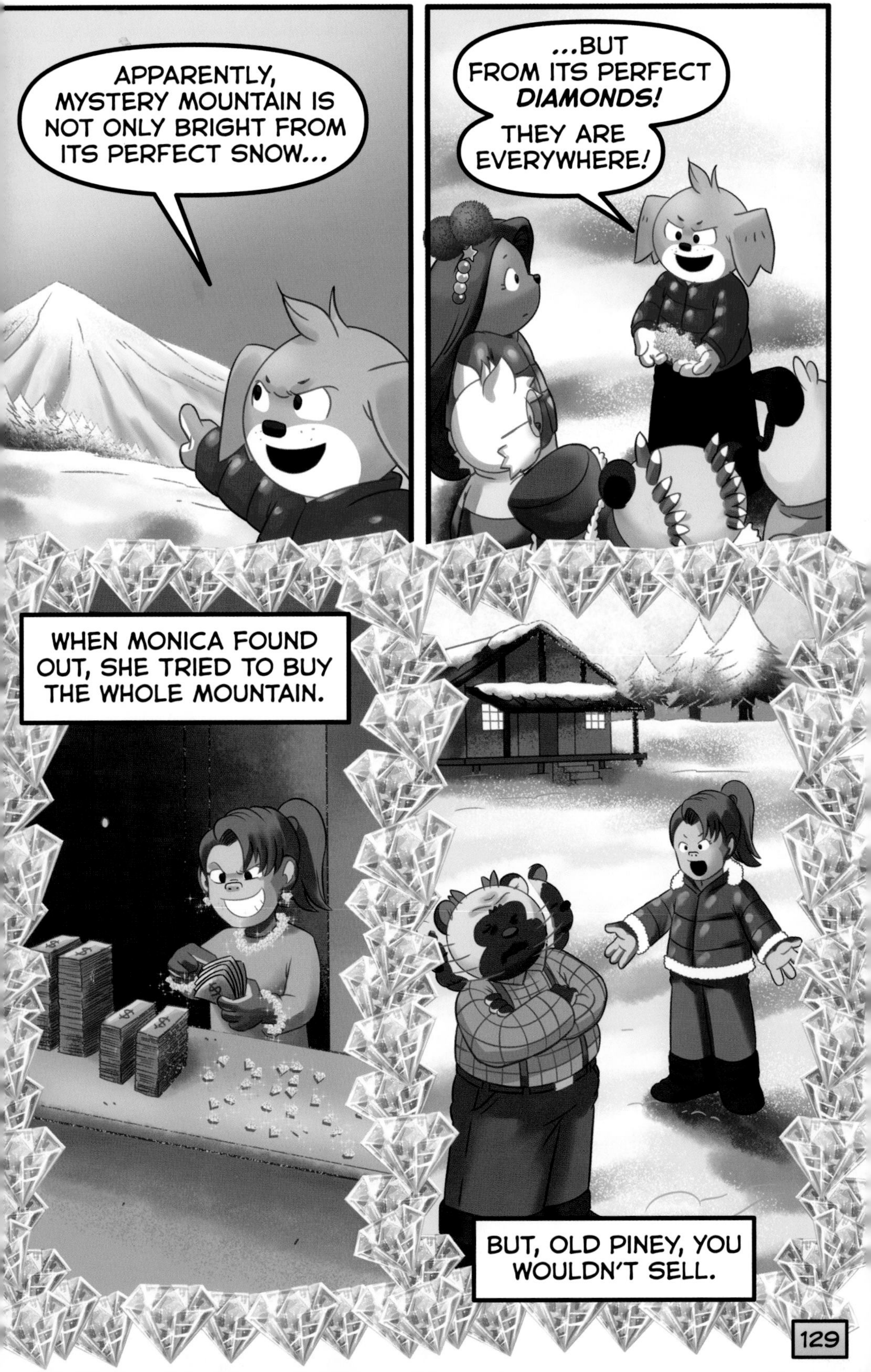
APPARENTLY, MYSTERY MOUNTAIN IS NOT ONLY BRIGHT FROM ITS PERFECT SNOW...
...BUT FROM ITS PERFECT *DIAMONDS!*
THEY ARE EVERYWHERE!
WHEN MONICA FOUND OUT, SHE TRIED TO BUY THE WHOLE MOUNTAIN.
BUT, OLD PINEY, YOU WOULDN'T SELL.

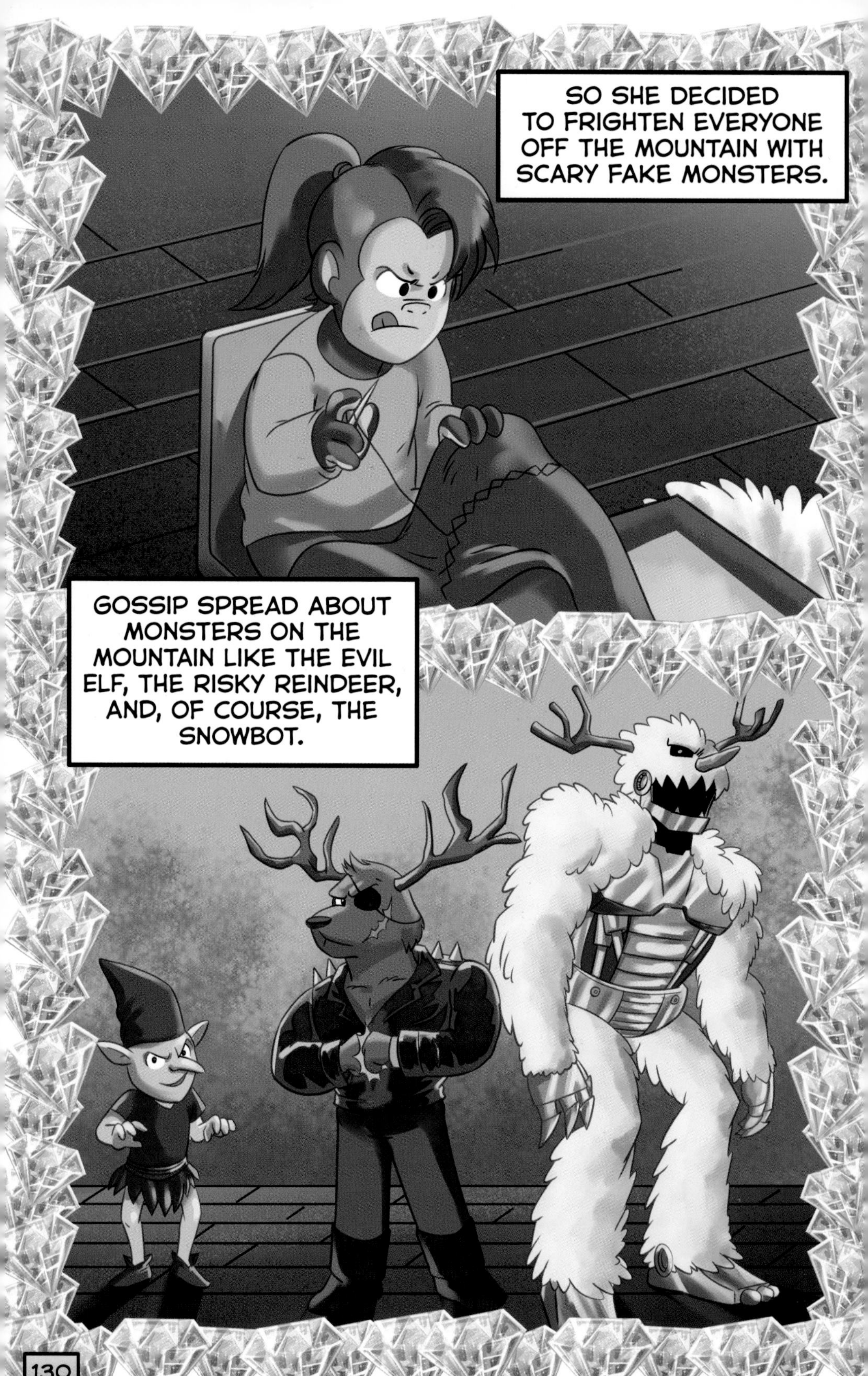
SO SHE DECIDED TO FRIGHTEN EVERYONE OFF THE MOUNTAIN WITH SCARY FAKE MONSTERS.
GOSSIP SPREAD ABOUT MONSTERS ON THE MOUNTAIN LIKE THE EVIL ELF, THE RISKY REINDEER, AND, OF COURSE, THE SNOWBOT.

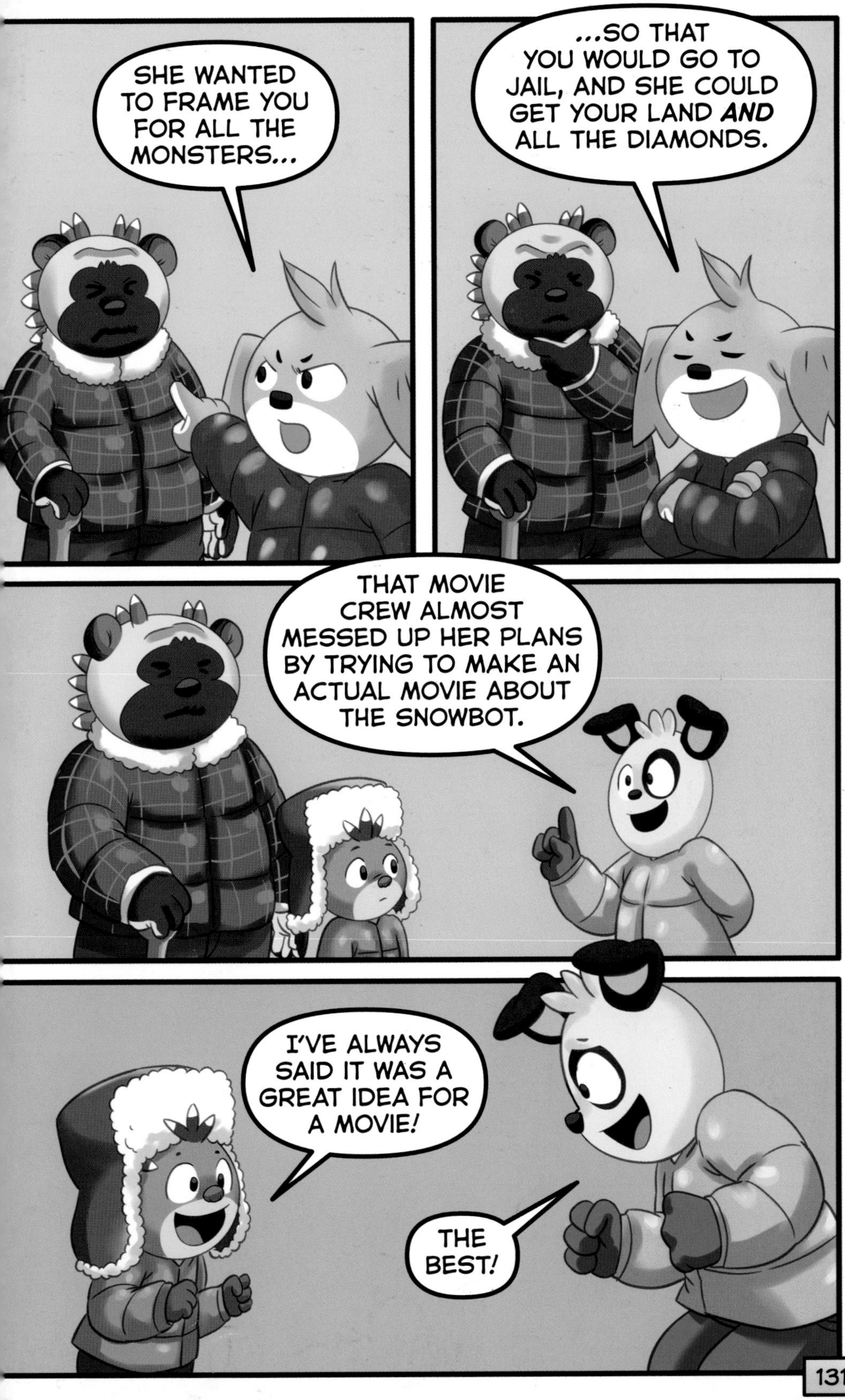
SHE WANTED TO FRAME YOU FOR ALL THE MONSTERS...
...SO THAT YOU WOULD GO TO JAIL, AND SHE COULD GET YOUR LAND **AND** ALL THE DIAMONDS.
THAT MOVIE CREW ALMOST MESSED UP HER PLANS BY TRYING TO MAKE AN ACTUAL MOVIE ABOUT THE SNOWBOT.
I'VE ALWAYS SAID IT WAS A GREAT IDEA FOR A MOVIE!
THE BEST!

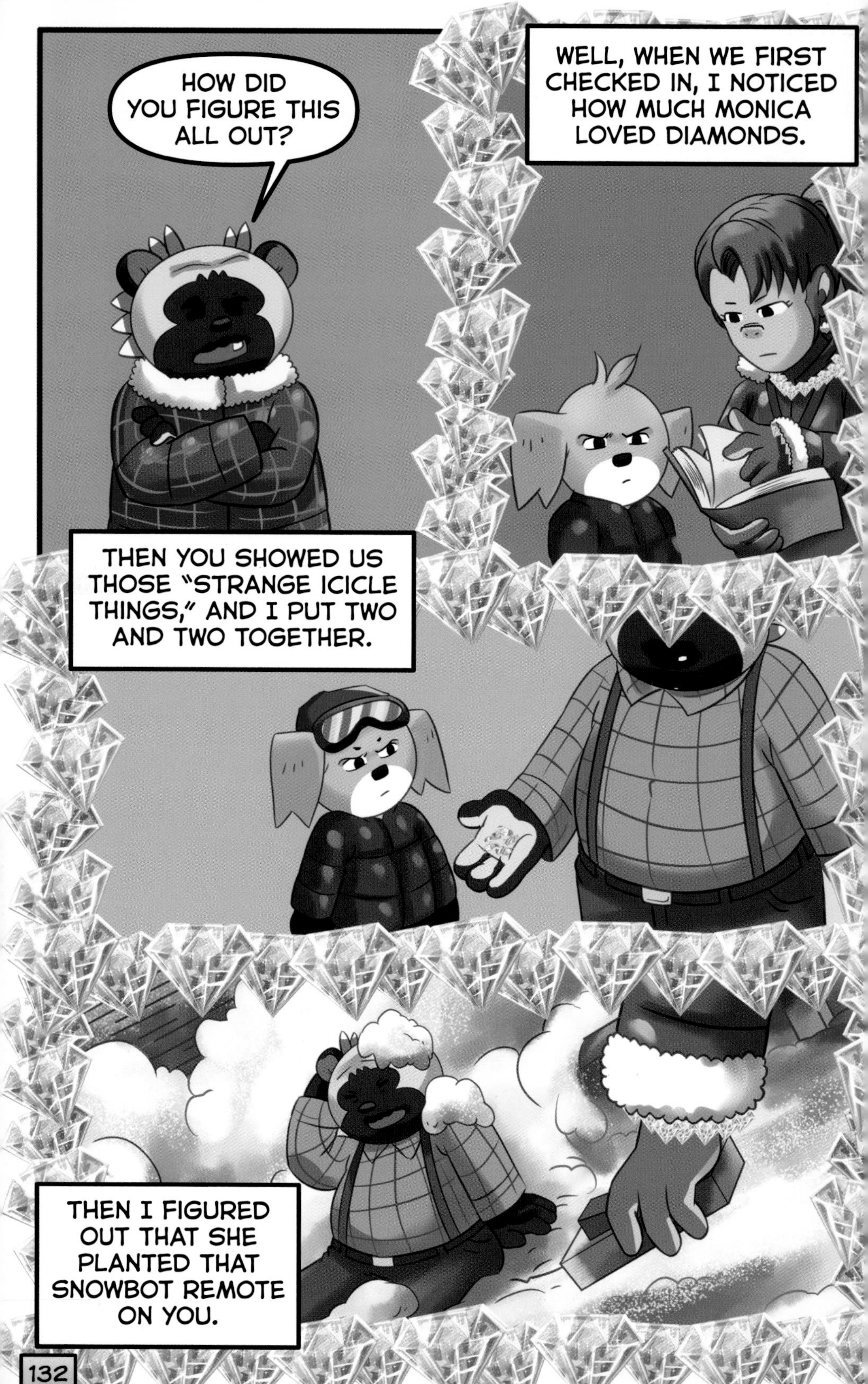
HOW DID YOU FIGURE THIS ALL OUT?
WELL, WHEN WE FIRST CHECKED IN, I NOTICED HOW MUCH MONICA LOVED DIAMONDS.
THEN YOU SHOWED US THOSE "STRANGE ICICLE THINGS," AND I PUT TWO AND TWO TOGETHER.
THEN I FIGURED OUT THAT SHE PLANTED THAT SNOWBOT REMOTE ON YOU.

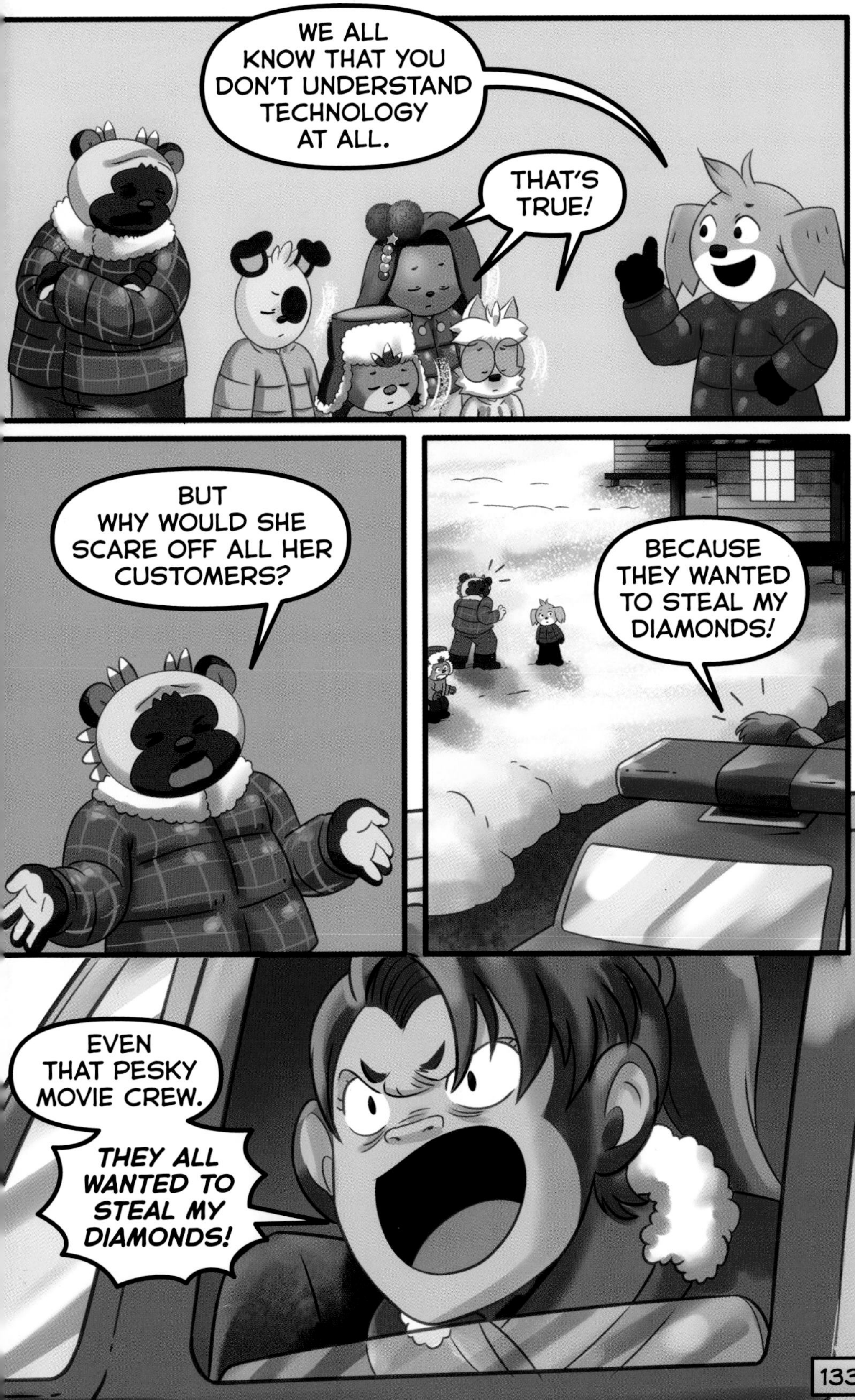
WE ALL KNOW THAT YOU DON'T UNDERSTAND TECHNOLOGY AT ALL.
THAT'S TRUE!
BUT WHY WOULD SHE SCARE OFF ALL HER CUSTOMERS?
BECAUSE THEY WANTED TO STEAL MY DIAMONDS!
EVEN THAT PESKY MOVIE CREW.
THEY ALL WANTED TO STEAL MY DIAMONDS!

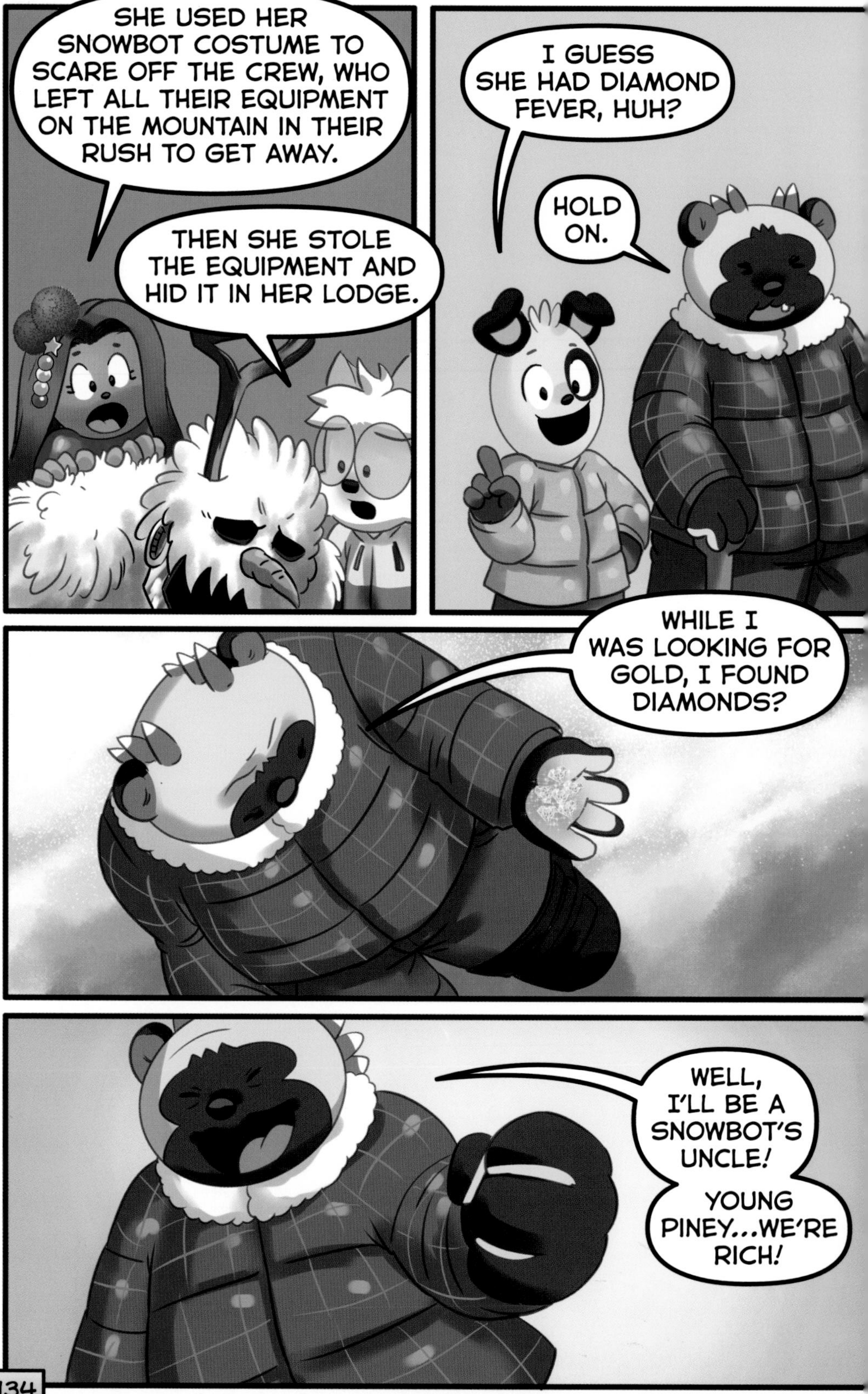
SHE USED HER SNOWBOT COSTUME TO SCARE OFF THE CREW, WHO LEFT ALL THEIR EQUIPMENT ON THE MOUNTAIN IN THEIR RUSH TO GET AWAY.
THEN SHE STOLE THE EQUIPMENT AND HID IT IN HER LODGE.
I GUESS SHE HAD DIAMOND FEVER, HUH?
HOLD ON.
WHILE I WAS LOOKING FOR GOLD, I FOUND DIAMONDS?
WELL, I'LL BE A SNOWBOT'S UNCLE!
YOUNG PINEY...WE'RE RICH!

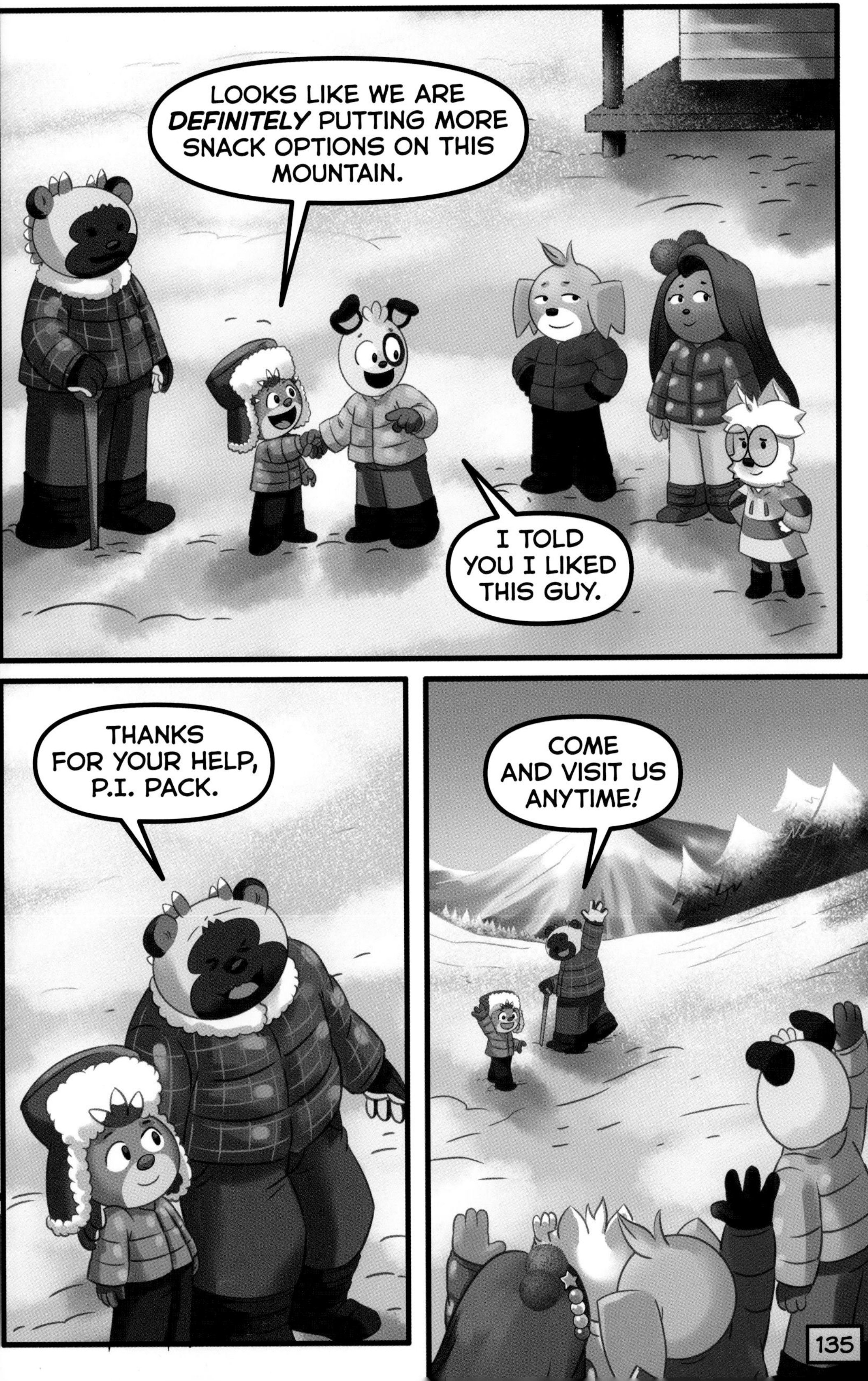
LOOKS LIKE WE ARE *DEFINITELY* PUTTING MORE SNACK OPTIONS ON THIS MOUNTAIN.
I TOLD YOU I LIKED THIS GUY.
THANKS FOR YOUR HELP, P.I. PACK.
COME AND VISIT US ANYTIME!

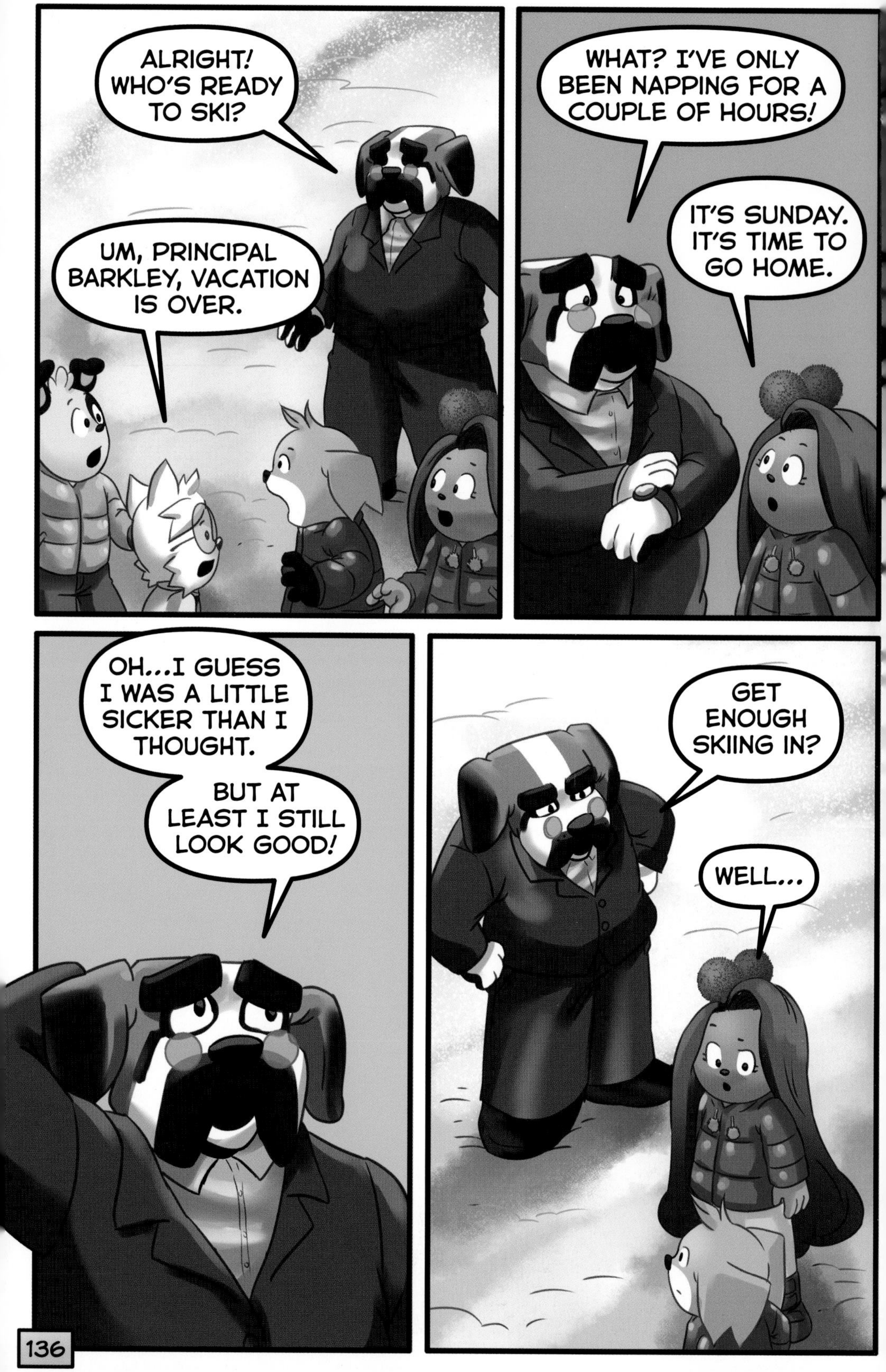
ALRIGHT! WHO'S READY TO SKI?
UM, PRINCIPAL BARKLEY, VACATION IS OVER.
WHAT? I'VE ONLY BEEN NAPPING FOR A COUPLE OF HOURS!
IT'S SUNDAY. IT'S TIME TO GO HOME.
OH...I GUESS I WAS A LITTLE SICKER THAN I THOUGHT.
BUT AT LEAST I STILL LOOK GOOD!
GET ENOUGH SKIING IN?
WELL...

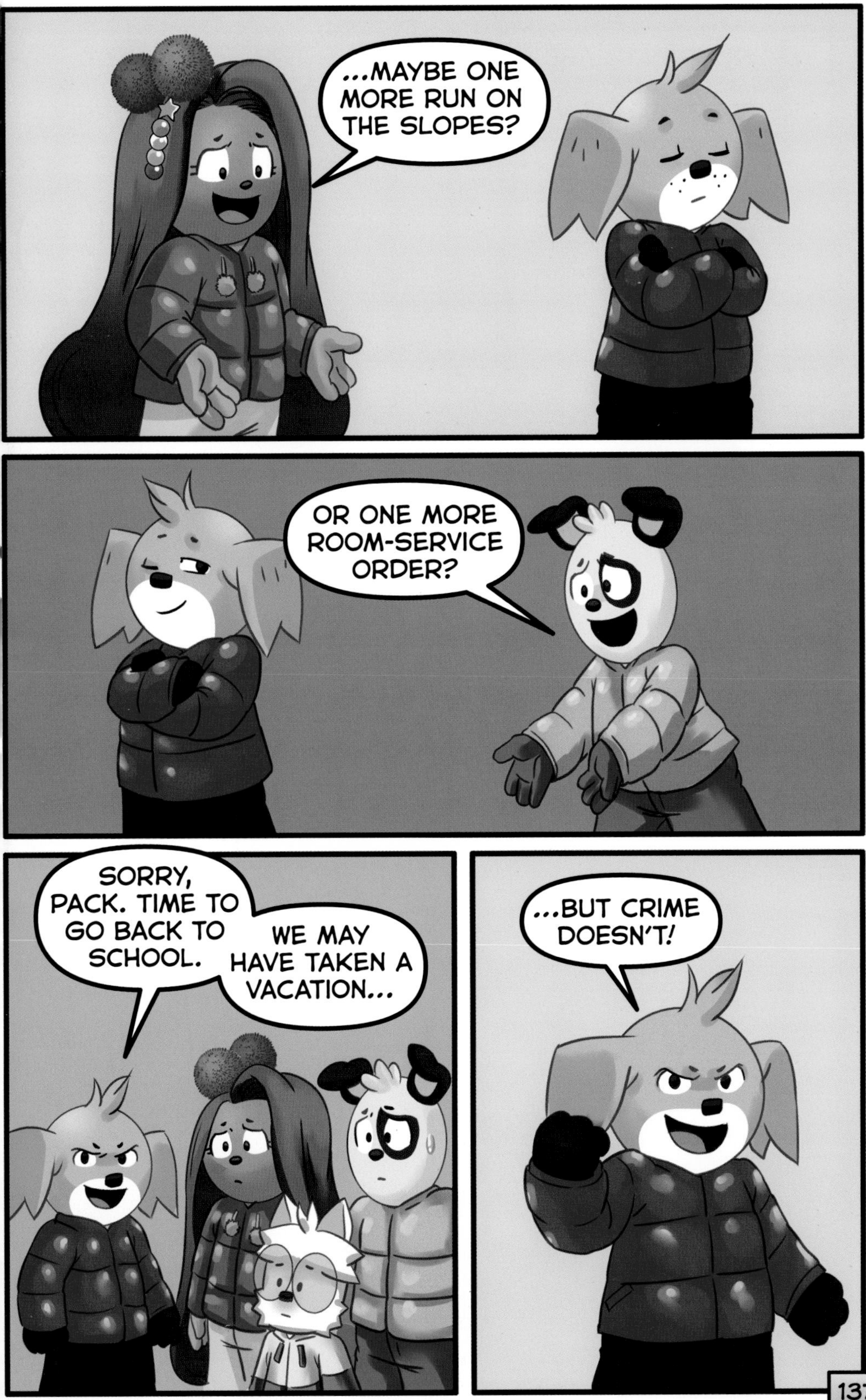
...MAYBE ONE MORE RUN ON THE SLOPES?
OR ONE MORE ROOM-SERVICE ORDER?
SORRY, PACK. TIME TO GO BACK TO SCHOOL.
WE MAY HAVE TAKEN A VACATION...
...BUT CRIME DOESN'T!

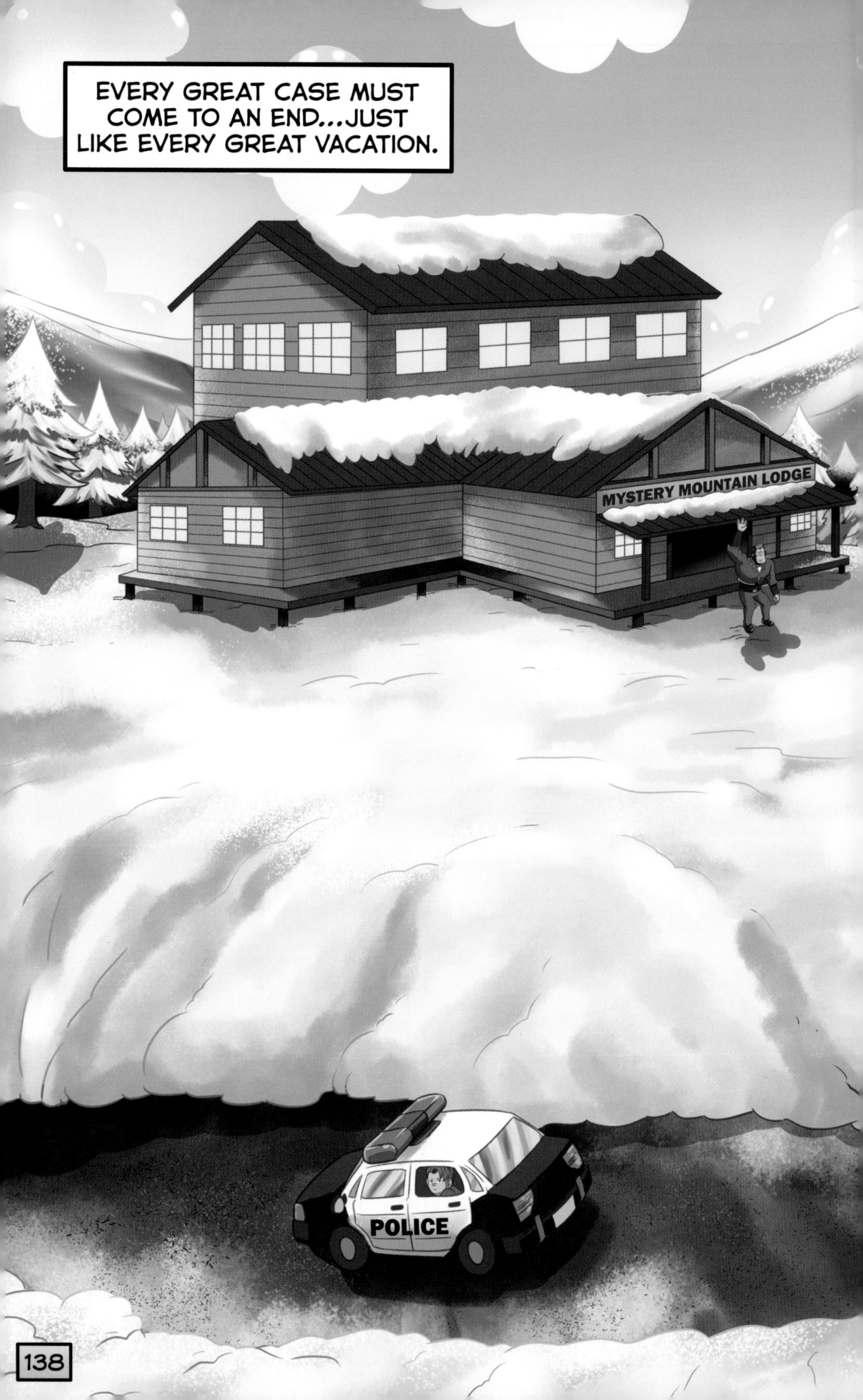
EVERY GREAT CASE MUST COME TO AN END...JUST LIKE EVERY GREAT VACATION.
MYSTERY MOUNTAIN LODGE
POLICE

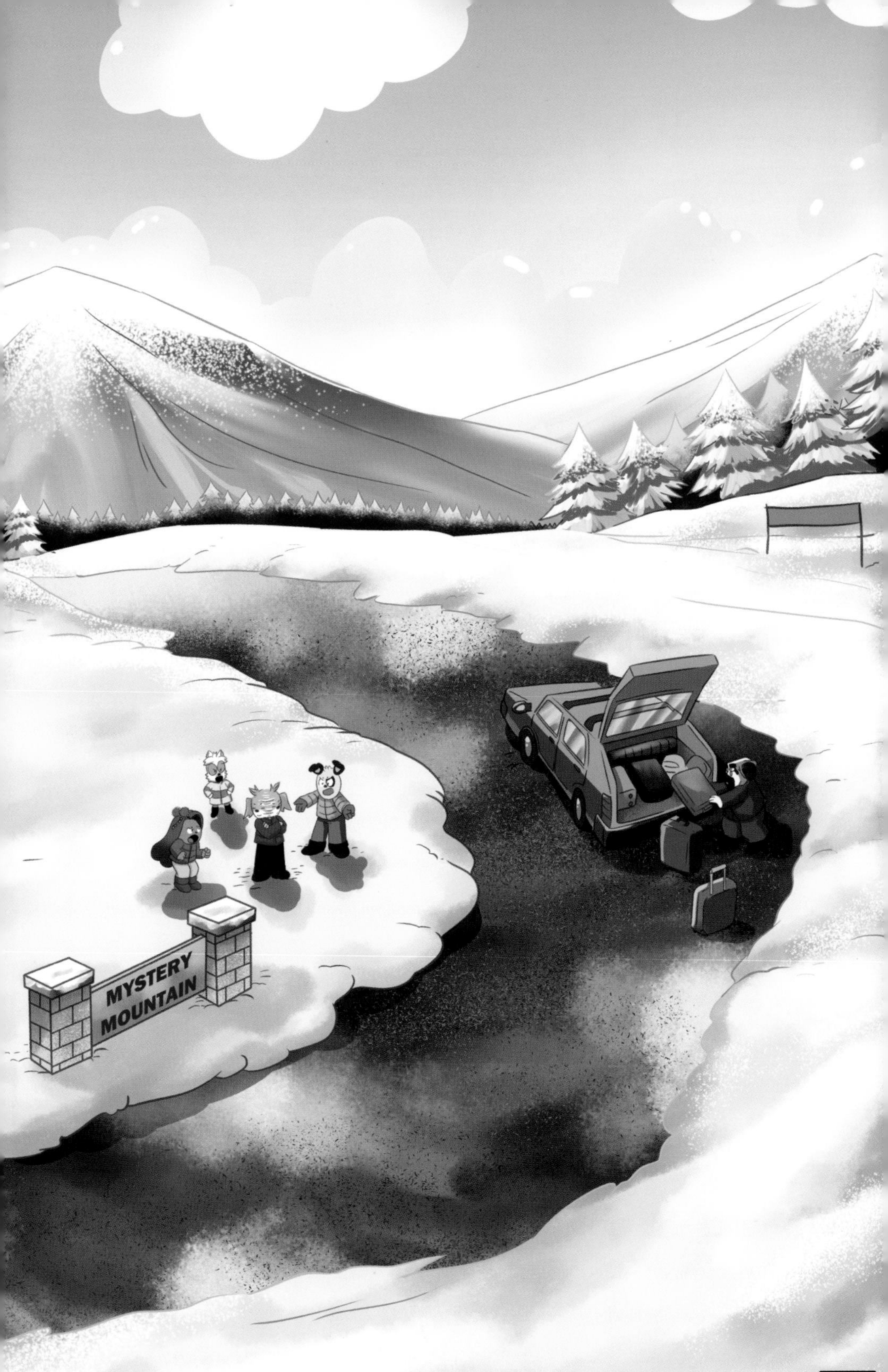
MYSTERY
MOUNTAIN

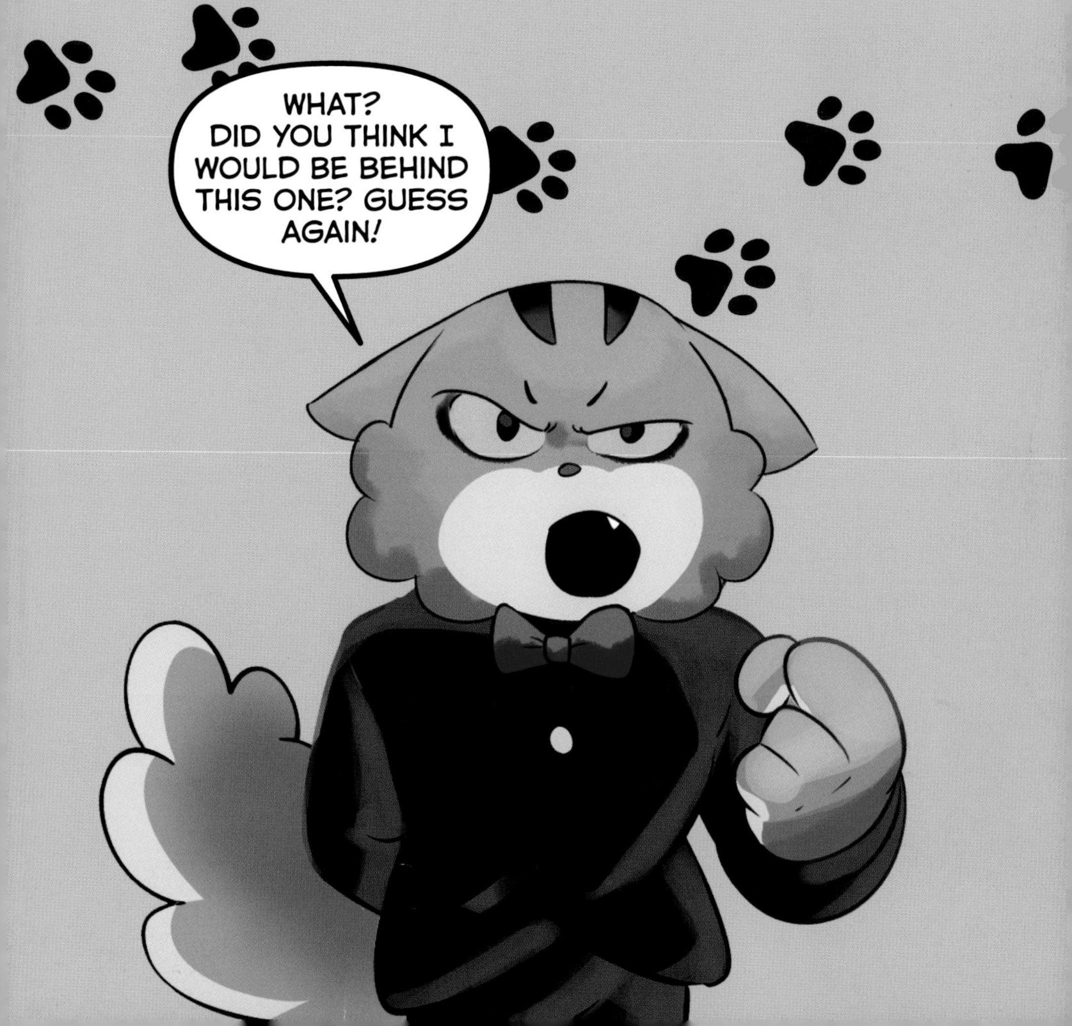
WHAT? DID YOU THINK I WOULD BE BEHIND THIS ONE? GUESS AGAIN!

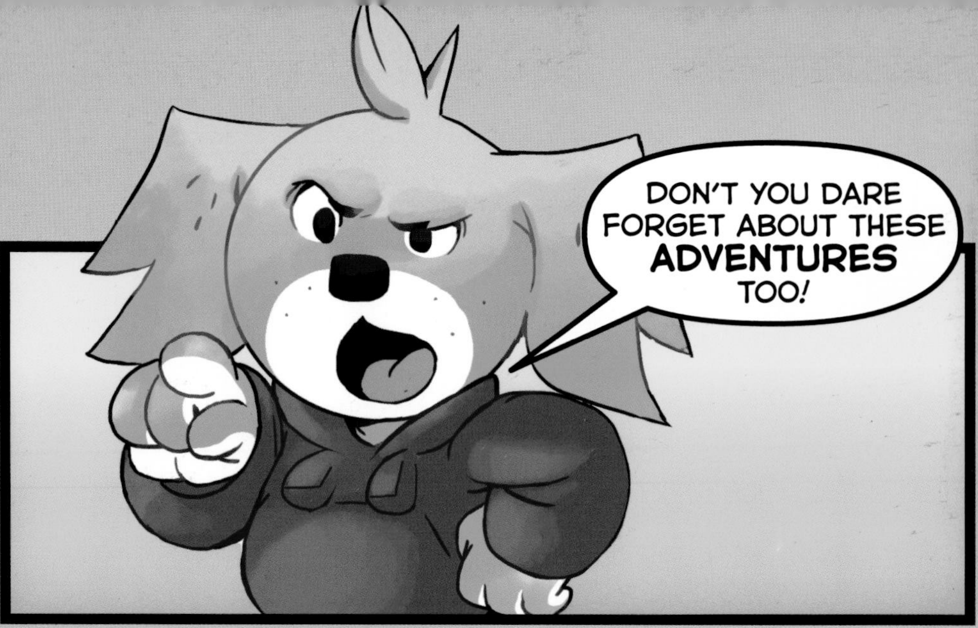
DON'T YOU DARE FORGET ABOUT THESE ADVENTURES TOO!

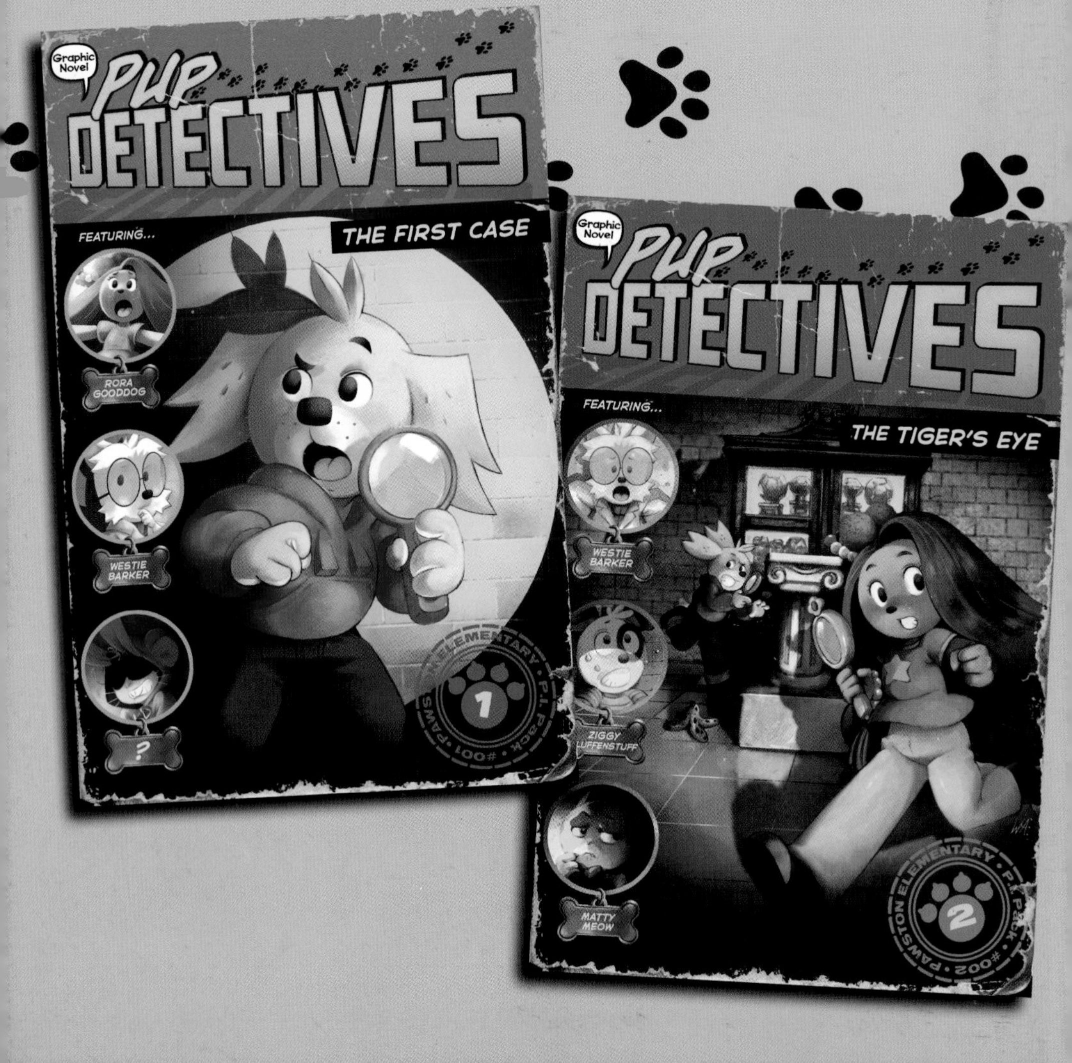
Graphic Novel
PUP DETECTIVES
FEATURING...
THE FIRST CASE
RORA GOODDOG
WESTIE BARKER
?
ELEMENTARY P.I. Pack #001
1
Graphic Novel
PUP DETECTIVES
FEATURING...
THE TIGER'S EYE
WESTIE BARKER
ZIGGY LUFFENSTUFF
MATTY MEOW
PAWSTON ELEMENTARY P.I. Pack #002
2